'Terrifying, fast-moving and exciting thriller'

Independent, Ireland

'A whirlwind of action, suspense and vivid excitement'

Irish Times

The Double Tap

'Masterful plotting . . . rapid-fire prose'

Sunday Express

'One of the most breathlessly exciting thrillers around . . . puts [Leather] in the frame to take over Jack Higgin's mantle'

The Evening Telegraph, Peterborough

'A fine tale, brilliantly told – excitement which is brilliantly orchestrated'

The Oxford Times

The Vets

'The book has all the ingredients for a successful blockbuster'

Sunday Telegraph

'If you feel a sleepless night coming on, here's something to help you meet it head on; Stephen Leather's fifth thriller. His last was praised by Jack Higgins who couldn't put it down. The same goes for this'

Daily Mail

The Chinaman

'Will leave you breathless'

Daily Mail

About the author

Stephen Leather has worked as a journalist for more than ten years, working for a number of newspapers, including *The Times* in London the *Glasgow Herald* and the *South China Morning Post* in Hong Kong. He is the author of ten highly acclaimed thrillers, PAY OFF, THE FIREMAN, HUNGRY GHOST, THE CHINAMAN, THE VETS, THE LONG SHOT, THE BIRTHDAY GIRL, THE DOUBLE TAP, THE SOLITARY MAN, and THE TUNNEL RATS (available from Hodder & Stoughton hardbacks). Stephen Leather lives in Dublin.

Also by Stephen Leather

Hungry Ghost

Stephen Leather

CORONET BOOKS

Hodder & Stoughton

Copyright © 1992 by Stephen Leather

First published in Great Britain in 1992
by Hodder and Stoughton
A division of Hodder Headline PLC
First published in paperback in 1992
by Hodder and Stoughton

The right of Stephen Leather to be identified as the Author
of the Work has been asserted by him in accordance with
the Copyright, Designs and Patents Act 1988.

A Coronet Paperback

20 19 18 17 16 15 14

A CIP catalogue record for this title is available
from the British Library

ISBN 0 340 67224 2

Typeset by Palimpsest Book Production Limited,
Polmont, Stirlingshire
Printed and bound in Great Britain by
Clays Ltd, St Ives plc

Hodder and Stoughton
A division of Hodder Headline PLC
338 Euston Road
London NW1 3BH

For Angela

The door opened with no sound on well-oiled brass hinges. Two men and a girl came in on tiptoe like students on a Rag Week stunt. The girl was dressed in a nurse's uniform, starched white with a pocket over her right breast, and white shoes. On her head was a white cap and she carried a small, black leather bag. She was barely five feet tall, but perfectly in proportion, so that standing alone and from a distance it was hard to judge her height. But with a man either side of her in the gloom it was obvious that she was petite, far too small to ever be a model but pretty enough to break hearts.

She moved over to the bottom of the bed and beckoned the men to move to either side. They wore dark business suits, but they wore them badly as if unused to the feel of heavy cloth and long sleeves. While the girl had the soft, well-cared-for skin of a city creature, the men looked weather-beaten and worn as if they'd spent their lives in the fields. And while the girl looked as if she'd never had to lift anything heavier than a lipstick, the men were well-muscled and strong.

The girl gently placed her bag on the foot of the bed, close to the sleeping man's feet and silently opened it. She nervously licked her upper lip, a quick showing of her small, pink tongue, and she took a deep breath, the soft mounds of her breasts pushing the uniform up. She nodded, once, and the two men moved at the same time

1

to grab an arm each. The man on the left, the slightly smaller of the two, reached across and clamped a hand firmly across the sleeper's mouth. He woke with a start and began kicking his legs up and down and twisting his shoulders, his eyes wide with fright and shock. He tried to scream, to force air out of his heaving chest, but the bitter-smelling hand muffled all sound except for a pig-like grunt, too quiet to be heard outside the room. He tried to thrash his head from side to side but the hand held him steady. He tried to bare his teeth to bite the flesh but the thumb was under his chin and painfully squeezing his mouth shut. The men, neither of whom he could see, pulled his arms to the side so that he lay crucified, rigidly held to the bed above the waist but still kicking his legs and grunting. They held him until his legs tired and the grunting stopped. The panic eased somewhat as he realized that they hadn't hurt him. Maybe they just wanted to give him a message, didn't want him to disturb the rest of the party. Perhaps if he lay quietly they'd move the hand and allow him to speak, perhaps they'd tell him what they wanted. He relaxed, let himself go loose to show that he wasn't struggling anymore. But they kept his arms outstretched and the hand stayed where it was, forcing him to breathe noisily through his nostrils.

He became aware of the girl then. He could just make out the top of her head, the white cap and below it two oval-shaped eyes. He felt a weight press down on the bottom of the bed and then saw her face clearly as she climbed up and knelt down with her knees either side of his legs. She had high cheekbones and finely arched eyebrows, and she watched him with a look of quiet amusement. She was gorgeous, no doubt about it, and

2

he couldn't take his eyes off her pouting lips. Her tongue came out and she licked them, slowly and sensuously, like a cat, and began to move up his body, moving one knee at a time. It was a hot night and he was naked under the sheet and he could feel the coolness of her thighs through the cotton. She looked like a nurse, he thought, but what was a nurse doing in his room in the middle of the night and who were the men? For a wild moment he thought he might be in hospital, suffering from amnesia or something, or perhaps he'd had a breakdown. But he knew he was still in the Embassy compound, in the bed he'd occupied for the past three nights. He wasn't in hospital and this wasn't a dream.

She reached his thighs and settled back, nestling her firm buttocks on his knees. Her lips drew back in a teasing smile and he saw white even teeth and behind them her small pointed tongue. Her ears had no lobes, he noticed, and her skin was flawless. She wasn't flat-chested like many Chinese girls, he could see the swell of her breasts under the white dress. His gaze wandered down the line of studs on the front of her dress, down between her breasts to her lap. The dress had ridden up her thighs and he could see her knees by squinting his eyes. Then he saw the hypodermic in her hand and he froze. It began to move upwards and he watched it like a rabbit hypnotized by a snake. The girl held it in front of her face, needle upwards. In her other hand she held a small vial, containing a colourless liquid, which she pushed onto the needle and extracted fluid from.

The man groaned and began to buck up and down and rock from side to side. The girl gripped him tightly with her thighs as if riding a horse, then she slid up his body until she was sitting on his groin. The dress rode higher up her legs and he caught a glimpse of suspenders and white lace panties. She finished filling the syringe and then popped the empty vial into her breast pocket. The man felt himself grow hard under the sheet, and the girl felt it too. She pressed down against him and smiled, enjoying the feel of his maleness, so close to her, just a sheet separating them. She reached down between her thighs and stroked him, just once. To tease him. Then she removed her hand and tapped the glass with a long, red-painted fingernail and watched the bubbles closely as they rose to the top, under the needle. She gently squeezed the plunger at the bottom, creating a miniature fountain that played over her hands.

The man panicked then, he thrust up and down, trying with all his might to throw her off. He shook his head violently from side to side, eyes rolling with fear, but the hand round his mouth tightened and locked him still. Her cap fell off and black hair tumbled down over her face and across her shoulders, a solid curtain of blackness. She flicked it back and it cascaded around her face. He tried rolling his hips but she just gripped him tighter and moved with him. She reached forward with her left hand and ran her fingertips down his cheek.

'I'm not going to hurt you. I promise,' she said in unaccented English that took him by surprise. He began to sob quietly but lay still, and then she leant forward and injected the contents of the hypodermic into his right arm. Tears rolled down his cheeks and trickled along the side of the hand that kept his mouth clamped shut. She put the empty hypodermic on the bed and he felt a coldness travel up his arm, like pins and needles. She moved forward, placed her hands on the pillow, and kissed him softly on the forehead. He caught the fragrance of jasmine and then it hit his heart and his chest exploded in pain and he died, no sound because his jaw was still locked tight.

The girl shuddered, either with pleasure or relief, and then slid off the bed, gathering up the hypodermic and replacing it in the bag. The men arranged the dead man's arms under the sheet, and then the three left the room as silently as they'd entered just three minutes earlier.

Sunday was a hell of a funny day to be summoned down to Suffolk to see your boss's boss, but it wasn't the sort of invitation that Donaldson could turn down. In fact invitation was the wrong word, he'd been ordered down by Grey, even though the order had come in a very obtuse form. Grey was his normal soft-spoken self on the phone, but there had been no doubt in Donaldson's mind that something was worrying the man.

When Donaldson took the call his first thought had been that he was about to be sacked, that the latest round of positive vetting had uncovered his little secret. He'd been careful to cover his tracks and whenever he met others who shared his tastes he'd used a false name, but these days you could never be sure; it was always a risk. And perhaps it was the possibility of being caught that added to the excitement. But Grey had simply said that he'd needed his help and that it was something that had to be dealt with out of the office.

He'd been given quite a complicated set of instructions

to follow to reach the house and once he'd left the main road he'd had to stop a couple of times to read the scribble he'd jotted down on the back of an internal memo. It had rained for a while, which hadn't helped. It was the height of summer but the weather owed more to November. It was almost chilly, and had been for the best part of a week. A freak north wind, said the forecasters. Bloody typical, thought Donaldson.

He was ten minutes late and Grey was waiting for him at the entrance to the drive. He was holding open a wooden gate which he closed behind Donaldson's Toyota as it pulled up in front of the thatched farmhouse.

As he climbed out of the car Donaldson instantly felt over-dressed in his light blue suit. Grey had swapped his customary Savile Row pinstripe for baggy cord trousers and a thick white fisherman's sweater. With his greying temples and weather-beaten face he looked more like the head of a farming family than an off-duty civil servant. He shook Donaldson limply by the hand and took him along the hall past a selection of tasteful hunting prints and into a sitting-room packed with plush settees and Victorian furniture. It was very much a woman's room, with pretty lace things on the backs of the chairs and a collection of old perfume bottles on a circular table in one corner. On top of a large television set was a collection of brass-framed photographs of the Grey clan. A fire was burning merrily in a white-painted metal fireplace that looked original and Grey gestured towards the two floral-patterned easy chairs either side of the blaze. In between the chairs was a low coffee table on which stood a fine bone china tea-set and a silver teapot. There was also a plateful of crumpets dripping with butter.

The two men sat down and made small talk while Grey poured. The conversation turned towards the office, and workloads and politics. Donaldson felt uneasy; Grey wouldn't normally even say hello to him if they passed in a corridor. Donaldson was a Grade 2 admin assistant, albeit with a high security classification. His main job was to keep track of expenses of agents in the field, he was always at arm's length from operations. The nearest he got to the sharp end of intelligence work was to read thrillers by Brian Freemantle and John le Carré.

The fire crackled in the grate, the logs moving against each other like uneasy lovers. A gust of wind blew down the chimney and a plume of smoke bellowed under the rim of the fireplace and wafted gently towards the ceiling, filling the air with the fragrant scent of burning pine.

'There's nothing like an open fire,' said Donaldson, settling back in the chair and enjoying the warmth but wishing that his host would just get on with it. Men of Donaldson's rank didn't get social invitations for tea and crumpets in deepest Suffolk.

'It's worth the effort,' replied Grey.

Sure, thought Donaldson. Grey probably kicked his wife out of bed in the morning to empty the ashes, fill the grate and blow on burning newspapers until the bloody thing was lit. Either that or he'd have a servant to do it. Grey wasn't the sort of man who'd be caught dead with a dustpan and brush in his liver-spotted hands.

'More tea?' asked Grey, proffering the silver teapot.

'Thank you, no, sir,' Donaldson replied politely. He already wanted to visit the toilet.

'I suppose you're wondering why I asked you here,' said Grey, as he poured himself another cup.

Of course not, you silly old fool, thought Donaldson, but he merely smiled and nodded, once.

'We have a problem in Hong Kong,' continued Grey. 'Or to be more precise, we have a problem over the border, in China.' He stirred his tea thoughtfully, the spoon clinking gently against the cup. 'You are of course aware of the massive loss of confidence in the colony, especially after what happened in Tiananmen Square. There has been a rush to get out, businesses are thinking twice about investing there, the place is a shambles. The British Government is struggling to make the transition in 1997 as smooth and painless as possible.'

He replaced the spoon in the saucer and sipped the tea with relish.

'The Government has already made it clear that we cannot offer sanctuary to all the six million Chinese who live in Hong Kong, so it's vital that we keep the lid on things, if you follow me. Once Hong Kong is part of China, of course, it is no longer our problem. Until then our intelligence services are doing everything they can to nip any trouble in the bud. We are actively seeking to dissuade those local politicians and businessmen who are trying to delay the handover, or to impose restrictions which we know the Chinese will find unacceptable.'

Grey gave his pale imitation of a smile and leant forward to place his cup and saucer on the table between them.

'That is background, background you are no doubt aware of. Now to the problem in hand. There is a nuclear power station in China, some six miles away from Hong Kong. The authorities in Beijing have received a threat to destroy it, to blow it up.'

8

'My God!' said Donaldson. 'A nuclear explosion six miles from Hong Kong?'

'Strictly speaking, it wouldn't actually be a nuclear explosion,' said Grey, clasping his hands and resting them in his lap. 'As I understand it, a conventional explosive device has been placed in the foundations, close to the reactor. If detonated it will crack open the reactor and lead to the sort of thing we saw at Three Mile Island and Chernobyl. Not a nuclear explosion, but the release of a cloud of radioactive material. Hong Kong, I should add, tends to be downwind of the power station.'

Donaldson fell silent as his mind tried to grasp the enormity of Grey's revelation. There were so many questions to ask that he didn't know where to start and he was relieved when the old man began speaking again.

'MI6 tells us that the ultimatum was delivered to Beijing by one of the triads in Hong Kong, the Chinese mafia if you like. They are especially fearful of what will happen when the colony comes under full Chinese jurisdiction. They execute criminals in China, you know. In football stadiums. Parents take their children to watch.' He shook his head sadly. 'It's a simple matter for the big hongs like Jardine Matheson to switch their domicile to Bermuda, or for the Hongkong and Shanghai Bank to invest money overseas and transfer its capital around the world, but the triads are firmly rooted in Hong Kong. They cannot afford to give up their illegal activities in the colony. They simply have too much to lose. So with only a few years to go before the British pull out they have decided that their only hope is to delay the handover. They want the *status quo* to continue, for fifty years at least.'

'Why fifty years, sir?' asked Donaldson.

9

Grey smiled thinly at the man's lack of knowledge. 'In 1997 Hong Kong will be given back to China, but for fifty years after handover it will operate under its own rules and regulations. It will have its own Government, including its own elected representatives, and its own laws, which are currently being drafted. It will be part of China, but at the same time separate from it. Special Administrative Region, I think they're going to call it. It will stay that way until 2047 when it will become just another part of China. But during those fifty years the policing of Hong Kong will be the responsibility of the Chinese. And it is that which is worrying the triads.'

'I thought they were bailing out along with anyone else who can afford to buy a passport, sir,' said Donaldson, and was rewarded with a nod from the older man.

'Yes, but it's not as simple as that. Any sort of criminal record will stop them getting into Canada, Australia or the United States. The middle classes and the rich have no problems buying second passports, but it's standard practice in most Western countries to cross-check with Special Branch in Hong Kong to ensure that applicants don't have triad connections. I've no doubt they could buy a passport from Andorra but most of them have nowhere to go. Some have managed to get out and as a result many of the triads are active overseas. They operate anywhere where there are Chinatowns . . . or Chinese restaurants. But the bulk of their income comes from vice, drugs and extortion in Hong Kong. And they are naturally reluctant to lose that revenue.'

'But surely, sir, contaminating Hong Kong is no answer?'

Grey shrugged and reached for his cup and saucer

again. 'It seems to be a sort of scorched-earth policy. If they can't have it, no one else will. But I suppose they assume that their demands will be met.'

'All they want is for the police force to remain British, you say?'

Grey drained his cup and sighed. 'You know what happens when you give in to blackmail, particularly where terrorists are involved. You submit once and the stakes are raised next time. The Chinese are not stupid. They know if they give in to this demand then more will follow. And to be frank, there is not one hope in hell of the Chinese – or the British – agreeing. The British Government just wants a clean withdrawal and the Chinese want complete control. No, their demands will not be met. The men behind it must be stopped.'

Donaldson nodded.

'That's why I need your help,' said Grey.

'I don't follow, sir,' said Donaldson, feeling out of his depth.

'On no account must the Chinese be aware that we know of the blackmail threat. We haven't been approached officially, nor will we be. That is why we cannot deal with this through normal channels, as news would soon filter back to Peking.'

'I hardly think we have any Chinese double-agents, sir,' said Donaldson smugly.

'If we have I wouldn't expect you to know about them,' said Grey, and Donaldson winced at the reprimand. 'No, our department cannot be involved officially. Or unofficially for that matter.'

'So you want me to arrange a freelance, sir?'

'No,' said Grey, carefully putting his cup and saucer

back on the table and looking wistfully at the now empty teapot. 'No, not a freelance.' He looked up at Donaldson, eyes shining like a ferret's. 'We want to use Howells.'

Donaldson stiffened as if he'd been plugged into the mains.

'Howells is dead,' he said.

'Retired,' stressed Grey.

'That's what I mean,' said Donaldson.

'No,' smiled Grey. 'I mean he really *was* retired. Pensioned off. He's alive, and available.'

Donaldson sank back into the easy chair, his mind whirling as it tried to come to terms with what he'd heard.

'Howells is a psychopath,' he spluttered.

'Actually, I think the phrase the psychologists use is sociopath, admittedly with homicidal tendencies. Though you'll have to take it from me that Geoff Howells is a changed man, for the moment at least. Have you seen the garden?'

The change in subject caught Donaldson by surprise. 'I'm sorry, sir?' he said.

'The garden, have you seen the garden? Come on, I feel like a walk.'

He led the younger man down along the hall to the back door where he pulled off his slippers and donned a pair of green Wellington boots. He gestured towards a matching pair.

'The grass is still wet. Try those for size. They're my son's, he's up at Oxford.'

He would be, thought Donaldson. The boots fitted, though.

Grey hauled open the door to be greeted by two heaving

12

Labradors, one black, one golden-brown, tongues lolling out of the corners of their mouths, tails wagging madly, overjoyed to see their master. Donaldson had seen similar reactions from section heads going into Grey's monthly think-tank meetings. Not that Donaldson had ever attended one. The black dog leapt up and tried to lick Grey's face and he pushed it away, though obviously pleased at the show of affection.

'Down, Lady,' he said, but there was no harshness in his voice.

The dogs ran in circles around the two men as they walked along the edge of the lawn which sloped gently down towards a small orchard. The grass formed a triangular shape with the base at the house and the clump of apple trees filling the apex. The garden was bordered by a thick privet hedge some ten feet high and between it and the lawn was a wide flower bed packed with plants and bushes. The air was cool and moist and Donaldson breathed in deeply, savouring its freshness.

'Do you live in the country?' asked Grey.

'Ealing, sir,' replied Donaldson.

'Ah,' said Grey quietly, as if he'd just heard that Donaldson was an orphan.

'I have a garden, though,' Donaldson added, and then inwardly squirmed as he realized how lame that sounded. They walked in silence for a while until Grey sniffed the air and turned to peer upward at the roof.

'Damn chimney's smoking too much, I'll have to get it swept. Have you any idea how much it costs to have a chimney swept?'

Donaldson didn't; his three-bedroomed semi had radiators in every room.

They wandered into the orchard, a dozen or so trees twice the height of a man, a mixture of apple, pear and plum, and Grey carefully inspected each one.

'Do you think they need spraying?' asked Grey, but Donaldson guessed it was rhetorical.

You never knew with Grey, that was the problem. He was often so subtle, so obtuse, that it was easy to miss what he was trying to say. He'd once called in one of his departmental heads for a half-hour chat and the poor man had walked out of the office without even realizing that he'd been sacked. It wasn't until Grey passed him in the corridor a week later that he discovered he was still on the payroll. It wasn't unusual for group meetings with Grey to be followed by a flurry of phone calls along the lines of 'what exactly did we decide?' Donaldson was on edge for any hint, any clue as to what it was that Grey wanted. All he knew so far was that it involved Geoff Howells, a man he thought had been dead for more than three years.

That was the last time one of his expense sheets had passed over his desk. Ridiculously high, as usual. Donaldson had enjoyed wielding the red pen, often slashing them by half. Until the day Howells had burst into Donaldson's office. Jesus, he'd been terrified. Damn near pissed himself.

'Did you ever work with Howells?' asked Grey.

Donaldson shook his head. 'No, but I followed his career with interest.'

'Short but eventful,' said Grey. 'He managed to gain quite a reputation in a relatively short period of time.'

'Captain in the SAS, wasn't he? Trained to kill.' And the bastard damn near killed me, thought Donaldson. He'd grabbed him by the throat and pinned him to the wall.

That's all Donaldson remembered until he woke up in the empty office with one of Howells' expense sheets shoved between his teeth. That was the last time he'd used the red pen.

'Special Boat Section, actually. One of the best. Did a superb job during the Falklands War, led one of the advance reconnaissance teams sent in to identify the Argentinian positions. Recorded nine kills during a four-day mission.'

'Impressive,' said Donaldson.

'Problem was,' said Grey, studying a small patch of green mould on the trunk of one of the plum trees, 'two of them were SAS troopers. That's when he came to our attention.'

'What!' exploded Donaldson.

'We hushed it all up of course, we were getting enough bad publicity at the time as it was.'

By 'we' Donaldson assumed he meant the British. 'What happened, sir?' he asked.

'He joined one of our more low profile departments.'

'No, sir, I mean what happened to the SAS men?'

'Howells was sitting in a hole a hundred yards or so from an Argentinian artillery unit when two SAS soldiers practically fell on top of him. According to Howells one of them was about to shoot and he reacted instinctively, killed one with a punch to the throat and knocked the other to the ground and broke his neck. It was over in seconds, apparently, and the Argentinians didn't hear a thing. He left the bodies in the hole. One of life's little tragedies.'

Donaldson thought for a moment that Grey had made a joke, but realized that he was serious.

'We took him in and trained him. He was good, very

15

good. One of the best, in fact. Ten clean kills in a two-year period. Never any problems, not as far as the technical side was concerned, anyway. I am going to have to speak to Perkins about this.'

'Perkins?' said Donaldson, totally confused.

'My gardener. He's going to have to do something about this mould. It can kill the tree if it isn't treated, you know.'

Donaldson didn't know, and frankly he didn't give a toss. He had only one tree at the end of his pocket-handkerchief of a garden.

'He started to enjoy the work, that was the trouble.' Donaldson realized Grey had switched back to Howells, though he was still studying the mould intently.

'The psychologists picked it up during his monthly check-up. He was fretting when he wasn't working and they discovered that he'd put a little too much, shall we say, effort into his last job. His target was a Libyan student who planted that messy bomb in Manchester some time back, you remember the one? Killed three people. Nothing we could prove in court so Howells' department was told to arrange a termination. Howells decided to make it look like a car accident. And he did, too. By the time they cut the Libyan out of the wreckage there was barely an unbroken bone in his body.'

'So?' said Donaldson, though he knew what was coming.

'So that's the way the Libyan went into the car. Howells killed him with his bare hands – slowly and very painfully.'

That was one of the crazy things about their line of work, mused Donaldson. You could do the job, and do it professionally, but once you started to enjoy it, you were finished. The psychologists reckoned that only a madman could enjoy killing, but they never asked if a truly sane man would do the job in the first place. Going by the names and expense sheets that went across Donaldson's desk, three years was as long as they normally lasted in the job, though some could go on for much longer. The CIA was rumoured to have a grandmother on their books who'd been active for nigh on thirty-five years.

'You know why he wasn't transferred?' Donaldson didn't, of course. 'We tried to shift him over to a desk job, but Howells wouldn't have any of it. Said he wanted to carry on doing what he was good at, what we had trained him to do. Said he wouldn't accept a transfer.'

That happened sometimes, when operatives got so addicted to the adrenalin rush that they couldn't bear to lose it. And if they were forcibly moved into another job they'd find another outlet for their frustrations and innocent bystanders would get hurt. It happened, but when it did the man, or woman, was swiftly retired. And retirement didn't mean a pension and a cottage in Devon. Retirement meant permanent. It was never spoken about openly, not at Donaldson's level, anyway. But every now and again a name would just disappear from the approved-expenses list and the file would be recalled by Personnel and never seen again. Donaldson had breathed a sigh of relief when Howells' name and file had gone. The man was a nutter, a dangerous nutter.

The two men walked out of the trees and back along the lawn towards the house. Grey picked up a small dead branch and threw it for the dogs. They rushed after it, barking and barging into each other. They reached it at the same time and grabbed an end each, pulling it and grunting with pleasure. Donaldson knew exactly how the stick felt.

'Where is he now, sir?'

'Bali.'

'Bali?'

'Indonesia.'

This was becoming bizarre, thought Donaldson. In the space of a few minutes the conversation had gone from a threat to destroy a Chinese power station to a retired killer lying on a beach in Indonesia. And somewhere in the middle, like the stick caught between two dogs, was Donaldson himself.

'We want to use Howells to clear up this Daya Bay business,' said Grey.

'Daya Bay?'

'That's where the nuclear reactor is. We want Howells to defuse the situation.'

He didn't seem to realize the pun. The black Labrador had won the tussle over the stick and came running over to Grey to present the trophy, and receive a pat on the head for her trouble. The other dog pretended to lose interest and wandered among the trees, sniffing at roots.

'Why Howells, sir?' asked Donaldson, hoping it didn't sound like criticism.

'We need someone who can't be traced back to us, someone who isn't on our books, and that rules out staffers and freelances. The Chinese mustn't know that we know, if you see what I mean. So any action we take must be completely covert.'

'But surely that would also rule out Howells, sir?' Donaldson though he knew what was coming and he prayed to God that he was wrong. He didn't want to meet Howells again – ever.

'Because he used to work for us? That isn't a problem. He's never worked in Hong Kong or China, so it's unlikely he would be recognized. His mental problems and his retirement are no secret, and if anything goes wrong it would be assumed that he'd just gone on the rampage. I can't think anybody would believe that the British Government would use such an agent.'

Donaldson agreed with that one. And his own involvement was starting to give him an uneasy feeling in the pit of his stomach. His urge to go to the toilet was increasing by the minute. Maybe it was the tea, maybe it was the cold air, or maybe it was the thought of working with Howells. That seemed to be what Grey was suggesting.

'I must repeat that it is crucial that the Chinese do not find out that the British Government is involved. The negotiations between the triads and the Chinese are being conducted at the highest level in Peking and there is only a handful of people involved. If they discover that we know what is going on, there is a good chance it will expose our source. There must be no connection at all seen between Howells and my department.'

Which, thought Donaldson, is why I'm here. To provide the distance.

'Howells isn't the man he was,' continued Grey.

'In what way, sir?'

Grey thought for a while, oblivious of the dog shuffling backwards and forwards at his feet waiting for the saliva-smeared stick to be thrown.

'Have you ever had a tooth capped?' he asked.

Donaldson shook his head. What the hell did teeth have

to do with this? There were times when he wondered if the older man really was starting to go gaga.

'It's worth doing if you've got a tooth that's so badly rotted that it can't be repaired with a normal amalgam filling. You build another tooth out of porcelain and metal and bond it to what's left of the original tooth. It looks real and it functions as normal.'

He threw the stick hard and high and the dog hurtled after it as it curved through the air. The dog in the orchard pretended not to notice, but its tail wasn't wagging.

'Howells had a personality that was rotten to the core. For whatever reason, he'd got to the stage where he enjoyed inflicting pain, enjoyed killing. He spent six months in a private sanatorium while some of the best psychologists in the country tried to undo the damage – but to no avail. Their conclusion was that Geoff Howells could never be returned to society. He was facing a lifetime in a Broadmoor cell weaving baskets.'

The dog was back, stick in mouth, but Grey ignored her. The two men had returned to the back door of the house but Grey made no move to open it. Donaldson's bladder was starting to hurt.

'We decided instead to try a different method, which brings us back to the dental analogy. They produced a new personality and in effect grafted it on to the old one, just like capping a bad tooth. They used deep hypnosis and God knows what drugs to suppress all his killer instincts, dampened his feelings and emotions and overlaid them with a new set. He has the memories of what went before, but it's as if they belong to someone else. To all intents and purposes Howells is now a confirmed pacifist, as docile as a lamb. We've done a few favours for the Indonesian

Government over the years so we arranged for him to live there.'

Until he was needed again, thought Donaldson. Until now.

'If he's been neutralized, surely he's no good to us now, sir,' said Donaldson, more in hope than belief.

Grey smiled. 'The conversion isn't permanent. In the same way that a cap can be pulled off a tooth, the new personality can be removed to reveal the man he used to be. And it's that man we need.'

'I still don't follow why it has to be Howells, sir. Surely we could use any freelance and just make sure our tracks are well covered.'

God, that sounded like a whine. Would Charlie Muffin have said that? Would Quiller refuse to take an assignment because it meant dealing with a psychopath/sociopath? If he had any bloody sense he would.

Grey shook his head. 'No, you know how they work. They all keep safety deposit boxes with envelopes to be opened in the event of their deaths. And they don't take kindly to being used, it can have a nasty habit of backfiring. No, Howells is perfect. He has no living relatives, he will follow instructions to the letter and he is . . .'

'Expendable?' asked Donaldson hopefully.

'Exactly. I am glad we understand each other.' He seized the doorknob and pushed open the wooden door, careful not to allow the panting Labrador in. He ushered Donaldson inside where they removed their boots, then led him into the sitting-room and picked up a manila file off a small mahogany side-table. 'Sit down and read this. It goes without saying that I don't want you to take notes.' If it goes without saying, thought Donaldson, why mention it? 'Come and see me when you've finished reading the file. I'll be in the garden.'

Grey closed the door gently. A minute or so later Donaldson heard him let himself out of the back door and call for the dogs. He settled down into the chair and began to read, all thoughts of his bladder gone.

Donaldson spent the best part of an hour reading and re-reading the report. It was sketchy in parts, but when he'd finished Donaldson felt he knew a lot more about what made Howells tick. And it didn't make him feel any easier about meeting the man.

The remoulding of his personality had been done by two top psychologists, one as part of a Government-sponsored research project he was doing at Bart's in London: the other was a young high-flyer on attachment from the CIA.

As Grey had said, it had taken some six months to make Howells safe, if not sane, but the trigger to reactivate him consisted of just three colour-coded cards which had to be produced in the correct order. According to the detailed instructions which came with the report, Donaldson was first to ask Howells if he was ready to take on the assignment, to appeal to the man's loyalty to his country. Then he was to offer him money. If the psychologists had done their job properly, Howells would spurn both offers. Donaldson was then to show him the cards which were contained in a white envelope. There would be little visible change but Donaldson was then to hand him a second envelope containing a full briefing. Simple, thought Donaldson. He slipped the two sealed envelopes into his inside jacket pocket and concentrated on memorizing the instructions. When he'd finished he took the file out into the back garden. This time he didn't bother with the Wellingtons.

Grey was at the bottom of the garden, to the right of the orchard, gathering up dead grass and fallen twigs with a rake. As Donaldson approached Grey sprinkled lighter fluid over the damp pile and dropped on a lighted match. He stepped back with a satisfied smile on his face as the bonfire flared into life.

'I've read the file, sir,' said Donaldson, handing it over. Grey reached into his back pocket and pulled out a third envelope.

'This contains your tickets and travelling expenses.'

Donaldson took it and put it into his pocket with the other two. He was starting to feel like a postman.

'Your flight leaves tomorrow, Cathay Pacific to Hong Kong and then Garuda to Bali. I suggest you phone in sick first thing tomorrow morning. On no account are you to tell anyone where you are going. You're not married, are you?'

'No, sir.'

'Family?'

'My mother and father live in Cheshire. They won't miss me.'

'Good man,' said Grey. 'Can you see yourself out?' he added, dismissing Donaldson with the rhetorical question.

When he heard the man's car start up and drive off

Grey dropped the file on top of the bonfire and watched as its edges browned and curled in the heat. As the pages shrivelled and burnt he absent-mindedly patted the black Labrador on the head.

'Two birds with one stone, Lady,' he said softly. 'Two birds with one stone.'

Much the same thought was going through Donaldson's mind some forty-eight hours later as his Garuda flight approached Denpasar airport. There were two things he liked best in the world. One was immersing himself in a good thriller and the other was having sex with small boys. Preferably small boys that were tied down and whimpering. The assignment from Grey looked set to satisfy both passions. He'd heard that the boys in Indonesia were simply gorgeous, big brown eyes and soft, smooth, brown bodies. Just the thought gave him a hard-on.

The Garuda Airbus looked new, the blue and grey interior trim sparkling clean. The plane seemed to be a cheap version, though, with none of the optional extras, no movie screen and no music. It was cold, too, bitterly cold. But instead of turning up the heat the cheerful stewardesses doled out blankets soon after they'd taken off from Hong Kong. His legs were cramped and he cursed Grey for only providing him with economy-class tickets. Cheapskate, he thought. It wasn't as if getting the expenses approved would be a problem.

It was pitch dark outside and there seemed to be hardly

any lights on the island below as the plane descended. He took a last look at the Garuda brochure, which told him that Indonesia consists of 165 million people spread among 13,677 islands. Half of the population are aged under twenty and, thought Donaldson eagerly, half of them are boys. The 300 ethnic groups speak 583 different languages, but he didn't plan to do much talking. His palms were sweating, despite the cold in the cabin.

Donaldson didn't see the airfield until the plane slammed into the ground, bounced fifty feet or so back into the air and then landed properly. Third bloody World, he thought sourly.

The Airbus came to a halt a hundred yards from the terminal building and Donaldson was annoyed to discover that he and his four dozen fellow passengers were expected to walk. God, it was hot, and humid, and before he'd even descended the mobile stairs to the tarmac he felt beads of sweat on his face and was gasping for breath. The air was filled with the sound of crickets and other night insects proclaiming territorial rights or offers of marriage or whatever it was that insects found so important to communicate after dark. A gaggle of Hong Kong Chinese tourists overtook Donaldson on his right and left before regrouping in front of him like fish passing a reef, talking incessantly.

The sweat was now pouring off his back and he could feel rivulets of water dripping down the backs of his legs underneath the lightweight grey Burtons suit he was wearing. He shifted his shoulder bag, wincing as the narrow plastic strap bit into his flesh through the thin material.

He reached the terminal building and gratefully sucked

in lungfuls of cold air which immediately made his skin feel clammy. Immigration and customs were a breeze; Bali was obviously well geared up for tourists, and Donaldson saw two uniformed teenagers who he'd quite happily have died for. Or paid for. They both had skin the colour of polished mahogany, and beautiful brown eyes that looked as if they were brimming with tears, though they both returned his smiles with pleasant grins. Down boy, thought Donaldson. Later, in Jakarta, on the way back. A couple of days of R&R, a well-deserved reward for a job well done. Christ, he was getting hard again.

As he walked from customs and into the arrivals lounge he was accosted on either side by Indonesian men, dressed in shabby T-shirts and frayed jeans and nowhere near as attractive as the uniformed youngsters from whom he'd had to tear himself away.

'Taxi? Taxi? You want taxi?' they chorused.

'Yeah, yeah,' said Donaldson, starting to sweat again. 'Which of you speaks the best English?'

He took off his glasses and wiped the condensation off with his handkerchief for the tenth time since leaving the flying fridge.

'I speak good English, sir,' said a man on his left, about the same height as Donaldson but much thinner and with a drooping moustache. Like Donaldson it appeared to be wilting in the heat.

The man seemed bright enough so Donaldson walked with him through the open doors towards a line of battered cars. Now that Donaldson had been claimed the rest of the drivers moved away in search of fresh blood. The Indonesian took Donaldson's bag for him and led him to an ageing car of indeterminate make that could have been green, or blue, or black. It was parked some distance away from the terminal and there was no lighting so it was hard to tell. Twice Donaldson slipped into holes in the road as he walked behind his guide and he swore loudly.

'Sir?' said the driver, opening the rear passenger door and throwing in the bag.

'Nothing,' said Donaldson, sliding into the car. It appeared to be lined with some sort of fur, and brass chimes dangled from the driving mirror.

'Go where?' asked the driver.

'Shit,' said Donaldson, suddenly remembering he had no local money. 'Wait here, I'll have to change some money.' He lurched out of the car and back to the terminal.

The driver, unwilling to let his fare out of his sight, scampered after him.

'No problem, hotel can change money,' he said to Donaldson's back.

'We're not going to a hotel.'

That worried the driver and he waited anxiously while Donaldson changed a handful of ten-pound notes. The Mickey Mouse money had a hell of a lot of zeros and it looked to Donaldson as if he had instantly become a millionaire in local terms.

On the way back to the taxi he explained to the driver where he wanted to go; to head for the Hotel Oberoi but to drive one mile past the hotel's entrance to a crossroads, then to turn left. Howells was living in a villa close to the beach where the road petered out.

'You want Oberoi Hotel,' nodded the driver and started the car.

'No, you idiot,' snapped Donaldson, and he repeated the instructions to the smiling driver.

When he'd finished the driver grinned even wider and said, 'No problem.'

'I bet,' said Donaldson.

The driver grated the car into gear and moved off, humming quietly to himself. It was sweltering. Donaldson tapped him on the shoulder. 'Switch the aircon on,' he said.

The driver turned and said smilingly, 'No aircon. Sorry. Open window.'

'Terrific,' said Donaldson, and flopped back into the seat. He wound the window fully down and let the breeze blow across his face. It felt like a blast from a hair-dryer and if anything it made him sweat even more.

They soon left the airport lights behind and drove along a double-track road with no pavements, the car constantly swerving to avoid pedestrians. God knows why so many people were out this late at night, thought Donaldson. Maybe the television was bad. There were women with brightly coloured dresses carrying sacks on their heads, children running around parents, kids walking hand in hand. The darkness beyond the headlights of the car was absolute, and the driver seemed to have some sixth sense that allowed him to hit the horn and start moving the car before they came into vision. Motor-cycles buzzed past constantly, young men without crash helmets crouched low over the handlebars with girls riding sidesaddle behind, hair flying in the wind and tears streaming from their eyes.

Donaldson closed his eyes and tried to relax, and when he opened them again the car was alone on the road.

Through the open window he could see the star-packed night sky, but there was no moon and the countryside to either side of the road was totally dark.

'How far?' he asked the driver.

'Not far. Soon,' the driver said. He pointed over to the left hand side of the road. 'Monkeys. Many monkeys.'

Donaldson peered into the blackness. Nothing. He squinted. Still nothing. He tried opening his eyes wide. Nothing. The driver was looking expectantly over his shoulder, waiting for some reaction.

'Super,' said Donaldson. The driver nodded, obviously pleased.

A few minutes later he gestured to the right. 'Rice fields,' he said.

Donaldson looked. Pitch black. 'Fantastic,' he said.

The driver took a left turn and the road narrowed, still supposedly a double track but with passing places every half mile or so. He pointed to the left. 'Very old temple,' he said to his passenger. 'Very famous.'

Donaldson didn't even bother to look. 'Marvellous,' he said, and settled back in his seat with his eyes closed. Maybe the guy would shut up if he thought he was asleep.

He didn't. He continued his guided tour, and Donaldson alternated between 'Super,' 'Fantastic,' and 'Marvellous.'

At one point in the journey they drove along a line of shops that seemed to stretch for miles, all of them open. They were a mixture of cheap and cheerful restaurants, boutiques selling T-shirts and cotton dresses and shops with no fronts that contained racks upon racks of cassette tapes. Obviously pirates, thought Donaldson, cheap counterfeits selling for one tenth the official price. The only customers seemed to be tourists, blonde women with chunky thighs and bra-less breasts and men with long hair and burnt skin uniformly wearing scruffy T-shirts, shorts and sandals. There were no food shops, no sellers of the essentials like soap powder or salt or vegetables. An Asian Golden Mile, without the funfair.

'You want to stop here?' asked the driver.

Donaldson shook his head. 'Are we nearly there?'

'Soon,' said the driver, honking his horn at a yellow jeep trying to push in from a darkened side-road.

The car slowed to a walking pace behind a queue of Land Rovers, jeeps and bicycles that seemed in no hurry to move any faster. Probably the heat, thought Donaldson, wiping his glasses again. A thin balding man with John Lennon glasses bought a bowl of noodles and pieces of meat on little wooden sticks from a street vendor and leant against the bonnet of a parked car to eat while his companion, a broad-hipped woman with cornflower hair tied in braids, watched. 'Don't you just love this food?' he said in a mid-Western drawl and she smiled. One case of hepatitis B coming right up, thought Donaldson. Serves the Yank right.

The air in the car was starting to stink of exhaust fumes but it was so hot that Donaldson didn't want to wind up the window. Instead he took his handkerchief out and held it over his mouth. It didn't seem to make any difference. He tried holding his breath but that made him feel even dizzier than the fumes.

Eventually they left the strip of shops and plunged into darkness again. The headlights picked out three roadside signs pointing the way to hotels on the left and then

they stopped. The driver pointed through the windshield.
'Oberoi,' he said.

'OK,' said Donaldson. 'Drive straight on.'

'Straight on?'

'Just drive,' he said, waving his hand towards the
bonnet of the car. He peered at the speedometer. It
was in kilometres and Grey had said to drive for one
mile past the hotel turn-off. They hit the crossroad at
1.4 kilometres and Donaldson told the driver to turn left.
The man was starting to get uneasy, but he remembered
the pile of foreign money Donaldson had changed. Just
another crazy tourist. Probably just had a bit too much to
drink on the plane.

The road quickly became a single track, and from what
Donaldson could see in the lights of the car there were
fields on either side with a scattering of tall trees. It felt a
little cooler and once or twice he thought he could smell
the sea, and then he saw thirty yards or so to the right of
the track, a pointed roof atop what looked like a square
building, silhouetted against the stars.

Donaldson tapped the driver on the shoulder. 'Stop
here,' he said.

'Here?' echoed the driver, but saw from the look on
Donaldson's face that the answer was yes so he slammed
on the brakes.

'How much?' asked Donaldson, suddenly realizing that
he hadn't agreed a price before getting into the cab. The
driver's eyes lit up, too, as he remembered the same thing.
The driver mumbled a figure with a lot of zeros on the
end and Donaldson was too damn tired to try and convert
it into real money. He quickly counted out a handful of
notes and threw them on to the front seat.

'Thanks a bunch,' he said.

'Don't mention it,' said the driver, nodding his head in time with each word. 'Good English, yes?'

'Marvellous,' agreed Donaldson, grabbing his bag and staggering out of the car. His right leg seemed to have gone to sleep.

The car did a jerky four-point turn and then lurched back down the track, leaving Donaldson alone in the dark with his sleepy leg. He limped towards the house.

As he got closer to the house he noticed that the bottom of the roof was illuminated with a warm glow, though the top was shrouded in darkness. Then he realized that what he was looking at was a wall, half as tall again as a man, which ran around the house itself. The light was inside. There was no doorway in the side of the wall he was approaching, so he followed it around to the left. Still no door. He was walking towards the sea, the waves breaking on the shore like thunder. He was walking on grass, but as his eyes became more accustomed to the starlight he could see a strip of white that must be the beach.

Donaldson stopped and listened. In between the watery crashes he could hear music. Pink Floyd. Dark Side of the Moon. God, that took him back.

He turned right and found the door, two slabs of weathered wood set into a stone arch. To the left was a brass bell-pull, like a stirrup attached to a long rod. Donaldson reached out his hand, then noticed that the door wasn't closed; light was shining through a two-inch gap. He pushed gently and the gap grew silently wider. He could hear the music more clearly now. Facing the doorway was another wall made of the same rough-hewn stones as the outer barrier, but about five feet tall. Sitting on top of it was a stone eagle, or chicken, or angel. Or perhaps it was a combination of all three, it was difficult to tell with the light behind it.

Donaldson had to turn sharp left for three yards or so and then right, into a small courtyard, surrounded by lush green plants. At the opposite side of the stone-flagged square was a small pool into which trickled water from the mouth of a stone lion set into the wall. Lily pads floated on the surface, moving gently around the dribble of water. Somewhere a frog croaked, but quietly, as if afraid to draw attention to itself. The pool was illuminated by three spotlights set into the wall and by a soft glow that came from large french windows that led into the house. Donaldson moved into the centre of the courtyard, sidestepping a brown-shelled snail that was meandering towards the water. From somewhere above his head a bird called into the night, a high-pitched whine that grew louder and deeper and then stopped, like incoming mortars in a war film. His right hand was tightly clenched around the strap of his shoulder bag, drenched in sweat. The heat, he told himself, ignoring the smell of fear that was pouring off him, the smell that dogs can scent and which raises their hackles and starts them growling and snarling. It was just the heat, thought Donaldson, just the heat. *Christ, what are you doing here?* asked a small voice inside, the voice of a threatened schoolboy. *Howells is an animal.* He ignored the whining voice and moved forward again, towards Pink Floyd and the window.

He could see into the room now, the french window framing a scene of domestic bliss, a man and two girls. The three were sitting at the far end of the room around a small table, the man with his back to the window, the girls to his right and left. The man's hair was tied back in a short ponytail by a rubber band, and his head bobbed forward and back as he spooned in food from a small bowl. He was sitting cross-legged on the floor, wearing faded jeans and a white shirt, sleeves rolled up past the elbows. The girls could have been twins, pretty in a boyish way, giggling to each other and with the man as they ate. They both had pageboy hair cuts and seemed achingly young, with smooth and unlined skins and bright, wide eyes with dark, fluttering lashes. Occasionally, one or the other would reach out to touch the man, or to ladle rice into his bowl or hand him a piece of meat. They were talking, Donaldson could see their mouths moving, but the music drowned out the words. The girls wore simple flowered print cotton dresses, open at the neck but covering their arms. One wore a thin gold chain around her neck, but other than that Donaldson wouldn't have been able to tell them apart. He found their boyishness over-poweringly provocative, but at the same time he was repelled by their obvious femininity. He took out his handkerchief and mopped his brow again. He replaced the wet square of linen and knocked gently against the glass with his knuckles.

Whatever the psychologists had done to Howells, they hadn't affected his reactions. In one smooth, flowing movement he'd replaced his bowl on the table, uncurled his legs and moved three paces to the side, away from the girls, side on to Donaldson but looking straight at him. Donaldson knew with a tight feeling in his stomach that if Howells had had a gun in his hand he'd have been dead. It was Howells, he was sure of that, but he'd changed. The face was thinner, and the soft beard and moustache were new. He'd lost weight, too. Not that Howells had ever been anything other than hard muscle, but now he looked almost emaciated. Donaldson could see his stomach was dead flat, and he had a marathon runner's backside and legs. Howells spoke quickly to the girls and they slowly moved away from the table, away from him, worried frowns on their faces. Howells seemed to be looking through Donaldson with impassive hazel eyes and for a moment Donaldson wondered whether reflections meant he couldn't see through the window. No, that couldn't be right, there were lights outside. He reached out and knocked again.

Howells walked forward slowly, balls of the feet touching the ground first, as if ready to spring at the slightest shock. He didn't look like a former SBS officer, or a professional killer, more like a junkie itching for a fix, but there was something in his cat-like walk that was unnerving. The room was still filled with music, but Donaldson knew that Howells was moving silently.

He stepped back as Howells slid the window open and Pink Floyd swelled out. Howells didn't say anything, but he reached up and gently smoothed the underside of his chin with the back of his hand as he studied Donaldson. Donaldson's bladder was suddenly heavy. His mind was whirling, wondering exactly what he should say. *Hiya Geoff, remember me?* Perhaps *Mr Howells, I presume?* How about '*I'm sorry I must have the wrong address*' and then getting the hell out of here said the voice in his head. He coughed quietly, trying to clear his throat. How could his body be soaking in sweat while his mouth was so dry, he thought.

'Geoff Howells?' he said hesitantly.

Howells nodded slowly, still stroking his beard.

'Er – can I come in?'

Howells said nothing.

'Grey sent me,' Donaldson added, almost as an after-thought. 'From London,' he continued lamely.

Howells smiled, a lazy confident smile that revealed white, even teeth. It seemed like a real smile, the smile of a friend, not the plastic version of a used-car salesman. Donaldson immediately felt easier and relaxed. Howells stood to one side and opened the french window further.

'Come in,' he said, and Donaldson was surprised at how soft and gentle the voice was. 'I'm afraid we don't get many visitors.'

Donaldson stepped over the threshold. He shivered as he passed Howells. Did he remember him? Probably not. Something to do with the brainwashing, maybe.

The room was square, about twenty feet by twenty. To the left were two doors of a dark red wood that looked as if it would be warm to the touch. There was no aircon, though a fan set into the white-painted ceiling was doing its best to keep the air moving. The walls were white, dotted with framed prints of what looked like Balinese gods. Tasteful, thought Donaldson, but somehow sinister. They weren't gods to help the unfortunate and protect the weak, they were vengeful gods who would kill and maim. Between the two doors was a large carved wooden chest with a big brass lock set into the front and a stack of newspapers and magazines on top. The furniture was made of the same red wood as the doors: a long, low sideboard, a bookcase full of paperbacks, and a rattan three-piece suite with cream coloured cushions. The girls were standing together behind one of the wooden chairs,

36

holding hands and looking at Donaldson from lowered eyes. To their left was a racked stereo system, matt black and expensive with waist-high speakers. He jumped as the window thumped shut behind him. He turned to find Howells watching him with an amused smile on his face. 'Sorry,' he said. 'Can I get you a drink?'

'No,' replied Donaldson. 'No, thanks, I'm fine.'

There was a sickly sweet smell in the air. Incense. It was coming from some sort of shrine set into the wall between the doors, a wooden box open at the front and painted a garish crimson. There were three sticks of incense smouldering away, and in front of them there seemed to be pieces of rotten fruit and a small garland of yellow flowers. Howells sat in one of the chairs and stretched his long legs out in front of him.

Donaldson sat down on the settee and balanced his bag on his knees. That felt uncomfortable so he put it by his side. 'Well,' he said, and Howells raised his eyebrows.

The album was almost finished, the second to last track, *Brain Damage*, and the words echoed through Donaldson's head. *'You raise the blade, you make the change, you rearrange me till I'm sane.'* Very apt, thought Donaldson, except that it hadn't been a surgeon's scalpel that had changed Howells' personality, it had been deep hypnosis and drugs, and in his pocket he had the colour code sequence that would bring the old Howells back to life. Howells the sociopath. Howells the killer.

'Well,' said Donaldson again. How to start, that was the problem. Grey had been quite specific; first he was to check how effective the programming had been, before showing him the cards. But what the hell was he supposed to say? There's a man we want

37

you to kill? To eliminate? To terminate with extreme prejudice?

The girls had grown bolder now and they scurried over to sit either side of Howells on the floor, looking up at him like adoring poodles. They were lovely. God, what must the young boys be like, thought Donaldson.

'Could I speak to you in private?' he asked.

'Sure,' said Howells, and he spoke quickly to the girls in some sing-song language. They looked as if they'd been whipped but he smiled and said something else and they nodded excitedly and, holding hands again, went through the other door. Probably the bedroom, Donaldson decided.

'Do I know you?' Howells asked, gently stroking his beard and studying Donaldson with what appeared to be quiet amusement.

Donaldson swallowed. 'I think we met a couple of times in London. You probably don't remember.' The smell of incense seemed to be getting stronger, filling the air and threatening to choke him.

'And you say Grey sent you?'

'Yes,' Donaldson replied, and then cleared his throat noisily. 'Do you remember him?'

'Of course.'

'I have a message from him.'

'Well?'

Donaldson was confused. 'Well what?'

'What is the message?' Howells asked patiently.

'He wants you to work for him again.'

'Like before?'

Donaldson nodded. 'Exactly.'

Howells looked pained. He slid down the chair and

rested his neck on the cushion, looking up at the ceiling. 'I don't do that sort of thing any more.'

'What sort of thing?'

'You know what I mean. I'm different now. I'm a Buddhist.' He fell silent for a few minutes, eyes closed. 'I can't do it. It's a part of my life that I'd rather forget. I just can't kill any more. I'm practically a vegetarian.'

Donaldson reached for his bag, and unzipped it. 'Grey asked me to give you something, he said it might make you change your mind.'

'Nothing can do that. Go back and tell him, thanks, but no thanks.'

Donaldson's hand groped around the bag like an inquisitive ferret until he located the two sealed envelopes Grey had given him back in England. The thicker of the two he left on top of the bag and he tore the other open. Inside, as Grey had said, were three coloured cards the size of beer-mats: one was lime green, one blue with a yellowish hue, and the third was a sort of silvery beige, but it seemed to change colour the longer you looked at it. On the back of each card was a number: 1, 2 and 3 in blue ballpoint.

'Grey said I was to show you these,' said Donaldson, getting to his feet. He stood in front of Howells, the cards in his hand, like a conjuror preparing to perform. With a weary sigh Howells raised an arm and took the card with number one written on the back.

'What is this supposed to be?' he asked, squinting at the green card. He turned it over and examined the number. Donaldson licked his upper lip and handed down card number two, the blue one. Howells frowned, and forced himself into a more upright sitting position, confused rather than worried. He shrugged and made to give them back to Donaldson.

'There's one more,' he said, and handed it down.

Donaldson wasn't sure what he expected to happen, though he'd played the scene through his mind time and time again on the journey from Heathrow. A minor epileptic fit, maybe, fluttering of the eyes, fainting, the look of a sleeper awakening, maybe a confused 'Where am I? Who am I?' Howells was a big disappointment; he did none of those things. His frown deepened, he examined all three cards again, turned them over and handed them back.

'And what is that supposed to mean? Is it some sort of code?'

Now it was Donaldson's turn to be confused. What had gone wrong? He checked the cards, confirmed that he'd passed them over in the correct order, and put them back into the envelope.

'Do you feel any different?'

Howells snorted, the sound of a cat sneezing.

Donaldson shook his head, trying in vain to clear away the thick smell of burning perfume. He weighed the second, bulkier, envelope in his hands and wondered whether it was worth giving it to Howells. The experiment had obviously failed dismally. Whatever Howells had been like before he now had the killer instincts of a pet rabbit. He dropped the sealed envelope on to the knees of the sitting man and walked dejectedly back to his own seat.

'What is it?' Howells asked.

'It's a letter. From Grey. My orders were to show you the cards and pass that envelope on to you.'

'Mission completed,' said Howells, opening the envelope.

'I suppose so,' said Donaldson. He watched Howells take out a sheaf of papers and what looked like a wad of currency. Howells sat and read in silence, once raising his eyebrows and snorting again.

'I suppose I'd better be going,' said Donaldson. 'Can I call a taxi from here?'

Howells shook his head without taking his eyes from the papers. 'No telephone,' he said. 'Let me finish this and I'll run you into town.'

Donaldson settled back into his chair, toying with the strap of his travel bag. Eventually Howells finished. He refolded the papers and replaced them in the envelope and placed it, and the money, on the table alongside the remains of the meal.

'Very interesting,' he said. 'And Grey expects me to do this for him?' He got to his feet, shaking his arms by his side as if restoring the circulation to cramped limbs. 'The callous bastard doesn't change, does he?'

Donaldson smiled nervously. 'He doesn't, but I think he expected you to have.' He stood up and slung the bag over his shoulder. 'Have you got a car?'

'A jeep, round the back.'

'It's very kind of you.'

Howells smiled and stepped forward, his right arm swinging quickly sideways and then twisting up, fingers curled back so that the heel of the hand made contact first, shearing off the cartilage that was Donaldson's nose and driving it into the centre of the man's brain. His legs gave way and he slumped to the floor, a trickle of blood running down his chin. It was a good clean kill, thought Howells,

41

a move he'd practised ten thousand times but never used, until today. He felt a glow of satisfaction at how easy it had been, the feel of the nose breaking, the speed of the blow, the fact that Donaldson hadn't had time to react or to make a sound. As he looked down at the body the glow turned into something else, something almost sexual, a shiver that ran down his backbone making him gasp. Like an orgasm. Only better. Howells wished he had more time, time to play, to prolong it, but the girls were in the bedroom and he didn't want to disturb them. The tremor of enjoyment passed, as it always did, leaving him with a sense of loss, an itch that he wanted to scratch again. He opened the chest, hefted the body on to his shoulder and dropped it in. Later, when the girls were asleep, he'd bury it. But first, he was hungry. He wanted a steak, a thick one, medium-rare. It had been a long time.

The road that Howells drove along to the airport was quieter than when Donaldson had arrived. It was light, but only just, and his jeep was the only vehicle to be seen. Hardly surprising, it was 4.30 in the morning, two hours before his flight was due to leave for Hong Kong. The rice fields were deserted, criss-crossed with lines of string to keep the birds away. Every hundred yards or so were small wooden platforms under roofs of reeds where farmworkers could shelter from the hot sun. The strings ran from platform to platform so that they could be pulled from the shade but at this time of the morning there were no sudden movements, just gentle swings in the wind. The wind blew through tin cans nailed to wooden posts making an unearthly wailing noise, another way of keeping the birds at bay.

It was three days since he'd killed Donaldson, now safely buried three feet below the courtyard, close to the pool. Howells had sent the two girls back to their village, promising them that he'd return in a few days and knowing it wasn't true. It felt good to be working again, to be following orders, to be able to use his initiative and his skills. He felt free. He stroked his chin, enjoying the feel of the bare skin now that he'd shaved off the beard and moustache. His hair was still longer than he liked, but he'd change that when he got to Hong Kong.

He'd been to Hong Kong twice before, but both times en route to other destinations. He'd never worked there, just visited a few bars and toured the shops. He remembered buying a camera there, a Pentax, but for the life of him he couldn't remember what had happened to it. Not that it mattered any more. Howells began whistling to himself quietly, his face a picture of contentment.

In his back pocket was the envelope from Grey that Donaldson had so faithfully delivered. It contained two photographs of a man called Simon Ng, three closely typed sheets of background information on him and ten thousand American dollars in large bills. Slightly less actually, because he'd used some of the cash to buy a ticket to Hong Kong. A one-way ticket.

Howells started smiling as he whistled, and the smile quickly widened into a grin. He began laughing out loud, an unnerving, disjointed sound.

It was eight o'clock in the morning when the *QE2* dropped its anchor above Patrick Dugan's head. That's what it sounded like anyway. The rattle of metal links against hard wood went on for twenty seconds or so and then stopped dead. God knows what they were doing, but whatever it was they did it every morning. And last thing at night it was furniture-moving, or footsteps, or the shower running. And sometimes it was at three or four o'clock in the morning. But always the anchor dropped at eight, on the dot. Dugan groaned and stuck his head under the pillow. He felt, rather than heard, the sound of lift doors closing several floors below him and knew that he wouldn't be able to get back to sleep.

His block was twenty-eight storeys high, and there were eight flats on each floor. If each flat had a average of one point five wage-earners, and most had two or three, then that meant 336 people would be leaving for work of a morning. And assuming they all left between 7.30 a.m. and 9.30 a.m., that meant an average of one every twenty seconds or so. And each departing resident meant a lift door opening and closing twice. There was no way he'd get back to sleep, not with the noise and the sun streaming in through the bedroom window.

'Shit,' he said with venom. He decided to make an effort to blank out the sound of the lift but the more he tried to ignore it, the more the vibration through the pillow annoyed him. He tossed on to his front and tried resting his forehead on the mattress. No good. He tried lying on his back. No good. 'Shit,' he said again. He decided to get up and groped for a towel to wrap around his waist. It was a thick blue and white striped one he'd stolen from the Shangri-La Hotel in Bangkok and he tied it around his thickening waistline. He'd never got around to buying curtains for his shoebox of a flat and he could be observed by the occupants of at least three dozen other homes during the short walk to the bathroom. He'd got used to the lack of privacy very quickly; it was just the noises which annoyed him now.

When he'd first moved into the flat the one above him had been empty and he'd actually enjoyed waking up in the mornings. Six months after he'd taken on the mortgage his peace and quiet had been rudely interrupted. The new occupants had embarked on a renovation programme that had taken the best part of twelve weeks, drilling, hammering and banging that started at daybreak and went on until early evening. God knows what they did because the biggest flats in the block had only three rooms, small ones by UK standards though fairly spacious in Hong Kong terms.

Then the building work stopped. Bliss. Then the *QE2* started docking every morning, bright and early, and the furniture began moving at night. And someone began arriving home in the early hours, pacing up and down in high heels before spending half an hour in the shower. A hooker, maybe, with carpenters for brothers. And shipbreaking parents. For a time he'd thought there might be a drugs ring operating from the flat and he'd toyed with the idea of flashing his warrant card and demanding a look inside, but thought better of it; not without probable cause, and there'd been no telltale vinegar smells. He had been up once, months ago, when the furniture moving had gone on for what seemed an interminable time, screeching and groaning and scraping until he hadn't been able to stand it any more. He'd rung the bell and it had been opened by a pretty Chinese girl in sweatshirt and jeans. Behind her were two young men holding opposite ends of a small wooden table.

'Please, it's very late,' he said in his very best Cantonese, not the street talk and triad slang he used at work but polite and all the tones spot on. 'I am trying to sleep. What are you doing to make so much noise?'

'We finish now,' she said in fractured English, smiled and closed the door.

They stopped. But the following night they were back at it again. Dugan had given serious thought to moving. Finding another flat wouldn't be a problem in Tai Koo Shing, there were thousands of them and a steady stream of vacancies as families packed up and emigrated to Canada or Australia. Trouble was he'd got a ninety per cent mortgage and the rest had taken every cent he had in the bank. There was no way he'd be able to raise the legal fees, stamp duty and estate agent fees to move again. And chances were he'd end up in exactly the same position. It was Hong Kong, when all was said and done. Six million people crammed into a few square miles. You had to expect noise, he told himself.

He'd spent almost ten years in rented flats before deciding to buy, encouraged by the fact that the mortgage costs were actually less than the rent he'd been paying for his flat in Happy Valley with half a view of the racetrack. He'd seen prices plunge before, in the 1980s when the thought of what would happen when the colony was given back to the Communists had put the shits up everybody, but there was an air of confidence in the place when he decided to buy. Sure, there were still queues to get out but for every family selling up there was another eager to get its first step on the home ownership rung, a huge Chinese middle class with money to spend. He'd done all the sums before he'd bought this place, but he had miscalculated on the costs of furnishing it even though it was tiny. In London it would have been described as a compact studio flat but in Hong Kong it was sold as a family-sized home. He'd had to arrange an overdraft to buy the air-conditioners which he'd foolishly assumed the previous owners would leave behind free of charge. He should have known better. When they moved out they even took the lightbulbs and shower curtain, and unscrewed the towel rail at the side of the washbasin.

Dugan had invested every cent he had in the flat and then the geriatric lunatics in Peking ordered the massacre of unarmed students in Tiananmen Square and the bottom fell out of the property market, and for a few agonizing months Dugan's flat was worth about a fifth less than his mortgage. It had climbed back since, but there was still an air of unease in the colony, based on a total mistrust of the Chinese Government and their trigger-happy soldiers.

The bathroom floor was damp again but he still couldn't work out if it was condensation or a leak. At least it didn't smell like piss. He reached for the flush handle but it swung uselessly in his hand and he realized with distaste that the water had been turned off again. It happened every week or so, every time someone in the block needed plumbing work done. The toilet supply was separate from the drinking water; all flushing was done with sea water held in a big tank on the roof, so at least he'd be able to shower and make a coffee – though sometimes they switched off the main water supply as well. He watched two turds gently circle each other like wary otters in the toilet bowl and he cursed quietly. What if he brought a girl back tonight? Great aphrodisiac, a toilet full of stale shit.

He walked into his galley kitchen and put the kettle on the single gas burner. That and a microwave were the only cooking gear he had. Usually he ate out, and all the fridge contained was milk, a few frozen TV dinners and a bar of Cadbury's fruit and nut chocolate. He spooned some Gold Blend granules into his 'I'm The Boss' mug and went back to the bedroom to put on a CD. He'd moved the CD player into his bedroom after the night noises started, using music to cover the sound of moving furniture, high-heeled shoes and opening and closing lifts. It almost worked. By the time he'd chosen Orchestral Manoeuvres In The Dark his kettle was starting to whistle feebly. He poured the water on to the brown granules and showered while it cooled. Mould was starting to grow in the cracks between the tiles and he groaned inwardly – another Sunday morning to be spent scrubbing the walls with an old toothbrush. As usual the hot water laboured to crawl out of the shower head and he had to move his broad back around to rinse off the suds. He shaved in the shower, being careful not to damage his moustache. He'd been growing it for three months now and it was in good shape, almost oblong with just a slight downturn at the edge of his lips. It made him look more serious, he reckoned, and also went some way to make up for the thinning thatch on top of his head. He checked his teeth at the mirror. At least they were OK. Dugan didn't look at himself through rose-coloured glasses: he knew all his faults; the thickening stomach, the thinning hair, the nose that had been broken once too often playing rugby for the police team. He wasn't good-looking, and he looked five years or so older than he really was, but his deep blue eyes and warm smile attracted more than enough girls. Girls rather than women; his escorts were usually at least ten years younger than he was, and usually Chinese. The blue eyes and fluent Cantonese usually won them over without too much trouble. Like plucking apples in an orchard. A frustrated gweipor had once asked him what it was about Chinese girls that attracted him so much. 'There are so many of them,' he'd answered, only half joking. He relaxed the bared grin into a gentle smile and winked at himself in the mirror.

'You smarmy bastard, you,' he said. He walked barefoot back to the kitchen, leaving behind a trail of wet footprints on the polished wooden floor. The hot coffee gave him a boost and the energy to dry himself and dress. His grey suit was sombre enough for a senior inspector in the Royal Hong Kong Police Force but it could do with dry cleaning. It was crumpled, but not stained, so he could live with it for a few days longer. His white shirt was clean and he wore his second-best rugby club tie. He stood in front of the fitted unit that stretched from the floor to the ceiling and used his reflection in one of the mirrored cupboard doors to help comb his hair over his bald patch. It didn't look too bad. A hell of a lot better than it looked in the changing-room after a game of rugby, that was for sure. Not that baldness worried him, but there was no harm in making the most of what he had left.

He switched off the CD player, double-locked the front door behind himself and waited for the lift. There were three, computer-controlled so that you never had to wait more than thirty seconds. There was a note in Chinese taped to one of the lift walls. He couldn't read it, his fluency was confined to spoken Cantonese, but he knew that it meant the water had been switched off.

Dugan's office was in Wan Chai, close to the bar area and the quickest way this time of the morning was to go by MTR, the Mass Transit Railway. Dugan could walk from his flat to the MTR station under cover every step of the way, thanks to the interlinking design of the Tai Koo Shing complex; tower blocks, schools, restaurants, department stores, all linked by covered walkways.

A small group of elderly women were practising t'ai chi on the podium, watching the moves of a white-haired frail grandmother in black silk trousers and white shirt and trying to copy them. The moves had started life as one of the most effective of the Oriental martial arts but through centuries of teaching, of being passed from instructor to pupil, they had lost all purpose and were now no more than a slow-motion dance, useful for keeping old folks supple but of little use in a fight. Dugan smiled as he imagined the grandmothers trying to fight off a mugger and wondering why they couldn't disable their attacker by standing on one leg and waving their hands in front of them.

Blankets and mattresses had been spread out around the fountains to air in the morning sun and he threaded his way through them to the entrance to Cityplaza, the estate's main shopping complex which also contained the MTR station.

It never ceased to amaze Dugan how clean it all was, the lack of litter and graffiti. If it had been in England the vandals would have long covered every flat white surface with spray-painted obscenities, but Tai Koo Shing looked pretty much as it did when Swires first built it on reclaimed land more than a decade earlier.

Dugan remembered the pictures in the *South China Morning Post* of the queues to buy flats in the first block, and ever since it had been a place where middle-class Chinese aspired to live, the two- and three-bedroomed flats often representing the pinnacle of a lifetime's work or the launch pad to emigration. And because it was a middle-class dormitory town and not a working-class dumping ground, and all the residents had to pay a fairly hefty monthly management charge, it was always well cared for and repairs were usually done promptly. It was an OK place to live, once you got used to the crowds. It was busy even first thing in the morning, and on weekends it wasn't worth trying to do any shopping there it was so crowded. They came from all over Hong Kong to wander around and window-shop, to gaze at the displays of high-priced fashion and state-of-the-art consumer electrical equipment. Some bright entrepreneurs had even started running bus trips from the villages in the New Territories, and on weekends you'd see lines of old men and women with dirt-encrusted hands and worn clothes being taken around in groups, wide-eyed at the bright, shiny affluence of it all. The MTR station was mobbed, as usual, and Dugan had to fight to get on to the first train that stopped. A small man in stained T-shirt and shorts called him a 'gweilo prick' but Dugan didn't let on that he'd understood. No point.

Dugan's only blessing being that he was virtually a head taller than most of the rush-hour crowd, at least he had the illusion of space from the neck up. The underground train was like a huge snake as it rumbled along, one long continuous chain of carriages. On the straight sections of track he could see from one end of the train to the other, every inch occupied by the great unwashed public. He tried to breathe through his nose as much as possible because he worried about catching flu or something. There must have been at least two dozen people within breathing distance and any one of them could have had something contagious, he thought.

Standing on the MTR and swaying as the train braked to a halt, he made the effort to concentrate his mind on the work that was piling up on his desk. There were at least ten cases that had to be treated as urgent, but there were two that he was particularly interested in. One was a complicated fraud case involving a small Chinese bank – a case of cheque kiting that involved three Hong Kong deposit-taking companies and banks in Texas, Geneva and the Cayman Islands. The stream of cheques, each one covering another, had totalled 160 million dollars before anyone had noticed, and the twenty-three-year-old cashier who looked as if butter wouldn't melt in her mouth had netted herself a cool $12 million with the scam. Dugan was putting a case together and, just as importantly, was trying to track down the missing money. The girl was out on bail, her passport confiscated, and Dugan was sure that at any moment she'd disappear into the mainland or to Taiwan. God, what he'd give to go with her – and the money.

The other case concerned a company that sold computers and then stole them back a couple of months later. Over a dozen firms, most of them in Sha Tin, had been hit, the same computers in each case. Dugan reckoned there'd be a triad link somewhere and privately nursed the hope that it would bring him to the attention of the top brass in the anti-triad squad. He was getting bloody nowhere, though. How was he expected to, for God's sake, when he was practically chained to his desk?

He brooded about the unfairness of it all as he got off the train and took the escalator to the surface of Wan Chai MTR station. The hot air took him by surprise as it always did when he left the air-conditioned station and stepped into the bright sunlight. By the time he got to his office he was sweating. He slumped into his chair, glared at the pile of pale green files on his desk and sighed deeply. Coffee, he thought, and wandered out into the corridor. His boss, a beanpole by the name of Chief Inspector Christopher Tomkins – Chief Inspector to his friends – was by the machine, gingerly removing a liquid-filled cup.

'Why the hell does this machine always fill right up to the brim?' he asked Dugan.

Dugan shoved a two-dollar coin into the slot. He pressed the button marked 'black coffee with sugar'. The machine vomited dark brown liquid into Dugan's plastic cup. It stopped half an inch from the top.

'It likes you,' said Tomkins, jealously.

Dugan took his coffee back to his laden desk and slumped down in the chair. It rocked dangerously; one of the wheels was loose – again. At least once a week he upended it and screwed the five castors in as tight as he could but it seemed to make no difference. Sometimes he worried that Tomkins might be sneaking into his office late at night and unscrewing them. As he sat down he realized that Tomkins had followed him. He seemed to have something on his mind, so Dugan looked at him expectantly.

'The computer case,' said Tomkins.

'It's going well,' said Dugan. 'I thought I might visit a few of the computer shops in Tsim Sha Tsui, rattle a few cages and see what falls out.'

'Actually Pat, I've had a call from the anti-triad squad. They want the file sent over.'

'What!' Dugan snapped. 'How the hell do they know about it?' It was obvious from the look on Tomkins' face that he'd told them. Dugan shook his head, lost for words. His big case. His chance to be noticed.

'Come on, Pat, you've got a heavy case load as it is. You should be glad they want to help.'

'Help?' said Dugan. 'You mean they'll let me work on the case with them?' Tomkins looked embarrassed at the hope in Dugan's voice.

'No,' he said. 'They'll handle it, but I guess they'll want to talk to you about it.'

'It's not fair!' said Dugan.

'Life's not fair, Dugan. Don't be dumb. You've plenty of cases.' He nodded at the stack of files on the desk.

'This one's different. It's a big one.'

'It's triad-related.'

'I know it's triad-related, that's why I want to work on it.'

'Look, Dugan, that's what the anti-triad unit is for.'

'There are plenty of guys in Commercial Crime working on triad cases, you know that.'

'Yeah, but they don't have relatives running one of the biggest triads in Hong Kong, do they?' said Tomkins, beginning to lose his temper.

'Is that what it's about, my brother-in-law?'

'There's nothing I can do, Pat. The word has come down from on high. You're to be kept off this case.'

'Christ! He only married my sister,' said Dugan. 'It's not as if I sleep with him or anything! What do they think I do, go over all my cases with him? Is that what they think?'

'Don't fight it, Pat, you'll be pissing into the wind.' He held out his hand and with a snort Dugan thrust the file at him. Tomkins took it and started to say something but Dugan waved him away.

'Forget it,' said Dugan. 'Just forget it.'

Howells booked into the Holiday Inn Harbour View. The hotel was about ten minutes' drive from the single runway of Kai Tak airport, on the mainland, close to the bustling shopping arcades of Tsim Sha Tsui. It was a modern, comfortable room with light teak furniture and a picture of a golden peacock on the wall.

It was early evening and Howells lay on the bed, his legs crossed at the ankles, slowly rereading the three sheets of papers that held the life, and death, of Simon Ng. Chinese name Ng Chao-huang, but to his friends and associates he was Simon Ng. Simon Ng was the Lung Tau – Dragon Head – controlling a drug and vice empire that pulled in tens of millions of dollars every year. Simon Ng, who lived with his family in a closely guarded complex in the New Territories, surrounded by triad soldiers. Simon Ng, who had to die. The two black and white photographs lay by his side. They showed a good-looking Chinese man in his early forties, smooth-skinned with a small dimple in the centre of his chin. The face was squarish, the hair closely cropped so that it stood up almost straight on the top of his head and was shaped around his ears. He had thin lips that didn't look as if they had the habit of forming a smile. Simon Ng looked hard. And if Grey's notes were to be believed, he was hard.

The triad leader had a wife, an English girl called Jill, and a daughter, eight years old, called Sophie. He had two brothers, one in San Francisco, the other in Vancouver, and a sister who'd stayed in Hong Kong and married a Chinese banker. Father had retired to a large house on the Peak where he spent his time polishing his collection of jade. The father used to be the head of the organization, but now the power lay with Simon Ng.

Howells rang down to reception and asked if he could hire a car through the hotel. It was easily arranged, said the girl who answered, and yes, the hotel could supply him with a road map, she'd send one right up.

He'd travelled on his own passport but booked into the hotel under Donaldson's name. He'd brought Donaldson's passport with him, and his credit cards, and his glasses, just to be on the safe side. He didn't look much like the man buried under the flagstones of the villa in Bali, but neither did the picture in the passport, and with the glasses on he was close enough.

The map arrived and he studied it until the phone rang and the receptionist said his car was downstairs. It was a blue Mazda, almost new, with a pine air-freshener fixed to the dashboard. The agent who'd delivered it to the hotel had left the aircon running so it was pleasantly cool. He dropped the map on to the passenger seat and edged out into the afternoon traffic of downtown Kowloon. The car was a right-hand-drive automatic and the traffic drove on the left so it confused him for a while. He'd been in Bali too long and grown accustomed to driving on the right. Cars and vans were bumper to bumper for the first mile or so as he drove past the tourist shops packed with cameras, electrical goods and clothes. Hong Kong looked a prosperous city, with none of the obvious poverty he'd seen in Indonesia, where the pavements were full of beggars and children in tattered clothes and the roads buzzed with motorcycles. Hong Kong had few bikes, all the cars seemed new, and the crowds on the pavements were well-dressed and affluent. The buildings were as clean and new as the cars, blocks of glass and steel and marble. Howells drove out of Tsim Sha Tsui, through the industrial areas of Kowloon and past towering residential blocks, thirty storeys high. He glanced at the map a couple of times, but only for reassurance. His sense of direction was unfailingly good and he'd been trained to memorize routes. He left the built-up areas behind him and was soon driving through countryside that reminded him of the Brecon Beacons, rolling hills and thickets of wind-stunted trees.

It was an hour's drive from the hotel to where Ng lived, halfway up a hill that looked down on the South China Sea. The house stood alone, a single storey H-shaped building, two long wings connected by a third block in which was set the main entrance. It was surrounded by green, well-kept lawns on all sides and enclosed by a ten-foot-high stone wall. That was what the file had said, anyway; all that Howells could see from the main road as he craned his neck out of the Mazda's window was the imposing wall. A single track side-road linked the main road to the compound, winding its way left and right up the wooded hill to a pair of black metal gates. The nearest houses were about half a mile away, red-roofed three-storey blocks that would have looked at home in a Spanish seaside town, but they were served by a separate road. There was only one way up, and there seemed to be no way of getting the car to the top of the hill from where he could look down on Ng's house. He'd be able to make it on foot, but he'd have some explaining to do if he got caught.

He drove the car off the main road and headed up the track but he'd barely travelled a hundred yards before the way was blocked by a horizontal pole painted in bright red and white. There was a large sign covered in foot-high Chinese characters and Howells didn't have to be a linguist to work out that it meant 'Halt' or 'Private Property' or 'Trespassers Will Have Their Balls Removed'. He stopped the car, but before he could open the door a man came out of a wooden gatehouse, hand moving towards the inside of his brown leather jacket. The hand didn't reappear, it lingered around his left armpit as if idly scratching. Howells wound down his window and grinned. 'I'm trying to get to Sai Kung,' he said to the guard. The man was about fifty, but stockily built and in good condition. He shook his head.

'Not this road,' he said, and pointed at the barrier. 'Private.' He took his hand away from the shoulder holster, confident that he was talking to a stupid tourist who'd just lost his way. He rested both hands on the car door and leant forward, smiling at Howells with yellowed teeth. 'You must go back.'

'Whatever you say, sunshine,' said Howells, conscious that another guard had moved out of the trees behind him and was standing at the rear offside wing of the car. Security was good, and he had no reason to doubt that there would be more men scattered through the woods. He reversed the Mazda back down the track and on to the road before driving around to the far side of the hill.

So far as he could see the road was the only way he'd be able to get up to the compound. And even if he got there, what then? This wasn't a James Bond movie, one man couldn't storm a fortress alone, no matter how heavily armed. The thought of free-falling in from 25,000 feet made him smile, bringing back fond memories of his days with the SBS. But even then it wouldn't have been considered without a team of four and stun grenades and Uzis and whatever else they could hold on to at 120 mph during the long drop. No, while he was at home, Ng was safe. Howells drove back to Kowloon deep in thought, whistling quietly to himself through clenched teeth.

Hot Gossip was jumping. It was one of Dugan's favourite bars and a hangout for many of the unmarried cops, gweilo and Chinese. A bar where you were reasonably sure of picking up a girl and reasonably sure of not picking up something contagious, where the food wasn't bad and the music was loud and the drinks were expensive enough to keep out the rabble. It was on two floors in Canton Road, the bar and dining area above and a trendy disco below. Dugan was upstairs, priming himself with half pints of lager before diving into the flesh market below.

He was standing by just about the longest bar in Kowloon, a polished black job that could seat a couple of dozen people without looking the least bit crowded. And behind the bar, at intervals of ten feet, were wall-mounted television screens all showing the same music video. At the far end of the bar, where it curved around to the left to the nook where the barmen mixed their high-priced cocktails, was a cluster of tables with pink tablecloths. They too were surrounded by television sets. No matter where you stood or sat you could see a screen without moving your head.

Dugan had left the office early and had walked in on his own but soon found friends in the form of three officers from the anti-triad squad who were also on the police rugby team. They'd begun teasing Dugan about his work, as they always did, and asking when his next quarry would be taking a one-way trip to Taiwan. Dugan was used to the ribbing, in the same way that he was used to suspects disappearing from Hong Kong as soon as the Commercial Crime boys got anywhere near ready to make an arrest.

'It's all right for you bastards,' he said, waving his half-filled glass at them. 'You can catch them with a gun in their hand or a pocket full of dope. Or you can kick down the door to a fishball stall and catch them with underage girls.'

'Chance'd be a fine thing,' howled Colin Burr, a hefty scrum-half with shoulders that looked as if they were made for bursting through doors.

'Deny it,' said Dugan. 'Deny it if you can.'

'You pen-pushers ought to give it a try some time,' said Nick Holt, a lanky Scot with a Hitler moustache who'd only been in Hong Kong three years.

'Yeah, have a go at real police work for a change,' echoed Jeff Bellamy, the oldest of the group and, like Dugan, starting to lose his hair. Unlike Dugan, though, he'd given up trying to comb what he had left over the bald patch and instead had it cut short, a brown fringe that ringed the back of his head.

'Real police work?' sneered Dugan. 'Don't make me laugh. When was the last time you put away one of the Dragon Heads? Name one.'

'Cheung Yiu-chung,' suggested Holt. 'He went down for seven years.'

'Bastard,' conceded Dugan. 'OK, name five. Go on, name me three.'

'Oh piss off, Dugan.'

'You know what I mean. Sure, your arrest records look better than ours, but almost all yours are small fry. Foot soldiers. But we go after the big fish. The real criminals, the ones who steal billions at a time.'

'Yeah, but Dugan, how many do you actually catch?' sniggered Burr as he drank.

'It takes time to build a case,' said Dugan. He fell silent and watched Patsy Kensit prance around on one of the screens behind the bar. She was gorgeous. What made him so argumentative was that he knew they were right. In the first place it often required months of painstaking research that owed more to accountancy than to police work before they had enough evidence to make a case. And by the time they'd got enough evidence together the suspect or suspects had usually had plenty of warning, and they were usually rich enough to be able to buy themselves an escape route. It could be frustrating. Bloody frustrating.

Dugan looked away from the screen and scanned the diners, taking in the whole restaurant area with one easy glance. He realized with a jolt that he too was being studied, by a petite Chinese girl with beautiful eyes. She was sitting at a table with two other girls, wearing a dress every bit as black and shiny as her hair. She seemed small, even for a Chinese girl, but the eyes were knowing and teasing. The eyes of a woman, the body of a young girl. She smiled at Dugan, catching him off balance. He looked away, embarrassed, as if he'd been caught peeking through the window of a schoolgirls' changing-room.

He shrugged. 'Downstairs?' he said.

'Now he's talking sense,' said Bellamy. They emptied their glasses and walked the length of the bar and down the stairs that led to the disco. The throbbing beat enveloped them like a clammy mist and they had to push their way through the crowd to reach the bar. Holt ordered a round of drinks and they stood together, watching like predatory sharks preparing to carve through a shoal of fish.

'What about those two?' said Holt, nodding at two girls dancing together.

'Tasty,' agreed Burr. 'Very tasty.'

The girls moved well together, obviously used to dancing with each other.

'Want to give it a go?' Holt asked Burr.

'Sure,' he replied, and the two men placed their glasses on the bar and edged their way on to the crowded dance floor, towards the girls.

'See anything you fancy?' Bellamy asked Dugan.

'Not yet,' said Dugan, 'but it's just a matter of time.'

Across the disco he saw three girls walk down the stairs and stand at the edge of the lights. One was the small Chinese with the beautiful eyes. She seemed to be looking right at him, though he knew he must be obscured in the gloom.

'You're staring,' laughed Bellamy.

'Pretty, isn't she?'

'The short one? Exquisite. But a big gweilo like you would tear her apart. Pick on someone your own size.'

Dugan looked at him and laughed and when he looked back to the stairs the girls had gone.

The two men stood by the bar, scanning the dance floor and tapping their feet to the beat. Burr and Holt seemed to be doing OK, they'd moved in on the two girls and now were gradually edging them apart like sheepdogs with nervous sheep.

Dugan thought about asking Bellamy how his application for a transfer was getting along, but decided against it. Wrong time, wrong place. God, he wished they'd pull their finger out. He was going slowly mad in Commercial Crime's A Division, even before today's disappointment. It wasn't police work, it was clerking, pure and simple. The straw that had broken the camel's back was the Carrian affair, a three-year investigation followed by an eighteen-month trial, the longest in Hong Kong's history, and the most expensive. It had ended abruptly when a single judge had decided that the defendants had no case to answer. Almost five years of hard work down the drain. Dugan had worked his balls off on that case, ten or twelve hours a day. He'd eaten, slept and breathed the Carrian case, only to see it dismissed by one man.

The night after the judge had stopped the trial Dugan

went out and got seriously drunk. A week later he'd put in his first application for a transfer, to switch from A Division to C Division. A Division handled the long, complex fraud cases, split into four taskforces to handle the big ones. B Division looked after general fraud; a move there would have been seen as a step down, a demotion. C Division had more kudos, chasing up counterfeit cases. That meant a lot of foreign travel, undercover work, the real *Miami Vice* stuff. Trouble was there were only forty officers and the competition to get in was cut-throat. When Dugan had applied he'd been told it would be three years at least until there'd be an opening. Dugan reckoned they were giving him the brush off, that they thought he was too valuable for A Division to lose.

Eventually his patience had snapped and he'd decided to break with CCB completely and try to get back to real police work. But nobody seemed to take his application to join the anti-triad squad seriously – and now he knew why.

Bellamy noticed his silence, and reached over to clink glasses with him. 'How's life?' he asked.

Dugan shrugged. 'Nothing changes. I'm still pissed off with CCB.'

Burr and Holt were back to back now, moving the girls further and further apart. They'd pulled, all right, and done it without talking, too, because they couldn't be heard over the driving beat. Dugan drank deeply. He didn't care any more that it was the wrong time, wrong place.

'I've got to get out,' he said.

'Music too loud?' said Bellamy.

'You know what I mean,' said Dugan. 'Out of Commercial Crime.'

Bellamy shook his head slowly. 'You're better off where you are, Dugan.'

'No,' hissed Dugan. 'I want out.'

The two men looked at each other over the tops of their glasses. Dugan wanted to push it, even though he knew by the older man's silence that he was going to be disappointed. Like phoning to ask a former lover if she'd give it one more try, knowing that he wasn't going to get what he wanted but determined to try nevertheless, even though the pain of rejection would be worse than maintaining the *status quo*.

Dugan explained about losing the computer case. 'I want to move to the anti-triad squad. I have to get back to real police work.'

'Commercial Crime is real police work,' answered Bellamy, avoiding Dugan's eyes.

'I don't understand why they're making it so difficult for me to move,' Dugan drove on stubbornly, knowing the answer. He saw Bellamy's lips move, but the words were lost in the music.

'What?' he shouted.

'You know why,' Bellamy yelled. 'Your bloody brother-in-law. That's what's stopping you. Simon bloody Ng and your sister.'

Dugan sighed and felt alternate waves of anger and frustration wash over him. The computer case was the first he'd lost because of Ng, but it was obvious that it wouldn't be the last. And now it was clear that the powers that be would not allow him to move out of Commercial Crime. Bellamy looked away, embarrassed.

'Fuck it,' said Dugan, and forced a grin. 'Let me buy you a drink. And then I want to get laid.'

When he turned to the bar, she was there. Small and cute and looking up at him with an amused grin on her face. Had she heard him? Dugan hoped not. He smiled. 'Hello,' he said. 'I saw you upstairs, didn't I?'

She nodded. 'And I saw you. Small world, isn't it?' She giggled. Pretty mouth, thought Dugan.

'Can I buy you a drink?' he asked, switching into Cantonese and enjoying the look of surprise on her face.

'I'd like a soft drink, something long and cool,' she said quickly in Cantonese and he knew he was being tested.

'How about me, will I do?' he asked, and she laughed again.

'How come your Cantonese is so good? You a cop?'

'Of course,' he said. 'What do you really want to drink?'

'Perrier,' she replied.

Dugan ordered himself a beer and a fizzy water for her, and then felt a thump in the small of his back.

'Don't forget your friends,' Bellamy growled.

Dugan ordered a lager for Bellamy and handed it to him without looking. His eyes stayed on the girl, worried in case she moved away.

'How about an introduction?' Bellamy asked.

'How about riding off into the sunset and letting me and this young filly get acquainted.' He talked in English, quickly, and he used slang so that the girl wouldn't be able to catch the meaning but she grinned and reached past Dugan, arm outstretched, and shook hands with Bellamy.

'My name's Petal,' she said.

'Pleased to meet you, Petal,' said Bellamy. 'I'm Jeff Bellamy. And this young reprobate is Patrick Dugan. A man to be avoided at all costs.'

'You can let go of her now, Jeff,' said Dugan. He took hold of the girl's hand. It was soft and cool. 'Nice to meet you, Petal.'

'Nice to meet you, Patrick Dugan.'

'It's my turn to ask,' he said. 'How come your English is so good?'

'I was a good student. A frightfully good student,' she said, and her accent was pure Cheltenham Ladies' College.

Dugan gestured at the drink in her hand, bubbles bursting against the slice of lime. 'Not drinking?'

'I'm here to dance, not to drink.'

He took the hint and together they moved to the dance floor. She moved well, and she kept close to him as she danced, touching him occasionally, by accident or by design, he couldn't tell. Just a nudge of an elbow, or their hands would meet as she turned to one side, and each time it was like receiving a small jolt of static electricity. He wondered where her friends were, now she seemed to be alone. The DJ switched to a slow ballad and made some crack about it getting to that time of the night; and Dugan made to leave the floor but she stepped forward and linked her arms around his waist and rested her head against his chest, eyes closed. God, she was tiny, like a schoolgirl, though the breasts that pressed against him were those of a woman. He circled her with his arms and he felt big and clumsy. She smelt of fresh flowers.

Howells was sitting at a bar some two miles south of Hot Gossip, in a Wan Chai dive called the Washington Club.

The brash signs above the head of the aged doorman who sat outside on a wooden stall promised topless dancers, but it had been many years since the place had seen a naked breast. The main drinking area was a circular bar surrounding a small raised dance floor where two girls wearing identical black and silver swimsuits and high-heeled shoes did their best to keep in time with the music. Between the dancers and the bar a group of middle-aged women in long evening dresses either served customers or sat on stools with faces like thunder.

When Howells had walked in through the door and past the large ornamental fish tank an hour earlier a woman old enough to be his great-grandmother led him to a stool and asked him what he wanted to drink. While she fetched him his lager two of the overweight women moved towards him like menacing bears. One of them reached for his hand and held it, rubbing the flesh gently. She felt like sandpaper, thought Howells. 'How long you been Hong Kong?' she asked, smiling with twisted teeth.

'Two days,' he answered. His drink arrived and he used it as an excuse to get his hand back. A white bill was folded into a plastic tumbler which the great-grandmother placed in front of him.

The second woman, plump with loosely permed hair and a prominent Kirk Douglas dimple on her chin, blinked and said: 'Where you stay?'

'Mandarin Oriental,' lied Howells.

'Good hotel,' she said, nodding. 'What your job?'

'Salesman.'

'What your name?' said the other woman. Bargirl was not the right description. Barwoman? Barhag? Howells wondered how she listed her profession in her passport.

'Tom,' said Howells, using the first name that popped into his head. The women introduced themselves, each formally shaking his hand.

'You buy me drink?' asked Dimple.

Howells could see a price list fixed to a pillar to the left of the dancers showing that his lager was about the same price as it would be in a five-star hotel and that the cheapest hostess drink was about three times as much.

He shook his head. 'Not tonight, thanks.'

'Not expensive,' she said.

'No,' said Howells, and pointedly ignored them. They spoke to each other in Cantonese, gave him a filthy look each and then walked off. Howells nursed his lager and concentrated on the dancers. One was short with long black hair and a small, upturned nose; the other was taller with a frizzy mane of hair and a curvier figure. Both had skin that was a darker brown than the middle-aged couple who had just tried to mug him. As he watched they moved into a synchronized dance routine, legs kicking and shoulders shaking. They'd obviously done it many times, no need to watch each other's steps. Real troupers. Another four girls with skin the same colour as the dancers' sat together at the back of the bar eating shelled peanuts. They were wearing T-shirts over their swimsuits and chattering in a bird-song language, probably Filipina.

There were a dozen or so customers drinking at the bar, all of them male. Three of them were drinking with hostesses, and they had blue slips in their tumblers alongside their own white receipts. One, a balding guy with horn-rimmed spectacles and the downtrodden look of a man who'd escaped from his wife for a few hours, was being given a real working-over by four of the hags, two in front of him and one either side. They were all drinking from champagne glasses and there was a wad of blue chits in his tumbler. They laughed at his every word and the women on his side of the bar took it in turns to massage his neck.

The two dancers came to the end of their routine and stepped off the stage, their places taken by two other girls. The one with the cute nose rubbed herself with a blue towel and shrugged on an orange shirt and sat on a stool opposite a tall, cadaverous man with slicked-back brown hair and a thin moustache. The great-grandmother placed a hostess drink in front of the girl without waiting for the man to agree. Obviously a regular. Probably in love.

Howells sat with both hands cupped around his lager, head slightly bowed but eyes taking everything in – the TV set suspended from the ceiling showing an Olivia Newton-John video that bore no relation to the Cantonese pop song to which the girls were dancing – the two tall and hefty-looking Chinese men standing together by the gents, obviously on standby in case there was trouble – the small Filipina girl in a black strapless dress whose large eyes switched to the door every time it opened – the bags on the floor behind the bar containing the girls' going-home clothes.

The dancing girls stood back to back, wriggling and rubbing their arses together, laughing as if they meant it. Olivia Newton-John was prancing around in jogging gear and a white headband. A girl came out of what Howells reckoned was probably a staff restroom at the far end of the bar, about five foot four with hair that curled under her chin, and eyes that were big and wide and more Western than Asian. She was wearing a clean white blouse with a lace collar and sleeves, a black string bow and a black skirt that reached to the floor.

Her eyes scanned the bar professionally and she smiled when she saw Howells. She seemed to have too many teeth for her mouth, the lips curled back like a horse about to neigh and they gleamed like ivory tombstones in the flashing lights above the dance floor. Howells raised his eyebrows and lifted his glass to her in mock salute. She laughed, her lips curling back even further showing even more teeth and she lifted a slender hand to cover her open mouth. She should have been taken to an orthodontist when she was a child, thought Howells. Maybe her parents didn't know better. Maybe they didn't care.

She walked over and stood next to him. 'Hi. What's your name?' The teeth flashed white.

'Tom,' he said, sticking to his first story.

She held out her hand and he shook it. It felt cool and dry. 'My name is Amy.'

'Pleased to meet you, Amy,' he said. 'Can I buy you a drink?'

She looked taken aback, surprised at the offer. Probably taken all the fun out of it, thought Howells. Maybe he should have played hard to get. She walked over to get her own drink and put a blue chit into Howells' tumbler.

She clinked her glass against his. 'Thank you,' she said.

'You're welcome. How long have you been in Hong Kong?'

She looked confused. 'I was born Hong Kong,' she said, her brow furrowed.

'Where do you live?'

'Tsim Sha Tsui,' she answered.

Howells kept a serious look on his face. 'What is your job?'

Now she really looked confused, and bit her lower lip. She didn't answer.

'You buy me drink?' Howells asked her, and suddenly she got the joke.

'You joking me,' she said, and pinched his forearm, hard. 'You play at bargirl. You very bad man.' She was attractive rather than pretty, her nose slightly flattened, her lips a little too thick, but her eyes were bright and mischievous and her skin was good. She could have been anywhere between twenty-five and thirty-five years old, which put her in a different generation to the rest of the barhags. 'You work in Hong Kong?' she asked.

Howells nodded. 'Salesman,' he said.

'Selling what?'

Death, he thought. 'Fridges,' he said, and she looked at him quizzically. 'Fridges,' he said again. 'To keep things cold.' He drew a box in the air with his hands and mimed opening its door.

She got it and smiled. 'Fridge,' she said, and repeated it a few times, committing the word to memory. That was probably how she picked up her English, thought Howells, talking to customers and getting them to explain the words she didn't understand. Her English wasn't that bad; she had no trouble understanding him so long as he didn't speak too quickly and he wondered how much was the result of pillow talk.

Amy earned her money. She listened carefully to his every word, her eyes never leaving his face, answered all his questions politely and took an interest in him; where did he live, where were his family, how did he like Hong Kong. Occasionally she'd reach across and run her fingertips along his arm and when he flattered her she'd lower her eyelashes and almost blush. She made her small drink last twenty minutes, but as soon as she'd sipped the last drop the great-grandmother sidled up and picked up the empty glass. She showed it to Howells like a detective producing evidence of a murder.

'You buy girl drink?' she asked, tilting the glass from side to side as if to prove that it really was empty.

Howells nodded. 'Sure, why not?'

'Thank you,' said Amy, and put her small hand on top of his as if he'd just done her a huge favour and it wasn't simply a business transaction. Howells wondered how many thousands of times she'd done that, whispered thank you and held hands. Her drink arrived and so did another blue chit.

'What about buy me a drink?' said the old woman.

'Not tonight,' he said. 'Next time.' He turned away from her and concentrated on Amy, asking her about her life.

'My story very sad,' she said.

It was too, a story about a big family and a drunken father who'd assaulted her when she was twelve years old. She'd run away and been befriended by a sixteen-year-old drugs dealer who encouraged her to start chasing the dragon – smoking heroin – and then put her to work in a fishball stall, an underage brothel. She'd escaped from him the day before her fourteenth birthday and fell into the arms of a money-lender who lent her money, set her up in a one-room flat and supplied her with half a dozen customers a night to pay off the interest. She'd eventually met a businessman, a plastic bag manufacturer, who'd promised to marry her but dropped her as soon as she got pregnant. She'd had an abortion but he still wanted nothing to do with her. Now she lived alone and had worked in a succession of bars, on Hong Kong island and over in Kowloon.

She told the story in a flat monotone and Howells wondered how many times she'd told it, and how much of it was true.

She told him how much commission she got from each drink, how many drinks she got a night, how all the girls had to work double shifts – fourteen hours a day – whenever there was an American ship in town. Howells asked her why she didn't dance and she scowled.

'Only Filipina or Thai girls dance,' she said, scornfully. 'Chinese girls not do that.'

That was rich, thought Howells. Mugging drunken tourists for drinks was respectable, going back to their hotels was a legitimate business transaction, but dancing in a swimsuit was beneath her. Amy seemed to have no feelings of shame or regret about her job, it was just business. He asked her how often she left with customers, and she shrugged.

'Depends,' she said. 'Sometimes one month four times, sometimes one month and I not go.'

Again, she had her own set of values. Americans were out 'because they not clean', and she didn't like Germans because a German had once beaten up her friend and stolen her purse. She was wary of tourists and never went with policemen because they wouldn't pay. What she liked best, she said, were married men who lived and worked in Hong Kong. 'They very careful because they not want wife to get sick, and they not stay all night,' she said. You couldn't fault her logic, Howells realized.

'You want to buy me out?' she asked Howells, finishing her second drink. The great-grandmother was by her side before she'd even had a chance to place it on the bar. Howells said yes to the drink, but no to the buy-out offer.

'I've very little money tonight,' he said. 'Maybe another time.'

'No problem,' she said. 'You can use credit card. And we give you receipt.' She pouted and pinched his arm gently, pulling at the hairs. 'I like you, Tom.'

Howells knew it was an act, an act she'd put on thousands of times before, but he was still half convinced that she thought he was special.

He shook his head, firmly. 'I like you too, Amy, but not tonight.'

Her drink and chit arrived, along with a fresh lager for Howells which he hadn't ordered but which he accepted anyway. Amy gently clinked his glass. 'Nice to meet you,' she said. Then she went back to work, talking and laughing and touching.

The dancing girls continued their rota, twenty minutes on and forty minutes off, taking drinks from customers during the rest periods. They seemed to have a different approach to Amy, greedily gulping down their hostess drinks whenever the customers looked away, pouring them into the sink when they went to the gents. Amy was as good as gold, making each drink last a full twenty minutes.

'Do many police come here?' asked Howells.

Amy shook her head. 'No. They go Club Superstar sometimes. It is a disco and you not have to buy girls drinks there.'

Howells smiled. 'Where else do they go? Where Kowloon side?'

Amy pouted again. 'You want to go? You tired of me?'

'No,' he laughed. 'Don't worry.' They touched glasses again. 'Where in Kowloon do they drink?'

'Rick's Café, Canton disco, Hot Gossip,' she said, 'many places.'

Howells remembered the names in the same way that Amy had memorized the word 'fridge'. He left her half an hour later, promising to see her again but not meaning it. She looked mournful as he said goodbye but he looked over his shoulder as he reached the door and saw that she was already on another stool talking to a bearded tourist wearing Union Jack shorts. Just business. Fickle cow, thought Howells.

Dugan was pleasantly surprised when Petal agreed to go home with him. He'd half expected her to play coy but she'd seemed eager and clutched his hand tightly as they sat in the back of the taxi, and when he leaned forward to kiss her, her lips parted and she moaned softly, her small hand gently caressing his thigh.

His luck was obviously in. Even getting the taxi had been fortuitous; normally late at night you had to fight the masses, every man for himself, but tonight one had pulled up just as they walked out into the night air. The gweilo in the back seat had even held the door open for them before disappearing into the disco.

Petal had laughed at all his jokes on the way back to Hong Kong island and she leant against him in the lift. Dugan's heart was pounding and his hands were actually shaking as he slotted the key into the lock and opened the door for her. She grinned as she walked past him, and he was suddenly ashamed of the smallness of the flat. He wanted to impress her and he knew that his shoebox of a home wouldn't impress anyone. God, the bedroom was a mess – and then with a jolt he remembered the unflushed toilet. He pushed past Petal and dashed into the bathroom. He took a deep breath and pushed the handle, sighing out loud as he heard the water flush. When he walked back into the lounge Petal was sitting on the sofa, smiling.

'You seemed in a hurry,' she said. 'Problems?'

'No,' said Dugan. 'When you've gotta go, you've gotta go.' Oh Jesus, had he really said that? 'Can I get you a drink?'

'Hmmm, that would be nice. Do you have any wine?'

Dugan couldn't believe the way things were going. Hiding at the bottom of the fridge was a bottle of Californian white that he'd never got round to drinking. 'Of course,' he said, 'white OK?'

'Fine,' she answered.

Even the cork came out smoothly and for once there were no bits floating on the top when he poured it into two matching glasses. Their fingers touched when Dugan handed her the glass and she smiled again. Dugan sat next to her. The flat was so small there was nowhere else to sit, unless he went into the bedroom.

'Very convenient,' she said.

'I'm sorry?'

She nodded out of the window. 'Very convenient,' she repeated. 'If you get bored watching your television you can always watch the neighbours.' From where they were sitting they could look right into next door's lounge, which was at right-angles to Dugan's. His face fell and she realized she'd hurt his feelings. 'It's a lovely flat,' she said.

'No it's not,' he said, and his voice had a brittle edge to it. 'It's small and it's noisy and if I could afford somewhere bigger I'd move but on an inspector's salary . . .'

She pressed her finger against his lips. 'I love it,' she said. 'Show me the bedroom.'

Howells held the door of the taxi open, not out of politeness but because he found it difficult to take his eyes off the girl who was waiting to take his place, a mixture of small-girl vulnerability and obvious sexuality that he found a little disturbing. She looked like a child but moved with the easy grace of a woman, and her face was that of an angel, albeit an Asian one. He envied the heavily built white guy she was with. She smiled at him as she moved past and murmured a thank you. He breathed in her perfume, the fragrance of jasmine, and then the taxi was gone.

He stood for a moment and then entered Hot Gossip and went upstairs to the bar, where he took an empty stool and ordered a lager. He drank it and looked around with the hungry look of a man on the make looking for a single girl, his eyes flitting from face to face. He made eye contact a couple of times as he checked out the whole bar, hopeful girls without dates, but they weren't what Howells was after.

He watched one of the television sets mounted on the wall, an old black-and-white video of the Beatles, a fresh-faced John Lennon shaking his head in time to the beat. Howells raised his glass to the screen. 'You'll go out with a bang, John,' he said. 'At the top. The best way to go.' He drained the glass and paid his bill and walked down to the hard driving noise of the disco.

He shouldered his way through the sweating crowd, helped by the fact that he was a few inches taller than most of the clientele. His gaze swept back and forth like a fighter pilot on patrol, and he found what he wanted standing by the bar: two Europeans, short haircuts, fit-looking with restless eyes. Howells stood about six feet from them as he ordered another lager, straining to hear them over the music. They looked like coppers and after ten minutes or so Howells had heard enough to know that they were. One was a big bastard, the other was tall and thin with a moustache. They each had a Chinese girl hanging on to their arms but they ignored them, talking over their heads as if they weren't there. They were joined by a third man, also a policeman, and they began discussing another man, something about wanting a transfer. Office politics.

The one with the moustache looked the best yet. Howells was now completely clean-shaven, but it wouldn't be a problem; men shaved and grew moustaches all the time.

Howells waited until he went to the toilet and caught up with him as he banged through the black door.

'Sorry,' muttered Holt.

'OK, no problem,' said Howells, keeping his head down. Holt stood in front of one of the urinals and unzipped his flies. It looked as if they were the only two in the room, but to be sure Howells ducked down and pretended to tie his shoelace while checking the toilet doors. Both unlocked. All clear. Holt had closed his eyes as he urinated. Howells swung his arm round and slammed the edge of his hand into Holt's temple, not hard enough to kill, but hard enough so that the policeman dropped without a sound, urine splashing down his left leg. Howells caught him under the arms and dragged him backwards into one of the compartments. He eased him on to the seat and then undid his belt and pulled the man's trousers down to his ankles. One of Holt's shoes had fallen off and Howells went back for it. He locked himself in with the unconscious man and was just replacing the shoe when the door to the washroom thudded open. Soundlessly Howells sprang up, placing his feet between Holt's thighs and balancing on the seat, arms outstretched against the walls.

When they were alone again Howells finished tying Holt's shoelace before going through his pockets. The warrant card was in a clear plastic pocket in Holt's brown pigskin wallet. Howells took the lot; there was more chance of it looking like a robbery that way. Holt's head had slumped down on his chest. He was breathing heavily through his nose, and apart from a red mark on the side on his head there was nothing to indicate that he hadn't just passed into a drunken stupor. Howells put his hands on top of the cubicle and heaved himself up and over. He stepped down on to the neighbouring toilet bowl and slipped through the door. He kept his head down as he walked back into the disco, nodding in time to the music and pretending to be slightly unsteady on his feet. Two minutes later he was in a taxi heading back to his hotel, gently rubbing his right hand.

Dugan awoke as the morning sunlight shafted through his bedroom window and pinned him to the bed. The aluminium window-frame began clicking as it warmed up and he rolled over in the double bed and opened his eyes. She was gone. For a moment he wondered if he'd dreamt her but there was a dip in the pillow and several long, black hairs, and the smell of her perfume.

'Petal,' he called. 'Are you there?'

There was no reply, and when he walked into the lounge he found a note on the circular dining table. *Pat – you looked so sweet I didn't want to wake you. Call me if you get time – Petal.* She'd left her telephone number and at the bottom of the sheet of notepaper was a flower, hastily drawn.

Dugan made himself a black coffee and sat in his bathrobe as he drank it. Normally he showered first, but this morning he wanted to put if off as long as possible; he knew it was stupid, adolescent even, but he didn't want to get rid of the smell of her.

'God, I'm wrecked,' he said out loud. He grinned stupidly. It had been a long time since a girl had made him feel the way Petal had. There had been a horrible moment when he thought that maybe he'd read the signs wrong and that she was on the game, she'd seemed almost too willing. Dugan was no stranger to hookers; many was the time he'd gone home with one to fill up an empty night, and he didn't begrudge them the money. A couple had even become friends, though he still had to pay them. But he'd wanted Petal as a lover, and as a friend, and anything else would have spoiled it for him. But she didn't force him to shower first, the way that hookers always did, nor did she insist that he wore a sheath. 'I'm on the pill,' she whispered. He'd been overcome by an animal passion that almost scared him with its intensity, but it had been coupled with an overwhelming feeling of tenderness. He'd wanted to squeeze her, bite her, eat her, to dominate her and yet at the same time be completely in her power. He'd stroked and caressed her and he was sure she'd come within seconds of his moving inside her, and eventually he'd cried out her name and afterwards she'd curled up next to him like a cat with his arms around her and he'd fallen asleep with her head under his chin.

He began to grow hard again as he thought of her and when he stepped into the shower he put it on full cold and gasped.

Howells sat in his rented car and yawned. The sky was smudged with the first light of dawn but he'd already been up an hour. He'd bolted down a room-service breakfast and driven out to Ng's house, where he'd parked about a quarter of a mile from the junction of the main road and the track that led up to the triad leader's compound.

There had been three deliveries: the papers, the milk and the post. Nothing else. Howells waited patiently. He didn't read a newspaper, or listen to the radio, or do anything else that might distract him from the job at hand – the waiting and the watching. Twenty minutes after the postman had left, an olive-green Mercedes 560 nosed down the track indicating that it was going to turn right, towards where Howells was sitting. The engine was already running because he'd needed the airconditioner to keep from melting. He waited until the Mercedes passed him, then began to follow it, never getting closer than fifty yards. It headed towards Kowloon and there was plenty of morning traffic so Howells wasn't worried about losing it.

They followed the road into the built-up area and then the car indicated a left turn as it approached a set of traffic lights and Howells did the same. The lights changed to amber as the Mercedes went through and by the time Howells made the turn they were red. The car in front braked suddenly and he had to swerve around it with a squeal of tortured tyres. He had no choice, he knew that, but he also realized that it was a sure way of attracting attention to himself. He should have waited, but he'd reacted instinctively, the way he usually did, letting his subconscious show the way. He stamped on the accelerator and caught up with the Mercedes, twenty feet from its bumper, then fifteen, and then he indicated he was going to overtake and rattled past it. There were three people in the car: a uniformed driver, a heavily built man in a leather bomber jacket in the front passenger seat, and a small girl in pigtails. She had blonde hair, Howells noticed with surprise. The girl was playing with something, her head down in concentration. The driver looked straight ahead but the passenger gave Howells the once-over and then looked scornfully at the rented car.

Howells accelerated until he was about a hundred yards ahead of the Mercedes and then he slowed to match its speed, watching it in the driving mirror. Another set of traffic lights came up and Howells slowed. The Mercedes indicated a right turn and Howells followed suit. They were driving through a commercial area now; shopkeepers were opening their small stores, pushing up metal grilles and sweeping floors. The traffic was denser; there were at least a dozen cars between them, and Howells was having trouble keeping the Mercedes in sight. He came to a busy crossroads and drove straight on, seeing too late that the Mercedes was indicating it was going to turn right again. Howells checked his watch. They'd been driving for twenty-five minutes and he doubted if the girl's school was much further away. He'd pick them up at the crossroads tomorrow morning. Now he had some shopping to do.

He found a diving shop in Tsim Sha Tsui, not far from the hotel. It used up about a third of the cash that had been left over after he'd paid for the ticket from Bali, but he got everything he needed. The guy in the shop must have thought it was Christmas – a customer who didn't bother bargaining and who paid in cash. He carried his purchases back to the hotel in two nylon bags and spread them out on his bed.

There was a single steel cylinder that the salesman had filled with a compressor at the back of the shop, a demand valve, flippers, a mask and a snorkel. Howells had thought about a wetsuit and discarded the idea, because he didn't plan on being in the water for long and the South China Sea wasn't particularly cold. And if he didn't wear a suit he wouldn't need a weight belt; the cylinder would just about balance his natural buoyancy. He'd bought a pair of trunks and a large knife and scabbard to strap to his calf. He already had a diving watch, a gold-plated Chronosport that he'd owned for going on fifteen years, but he'd paid for a good underwater compass. He didn't need a depth gauge.

He'd been prowling among the shelves when he spotted a small metal cylinder with a mouthpiece attached to its mid-point that he'd never seen before. He'd seen one in a James Bond movie once – *Thunderball*, he thought – but that had obviously been faked because it had only been six inches or so long, hardly enough for a couple of breaths even under very high pressure. The packaging on this one said that it was an emergency air supply and could be used for approximately thirty deep breaths. It was, the blurb stressed, only for emergency use. Howells bought one. The shop also sold a range of security equipment: truncheons, torches, Mace sprays and the like. Howells included a pair of handcuffs in his purchases.

He laid them all out on the bed and checked each item again before repacking them and putting the bags in the bottom of the wardrobe. Then he got the Yellow Pages out of the cabinet under the TV and began looking for a firm that hired out boats.

The first one he went to see was moored a couple of hundred yards from the shore of a place called Hebe Haven, about half an hour's drive from the hotel. There were hundreds of boats there, all shapes and sizes, yachts and junks, but the nearest was at least fifty metres away, a small, white and red cruiser that obviously wasn't lived on. He wouldn't be disturbed, he was sure of that, and if pushed he could always move it.

It was built in the style of an old-fashioned junk, shiny teak boards with a raised deck at the back and a single mast, but no sail because down below there was a powerful diesel engine. It bobbed in the water to the sound of ripples slapping against seasoned wood.

'You like?' asked the tall, gaunt Chinese boy standing next to Howells, leaning over the rail and staring at the sea.

'It's a good boat,' said Howells. 'How old is it?'

'Four years,' said the boy. 'Built Kowloon-side. For banker.'

'What happened to him? Emigrate?'

The boy laughed, showing yellowed teeth. 'No emigrate. He steal from bank. Go Taiwan. Bank sell boat. Now I rent.'

It seemed perfect, thought Howells. The hull looked solid, and the portholes were small, too small for even a child to climb through. Below decks was a large master bedroom and a thick, teak door which opened to reveal a small chemical toilet, and there was a lounge area with seats either side that pulled out to form two more beds. A galley kitchen lay to the left of the wooden stairway that led down from the main deck and at the rear was the engine-room.

By the look of the state of the engine it had hardly been used; the banker had probably only bought it for show. The upper deck at the back was perfect for a drinks party, and Howells could imagine a gathering of beautiful people out in the moonlight, drinking pink gins and making small talk.

The boy said that for a price he could arrange a place in one of the typhoon shelters, or even a berth at one of the yacht clubs, but Howells said no, where it was was just fine.

'You sleep here?' the boy asked.

Howells nodded. 'Sometimes.'

'You cannot sail, you must have boatboy to sail. Understand?'

Howells said yes, he understood. He paid a month's charter and a deposit, in cash. Then the boy climbed down to his black and red speedboat and roared off, the boat rocking in his wake. There was a small white glass-fibre dinghy tethered to the back of the junk so that Howells could row himself to the shore. The main landing-place was a large, L-shaped concrete pier that jutted into the water but to either side of it were ungainly, rickety old wooden jetties to which were moored lines of small boats waiting for their owners. Most of them were probably weekend sailors – and by the weekend it should all be over, thought Howells. Bar the shouting.

Dugan's head was starting to hurt, a dull thudding pain behind his left eye. Maybe he needed glasses. Sometimes he had to squint a little when watching television and he had trouble reading the signs down in the MTR stations, but he had no trouble reading, no trouble at all. He rubbed his temples, making small circles with his fingertips, and closed his eyes.

'Sleeping, huh?' said a laconic voice at the door. It was Burr. Dugan kept his eyes closed.

'I'm not sleeping, you wanker. I've just got the mother and father of all headaches.'

'Just behind the eyes, is it?' asked Burr, sympathetically.

'Yes,' growled Dugan.

'A sort of sharp, searing pain, like a nerve pain?'

'Yes.'

'First symptom of a brain tumour,' laughed Burr. 'You're fucked.'

Dugan opened his eyes, but continued to massage the sides of his aching head. 'Can I help you, Colin?' he asked.

'Just popped in to see if you'd heard about Holt.'

'What happened?'

'Stupid bastard got mugged. After you left. In the toilets. They found him sitting on the pan with his trousers round his ankles. They had to break the door down. He reckons somebody walloped him from behind. They took his wallet.'

'He's OK, though?' Dugan was genuinely worried; Holt was a friend.

'Yeah, he's all right. They took him to casualty for a checkup and they gave him the all clear. He'll probably be in Hot Gossip tonight as usual. Are you on for a bevy tonight?'

'I suppose I could be persuaded to force down a pint or two.'

The phone rang and Burr waved goodbye as Dugan picked it up.

'Hi,' said Petal. 'How's your day going so far?'

'It was OK,' lied Dugan. His head was still throbbing. 'Yours?'

'*Ma ma, fu fu,*' she said, Mandarin Chinese for horse horse, tiger tiger – not so good, not so bad. 'Same as usual.'

Dugan realized he didn't even know what she did. But then again, she hadn't asked too many questions about what his job involved. He'd spent what, nine hours in her company, four of them in bed, and yet he knew next to nothing about her. But at the same time he seemed to know everything, a sort of empathy, knowledge by osmosis.

'Are you doing anything tonight?' he asked.

'Nothing planned.'

Dugan cleared his throat. 'Do you fancy going out?'

'With you, you mean?'

Dugan laughed. 'That's what I had in mind.'

'Well . . .' she sighed, but Dugan knew he was being teased.

'Of course, if you've got something else on . . .'

'I'd love to see you,' she said.

'Dinner?'

'Mmm. Where?'

'There's an Italian restaurant in Tsim Sha Tsui, great food.'

'That sounds fine, I love Italian food.'

'OK, I'll meet you opposite the Hang Seng Bank inside the Tsim Sha Tsui MTR station at eight.'

'See you then.'

She put the receiver down first, and Dugan held it

to his ear for a few seconds, listening to the electronic tone.

Howells lay on the bed, flicking the remote control from channel to channel, but there was nothing to hold his attention for more than a few minutes. He'd eaten a room-service sirloin steak an hour earlier. There was nothing in the room worth reading and he didn't feel like sleep.

He'd transferred all the equipment to the junk, and he'd bought a strong lock and bolt which he'd screwed into the toilet door so that it could be locked from the outside. He'd stocked the galley with the bare essentials: bread, milk, and cans of soup and stew. He'd tested the aqualung and spent half an hour snorkelling around the boat, enjoying the feel of the water. But there was nothing he could do now. First he had to find out which school Ng's daughter went to, and he couldn't do that until tomorrow. It wasn't that Howells was nervous; there was no adrenalin rush, just empty hours to fill. He decided to go back to the Washington Club.

The taxi dropped him close to the bar and the moist, humid atmosphere wrapped itself around him like a damp towel as he stepped out of the air-conditioned environment. He was wearing light brown cotton trousers and a dark blue fake Lacoste T-shirt, yet he still felt as if he was overdressed. It wasn't just that it was hot, it was the humidity that made it uncomfortable. He'd spent three weeks in the deserts of Oman a few years back, helping the Government do a favour for the Sultan, and he hadn't felt half as hot as he did now. He wiped his forehead and when he took his hand away it was wet.

At several points along the length of the busy road were small groups of people lighting fires in the gutter. One group was a few steps away from the entrance to Popeye's, and Howells stood for a minute to watch. There was a mother with a young baby strapped to her back, her husband and two small boys gathered around a cluster of joss sticks that had been stuck into a large orange. The man was crouched down, squatting on his heels watching a pile of sheets of paper crinkle and burn. He was holding what at first glance looked like orange banknotes, but there were so many zeros on them that Howells realized they were play money. As the pile in front of him died down, the man fed more notes on to it. To the left of the burning paper was a cardboard plate on which were two pieces of meat, some grapes and a bread roll. The two boys were skipping around their mother, clapping their hands in excitement. Howells couldn't work it out; they were a well-dressed family, and the man was wearing an expensive wristwatch. Some religious festival, maybe. He left them to it.

Amy spotted him as soon as he walked in. She came over and gave him her tombstone smile. 'Nice to see you, Tom.'

She caught him by surprise until he remembered that Tom was the name he'd used the previous night. He was impressed that she'd taken the trouble to remember his name, but then realized that it was part of her job – make the customer feel wanted and important and special and chances are that he'd buy you a drink. Sound commercial sense, nothing else.

'Hiya, Amy. How are you?'

'Happy to see you,' she said, and linked her arm through his, leading him to the circular bar. It was crowded and there were only two empty seats, one either side of a bulky giant of a man with a crew cut and bulging forearms. Amy touched him lightly on the arm and asked him to move to the right, and he did so with a beaming, drunken smile. Amy guided Howells to one of the seats and sat down next to him. 'Beer?' she said.

Howells nodded. 'What's the best local beer?'

'San Mig,' she said. 'You want?'

'Sure, I'll try it.'

There were two girls dancing, with three sitting on stools chattering. The cadaverous man was there talking to his girl-friend, a sheaf of blue chits in the glass on the bar in front of him. Must be love, thought Howells sourly. Most of the men in the bar were soldiers or sailors, youngsters with cropped hair and pimples, laughing and shouting above the pulse of the music, ogling the girls and heckling each other. American accents everywhere. Amy returned with his drink.

'Get yourself one, Amy,' he said.

The girls dancing were Filipina, short and slightly chubby, mahogany skin and black eyes, flirting madly with their adoring audience. The record changed to a Beach Boys number, *Surfing USA* or something, and with whoops of delight three of the young men jumped on to their stools, waving their arms and swaying from side to side in a pretty good imitation of surfing. The girls stopped dancing and stood there pouting with their hands on their hips. Amy put a plastic tumbler in front of him with a white chit for his beer and a blue one for her hostess drink.

'Sailors,' she said. 'Americans.' As if that explained everything.

'Good business,' he said.

'No,' she said, with surprising venom. 'Just trouble. They come from PI. No money left.'

'PI?'

'Philippine Islands. Girls there very cheap. When they come here no money left. And they not buy drinks for girls, just themselves. And usually they very impolite.'

Howells nodded sympathetically. 'How long are they here for?'

'Four days. I think I try to take holiday tomorrow. I ask mamasan.'

'Probably a good idea. What sort of ship are they on?'

'Submarine. Nuclear submarine. They stay about five miles away and come in on small boat. Stay four days and then go.'

'To where?'

'Supposed to be secret, but one of them said they go to Korea. They talk all the time, boasting. See that boy?' She nodded towards the middle of the three barstool-surfers. 'He weapons officer. His job is to fire the missiles.'

He looked to be barely out of his teens, a faceful of freckles and ginger hair, flushed with drink and frowning as he tried to maintain his balance. He whooped and attempted to spin his stool around, his arms windmilling through the air and knocking his two mates over. The three of them tumbled backwards, crashing into the wall behind them and falling into a pile of arms and legs and stools.

One of the girls screamed but they were OK, too drunk to hurt themselves with anything less than a fall from an eight-storey building.

'You look fierce,' said Amy, concern in her voice. 'What is wrong?'

Howells forced a smile. 'Nothing,' he said. 'Just a hard day, that's all. Hey, what's going on outside?'

'What do you mean?'

'Families burning paper and putting food in the street.'

'Festival,' she said. 'Festival of the Hungry Ghosts.'

Howells looked bemused and Amy laughed. 'This is the time of the year when the gates to Hell are opened and all the ghosts come back to earth. You must keep them out of your houses, so you feed them in the street. And burn money for them. You must keep them happy so that they bring good luck.' She lifted her glass and looked at Howells through it. 'Nice to meet you, Tom,' she said. Over the other side of the bar the three surfers had climbed back on to their stools and were busy drinking themselves into oblivion.

The meal had gone well, very well. The pasta had been cooked to perfection, an unusual feat in Hong Kong, the veal was as tender as he'd ever eaten and the bottle of red wine they'd put away had relaxed Dugan completely. The only black spot on the evening had been when the waiter had returned with his Access card and told him that it hadn't been accepted. Dugan realized he hadn't paid the last account from the card company. There hadn't been enough in his bank account to cover it. He handed over his Amex card and smiled apologetically at Petal.

'Let's split it,' she said.

'No, it's OK. It's just an administrative foul-up, that's all. And my salary cheque went in a couple of days ago. Don't worry, I'm solvent.'

Until the bank took his mortgage payment out, and the management charges for his flat, and the electricity, gas and phone bills all got whipped out by the magic of direct debit. And he'd have to pay something on his credit cards or they'd be repossessed this time, he was sure of it. Shit. At least if he was in the private sector he could go and ask his boss for a raise.

'Well, I insist on you letting me buy you a nightcap,' she said. 'How about going back to Hot Gossip?'

'Fine by me,' Dugan answered, though with just a tinge of regret. He wanted to get back into bed with her as quickly as possible. She looked stunning; tight black velvet trousers and a jacket made of some glossy, gold-coloured material, with padded shoulders and a thin collar that was turned up at the back. She had on open-toed shoes and he noticed for the first time that she'd painted her toenails bright pink. God, she was sexy, even more so by virtue of the fact she seemed so small and vulnerable. Still, if the lady wanted Hot Gossip, that's what the lady would get.

They walked through the crowded streets of Tsim Sha Tsui, Dugan taking pride in the fact that Petal turned a lot of heads, Chinese and gweilo. He wanted the whole world to know that she was with him, wanted to label her as spoken for. He made do by holding her hand. It felt small and cool and was lost in his.

Most of the shops they walked past were for tourists: electric goods, jewellers, high fashion, with a sprinkling of topless bars, but even here families were out in force with their offerings to the ghosts.

'Do your family do this?' asked Dugan.

Petal nodded earnestly. 'Of course. It's part of our heritage. Even more so on the mainland. I help clean my ancestors' graves each year, I eat moon cake during the moon festival, I feed the ghosts.' He still couldn't get used to the cut-glass accent coming from such an obviously Chinese girl.

'But do you believe in it all?'

'It doesn't matter whether I believe it or not. That's not the point. It's part of being Chinese. You wouldn't understand, and I don't mean that nastily.' She squeezed his hand. 'I'm not explaining it very well,' she said.

'Are your family in Hong Kong?' he asked.

'No,' she said. 'Manchuria, northern China. What about your parents? Where are they?'

Dugan noticed the sharp change in subject, as if he'd touched a nerve. It was understandable, though; many Hong Kong Chinese were sensitive about their origins. Most were refugees, or the children of refugees, and the richer families didn't like anyone taking too close a look at their backgrounds because a great many of the old fortunes were based on opium or drug smuggling.

'They live in a town called Cheadle Hulme, near Manchester.'

'The north of England.'

'That's right. They have a shop there, a bookshop.'

'Are you from a big family?'

Dugan shook his head. 'No, just one sister, Jill.'

They'd reached the entrance to the disco, but went upstairs to the bar. Standing at their usual place were Bellamy and Burr, and Bellamy raised his eyebrows as he saw who Dugan was with.

'Petal,' he said, stepping forward to meet her. 'So nice to see you again. It seems like only yesterday . . .'

'It was only yesterday, Jeff,' said Colin.

Bellamy took her elfin hand and kissed it gently. Dugan felt a flash of jealousy but let it pass. Bellamy tried it on with every girl he met. His theory was that the more times you tried, the more often you'd succeed – it was just a matter of statistics.

'How's Holt?' asked Dugan.

'He'll be OK, it's his pride that hurts more than anything,' said Burr.

Dugan put his arm protectively around Petal's shoulders. She smiled up at him and held him around the waist. Bellamy and Burr looked at each other with mock horror on their faces.

'The boy's in love,' gasped Burr.

'Throw a bucket of water over them, somebody,' yelled Bellamy.

'Christ,' said Dugan, and he looked up at the ceiling in exasperation.

Petal seemed to revel in the company of the three men, laughing at Bellamy's corny jokes and listening with rapt attention to Burr's stories of police work. Dugan began to show his impatience; he didn't want to be standing at the bar with just one third of her attention, he wanted one hundred per cent of her, ideally naked and preferably in bed. He kept his arm around her shoulder and occasionally he'd give her an encouraging squeeze, but she made no move to go. The bar was busy, buzzing with its usual night-time mix of off-duty coppers, television starlets, Chinese yuppies and underworld figures. For once Dugan's eyes weren't prowling the crowd looking for possible conquests – he'd got all he wanted right under his arm. Petal was all he wanted to look at. It had been a long time since he'd felt like that about a girl.

'But aren't you frightened, taking on the triads?' she asked Burr.

'What's to be frightened about?' he said.

'Well,' she hesitated, 'don't they try to stop you?'

'Of course,' he said. 'But not with violence. They wouldn't dream of hurting a copper, not a gweilo anyway. The whole force would come down on them like a ton of bricks. They fight each other all the time, hatchets, guns, acid, the works. But it's always in-house violence, the public hardly ever gets hurt. And they leave the cops alone.'

Bellamy nodded in agreement. 'Most of the top triads are OK guys when you meet them socially. Wouldn't you say so, Dugan?'

Dugan grinned, a smile with no warmth. Bellamy was a bit tight, but even when sober he took a malicious glee at picking away at people's sore points, and right now friendships with triads was a definite touchy subject so far as Dugan was concerned.

'Take a look around you,' said Burr, waving theatrically with his arm. He pointed at a Chinese youth, late twenties, in a snappy blue silk suit, who was eating a steak and talking at the same time to a demure girl in a tight-fitting black dress that left little to the imagination. On the table in front of the man was a mobile telephone.

Petal raised an eyebrow expectantly. 'What about him?'

'Triad,' he said. 'Danny Lam. Very big in drugs, and I mean big. Danny Boy drives a very pretty little Ferrari, and he's partial to young Chinese girls – and I mean young. That one he's with now is twice the age he normally goes for. He gets them hooked on cocaine and when he's finished with them he hands them over to one of the fishball stalls.'

Petal wrinkled her nose. 'The what?'

'You've never heard of fishball stalls?' said Bellamy in disbelief. 'Under-age brothels. Chinese only, gweilos are never allowed in. We raid about five a week, charge the organizers and send the girls back to their parents. A few days later the girls run away again and the bad guys are out on bail. And so it goes on. See that guy over there?' This time he gestured towards another young man, this one with slicked-back hair and an expensive leather jacket. Under one arm he carried a small Gucci case from which protruded the aerial of a portable telephone. He was laughing with two teenage girls, one either side. Not exactly twins, but close. Petal looked at Bellamy for an explanation.

'Stockbroker,' he said. 'One of the best. Drives a Porsche. Now, can you tell them apart? Neither can I. They look the same, they drink in the same bars, they're members of the same clubs, they eat at the same restaurants. Chances are they even went to the same school.'

'What are you getting at?' said Dugan, angrily. He felt as if Bellamy was setting him up for something, but he wasn't sure what.

'The point I'm trying to make to Petal, Patrick my boy, is that triads are no different to any other local businessmen.'

'In fact,' added Burr, 'we actually get on quite well with some of them.'

'You're friends with them?' said Petal.

'No, not friends,' said Bellamy. 'Never friends. But we drink with them. It's part of the game. They'll stand and talk with us, part of the macho image, it gives them a boost to be seen drinking with cops. And sometimes they'll give you info about one of their competitors.'

'Part of the job,' said Burr.

'Sounds crazy,' said Petal, slipping into Cantonese.

'The world is crazy,' replied Burr, also in Chinese. All three of the men were good enough to be able to flit between the two languages without hesitation.

'Don't your bosses mind you mixing with the guys you're supposed to be trying to catch?' asked Petal, genuinely puzzled.

'There's a line that we don't cross, Petal. We drink with them, we laugh and joke with them, but that's as far as it goes,' said Burr. 'At the end of the day we're trying to put them away.'

'Listen to the Lone Ranger,' laughed Bellamy.

Dugan felt a fingernail run down his spine, and for a moment he thought it was Petal until he realized that her arm was around his waist. He turned to look over his left shoulder and found himself looking into a pair of green, knowing eyes above a slightly upturned nose and a wide, smiling mouth. The smile grew wider and dimples appeared in both cheeks, and as she tilted her head to one side her long blonde hair rippled.

'How's it going, brother of mine?'

'Hiya, Jill. Business as usual, nothing changes. You look good.'

She did, too. The white silk blouse and hip-hugging grey skirt she was wearing had exclusive designer labels and she had several ounces of gold hanging around her neck. The gold Rolex was new, and he didn't recognize the small pearl earrings. It seemed that every time he saw his sister these days she had something new, either clothes or jewellery. She wore her wealth like a badge of office. With pride.

She looked at Dugan's companions. 'Jeff,' she said, 'nice to see you. And you, Colin. Long time no see.'

They raised their glasses to her in unison.

'The lovely Mrs Ng,' said Bellamy. 'Where's your better half?'

'Speak of the devil,' said Burr. 'Here he comes now.'

A tall, well-built Chinese walked along the bar, confidently, like a male model on a catwalk, shoulders swaying slightly, one hand in the trouser pocket of his grey double-breasted suit, the other outstretched towards the girl. He was about forty years old, his hair short and trimmed around his ears, making his face seem even squarer than it was. He looked like a man who was used to wielding power, a man who expected to be obeyed.

He took Jill's hand and smiled, his thin lips pulling back into a smile that would have been cruel if the eyes hadn't been so warm as he looked at her. 'Sorry,' he said. 'He wouldn't let me go.' She tilted her chin up and kissed him on the cheek. Behind him were two men with hard eyes and unsmiling faces. They were never far from Simon Ng or his wife. Bodyguards. Ng looked past his wife at Dugan and nodded.

'Hello Pat,' he said.

'Simon,' he replied.

'And Mr Bellamy and Mr Burr. My favourite policemen. Can I buy you gentlemen a drink?'

The two cops beamed at him, and together drained their glasses. 'I'll have a brandy and Coke. A double,' said Bellamy.

'And I'll have a malt whisky,' said Burr. 'A treble.' It was a game they'd played many times with the triad leader.

A barman had followed Ng as he walked along the bar and was waiting patiently for him to order, ignoring several other thirsty customers. Ng ordered drinks for the two cops and a bottle of champagne and the barman moved off in double time. Ng had that effect on most people.

'What can I get you, Pat?'

Dugan lifted his half-filled glass. 'I'm OK, Simon, Thanks.' Ng looked at Petal, and then back to Dugan. 'I'm sorry,' said Dugan. 'This is Petal. Petal, this is my sister, Jill, and her husband, Simon.'

'Nice to meet you,' she said.

'If you'll excuse me, there's someone I have to see,' said Ng, and he walked over to the table where the blue-suited man was deep in conversation with the girl in the tight black dress. The man practically jumped to his feet and shook hands energetically with Ng, inviting him to sit with them.

'So how long have you known my little brother?' Jill asked Petal.

'Not so little,' interrupted Burr.

'I used to change his nappy, he'll always be my little brother,' said Jill.

'For God's sake, you were three years old at the time,' said Dugan, reddening. Ng was using the man's portable phone, talking and nodding. The girl was watching one of the television screens and pouting.

'Not long,' said Petal.

'Don't worry, he grows on you,' said Jill.

'Like mould,' said Bellamy, and Burr spluttered into his whisky.

Petal smiled at Jill. 'I know what you mean,' she said.

'What do you do, Petal?' asked Jill.

'I'm with the Bank of China. And you?'

'A lady of leisure,' she laughed. 'Bringing up an eight-year-old girl and looking after Simon.'

'You have an eight-year-old daughter?' said Petal, surprised.

'I married young.'

'Too young,' said Dugan.

'Pat didn't approve,' said Jill. 'Nor did our parents.'

'For different reasons,' said Dugan, sourly.

Dugan's objection had been that Simon Ng was a triad member. Their parents didn't want the marriage to go ahead because Ng was Chinese. One of the crueller things they'd said was that they didn't want Chinese grandchildren. Subtle. Jill had gone ahead regardless and she hadn't seen them since. In a way she'd had the last laugh, for when Sophie had been born she'd taken most of her genes from her mother and had curly blonde hair and European features – only the soft brown eyes had come from her father. But it made no difference, because by then the damage had been done.

'Come on, Petal, come and sit down with me and I'll tell you a few things about my little brother,' said Jill, leading her to a table close to where Ng was sitting.

Dugan sighed deeply. It just wasn't turning out to be his night.

The Navy boys were getting frisky. Two of them were on their knees behind the bar forming periscopes with their arms and making sonar noises. Their pals thought it was hysterical, and the dancers were laughing too until one of the glasses of lager was knocked over. The mamasan went over and asked them to be quiet, and the barhags moved away. The boys behaved for all of ten minutes before the horseplay started again, a game of tag with the freckle-faced weapons officer as 'It'.

He ran around the fish tank, feinted to dash out through the entrance and then lurched back to the bar. His mates were hard on his heels as he ran around the bar and ducked into the changing-room, from where he emerged five seconds later chased by two semi-naked dancers, shrieking and hitting him with towels.

He cannoned into the giant with bulging forearms, spilling his drink down the front of his T-shirt. The man growled angrily, grabbed Freckle-face by the throat and banged him against the wall. Amy slid off her stool and moved behind Howells, just in time because the younger man brought up his knee into the giant's groin and pushed him backwards. All the girls started screaming as the giant fell against Howells and overbalanced the stool. They fell to the floor together, Howells underneath, and the weight of the big man winded him. The giant rolled off and went after the weapons officer while Amy helped Howells to his feet.

By the time Howells was up Freckle-face was back with his head being pounded against the wall, his eyes rolling and his neck limp. Two other youngsters were trying to pry the big man's fingers from around their friend's throat, but with little success.

'He's killing him,' gasped Amy.

She was right, Howells realized. There was manic gleam in the man's eyes, a combination of alcohol and bloodlust that by the look of it was only going to end one way. And if the boy was seriously hurt or even killed then the police would come, and that was the last thing he needed.

'Tom, you must stop them,' said Amy, as if she'd read his mind. He looked at her, frowning, and she took him by the arm. 'Mamasan not here, she go to other bar. She leave me in charge.'

Howells realized then that the Chinese heavies he'd seen on his earlier visit weren't there either.

'Please, Tom. I be in big trouble. Some of the dancers do not have visas. Please stop them now.' She practically pulled him off his stool.

Howells decided he'd help; partly because she was so insistent, but also because he could see that Freckle-face was going to get hurt and he knew that if the police did come they'd take names and addresses and ask for identification and he didn't want anyone to know where he was.

Freckle-face's breath was rasping now, his eyes beginning to glaze and spittle foaming on his lips. The big man was breathing heavily through his nose as Howells moved up behind him and slammed his cupped hands against his ears, hard enough to stun but not hard enough to burst his eardrums. He bellowed and released his grip immediately, turning to face Howells with murder in his eyes. Howells smiled, relishing as he always did the way time seemed to almost stop when he was in combat. He could see each drop of sweat on his opponent's forehead, the red tinge to the whites of his eyes, the throbbing veins in his arms. He saw him step forward as if in slow motion and reach out with splayed fingers.

Howells let him come, taking a step backwards and dropping down as he put most of his weight on his rear leg, ready to spring forward. His right hand was clenched and in the ready position on his hip, his left hand slightly crooked, fingertips pointing at the man's face. He was still smiling. Relaxed – Howells had long passed the stage where he tensed up during a fight. There was only one time for tension, and that was when you made contact.

He knew it was a lot easier to kill a man or cripple him than it was to stop him without causing too much damage, and from his cat stance he could put together fifty or sixty combinations of moves that would end the life of the big sailor as easily as stepping on a cockroach. Part of Howells wanted to do it, to bring the side of his palm crashing against the man's temple, to hammer his knee with the side of the foot and then slam his elbow into the man's throat and feel the cartilage splinter. But the rational part of him knew that now wasn't the time. Best bet would be the solar plexus, but he wouldn't risk his fist because too hard and he'd break the sternum. He let the man move until he was almost on top of him, then he went under the outstretched arms, still in his crouch, and threw his right hip forward and thrust his arm towards the centre of the man's chest, dead centre between the base of his ribs. The fist unclenched as his arm moved and when he hit it was with the palm of his hand and it was controlled, but even so the sailor moved back a full yard in small shuffling steps, bent double. He slumped sideways against the wall and then slid down it to the floor, conscious but totally unable to move, his arms clasped around his stomach. The bloodlust had gone from his eyes; now he just looked pained.

Howells gestured to the two young sailors who'd been trying to help their friend. 'Dump him in a cab, now,' he said. 'With any luck, by the time he's recovered he'll have forgotten where he was when it happened.'

The two of them had to strain to lift him, and they half carried, half dragged him out of the bar.

'Thanks mister,' said Freckle-face. 'Thanks a lot.'

He went back to the other side of the bar as Howells picked up his stool and sat on it. Amy stood close to him, and slipped her arms around his waist. 'Thank you,' she said looking up at him. 'Where you learn to fight like that?'

'I had a rough upbringing,' he said, but saw from the look on her face that she didn't understand.

'You looked so peaceful when you were fighting. What style do you fight?'

'No style,' Howells answered. He knew what she meant by peaceful. That's how he felt when he was fighting – at peace. With himself and with the world. Only one thing gave him more satisfaction, more contentment, than fighting. And that was killing.

There was a strong smell of burning as Dugan and Petal stepped out of the lift.

'Jesus Christ,' said Dugan.

'What's wrong?' said Petal. 'Is the building on fire?'

'No,' answered Dugan. 'Just one of the neighbours appeasing his ancestors. It's too much trouble to go outside so they use the stairwell.'

He took her to a wooden door and pushed it open. It led to a small landing where the occupants of his floor left their rubbish to be collected in a large plastic bin. Dusty concrete stairs zig-zagged down to the entrance hall far below. They were supposed to be for emergency use only but Dugan had trudged up and down several times when the lifts had failed. Where the stairs angled to the right at the floor below, an old lady in a blue flowery-patterned trouser suit bent over a chipped enamel bowl, inside which sheets of paper money burnt with a reddish flame. She looked up, startled, like a child caught shoplifting, then relaxed as she saw it wasn't a security guard. She shouted a greeting up to Dugan and he answered.

'Mrs Chan, she lives in the flat directly below me. She's a nice old lady, almost stone-deaf.'

'That must be useful if you want to play your stereo loud,' said Petal.

They left Mrs Chan to it. 'It's a strange place, Hong Kong,' said Dugan as he unlocked the door to his flat. 'Twenty-odd floors up in a modern tower block and a little old lady carries out a tradition that goes back thousands of years without a thought to the fire risk. The management sent around a letter a few days back specifically telling residents not to light fires and joss-sticks inside the buildings and pointing out that there were specific areas on the podium outside where they could do it. But does anyone take any notice? Do they hell. Sometimes I lie awake at night worrying what would happen if one of the flats below went up in flames. You know the ladders of the fire engines only go up eight floors? Any higher than that and you're on your own.'

'I think you worry too much, Pat,' said Petal, flopping down on to the settee.

'Yeah, maybe you're right. Coffee?'

'Please. I liked your sister,' she called after him as he went into the kitchen and switched on the electric kettle.

'Sorry?' he said, popping his head around the door.

'I said I liked Jill. And Simon. They seem a very happy couple.'

'They are. I was a bit worried at first when they married, but it's worked out really well.'

'Worried about what?'

'You know, Chinese guy and English girl. It can lead to problems.'

'It happens all the time,' said Petal.

'No it doesn't. Sure, lots of gweilos take Chinese wives, but not the other way around.'

'Sexist pig,' she laughed. 'Or do I mean racist pig?'

'You know what I mean. A pretty girl is a pretty girl, it doesn't matter where she's from. Wherever in the world she goes she'll be looked at as a pretty girl.'

'And?'

'And it doesn't work the other way. They look at the girl and wonder why she's with a Chinese. Then straight away they'll assume it's for money.'

'Who's they, Pat?' Petal asked in a soft voice. He could feel that he was forcing himself into a corner.

'You know, Petal. Everybody. And I'm not just talking about gweilos, the Chinese themselves are just as bad, just as racist. You know what the Chinese call the children of all mixed marriages.'

'Bastards,' said Petal.

'Bastards,' repeated Dugan. 'Neither one nor the other. And when they die, only the Chinese half goes to Heaven.'

'It's folklore, Pat, just that. Nobody means it any more.' The kettle began to whistle, and Dugan leapt at the opportunity to cut the conversation short. Jesus, second date and already he was arguing with her – over race, of all things.

He put his head around the door again. 'Milk and sugar?'

'Please,' she said. 'Three sugars.'

Dugan brought the coffee in and handed it to her in his Mickey Mouse mug.

'Careful,' he said, 'it's hot.' She took the mug from him.

'Jill invited us to Sophie's birthday party tomorrow evening, and on Sunday for a barbecue at their house,' she said, and sipped the hot liquid.

Just like Jill, thought Dugan, she'd already tagged Petal and him as an item. In a couple of days she'd have them up to the altar and married.

'House?' he said. 'More like a fortress.'

'What do you mean?'

Dugan looked at her through narrowed eyes. 'You do realize what my brother-in-law is?' he asked. He mentally kicked himself, because of course she didn't. He hadn't mentioned it, and Hot Gossip wasn't the right place to start talking about it, certainly not in front of Bellamy and Burr, anyway. He sat down on the couch next to her. 'He's a triad leader, a Dragon Head. Or to be more accurate, the son of a triad leader. One of the most powerful in Hong Kong, Ng Wai-sun, now living in quiet retirement on the Peak and waiting to join his ancestors. Ng Wai-sun has three sons, Simon, Charles and Thomas. Charles is into property development in Canada, legitimate by all accounts, Thomas is in San Francisco looking after the American end of the business, and Simon runs the show in Hong Kong.'

'But what exactly does he do?'

'The same as every other triad in Hong Kong – extortion, protection, illegal gambling, prostitution, drugs. Remember that smooth-looking character that he went up to talk to, Danny Lam?'

Petal nodded. 'The one who likes young girls?'

'That one. He works for Simon. Simon's not a good guy, Petal, don't be deceived by appearances. He's never done me any harm, not intentionally anyway, and he worships Jill and Sophie, but I trust him about as far as I can throw him.'

'What do you mean "intentionally"?'

'I mean he hasn't ever set out to hurt me. But because of him I'm stuck in a job I hate and I can't move.'

'Commercial Crime?'

'Yeah. I want action, Petal, I want to be where the

bullets fly, I want to be a real policeman and not a paper shuffler. But with a triad leader as a brother-in-law they're hardly likely to trust me, are they?'

'Is it that bad?'

'Yes, it's that bad. But what can I do? Jill loves him, she always has done, ever since they met almost ten years ago.'

'You were a cop when they married?'

'Yeah. Just out of my probation. Jill knew the damage that marrying him would do, hell, we talked about it often enough. She loves him, that's the end of it. And the end of my chance of getting involved in real policework. I only got told semi-officially last night, just before I met you. I'd always known it, but I'd always hoped that if I kept my nose clean I'd prove myself. But apparently that's not to be. I stay where I am, or I leave the force.'

'And you don't want to?'

'There's not much else I can do, Petal. Being a private detective looks glamorous on the TV, but real life is different. I suppose I could go and work for Simon.' He laughed bitterly, and Petal placed her mug on a side-table and put her hands on his shoulders. She put her face up close to his, close enough so he could feel her warm breath on his lips.

'I'm sorry, Patrick Dugan. Sorry that you aren't happier.'

She kissed him full on the lips, her small pointed tongue probing between his teeth. She moved against him and slowly straddled him, sitting in his lap and squeezing him with her thighs. Dugan groaned and closed his eyes.

Howells looked at his watch and tapped the steering wheel impatiently. There was no way he could have missed the Mercedes; he'd arrived at the crossroads well before seven o'clock and tucked the Mazda into a layby while he waited, but two hours later there was still no sign of Ng's car. Either the girl wasn't being taken to school today, or the driver kept changing routes.

He drove back to the side-road leading up to Ng's house but he couldn't see if the Mercedes was there or not. He couldn't risk hanging around because the guards would be sure to spot him, so instead he began to explore the surrounding area to get a feel of the roads.

He got back to the hotel early in the afternoon. He wolfed down a hamburger and chips in the coffee shop before walking over to the tourist area of Tsim Sha Tsui. He wanted a tape recorder and he found one quickly, a Sony about the size of a paperback book with a decent speaker. He didn't bother bargaining, but got the surly teenage assistant to throw in batteries and a C90 tape for the price. He paid in cash and went back to his room.

He spent the next forty-five minutes lying on his bed with the tape recorder switched on to record, the red light glaring at him accusingly as he read aloud listings from the Yellow Pages, a continuous monologue of names, addresses and telephone numbers. He kept varying the speed and tone of his delivery, but even so he was flagging towards the end of the tape and sighed with relief when it eventually clicked to a halt. He helped himself to a Coke from the minibar as the machine rewound the forty-five minutes' worth of verbal garbage.

For the first time in months Patrick Dugan overslept. Despite the searing sunshine, the clicking window-frame and the echoing lift doors, it was past 10.30 a.m. when he opened his eyes. He was alone, though Petal had left a note saying she'd call him about Sophie's birthday party and underneath it her signature flower.

He'd bought Sophie's present earlier in the week, a big floppy Old English Sheepdog toy with hair hanging over its eyes and a red bow tied behind one ear. He'd wrapped it as best he could and put it on the top shelf of his wardrobe, and after he had shaved and showered he put the parcel on his bed. A paw had come loose and was poking out but it looked kind of cute so he left it as it was. He thought of taking it into the office with him but knew that he'd get his leg pulled so he left it where it was. He'd come back and pick it up after work. Jill hadn't told him where Sophie's party was going to be, but he doubted if it would be at home. Simon Ng would want to be seen to be spending a great deal of money on his daughter and doing it at home would be interpreted as doing it on the cheap, as a massive loss of face. Ng would probably book a function room at one of the big hotels in Tsim Sha Tsui, so Dugan would be able to come back to Tai Koo Shing to change and then get the MTR over the harbour.

He got through most of the morning on autopilot. His headache had returned, with a vengeance. He'd swallowed

114

a couple of aspirins but they hadn't made him feel any better. Maybe it was his eyes – sometimes headaches were a sign that you needed glasses. He closed his left eye and looked at the type-written sheet in front of him. He had no problem reading it. He tried it with his right eye closed and the left open, and he could still read it. He held the sheet at arm's length and squinted at it.

'What the hell are you doing?' It was Tomkins, standing in the doorway with a file under his arm.

'I'm trying to work out if I need glasses or not.'

'Headache again? It could be the airconditioning,' said Tomkins.

Dugan put the paper down on his cluttered desk. 'What do you mean?'

'I read an article somewhere that they put ions into the air, or take them out, or something. Or was that aerosols? What the fuck, who cares anyway. How are you getting on with the kite-flyer?'

'Uphill all the bloody way. I'm still no nearer finding where the money went. Why?'

Tomkins waved the file triumphantly. 'Lee Ling-ling is her name, isn't it?'

Dugan said yes, brow furrowed. 'You on to something?'

'There can't be too many Lee Ling-lings around. And I've just come across one who's a director of a futures trading company that appears to be trading without any clients.'

'Hardly surprising, considering the lack of interest in the futures market here. Hang Seng Index futures aren't actually flavour of the month, are they?'

'Yes, but this firm has been buying Standard and Poors

500 futures quite heavily, so much so that the authorities in New York asked us to take a look. And up crops little Ling-ling. Maybe that's where she's been putting her ill-gotten gains.'

'She's a greedy little cow if she has. If I'd been her I'd have salted it away in a Swiss bank account somewhere.'

'Yeah, well, not everyone is as careful with their money as you, are they?'

'Is that the file?'

Tomkins nodded. 'I need it though, so just photocopy anything you need.' He threw it on to Dugan's desk. 'Let me have it back when you've finished.'

He left the office, walking as he always did as if someone had grabbed him by the back of his belt and was jerking him up and down. His buttocks were clenched, as if he expected at any minute to be the victim of anal rape. Some of the guys called him God because he moved in such a mysterious way. Tomkins outranked Dugan, but they were the same age and had been in the force for the same length of time, so they tended to operate as equals unless Tomkins was in a particularly foul mood. Both men knew that if it wasn't for Dugan's brother-in-law their positions could easily have been reversed.

Dugan massaged his temples with his knuckles. Thinking of Lee Ling-ling reminded him of Petal and he cursed himself again for not getting her office number. The phone rang and he grabbed for it, hoping it was Petal but not too disappointed to find it was his sister. He got a small glow of satisfaction when she told him that Sophie's birthday party was being held at the Regent Hotel.

'Seven o'clock,' she said. 'And I should have told you before, it's a theme party.'

'And the theme?'

'Pirates,' she said.

'Yeah, that'd be right,' he said.

'Behave, brother of mine.'

'Or you'll have my legs broken?' said Dugan, laughing.

'Are your phones tapped?' she said. 'Because I'd hate anyone to hear what I'm about to say to you.'

'I'll see you tonight, you can say it to my face.'

'Be there or be square,' she said, and hung up.

Dugan had barely replaced the receiver before it rang again. It was Petal.

'I overslept,' said Dugan.

'You had a hectic night,' she laughed.

'You should have woken me up,' he said. 'When you left.'

'I didn't have the heart to disturb you. You sleep like a small boy. Anyway, I'm just calling to see what time we're going to Sophie's party.'

'That's a coincidence, I'm just this minute off the phone with my sister. It's at the Regent Hotel. How about I meet you there, just before seven – is that OK?'

'Fine. It should be great fun, the pirate theme is a terrific idea.'

'How did you know?'

'Jill told me last night. I'm really looking forward to it.'

Then she said she had to go and the line clicked off, almost in mid-conversation, as if someone had come near her and she didn't want to be overheard. Maybe they didn't like her making personal phone calls. He bent down over the files. The evening seemed an eternity away.

Howells looked at his watch. Half past six. There was nothing he could do now until the following morning. He had a good working knowledge of the roads in the New Territories and the scuba gear had been tested. He stood at the window and looked across the harbour to the office blocks of Central. There were still lights in many of the windows, and behind the business district towered the mountains of Hong Kong island, dotted with the houses of the rich.

Below the hotel, between the road and the bustling harbour, was a wide walkway that followed the water, dotted with courting couples and tourists taking the evening air. There were fishermen too, old men and teenagers, squatting by the water's edge and throwing in baited lines. He saw one youngster yank in his line and pull up a small, struggling fish. Behind him stood an old man with a walking stick, which he was waving in the air in wide circles as he shifted his weight from foot to foot. At first glance Howells thought that perhaps he was just a senile old man throwing a fit, but as he watched he began to tune in to his rhythm. The stick was being used to block and to strike, and the old man was constantly moving his centre of gravity but was always in a stable position. He flowed from one position to another, and Howells saw the stick strike at head height, then down low as if tripping an attacker, then the man slowly spun around and used the stick in a scythe-like motion. It wasn't a form of martial arts that Howells recognized, but he could sense the purpose of the movements and could differentiate the killing blows from the blocks. He began to mimic the man as he watched, pacing his breathing as he twisted and turned in time with the old master. It felt good.

The adrenalin began to flow as he exercised, and he knew that he wouldn't be able to stay confined in the room all evening. He decided to go for a walk and left the hotel to stroll along the main road, towards the Star Ferry terminal. The pavements were so densely packed that he was constantly jostled and banged. He hated to be touched; it was bad enough that his personal space was constantly being invaded, but physical contact really put him on edge. At the first pedestrian crossing he came to he went over to the other side of the road where there seemed to be fewer people. He walked past a huge shopping complex, the New World Shopping Centre, the air filled with rattling chimes as the warm wind blew through a high-tech chrome sculpture. Cars were turning off the main road to drive up to the Regent Hotel on his left and Howells stopped to let them go.

As the last car accelerated away he stepped into the road, and then a big Mercedes sounded its horn and turned the corner and he stood back on the pavement. His mouth dropped in surprise as he recognized Simon Ng sitting in the back seat, next to the little girl. He couldn't see who else was in the back seat but he was sure it would be Jill Ng. The Mercedes drove up to the hotel, followed by a dark blue saloon car. Howells briskly walked after them and arrived as Simon Ng was helping his daughter out of the car. She was dressed as a pirate and was chattering excitedly, this time without pigtails, her hair loose around her face. A striking blonde woman in expensive clothes waited until a doorman in a gleaming white uniform opened the door for her before stepping out of the car. Jill Ng. The passenger in the front seat was the heavily built man he'd seen last time he followed the Merc, but he'd forsaken the leather bomber jacket for a dark green suit and a black velvet bow tie. The occupants of the saloon car also got out, three of them, young men who looked as if they could handle themselves. Howells could see that they weren't carrying guns but he had no doubt that they'd have knives concealed under the expensive suits. Two of them walked into the hotel lobby and looked around as the little girl slipped her hand into Ng's and tried to pull him along. He waited until one of the bodyguards turned and nodded before allowing her to drag him inside. Jill Ng walked with him and they were followed in by the other two men with watchful eyes. One of them slipped the doorman a tip as the two cars drove off, and then looked at Howells as he too walked into the lobby. Howells knew they wouldn't regard him as a threat – they'd be on the lookout for rival triads, not a gweilo.

Howells' mind was racing. All his planning had been based on catching Ng alone, and he knew it would be foolish to risk an attack when Ng had so many bodyguards around. But he also knew how often in the past he'd been able to take advantage of luck, to deviate from a set strategy because an opportunity presented itself. The group walked across the lobby, heading for a large white marble staircase. Howells walked at an angle to them as if heading for a newspaper counter to the left of the reception desk.

He saw Jill Ng say something to her husband, who nodded and smiled and freed his hand from the small girl's and came back down the stairs, heading for where Howells stood flicking through the newspapers. The bodyguards stood on the stairs and watched as Ng walked across the lobby. Howells dropped his left hand slightly and clenched and unclenched his hand, controlling his breathing. *Yes or no?* his mind screamed. The lack of a weapon didn't worry him: a fist to the temple, or the side of the hand to the throat, or the neck, one blow would do it. He wanted to, God he wanted to, he could feel the blood-lust rising like a sexual urge. Why was Ng on his own, what was he doing? What were his bodyguards playing at?

Ng reached the counter and spoke to the girl in Chinese. She pointed to a bank of phones and smiled and as Ng thanked her Howells stepped back, his mind screaming *Yes! Yes! Now!* He began to move his arm and then over Ng's shoulder he saw two of the bodyguards coming up, concern on their faces; Howells relaxed, picked up a copy of the *South China Morning Post* and paid the girl for it.

Ng's bodyguards walked with him as he went over to the telephones. Howells took the paper and sat down on one of the large leather sofas where he had a view of the stairs and could also watch Ng make his call. Had the bodyguards simply slipped, or were they normally so careless? Maybe they were over-confident, or perhaps they'd relaxed once they'd checked that the lobby was clear. Either way, it was a good omen for what was to come. But God, how he would have loved to have done it there and then, to have taken Ng's life with his bare hands and then slipped away.

Ng finished his call and the three men went back up the stairs after Jill and the girl. Howells decided to stay put for a while. Over the next half an hour he saw a number of children dressed as pirates being escorted up the stairs by doting parents, and he realized that it must be a party of some sort. Perhaps it was Sophie Ng's birthday, which would explain why she hadn't gone to school. Another good omen for the following day. He decided not to push his luck and to go back to the Holiday Inn.

Five minutes after Howells left the lobby of the Regent Hotel, Dugan arrived. He felt a complete and utter prat. The only item of clothing he could find that resembled a pirate's stripy jumper was his rugby shirt, so he'd put that on along with the bottom of his black track suit and tucked the legs into an old pair of black cowboy boots. He'd ripped a piece of black card from a file in the office and back in his flat he'd cut it into the shape of an eye-patch and tied it around his head with string. Then he'd twisted a dishcloth around his head, but one look in the mirror showed him that he'd gone too far so he took it off. He was lucky, he'd caught a cab as soon as he stepped out of his tower block, but the driver kept giving him funny looks over his shoulder.

He stood by a pillar and wished that the ground would swallow him up. Under his arm was the badly wrapped parcel from which protruded a thick, furry paw. Dugan loved his niece with all his heart, but even so he was beginning to have second thoughts. There was a reception to mark the opening of a new range of Dickson Poon boutiques in progress in the main ballroom, and a constant procession of dinner-jacketed businessmen and their glamorous wives and girlfriends walked past and up the huge staircase; it seemed as if every one looked at Dugan and smiled. A couple laughed out loud and one Chinese girl in a tight gold-coloured dress pointed at him and shrieked as if she'd seen a murder.

He pressed closer to the pillar, but his brightly striped rugby shirt was not exactly conducive to camouflage. Every now and then parents arrived with little pirates in tow, but Dugan was dismayed to see that all the adults were wearing normal casual clothes. The children giggled and waved at him and the adults just giggled.

'Oh my God,' said a small voice to his left.

He turned to see Petal, eyes wide and unbelieving, her small hands flat against her cheeks. 'Oh my God, Patrick, is that you?'

Her whole body began to shake with laughter and she bent forward at the waist, overcome with the funniness of it. Dugan was even more embarrassed.

'I had sort of hoped that you'd be dressed as a pirate, too,' he said glumly.

Petal straightened up and there were tears streaming from her eyes. Her large, gold hooped earrings were swinging backwards and forwards as she laughed. She wiped the tears away with the backs of her hands, giggling and snuffling all the time, and fought to get herself under control but failed abysmally. She deteriorated into whoops of uncontrollable laughter, leant against the pillar for support and put her hands over her mouth, turning her head away from him and then looking back and creasing up again.

Under normal circumstances Dugan would have been knocked out by Petal's outfit, a white, slinky dress, demure at the front but cut deep behind so that it showed most of her shoulder blades and back. It made her hair seem even blacker than usual and it ended at her knees, emphasizing the curve of her legs and her petite feet. She looked absolutely beautiful, but she looked nothing like a pirate.

'Patrick, you look fantastic,' she said when the giggles had finally subsided.

'Jill said it was a pirate party,' said Dugan lamely.

She began laughing again, her eyes moistening and her cheeks going red. 'For the children, Patrick. For the children!' She leant back against the pillar, her shoulder next to his and hugged herself as she laughed. She looked down, caught sight of the paw sticking out of the badly wrapped parcel and went into fits of laughter again.

'I'm going,' said Dugan, but she grabbed him by the arm and pulled him back.

'Don't you dare,' she said and held him close, her head up, asking to be kissed. Dugan kissed her softly, full on the lips as she stood on tiptoe. It made him feel a lot better. 'Come on,' she said. 'Let's go and see Sophie.'

They began to walk through the reception area when she suddenly stopped. She removed one of her gold earrings and helped Dugan attach it to his ear. She stepped back to admire her handiwork and with a straight face said it looked perfect, then she linked her arm through his and together they walked to the function room where the party was, guided by signs bearing a skull and crossbones with the words 'Sophie's Boarding Party' underneath.

Jill and Simon were standing at the double doors to greet the guests and Dugan saw with a heavy heart that they had also forsaken the pirate theme. Simon was wearing well-fitting slacks and a Dunhill shirt and Jill had on one of her favourite Chanel dresses and several ounces of gold jewellery.

'Don't say anything,' he growled. 'Just don't say anything.'

Sophie was standing with a group of friends by a large table laden with food set into a mock-up of a pirate ship. She beamed when she caught sight of him.

'Uncle Patrick!' she screamed and came running over, her blonde hair streaming behind her. He picked her up with his free arm and hugged her. She put her arms around his neck and squeezed the breath from him. 'Wow,' she said. 'You look great! Come and see my friends.'

She wriggled out of his grip and slid down his body. She was wearing a red and white silk shirt and black baggy trousers and she had a pink plastic sword thrust into a black leather belt with a big silver buckle. Around her neck was a diamond and gold necklace he hadn't seen before.

She saw him looking at it and fingered it. 'It's a birthday present from Daddy,' she said. 'Isn't it nice?'

'It's beautiful,' he said. It must have cost a thousand times more than his dog. He held his parcel out to her. She grabbed it and ripped off the paper and gasped as she saw the toy.

'Oh, Uncle Patrick, it's lovely.' She hugged it, rubbed her face against the fur and then held it at arm's length to look at it. 'It's so cute, it's my absolutely best present. Thank you.'

Dugan felt better and he allowed her to take his hand and pull him over to her friends.

'I'll stay with the adults,' Petal called after him.

Dugan eventually managed to untangle himself from

the mass of young pirates and made his way over to Jill, brandishing a plastic cutlass. She laughed and handed him a glass of lager. 'Thirsty work, being a pirate?' she said.

Dugan drank deeply and grinned. 'This is more fun than I thought it would be,' he said. There was a line of foam along his moustache and Jill reached across and wiped it away with a napkin.

The parents, mainly Chinese but with a sprinkling of Europeans, were standing by the impressive buffet while waiters hovered with trays of drinks, and the children were being entertained by a conjuror who kept producing green and yellow budgies from his clothing. He was dressed as a pirate, as had been the juggler who'd made the children gasp with his sword-juggling and rapier-swallowing. On a table next to the double doors was a display of small wooden chests each containing a parchment treasure map and a gold sovereign, going-home presents for the children.

'Did you arrange all this?' asked Dugan.

Jill shook her head. 'No, Simon found a designer to do it, some sort of professional party planner. You give him the theme you want and he does the rest. Do you fancy something special for your next birthday?'

'Don't even think about it. Where's Petal?'

She pointed over to the buffet. 'There, with Simon. Pat, she's delightful. Were did you find her?'

He shrugged. 'I guess she sort of found me. She is beautiful, isn't she?'

'She's lovely, but she's so sweet as well. She seems so interested in everything and everybody, she's completely different from the bimbos you normally go out with.'

'Thanks, kid.'

'You know what I mean. You've been out with some fantastic-looking girls but their IQs are rarely above room temperature. Petal is very sharp, but so gentle with it. Simon is quite taken with her.'

They stood and watched Petal talking to the triad leader, hanging on his every word as she held her glass with both hands. Dugan fingered his earring. 'She is different, isn't she?' he said quietly. 'To be honest, I can't understand why she does go out with me.'

Jill sighed with exasperation. 'For God's sake, stop being so hard on yourself! All I ever hear you do is complain about how you're getting old and how you're stuck in a rut. Petal thinks the world of you. All the time she was talking to us she kept looking at you and smiling, but you were so busy playing at being the pirate leader that you didn't notice. You should take a good look at yourself, brother of mine. You're tall, goodlooking, and you're a hell of a lot more fun than those deadhead cops you hang out with. All you need is a woman to show you how to make more of what you've got and to get you off junk food.' She looked him up and down coolly. 'And, it has to be said, your dress sense is a little suspect.'

They laughed together and Petal turned and waved to Dugan. She said something to Simon and they came over together. Petal linked her arm through Dugan's and kissed him on the cheek, then leant up, put her mouth close to his ear and whispered, 'Shall we go?'

'Sure,' he said, and he made to go but she pulled him back.

'Promise me one thing,' she said.

'What?'

'That you'll wear your eye-patch tonight,' she giggled. 'It looks really sinister.'

Dugan was suddenly overcome with affection for her and he held her close, resting his chin on top of her head as Jill and Simon looked on. 'We're going,' he said.

'Thanks for coming,' said Simon. 'And for getting into the spirit of it.'

They said their goodbyes and left, and as they walked out of the hotel Dugan didn't care about the looks or the giggles. He was with the prettiest girl in the world and that was all that mattered.

In the taxi Petal leant against him and sighed. 'I saw a different side to you tonight, Patrick Dugan,' she said softly. 'I didn't realize you liked children so much. They adored you.'

Dugan put his arm around her and kissed her forehead. He wanted to tell her that he adored her, but somehow he didn't think it would sound right coming from a man dressed as a buccaneer so he decided he'd save it until later.

The following morning the Mercedes arrived at the crossroads and with a sense of relief Howells slipped in behind it. He could see the uniformed chauffeur, the heavily built bodyguard in the front passenger seat, the girl in the back seat.

Five minutes later the car pulled up in front of a four-storey white-painted stone building surrounded by a tarmac playground. The girl opened the door herself and slipped off the seat, pulling a brown leather satchel after her. She slammed the door shut and ran over to a group of girls in white uniforms and blue belts without even a backward glance. Ng's daughter walked into the building chattering with her friends and the men in the Mercedes watched her until she was out of sight before driving off.

There was a large wooden sign fixed to the railings at the entrance to the playground and Howells noted down the name of the school, its headmistress and the telephone number.

He drove back to the Holiday Inn and ate eggs and bacon in the coffee shop before going up to his room. He sat on the bed with the phone, and placed two pieces of paper in front of him; one bore the name and number of the girl's school, the other the number of Ng's home. In between them he put Holt's warrant card.

He went to the wardrobe and took out his one suit. It was still a little rumpled after the trip from Bali, and he was surprised at how well it still fitted, considering the amount of weight he'd lost. He wore it with a light blue shirt and a navy blue tie with a yellow crest on it, and with his short hair and cold eyes he knew he'd have no trouble passing for a cop. He combed his hair in the bathroom and checked himself over again.

He had his wallet and he had the car keys. Everything else was on the junk. He sat down on the bed again and dialled the first number, the school. He asked the switchboard girl for the headmistress and was put through to her secretary. He told her he was Chief Inspector Caine and that he had to speak to the headmistress immediately.

He was put on hold and then a crisp female voice came on the line.

'Good morning, Chief Inspector. How can I help you?'

Howells spoke slowly and with a voice deeper than normal, phrasing each word carefully and precisely. 'Good morning, Miss Quinlan. I am sorry to bother you but I am calling in connection with one of your pupils, Sophie Ng.'

'Yes, she is one of my pupils. Is she in some sort of trouble?'

'No, no, she isn't in trouble, Miss Quinlan. But I am afraid there has been an accident involving her parents, a car crash.'

'Oh my Lord, no,' said the headmistress. 'Is it serious?'

'Yes, I am rather afraid that it is. They are both in intensive care and we are in the process of contacting the members of the family. Mr Ng's father is on the way to the hospital now. My reason for ringing you is to let you know that we have been asked to get Sophie to the hospital as quickly as possible. One of my men, an Inspector Holt, has already left and he should be with you shortly. Could you please arrange to have Sophie ready?'

'Of course, of course,' she said. 'Oh dear Lord. The poor girl.'

'And Miss Quinlan?'

'Yes, Chief Inspector?'

'I'd be grateful if you said as little as possible to the girl at this stage. It would be best not to upset her. Better to allow her grandfather to explain.'

'I quite understand.'

'Thank you for your help. Inspector Holt should be there soon. Goodbye.'

Howells replaced the receiver then immediately picked it up again and dialled Ng's home. It rang three times and then a guttural Chinese voice answered.

'*Wei. Wan binwai?*'

'Mary had a little lamb, its fleece as white as snow,' said Howells.

'*Wan binwai?*'

'And everywhere that Mary went, the lamb was sure to go.'

'*Neih daapcho sin la,*' said the voice and hung up. Howells switched the tape recorder on to play and left the receiver next to the speaker. On the way out he put the Do Not Disturb sign on the door handle. Miss Quinlan probably wouldn't bother to call the house to check, and if she did she'd find the phone engaged. Hardly surprising, what with the accident and all. And if the hotel switchboard should listen in to the call she'd just hear a crazy gweilo dictating a list of names and addresses. He retrieved his car from the hotel car park and drove to the school.

Miss Quinlan looked pretty much as Howells had expected from her voice: prim and proper, greying hair and horn-rimmed spectacles. Her features were sharp and pointed and she had a slight moustache of straggly black hairs. Howells didn't have to look to know that there wasn't a wedding ring on her finger. Miss Quinlan was the sort of woman who preferred to be married to her work and God help any of her little charges if they ever let her down. Howells didn't know if corporal punishment was allowed in Hong Kong, but he was sure that Miss Quinlan would be more than happy to administer a few strokes of the cane across bare buttocks.

'Inspector Holt,' he said, and offered his hand. She took it and shook it firmly. He could feel the bones under papery skin.

'I've been expecting you,' she said. 'Sophie is next door with my secretary.'

She walked back behind her large oak desk, seeking the reassurance it offered, something to hide behind. It was a masculine desk and on it there were no feminine touches to indicate that it was used by a woman. There was a brown leather-bound diary, a heavy crystal paperweight, a brass paperknife and two paper-filled wire trays, a black telephone and a grey plastic intercom. No flowers, no family photographs.

'Is there anything I can do?' she asked, tilting her head down so that she could look at him over the top of her glasses.

'No, everything is being looked after,' said Howells. 'The important thing now is to get Sophie to the hospital.'

The headmistress nodded. She pressed a button on the intercom and bobbed her head down like a pecking bird to talk into it. 'Can you bring Sophie Ng in, please.'

There was a double knock on the door and it opened to reveal a young Chinese girl in a charcoal-grey suit who was holding the hand of the little blonde schoolgirl. Miss Quinlan came out from behind her desk and smiled at the girl.

'Sophie,' she said, 'this gentleman is Inspector Holt. He's a policeman. He's come to take you to see your grandfather.'

The girl's eyes widened. 'Is something wrong?' she said.

Miss Quinlan turned to look at Howells and he knew she was going to suggest they tell the girl there and then so he quickly shook his head.

'No, everything is all right,' he said, reaching forward and patting her on the head.

The headmistress followed his example and nodded reassuringly. 'Your grandfather will explain,' she said.

The girl still looked worried, so Howells took her hand and led her to the door. He stepped to one side to let her through first, and as he did so he mouthed 'thank you' to the headmistress.

As the door closed behind them Miss Quinlan sat down and picked up the telephone. She tapped out the number of the Ng house, but it was still engaged.

Howells took Sophie to the car and made sure she'd fastened her seat belt before starting the engine.

'Where are we going?' she asked.

'To see your grandfather,' he replied.

'Why?' She was polite but insistent, her head tilted side-on, resting against the back of the car seat as she watched him and waited for an answer.

'He wants to see you.'

'Why couldn't Daddy or Mummy come?'

'They're busy,' he said.

'There's nothing wrong, is there?'

'No, of course not. Look, your grandfather will explain everything.'

'But why did they send you to get me?'

'What do you mean, Sophie?'

'You're a policeman.'

'Yes. You know I am. Miss Quinlan told you so.'

'So why did they have to send a policeman to get me?'

'Because it was quicker to send me.'

'Why don't you have a uniform?'

'I'm a plain clothes policeman,' he said. 'Not all policemen wear uniforms.'

She thought about that for a while, then she spoke to him in rapid Cantonese.

Howells grinned. 'And not all policemen speak Cantonese, Sophie,' he said.

'I thought they did,' she said. 'And this isn't a police car.'

Howells hadn't banked on this, interrogation from an eight-year-old girl. They were still driving through crowded city centre streets so there was no way he could use force to shut her up. He'd just have to keep talking until they were on their own.

'Where are we going?' Sophie asked, running her fingers along the dashboard and checking them for dust, the way she'd seen her mother do after the amahs had finished cleaning. 'To a police station?'

'No,' said Howells softly, 'to a boat. Your grandfather is waiting for you there.'

'Daddy's boat, you mean?'

'No, another one.'

There was less traffic about now; the nearest car was about a hundred yards behind.

'What sort of boat is it?'

'A junk. Like one of the old-fashioned ones.'

'How big is it?'

'I don't know. Thirty feet or so, I suppose.'

'Ha! My daddy's boat is forty-five feet long. It's an ocean-going cruiser.' She was obviously pleased by this show of one-upmanship and sat back in her seat, arms folded across her chest with a 'so there' look on her face. At least it stopped the torrent of questions.

'Mrs Ng?' Jill would never, ever, get used to the surname. The sound had no real equivalent in English, a sort of nasal grunt that Westerners just couldn't cope with. On the occasions she'd been to America or back home to Britain she'd switched to her maiden name when Simon hadn't been around. It solved a lot of problems.

'Mrs Ng?' repeated the amah.

'Yes, Rose, what is it?' Rose was one of two Filipina maids who lived in the house, cooking and cleaning and looking after Sophie.

'The phone isn't working. There is somebody talking on the line.'

'A crossed line?' said Jill. 'Leave it for a while, Rose, it might sort itself out.'

'Yes, Mrs Ng. Do you have the shopping list for me?'

'It's in the kitchen, Rose. On the table. Is Manny back with the car yet?'

'Yes,' said Rose.

'You might as well go with him, then. And can you buy some more gin, please.' Rose nodded and left Jill alone in the lounge, curled up on the white leather sofa with the *Hong Kong Standard*.

In Howells' bedroom in the Holiday Inn the tape

reached the end and the recorder automatically clicked off.

After a few minutes the switchboard girl came on the line. 'Excuse me, Mr Donaldson, are you still using the phone?' she asked. There was no reply, yet the receiver was definitely off the hook. Probably didn't want to be disturbed, the girl thought. Strange that it was still connected to an outside line, though. She disconnected it without a second thought.

Howells stopped the car and walked round to open the door for the girl. There was one road that led from the Clearwater Bay Road to Hebe Haven pier. It ended at a row of metal bollards so that cars couldn't drive on to the pier, but just before were parking bays. His was the only car there. Sophie ran through the bollards, past a long-abandoned canoe that seemed long enough to seat twenty people in single file, propped against a wall.

'Where is it?' she asked, squinting out across the shimmering blue sea at the forest of yacht masts. 'There are so many.'

'Over there.' Howells pointed to the left of the pier.

'Is that it, the wooden one?'

'Yes,' said Howells, 'that's it. Come on.'

'It's small,' she said. 'Where is Grandfather?'

'He's there. Maybe he's down below.'

Sophie cupped her hands round her mouth and yelled at the top of her voice. 'Grandfather . . . we're here.' Then she called again in Cantonese, her shrill child's voice echoing around the beach.

'Sophie, no,' said Howells, and grabbed her by the shoulder tightly.

'Ouch,' she squealed, 'you're hurting me. Let go.'

'I'm sorry,' he said. 'But you mustn't shout.'

'But I wanted to let Grandfather know we'd arrived.'

She was quiet now, and there was suspicion in her eyes, the mistrust of a hurt child. An old, balding man was sitting on the edge of the pier on a bleached wooden stool, threading earthworms on to a hook. By his side was a small wooden birdcage and as he impaled the worms he was talking to a small brown bird with a bright red beak.

Howells smiled at the girl. 'Come on,' he said, 'that's our dinghy there.'

He pointed to the jetty nearest the pier, where the little boat bobbed up and down where he'd left it. She looked as if she was going to argue so Howells forced a beaming smile and held her tightly by the hand. He took her back down the pier and along the shore, through a boatyard where large gleaming white cruisers lay cheek by jowl with battered old fishing boats that had seen better days. He let her go first along the wooden planks. From a distance they looked spindly and positively unsafe, a ragbag collection of pieces of wood that had been haphazardly nailed together, but close up he could see that the wood was sound and the nails unrusted, and there was very little give as they walked along.

They reached the dinghy and Howells lifted her in. As he pushed it away from the jetty his arm slipped into the water and his jacket sleeve was soaked. Sophie laughed at his comfort, her fear forgotten, for a moment at least.

He tilted the outboard motor into the surf and tugged at the starter until it kicked into life. Sophie sat at the prow, head over the edge, and trailed her hand in the water as Howells guided the boat towards the junk.

When they got close he cut the engine. He tied the boat up and held it steady while Sophie made her way up the wooden ladder, and quickly followed as she ran down the deck shouting for her grandfather. She went down below, past the galley, through the main cabin and into the bedroom, where Howells caught up with her. She turned round and ran into him, then stepped back, a look of panic on her face.

'Where is he? Where is my grandfather?' she screamed, tears brimming in her eyes.

Howells pressed his forefinger against his lips. 'Shh,' he said softly. 'There's nothing to cry about.'

Sophie began sobbing and backed away from Howells until she was up against the bed.

'Who are you?' she said haltingly between sobs. 'What are you going to do?'

'You have to stay with me for a while,' he said. 'Not for long, but you have to stay on the boat.'

He stepped forward and stroked the top of her head. Sophie flinched. She was suddenly furious with herself. Her mother had told her time and time again never to go with strangers, and once a policeman had come to the school and given a talk about what to do if someone tried to make you go with them. There were bad men who wanted to hurt children, he had said, but he'd never said why or what it was that they did. Neither had her mother. They'd never said why, only that she was never to trust strangers – but Miss

Quinlan had said it was all right. Sophie began to shake uncontrollably.

She couldn't look up at Howells; she didn't want to see his face. In a quiet, trembling voice she said: 'Please don't hurt me.'

Howells smiled down at her and ran his hand down her soft, blonde hair to the nape of her neck. 'Don't be silly,' he soothed. 'I'm not going to hurt you.'

The phone rang out, the sudden noise surprising Jill. She uncurled her legs and padded over the parquet floor to the black wooden sideboard. So much for the phone not working, she thought, lifting the receiver. God save me from stupid amahs. It was Simon, inviting her out to lunch at the Excelsior Hotel, and she accepted eagerly. It'd give her the chance to take the new Porsche out for a run; at this time of the day there wouldn't be much traffic using the cross-harbour tunnel.

She changed quickly, choosing clothes that she knew he'd like, and three-quarters of an hour later she was in the Grill Room. Simon was already seated at the corner table and halfway through his Perrier water when Jill arrived, slightly out of breath, with the head waiter in tow.

He stood and kissed her on the cheek. 'You look fabulous,' he said in Cantonese.

'You flatterer,' she replied, also in Cantonese. 'You are twice a liar. I look a mess and you have been waiting for some time. But thank you for lying so beautifully.'

The waiter raised his eyebrows, impressed with her fluency, and held the chair for her as she sat down.

'Can I get you a drink?' he said, in English.

'Campari and soda,' she said, her eyes on her husband. For the millionth time she marvelled at how good-looking he was. There really wasn't anything she didn't like about him physically. His hair was thick and black and his eyes a deep brown, his teeth strong and white, his shoulders broad and his skin the same light brown colour as a cocker spaniel her parents had owned in her childhood. His hands were squarish and strong; she could always feel their suppressed strength when he touched her, yet he'd never once hurt her, physically or mentally. He was immaculately dressed as usual, a black light-weight wool suit with a faint grey pinstripe running through it and a white shirt with his Hong Kong Club tie. His shoes were shining and she knew he'd gone to his regular shoe-shine boy, a wrinkled old man whose patch was in an alley near the Mandarin Hotel.

She'd learnt a lot from living with Simon Ng, not the least being the way her dress sense had improved. There was no doubt that was partly because as his wife she had a hell of a lot more money at her fingertips and several gold credit cards and charge accounts, but it was also as a result of going shopping with him. He had a good eye for design, always insisted on buying the best, and he knew what suited Jill. It had been hard for her to admit at first, but after a while she came to realize that on the occasions she met people when she was wearing an outfit he'd chosen the compliments came thick and fast. When she dressed in clothes she herself had chosen nothing was said. Under his guidance she'd gradually changed her whole wardrobe, and now it consisted mainly of the sort of names she'd only read about in the fashion magazines before she got married – Chanel, Kenzo, Charles Jourdan. She'd also acquired his love of expensive accessories. She had more than a dozen watches and three times as many rings, though she wore only one chain around her neck, a think strand of seamless gold that he'd given her when Sophie was born.

Today she was wearing a beige silk two-piece suit that stopped just below her knee; she carried a small matching Gucci bag and had her hair tied back with a small black bow, the way he liked it. She enjoyed dressing up for him. She was even wearing the white suspenders he liked, though he wouldn't see them. Until later. Her drink arrived and Simon raised his glass to her, the way he always did.

'To the prettiest girl in Hong Kong,' he said.

She snorted. 'I wish,' she said. 'I'm way past the age when I can be called a girl.'

'You'll have to excuse my lousy English,' he joked. A waiter handed them menus. 'What would you like?' Simon asked.

'You choose,' she said. 'You know what I like.'

He ordered for her and waited until the waiter had left before speaking.

'I have to go to Beijing next week,' he said.

'Again? You were there last week.'

He shrugged. 'Business,' he said. 'You know how it is.'

She knew. Jill knew all too well the business he was in, she'd known about his triad activities long before she married him. She'd known of them and she'd accepted them. She loved the man and so turned a blind eye to the comings and goings at their home, to her husband's frequent absences, the late-night phone calls, the ever-present bodyguards. The papers were filled with stories about triad killings, drug seizures, raids on under-age brothels, the bread and butter of the criminal empires, but even though she knew Simon was head of one of the most successful triads she didn't believe that he was personally involved in the violence. He was always so gentle and considerate with her, and when she watched him with Sophie her heart ached.

She reached over and stroked his hand on the table. 'Must you go?'

He nodded.

'Why Beijing?' she asked. 'Surely there's no business to be done there, not now.'

He pulled his hand away and there was a coldness in his eyes. 'It's business, Jill. Just leave it at that.'

It was always this way, Jill thought. He gave her everything she could want, he protected her and took care of her and he loved her, but there was a part of him that would be always unattainable and sometimes that frightened her. Her link with Simon Ng went back less than a decade, but the Ng family had ruled the traid for centuries. Jill often wondered what would happen if she pushed him to make a choice – her or the triad? She'd never put it to the test, because in her heart of hearts she knew which he would choose – and she could not bear to lose him.

She smiled and stroked his cheek. 'I just miss you so much when you're away,' she said, 'that's all.'

He took her hand and raised it to his lips, kissing

it softly. His eyes warmed and he squeezed her. 'I won't be long. And I'll bring you back a present,' he said.

The room was just as he'd left it when Howells returned. He replaced the receiver and put the tape recorder in the drawer of the bedside table. He stripped off his clothes, dropped them on to the bed and walked naked to the shower.

Later, as he sat on the bed wrapped in one of the hotel's thick white bathrobes, he dialled the number of Ng's house. It was answered on the third ring and a female Filipina voice recited the number in a sing-song voice. Howells asked to speak to Simon Ng and was told he wasn't at home.

'Is Mrs Ng there?' asked Howells.

Again he was told no. When would they be back? She didn't know. Howells hung up and lay back on the bed, fingers intertwined behind his neck, legs crossed at the ankles.

He waited a full two hours before calling the Ng house again. The Filipina girl answered again, and this time she said that yes, Mrs Ng was at home. She asked who was calling and he said Inspector Holt. He waited while the amah relayed the message to her mistress and handed her the receiver.

'Nick,' she said. 'How are you feeling?'

Howells was caught off guard. The last thing he'd expected was for the woman to know the copper he'd taken the ID from. He sat bolt upright on the bed, his mouth open and his mind racing.

'Nick, are you there?'

Part of Howells wanted to slam the phone down while he got his act together, but he realized that wouldn't solve anything, he'd only have to call back. All that mattered was that he spoke to Simon Ng; it didn't matter who he said he was or whether or not the stupid cow knew the copper or not.

'I'm sorry, Mrs Ng, I think you've got the wrong person. I'm trying to get hold of your husband.'

'He's not here at the moment. Didn't you say your name was Holt? Inspector Holt?'

'When will he be back?'

'I really can't say. Look, who is calling?'

'It is important that I get in touch with him, Mrs Ng. Does he have a mobile phone or a pager, or do you know where he is?'

'Is something wrong?'

Everything was going wrong, thought Howells. She was suspicious, Simon Ng wasn't there and in all probability she'd be on the phone to the real Inspector Holt as soon as he was off the line.

'No, nothing is wrong. But this is urgent, Mrs Ng.'

'Well, if you leave your number I'll ask him to phone you when he gets in.'

'Actually, I'm just about to leave the office – better I call him. What time do you think he'll be back?'

'I don't know,' snapped Jill, and she slammed the receiver down.

All Howells heard was the click of the line going dead; he had no idea of the venom with which the woman had cut short the conversation or the way she cursed him afterwards, but he knew that she hadn't been fooled.

Dugan winced as his phone rang. It was Petal. She wanted to see a movie and was Dugan free? Of course, he said, and they arranged to meet outside the cinema later on.

'How's your day?' he asked. That morning she had left without waking him, leaving only an indentation in the pillow and her signature flower.

'Busy,' she said. 'I've been tied up all day, that's why I'm so late calling you.'

'What is it you do for the Bank of China?'

'Marketing,' she said. 'Promoting their financial services. Nothing exciting. I'm sure my work isn't anywhere near as fun as yours. What case are you on today? That woman with the cheques?'

He was pleased and flattered that she took an interest in his work and that she'd bothered to remember what he was working on, but all the same he was aware that once again she'd given him the brush-off as soon as he'd asked about what she did. She'd done it pleasantly enough, but he still got the feeling that she was being evasive, that there was something she didn't want him to know.

'Yeah, but it's an uphill struggle.'

'Think of me and smile a bit,' she said. 'I'll see you tonight.'

After they'd said their goodbyes, Dugan sat with his head down over Lee Ling-ling's file and rubbed his forehead with the palms of his hands. His headache was worse. He drained his fifth paper cup of coffee and was just getting to his feet for another visit to the vending machine when his phone rang again.

'Pat?' It was his sister.

'Jill, how are you?'

'Fine,' she said. 'How about you?'

'Lousy headache, lousy job, and I think the airconditioner in my bedroom is about to pack up. Nothing changes.'

'Pat,' she said, and Dugan could tell by the change in her tone that she was serious. 'Pat, do you know an Inspector Holt?'

'Only Nick, Nick with the wounded pride and the surgical collar.'

'No, I don't mean Nick. Another Inspector Holt. Is there anyone else on the force called Holt?'

'Not that I know of. Why?'

'I've just had a phone call from someone calling himself Holt, wanting to speak to Simon. He was very evasive when I asked him what he wanted.'

'Are you sure he said he was a cop?'

'He called himself Inspector Holt. But he wouldn't give me his phone number.'

'Let me check it out, I'll get back to you as soon as I can.' It wasn't like Jill to get upset at something like that. Dugan was the worrier of the family, and over the years since Jill had married Simon Ng she'd grown increasingly more confident, so much so that occasionally the confidence crossed over to arrogance.

'OK, Pat. Thanks. It'd put my mind at rest. It's probably nothing.'

As soon as she hung up Dugan called Personnel and

asked them to check their files. There was no Inspector Holt, other than Nick. He called the ICAC and they said they'd check and get back to him.

Jill Ng was sitting on her white leather sofa with the phone next to her, and even though she was waiting for her brother to call her she still jumped when it rang.

'Pat?' she said. It wasn't, it was Miss Quinlan, the headmistress of Sophie's school.

'That's not Mrs Ng, is it?' asked the old woman, obviously confused.

'Of course,' said Jill, equally surprised. 'Who did you expect?'

The headmistress stuttered and stumbled for words and for a fleeting moment Jill wondered if she'd been drinking.

'To be honest, Mrs Ng, I'd heard that you and your husband had been involved in an accident. I was calling to see if there was anything I could do. I am rather surprised to find you at home. Inspector Holt said you were in the hospital.'

Jill's heart froze at the name. She gripped the phone tightly. 'Inspector Holt?' she said. 'He called you?'

'No, Mrs Ng. He came round. To pick up Sophie.'

Jill sagged back into the leather sofa, her mouth opening and closing soundlessly.

The headmistress realized that something was badly wrong. Her voice began to tremble. 'He showed me his identification, he was definitely a policeman, I know he was, I had no reason to . . .' Her voice tailed off.

Jill's voice was flat and emotionless when she spoke again. 'Why didn't you call me first, before you let him take my daughter?'

'Mrs Ng, I tried to call, but the phone was engaged. I did try.' The pleading whine annoyed Jill and she felt a red wave of anger.

'You're not fit to be in charge of children,' she hissed. 'You let a complete stranger take my child. Oh God, what have you done? What have you done, you old bitch?'

Miss Quinlan began to cry as she felt her world collapse around her. The sound of her tears made Jill hate the old woman even more, but she was so consumed with anger that words failed her. She quietly replaced the receiver, tears welling up in her eyes. She rose unsteadily to her feet and tottered over to a chrome and glass drinks trolley where, with shaking hands, she poured herself a tumbler full of brandy. She gulped it down, the alcohol making her eyes sting, and then refilled it.

She was finding it hard to breathe, as if there were steel bands around her chest and neck that were being slowly tightened. A thousand images of Sophie flashed through her mind: Sophie on Christmas Eve opening her presents, building sandcastles on the beach, riding piggy-back on Simon, playing pirates with Patrick.

She practically ran back to the phone and tapped out the number of her husband's portable phone, tears streaming from her eyes.

Simon Ng was standing stock-still with his arms out-stretched like a man crucified. Before him a small, portly old man with skin like an old chamois leather ran a tape measure around his waist.

'Same as always,' he nodded approvingly at his teenage assistant. He measured the length of the arms, the shoulders, and then he knelt down in front of Ng and ran the tape up his inside leg, calling out the measurements to the boy, who wrote them down in a small notebook.

They were in a poky room on the second floor of an ageing building in Tsim Sha Tsui, the walls lined with shelves piled with rolls of cloth. Ng was facing a large oak desk on which were stacks of cloth sample books and to his left was a tall, thin free-standing mirror in which he'd be able to examine the finished product. It took Mr Cheung five days to complete a made-to-measure suit, three days for favoured customers. Simon Ng had been taken to Mr Cheung by his father for his first suit the day before his fourteenth birthday. Mr Cheung never took longer than forty-eight hours with his order.

There were two men sitting on high-backed chairs, one by the door and one by the desk, solid-looking men with calloused hands and hard eyes, bodyguards who'd both been with him for many years. They held the rank of Red Pole in the triad, fighters who had proved their worth. Both had killed for Simon Ng.

The one by the door in a brown suit and wearing brown brogues that wouldn't have been out of place on the feet of a Scottish landowner was Ricky Lam, forty-eight years old but with not a single wrinkle on his face. Lam had served Ng's father for more than two decades and still paid regular visits to the old man on the Peak where they would relive old times over a pot of jasmine tea. In the inside pocket of his jacket he carried an ivory-handled stiletto and he had a throwing knife strapped to each arm. Lam could use all three with deadly accuracy, but he could just as easily kill with his bare hands and feet.

The man in the other chair was Lam's cousin, on his mother's side, a twenty-nine-year-old kung fu master called Franc Tse. If Ricky Lam represented the traditional triad way of life, then Franc Tse was positively New Wave. He wore pristine white Nike training shoes, skin-tight Levi jeans and an expensive dark brown Italian leather jacket, the sleeves pulled up almost to his elbows and the collar turned up. Whereas Lam's hair was in the traditional mainland 'pudding basin' style, Tse's was lightly permed and swept back off his forehead. Tucked into the back of his belt was a nunchakyu, two lengths of hard wood separated by a short piece of chain, a martial arts weapon derived from a rice flail. At night, when he couldn't sleep, Tse would stand in the middle of his room and practise using the flail with his eyes closed, enjoying the hard slap of the wood against his hands and hearing it whistle through the air. He was an expert with the spear, the long knife, the three-section staff and the throwing stars, but the nunchakyu was his favourite.

Both men were fiercely loyal to Simon Ng, and would have had no hesitation in giving up their lives for him, or for his family. Ng in turn trusted them completely. It was a relationship that went far beyond employer–employee, or master and servant; it was bound up with the oaths each had sworn to the triad, the triad that existed before them and would exist long after they were gone from the world. Each had sworn a blood oath to put the triad and its members before family, before friends, before life itself, and each knew they had a part to play in the triad. Lam's and Tse's role was to protect the Dragon Head, Simon Ng. And they would – to the death.

Ng had left his portable phone on the desk and he stepped around Mr Cheung to pick it up when it warbled. It was Jill.

'Simon?'

He wanted to chide her for asking the obvious, but he could tell from the tone that something was wrong. Badly wrong. He listened intently as she told him about the phone calls from the gweilo and the schoolteacher.

'Simon, what's happening?' she asked.

'I don't know,' he said. His mind was racing, his brow furrowed, and his two bodyguards fidgeted, picking up his nervousness. Even Mr Cheung walked over to his rolls of cloth and pretended to study them. His assistant stood at Ng's elbow openly listening, until Mr Cheung angrily waved him away with a flick of his tape measure.

'I'm coming home now, stay there until I get back,' he said. 'Don't ring anyone, don't talk to anyone. And don't answer the phone; if Sophie has been kidnapped it will be better if I speak to them. Do you understand?'

Jill didn't answer. All Ng could hear were her sobs.

'Jill,' he hissed. 'Do you understand?'

'Yes,' she said eventually.

Ng broke the connection and weighed the phone in the

palm of his hand as his men looked on anxiously. First things first – he had to limit the damage. He called the school and spoke to the headmistress, who was every bit as distraught as Jill. He calmly explained that there had been a misunderstanding, that the police had indeed been asked to collect Sophie from school, that it was Ng's grandfather who had been hurt in a car accident, and that Sophie was now back with the family at the hospital.

'It was all my fault, I'm afraid, Miss Quinlan,' said Ng. 'I went straight to the hospital and phoned a friend in the force asking them to fetch Sophie before I could get hold of my wife. She didn't know my father was in hospital and she seems to have panicked when you spoke to her. She feels very badly about the way she spoke to you, but I'm sure you understand how upset she was.'

The relief in her voice was obvious now that the old woman believed that her job and her pension and her conscience were safe, but Ng wasn't one hundred per cent sure that she was convinced by his story. With any luck she'd just let it lie and wouldn't contact the police.

Ng realized Lam and Tse were looking at him like dogs waiting to be thrown a bone. He nodded curtly. 'Let's go,' he said, picking up his jacket. 'Mr Cheung, I am afraid I must cut short the fitting.'

Mr Cheung slung his tape measure around his neck and cupped his hands together in front of his chest, bobbing his head backward and forward. 'Not at all, not at all, not at all,' he chanted, following on Ng's heels as the three triads left his shop.

Ng waited on the pavement, Lam watching his back as Tse stepped into the road and waved at the driver of their car. He was another old retainer, Hui Ying-chuen, who still insisted on wearing an old chauffeur's cap that Ng's father had given him thirty years ago. There was no need for Tse to wave; Hui wasn't the sort of driver to sit at the wheel reading a racing paper or to pop into a tea house to yam cha. He already had the Daimler in gear and glided to a halt so that the rear passenger door was exactly opposite Ng. Tse opened the door for Ng and then slid in beside him while Lam took the front seat, eyes ever watchful.

Hui drove quickly but smoothly, his liver-spotted and wrinkled hands light on the wheel and deft with the gear stick. The Daimler was the only one of Ng's five cars not to have automatic transmission, in deference to the old driver who'd never managed to get the hang of driving without a clutch. The four drove in silence, Hui because he never spoke unless spoken to, Tse and Lam because they knew that during periods of stress their boss often retreated into himself, deep in thought while he considered all his options.

The gates to the compound were already open as they arrived and Jill was at the front door of the house to greet them, her face stained with tears, her eyes red. She threw herself at her husband and hugged him hard. 'What are we going to do?' she wailed.

He put his hands on either side of her face and held her in front of him. Her lower lip was trembling and she tried to stop it by gently biting down. 'We're going to start by keeping calm,' he said evenly. 'We're not going to help Sophie by crying. Come with me.' He put his arm around her shaking shoulders and led her through the front door and into the lounge. One of the dogs, he couldn't remember its name, sniffed at Jill's legs in puzzlement and Ng glared at it until it backed away, its tail twitching between its legs. He sat her down on the sofa and stood over her so that he had to raise her head up to see him. 'Tell me again what happened.'

She went through it, the phone call from the man calling himself Holt, and call to her brother, and then the one from the headmistress. He could smell alcohol on her breath.

'Has anyone called since you spoke to me?'

'The phone rang twice, but I did as you said and didn't answer it.'

'Good girl,' he said. 'Don't worry, it's going to be all right.' He tried to sound confident but it belied the cold dread in his heart and Jill knew it. 'Wait here, I have to speak to Franc and Ricky. Do you want another drink?'

She shook her head fiercely. Alcohol wasn't a crutch she needed when he was there.

Lam and Tse were standing in the hall, unwilling to intrude on the family's grief. They'd heard enough from the phone conversation in the tailor's shop to know what was going on but he quickly explained anyway.

'I need Double Flower White Paper Fan. And tell Elder Brother to be ready.' Ready for what, he didn't know. Lam and Tse scurried off.

Elder Brother wasn't related to Ng, it was slang for the triad's Hung Kwan official, the man who controlled the twelve fighting sections, almost 250 fighters in all, Red Poles like Lam and Tse. White Paper Fan meant adviser, and the prefix Double Flower identified Ng's most senior confidant, Cheng Yuk-lin. Cheng had been appointed White Paper Fan by Ng's father and Ng himself had promoted him to Double Flower soon after his father had retreated to the Peak and handed over the mantle of Lung Tau – Dragon Head.

Ng went into the kitchen and helped himself to a Coke from the fridge before joining Jill in the lounge. She was still wearing the silk suit, but the black bow had disappeared and her hair was a mess; yet she was still the most attractive woman he'd ever seen and he loved her passionately. She was looking straight ahead with blank eyes and at first he thought she was in shock until he realized she was looking at Sophie's photograph in the bookcase. He walked over and picked it up, a colour picture of her in her school uniform taken six months earlier. He handed the brass-framed portrait to her and she sat with it in her lap.

Neither of them knew what to say, how to put their grief into words. It had been a difficult birth eight years ago, one that had nearly killed Jill and which had left doctors in no doubt that Sophie would be an only child. To have her taken from them now was more than they could bear. Ng would pay, or do, anything to get her back. He sat down next to Jill and rested his head against her cheek.

'I'm sorry,' was all he could say, and then she started crying again, tears plopping down on to the glass covering the photograph. He reached for her but the phone rang, startling them both.

Ng picked it up. 'Yes?' he said, using English. Jill clasped the photograph to her chest.

'Simon?' said Dugan. Ng cursed inwardly but kept his voice pleasant.

'Pat, how are you?' He'd have checked up on Holt by now.

'Fine, is Jill there?'

'She's upstairs, can I take a message?'

155

'Er – I'd rather speak to her if she's there, Simon. She rang me earlier.'

Ng knew that if he tried to stop him he'd set alarm bells ringing so he placed his hand over the receiver and said quietly to his wife: 'It's your brother, you'll have to talk to him. Don't let him know there's anything wrong. Understand?'

She nodded and wiped her eyes on the back of one hand. Ng handed her the phone.

'Hiya, brother of mine,' she said. Her voice wavered slightly so she shook herself and sat bolt upright.

'Are you OK?' asked Dugan.

'Of course,' she said brightly. Ng could see the tears were about to start again.

'I'm ringing about that Holt thing. Just as I thought, there is only one Holt. I've checked all the departments and the ICAC.'

'Must be somebody fooling around,' said Jill. She closed her eyes tightly to hold back the tears.

'Maybe, and maybe not,' said Dugan. 'But it seems a bit more than coincidence that someone steals his warrant card and then you get a call from an imposter wanting to speak to Simon. Have you told him?'

'No, I mean yes.' Christ, she was getting confused. 'I just told him. He said it was probably a joke, one of his friends trying to fool him.'

'Simon doesn't have too many gweilo friends, does he?'

'No but, oh I don't know, Pat. I'm sure it's nothing worth bothering about. Thanks for checking but just drop it.'

'OK,' said Dugan. 'I'll see you Sunday then.'

'Sunday?' said Jill.

'Yeah, you invited Petal and me around for a barbecue. It's still on, isn't it?'

'Yes, yes of course. Look, Pat, I have to go. See you.'

She hung up and began sobbing again as she rocked backwards and forwards on the sofa. Ng sat down next to her and held her hands, waiting for the tears to subside. A discreet cough from the doorway made him look up. An old man stood there, dressed in the traditional Mao-style jacket and trousers made from black Chinese silk, plastic flip-flop sandals on his feet. His head was egg-shaped and totally bald, the eyebrows thin and stiffly arched, the eyes pale and watery, the lips bloodless and curling downwards. It was not a friendly face, it was a face that led to some of the younger and more irreverent triad members calling Cheng Yuk-lin 'The Vampire' behind his back. It was a face that had barely changed over the thirty years or so that Simon Ng had known it; there was nothing left to age, no more hair to lose, no smooth skin left to be wrinkled. The only step left in the ageing process for the triad's trusted Double Flower White Paper Fan was death.

'Cheng Bak-bak, thank you for coming,' said Ng, getting to his feet and walking over to greet him. The old man nodded slowly and gravely and Ng knew that he'd already been told about Sophie. Only in private did he call his adviser Bak-bak, or uncle. It would give neither of them face to be so informal in front of other triad members, but there was a bond between them that went way beyond the normal relationship between a Dragon Head and a White Paper Fan. If Cheng hadn't loved Ng like a son he would have retired long ago and Ng had always been grateful for his guidance. Cheng had his own cottage on the opposite side of the compound, screened by a clump of palm trees; there he could tend his small garden and listen to his collection of songbirds in peace.

Ng took Cheng through the hall and into the book-lined study. It was an incongruity in the hi-tech house; old-fashioned, heavy English furniture that would have been more at home in a London club. There were framed hunting prints on the walls and a brass swan-necked lamp on the leather-topped walnut desk. The windows overlooked the gate and guardhouse where Ng could see Lam talking earnestly to the three men on duty. Locking the stable door after the horse had bolted, Ng thought ruefully. He sat on the captain's chair behind the desk and rested his elbows either side of the blotter as Cheng carefully lowered himself on to a generously upholstered Chesterfield.

'Would you care for tea, Bak-bak?'

'No thank you, Chao-huang.' Cheng was the only person, apart from his father, who called Ng by his Chinese name. 'Just tell me what happened.'

Ng went over it for the old man, and when he finished he realized how little information they had.

'Your wife is sure it was a gweilo?'

'Definitely. And he used the name Inspector Holt.'

'Then you realize this is not a brotherhood problem. It is either a simple matter of extortion, or something personal, an individual or organization trying to hurt you, almost certainly from outside Hong Kong. Locals would surely not bring in gweilos, not when help is so readily available from Taiwan or the mainland. I suggest you compile a list of all those non-Chinese who might want to cause you harm. And your fathers and brothers should do the same. Other than that there is nothing to do but wait until he calls again.'

'He might have done that already,' said Ng. 'I told Jill not to answer the phone and it rang before I returned home.'

The old man nodded, and as he did so the phone on the desk rang, giving them both a start. Ng grabbed for it and had the receiver to his ear before the echo of the first ring had faded.

'Yes?' he said. It was the gweilo.

'Simon Ng?'

'Yes.'

'Listen and listen well,' said Howells. Ng scrambled in his right-hand desk drawer for a writing tablet and took a pen from the crystal pen stand in front of him. He gestured towards the door and mouthed the word 'extension' and Cheng eased himself off the sofa and padded out. Before he'd crossed the hall Ng heard a click on the line and realized that Jill had picked it up. He hoped she'd be sensible enough to keep quiet.

'I have your daughter,' said Howells.

'I know,' said Ng.

'This is what you must do if you want her back. Do you have a pen?'

'Yes.' The monosyllabic answers were clipped and efficient. Ng was not a man to waste time.

'I want one million dollars from you. One million Hong Kong dollars. I want it by tomorrow morning, seven o'clock.'

Ng began to protest, trying to play for time, but Howells interrupted. 'Don't insult my intelligence, most of your

159

businesses involve cash. I will call you at six o'clock tomorrow morning. If you do not have the money by then, she dies. Is that clear?'

'How do I know you have her?'

'How many ransom demands have you had today?'

'Then how do I know she is all right?'

'You don't. But if I do not have the money by seven o'clock I can guarantee that she will not be all right.' The connection went dead.

Ng joined Jill and Cheng in the lounge. She was drying her eyes with a white linen handkerchief. She blew her nose loudly. Rose came in and stood by the sofa, wringing her hands, knowing that something was wrong but not sure what it was.

'Sorry to bother you, Mrs Ng, but Manny wants to know if there is anything you want collecting from town when he goes to pick up Sophie,' she said.

'Tell Manny that Sophie won't need picking up today,' said Ng. 'She's going to a party with one of her schoolfriends straight from school. And could you fetch my wife a cup of tea, please.'

When the amah had left, Ng asked Cheng what he thought. The old man held his arms out at his sides, hands wide open, palms up.

'One million dollars is not a lot of money,' he said simply.

The thought had already occurred to Ng. Anyone who knew him would know that he would pay a lot more than that for his daughter's life. Why not two million? Or five? There were a hundred other families in Hong Kong that could just as easily be hit for a million bucks – why risk the wrath of a triad?

Unless it was personal. That was the only thing that made sense.

'What's wrong?' asked Jill. 'What do you mean, it's not a lot of money?'

'Mr Cheng means that we'll have no problems raising it,' said Ng, pacifying her. There was no sense in getting her even more agitated. In fact, he already had at least a million in the safe in their bedroom. Getting the money was the least of his problems.

'I will come back tomorrow morning,' said Cheng, taking his leave as Rose returned with Jill's tea. Ng took it off the tray and lifted it to his wife's lips and waited while she drank. She wiped her eyes again and sniffed.

'I'm sorry,' she said.

'What for?'

'For being so weak.'

'Don't be silly,' he said, hugging her and burying his face in her hair. 'It'll be all right, I promise I won't let anything happen to her.' He wished he felt as confident as he sounded.

'You seem miles away tonight,' said Petal.

Her voice jolted him out of his reverie and Dugan smiled. 'Just tired I guess,' he said. They were in a noisy, boisterous Taiwanese restaurant in Causeway Bay. The cinema had been packed, not a seat to be had, and they had decided to go and eat instead.

'You must be exhausted to daydream in a place like this,' she laughed.

It was true. The restaurant was packed to the red velvet-lined walls with Chinese families, never quiet eaters at the best of times. At the table nearest them were three squabbling children, one playing with a small electronic game that had an annoying 'beep beep' and the others having a shoot-out with plastic guns that flashed lights and whirred. Two old men were shrieking at each other and jabbing their chopsticks into the air as if impaling flying insects while a middle-aged woman lowered her head to the grubby pink tablecloth and noisily spat out a mouthful of chewed chicken bones. A waiter swaggered up and slopped tea into their cups from a stained and chipped teapot, the lid tied to the handle with plastic twine. The air was alive with arguments and laughter, with the clicking of chopsticks and the clunking of bowls, and the rattle of metal trolleys piled high with dirty crockery being pushed to the kitchen. Even the fans overhead grated and shook as they tried in vain to stir the smoky atmosphere.

Petal and Dugan were sitting side by side at a table big enough for six. They'd polished off prawns fried in garlic, sweet and sour soup and beef with green peppers and white cabbage in a creamy sauce and were now filling what little space was left in their stomachs with fried rice. Dugan's chopsticks had been suspended three inches above his bowl of rice before Petal broke into his thoughts.

'I miss the old Berni Inns,' he said.

'Huh?' She made the soft grunt that the Chinese used to mean a thousand different things, anything from 'Pardon' to 'I agree' to 'The Restaurant's On Fire But We've Still Got Time To Finish The Rice.' Dugan guessed that in Petal's case it meant she didn't understand.

'A restaurant chain in England,' he explained. 'Steak, chips and frozen peas, a prawn cocktail to start and Black Forest Gâteau to finish. And virtual silence throughout your meal. Bliss.'

'Do you miss England that much?' she asked.

'No, I'm only joking. And the food is one of the best things about living in Hong Kong, being able to choose any one of a hundred sorts of cuisine: Thai, Korean, all the different kinds of Chinese, Japanese, and even British pub food. No, I don't miss England that much.'

'So what happened at work to put you in such a gloomy mood?' she said, pouring beer from a large bottle for him.

'It wasn't so much work, I was just thinking about Jill . . .' He left the sentence hanging and Petal saw his eyes glaze again. Dugan snapped himself out of it, and grinned sheepishly. 'I'm sorry, I was off again, wasn't I?'

'It doesn't matter,' Petal said. 'Is there anything I can do to help?'

'No, I'm probably worrying about nothing. She rang me this morning and said someone had called her claiming to be Inspector Holt, the friend of mine who was mugged in Hot Gossip. She asked me to check out if there were two guys called Holt and when I called her back she said I was to drop it. But she sounded strained, as if she'd been crying.'

'And you think she's in trouble?'

Dugan shrugged and dropped his chopsticks on the table. He leant back in his chair and sighed deeply.

'I don't know. When we were teenagers we were so close that I knew without asking what was troubling her. Once she married that all changed.'

'That happens. A husband has got to be closer than a brother.'

'Yeah, I know.'

'Perhaps she's having problems with her husband, perhaps that's why she was upset. They could have had a row or something.'

'No, he was there with her, he answered the phone. And he didn't sound as if they were in the middle of an argument. They're not the fighting kind, anyway.'

'You said he was a triad leader. That's a violent way of life.'

'No,' said Dugan, his jaw tight with conviction. 'He's never hurt her, and he never will. He loves Jill totally, and Sophie. Outside the family he's a hard man, a killer, and he's got his fingers in some very dirty pies. But he keeps Jill and Sophie right out of it.'

Petal smiled and nodded. 'OK,' she said. 'She's your sister.'

'I'm sorry,' he said. 'I didn't mean to steamroller over your opinions.'

'You didn't, you were sticking up for her, that's all. I wish I had a brother around to stand up for me.'

A waiter was hovering nearby, a teenager in a tatty blue waistcoat and black trousers that he'd outgrown. Dugan made a scribbling motion with his hand and asked for the bill.

'I'll call her again tomorrow, maybe.'

'We could go round and see her if you want.'

Dugan liked the way she said 'we', as if taking it for granted that they were a partnership, a team. But going round to the Ng house wasn't his favourite pastime. Driving past the guards was a sharp reminder that he was entering enemy territory, and the obvious signs of wealth made him nervous and a little angry. What annoyed him most was the way in which Jill revelled in it; the expensive furniture, the works of art and oriental relics that she so enjoyed collecting, the staff at her beck and call. The house didn't feel like a home, not to Dugan anyway. It felt like a cage, a moneyed cage.

The waiter returned with the bill on an oblong aluminium tray. He paid with cash, conscious that both his credit cards were too close to their limit for comfort. The last thing he wanted now was for the waiter to come back with a sly grin on his face to tell him that there was a problem with his card.

'Do you fancy going anywhere for a drink?' he asked, pushing back his chair and standing up.

'I don't feel like drinking tonight,' she said. 'How about we just go home?' It was 9 p.m. Dugan's smile widened, and he took her arm. The waiter came back with a couple of green notes and a handful of coins on the tray and Dugan waved him away as he followed Petal to the door, watching her hips sway as she walked, the way her hair rippled and shone as it moved against her shoulders.

The slight rocking of the boat and the sloshing of water against the hull was soporific and Howells knew that he'd soon be asleep. He was sitting on a wooden rattan chair that he'd wedged against the door that led out of the main sleeping cabin. The girl was sitting cross-legged in the middle of the bed, staring at him. She'd got past the crying stage and Howells had made no move to hurt her so the fear had subsided. She'd stopped whining for him to let her go, she'd stopped promising that she wouldn't say anything. At one point she'd pretended to faint and lay on her back making wheezing noises like an upturned turtle. Now she was indignant. She'd threatened him with the police, with her father, and with his bodyguards, eyes flashing fire. Any moment now and Howells reckoned she'd attack him. The kid had spunk.

'You'll be sorry,' she said.

'I'm sorry now,' laughed Howells. 'If you're not quiet you can sleep in the toilet.'

He'd kept her locked in the toilet while he'd been in Tsim Sha Tsui. He'd thought of tying and gagging her but decided against it in case she panicked and choked. The cubby-hole was wood-lined with no window and the nearest boat was far enough away that her cries couldn't possibly be heard, and she'd soon tire of yelling. But if she didn't let him sleep he was serious about putting her back there.

'Sleep,' he said.

'I don't want to sleep,' she said. 'I want to go home.'

'You will go home. Tomorrow,' said Howells, the lie tripping easily off his tongue. He still hadn't decided what he would do with her. He'd never killed a child before but he knew he was quite capable of it. A lot depended on how well his plan worked out. At the moment he needed her alive in case Ng totally refused to co-operate unless he spoke to her. He shifted in the chair and slipped his shoes off his feet.

'My parents will be worried. They'll be looking for me.'

'They know you're with me,' said Howells patiently. 'They're not worried.'

She was persistent. Howells had never married and had no children, and he'd never known his mother or father, he'd been abandoned as a baby and spent his whole childhood in institutions and with a succession of foster-parents. The kids he'd met there weren't like Sophie Ng at all, they were usually one of two extremes, either browbeaten into meek subservience or delinquents who were forever bucking authority just for the hell of it. Sophie's social skills and self-assurance were the result of a childhood where there was no shortage of love or money and he envied her that. Howells spent his life looking forward, not back, and he had no regrets about his lot, but he knew that if he'd had a better start in life things would have turned out differently for him. He wouldn't have had to escape into the Royal Marines, he wouldn't have been selected for the SBS, he wouldn't have fought in the Falklands and he wouldn't have been spotted by a man called Grey at a time when Britain's intelligence services had decided that it was better to use the highly trained killers of the SAS and SBS to do their dirty work than to put their own Oxbridge paper-shufflers at risk.

'Are you hungry?' asked Howells. He'd already made her a mug of oxtail soup and a cheese sandwich but she hadn't finished either.

Sophie shook her head. 'I want to go home,' she said.

'So do I, kid,' said Howells. 'So do I.' He wondered what it would be like to kill a child, to feel his hands tighten around her thin, white neck, to hear her small bones snap and to see the fear in her wide, brown eyes just before she died.

Jill shifted her position for the ten-thousandth time and kicked her legs from under the pale pink silk sheets. Once or twice she'd drifted off into a restless sleep but each time she'd suddenly woken up with her heart pounding and a dull ache in her chest that she knew only the return of her daughter would soothe. Sophie filled her mind incessantly, a labyrinth of thoughts that kept her mind trapped and refused her the luxury of rest. She opened her eyes and looked across at her husband. He was asleep and she felt a wave of resentment. He was lying on his front as usual, head turned to his left, towards her. He was breathing deeply and evenly, his brow untroubled, the sleep of the innocent – the unworried. How could he? How could he sleep at a time like this? As if he were reading her thoughts Ng opened his eyes.

'Can't sleep?' he asked.

'No. What time is it?'

He pulled his left arm from under the sheet and squinted at the slim Cartier watch on his wrist, the one Jill had bought for Sophie to give him last Father's Day. 'It's almost five.' He sat up and rubbed the sleep from his eyes. 'You stay in bed,' he said. 'I'll get you a cup of tea. Are you hungry?'

She shook her head. 'He'll call soon,' she said.

'I know,' said Ng, sliding off the bed. He grabbed his robe and headed for the kitchen. Jill lay on her back and stared at the ceiling, her arm across her forehead.

*　　*　　*

Dugan awoke to the sound of high heels clicking on a wooden floor above his head, pacing backwards and forwards, tap, tap, tap. He groped across the bed but he was alone. He listened, but there was no noise from the bathroom or kitchen. 'Petal?' he called hopefully, but she'd gone. She had a cat burglar's skill for getting out of his bed and the flat without waking him up. He knew without looking that there was a note on the table. All things being equal he'd rather have had a good-morning kiss and a cup of freshly made coffee, but at least the few scribbled words and the flower showed that she'd thought of him as she left.

At first he'd thought it quite cute that she slipped away without waking him, but now Dugan was worried that perhaps she had to be somewhere else when dawn broke. She seemed to be happy with him, and God knows she seemed to enjoy being in bed with him, so what could it be? She couldn't be married, and it wasn't as if she rushed to get home before midnight or anything, it was just that when dawn broke she was never there.

He looked at his watch, and groaned when he saw it was only quarter past five. It had been after two when Petal had eventually flopped down next to him, skin damp with sweat, panting like an exhausted dog. Dugan had felt like he'd been hit by a train at the time and he didn't feel much better now, but he knew he wouldn't be able to get any more sleep. The distant clunking of lift doors opening and closing would ensure that. He switched on his CD player and Ultravox filled the air. He twisted the volume button savagely. If he wasn't going to get any more sleep he was damned if anyone else should.

Howells' internal clock woke him up at 5.20 a.m. Early rising was a habit he'd picked up living in a children's home and which had continued in the Royal Marines, but this was something else, a natural ability to wake up on command that had never failed him. He was still slumped on the chair, though he'd used one of the pillows to support his back. The other was wrapped in Sophie's arms as she slept on the bed, still in her school uniform.

His neck ached and his mouth was uncomfortably dry but he'd woken up in worse positions, in peaty trenches in the Falklands or under the blisteringly hot sun of the Libyan desert. A luxury junk was nothing to complain about. He used the bathroom, leaving the door open so he could keep an eye on the girl. He washed himself with a flannel, and shaved using a can of shaving foam and a disposable razor he'd brought with him, but then realized he'd forgotten his toothbrush. No matter, he'd gone without cleaning his teeth for weeks at a time before when out in the field. Toothpaste was a chemical signature that even humans could detect in the jungle or the desert. Soap, too. He swilled his mouth out with warm water and rubbed his teeth with the flannel to get rid of the sour taste of sleep.

Sophie slept through his ablutions and didn't even react when he opened the door and went into the galley to boil a pan full of water. He made a pot of coffee, put three sugars into hers and made it half and half with milk, the way he used to like it when he was a kid. His own was black and bitter, the way he liked it now. There had to be a moral there somewhere, he thought, as he carried the mugs into the bedroom.

He put Sophie's mug on the floor and gently shook her. She moaned quietly and hugged her pillow tightly. 'Wake up, kid,' he said. She murmured something in Chinese and curled up into a foetal ball. Howells checked his watch. It was five thirty-five and it would take him exactly twenty minutes to get the dinghy to the shore and get to the public telephone. He gathered her up in his arms, pillow and all, and carried her through to the toilet. There was just enough room for her to lie on the floor. He closed the door and locked it, then took her untouched coffee back into the galley and poured it down the sink.

Simon Ng waited for the call in his study, sitting calmly behind his desk with his hands clasped on the blotter. His face was impassive, seemingly unworried; the only sign of tension was the fact that he was unconsciously toying with his wedding ring. His wife's distress was more evident. She sat on the Chesterfield, her face pale and drawn and her hands trembling. Jill was rarely up at this time of the day, she'd always been a late riser and living with Ng meant that a nine-to-five existence wasn't exactly at the top of life's priorities. She'd dressed in an old pair of jeans and a grey sweatshirt, and her hair was dull and lifeless. Ng was immaculate as always in a dark blue double-breasted suit, a crisp white shirt and his Hong Kong Club tie. Dressed to kill, thought Jill ruefully, conscious of the fact that by letting her appearance slide she was causing her husband to lose face in front of his men. She tried to force a smile but Ng seemed not to notice as he sat there, deep in thought. On the left-hand side of the desk was a slim, brown leather briefcase. Ng hadn't opened it but Jill knew it contained one million dollars.

Next to her was Cheng. He was well-used to rising early; he was often up to watch the dawn and listen to his birds proclaiming dominance over the little territory they had. He too seemed untroubled, sitting with his back ramrod straight, his hands resting on his knees.

Standing by the open door was a big bruiser of a man, well over six feet with thick forearms that were a tailor's nightmare. His name was Lin Wing-wah, but for five years or more he'd been the triad's Hung Kwan and everybody called him Elder Brother. He'd started off as a tough street fighter, a basic 49 Red Pole in charge of one of Ng's Mong Kok fishball stalls. He'd spent some time as the Cho Hai official, in charge of organizing the triad's rapidly expanding protection rackets, but when the Hung Kwan slot fell vacant Ng moved Lin into it. His sheer physical presence meant that Elder Brother was rarely disobeyed. His hair was parted in the middle and tied back in a small pigtail and he had a thin, drooping moustache under a nose that had been broken more times than was good for it. There was a black wart with a clump of hairs sprouting from it just above the middle of his lips. He called it his beauty spot. Lin was big and ugly, but Ng didn't pay him to win beauty competitions. He was paid to be the triad's strong-arm man and he did the job perfectly, and enthusiastically.

Lin's soldiers were split into a dozen fighting sections of between twenty and twenty-five men, and he had two of his best units waiting outside. There were four Mercedes in the drive in addition to Jill's Porsche, Ng's Daimler and the 560SEL that Manny drove. There were another six cars lined up on the single-track road leading from the compound. Lin was as prepared as he could be, but he still had no idea who the enemy was, or where the handover was to take place. Howells had told Ng that he wanted the money by seven o'clock and that he would call one hour earlier. That meant that Howells wanted the swap to take place within an hour's drive from the house, but at this time of the morning that just about covered the whole of Hong Kong island, Kowloon and the New Territories. A map of the territory had been pinned to the wall opposite the window and though it was small in area Lin knew there were a million places to hide, even for a gweilo.

There were only four of them in the study, but the room felt crowded, oppressive. They were careful to avoid eye contact with each other, like warring relatives at the reading of a will. Jill couldn't understand it, the crisis should have brought them closer together but instead it seemed to have isolated them, locked each of them into their own private world. Right now what she needed most was physical contact with her husband, his arm around her, the reassuring feel of his flesh, but she was reluctant to show her feelings in front of his men. Worse than that, she was afraid that he would refuse to comfort her, that he would be embarrassed by her and reject her. She could see now the power he had, how hard and controlled he was when dealing with a crisis. It wasn't the Simon she knew, despite the occasional smiles he threw her way. For the first time she was a little frightened of him. She had to be like him, strong and controlled. Public displays of hysteria wouldn't get her anywhere.

The phone rang and they all jumped, even Cheng. Ng let it ring, three times, four times, before he picked it up, so as not to appear to be too anxious. Lin slipped out of the room to pick up the extension.

'You have the money?' asked Howells.

'Yes. I want to speak to my daughter.'

'You can talk to her all you want once I have the money,' said Howells. The line clicked as Lin picked up the phone in the lounge.

'I want to talk to her now,' said Ng, firmly.

'She isn't with me now. Once you have given me the money I will tell you where she is.'

'How can I believe you?'

'You have no choice. Now listen and listen carefully. I will only tell you once.'

'I am listening.'

'You know a place called Hebe Haven, about half an hour's drive from your house?'

'Yes, I know it.'

'There is a pier there, an L-shaped pier.'

'Yes.'

'You are to park your car on the road and walk to the pier. To the right, as you face the sea, is a row of concrete steps that lead down to the water. I want you to wait there at exactly seven o'clock. Alone. With the money. If you are not there the girl will die. If you are not alone, the girl will die. If you do not have the money with you, the girl will die. Do you understand?'

'Yes.' Click. The line went dead.

Ng got up from behind the desk and walked over to the map.

'What did he say? What did he say?' asked Jill.

'Hebe Haven,' said Ng. 'I have to deliver the money to Hebe Haven in one hour.'

Lin walked back into the room. There was a low groan from Cheng as he pushed himself up off the sofa. He massaged his left knee and then slowly kicked his leg backwards and forwards. 'By sea or by land,' he said quietly, as if to himself. 'He could come either way.'

Ng nodded in agreement. He turned to Lin. 'I must arrive alone, but if we are careful we might be able to get one or two men near the pier, maybe even on it. Pretending to fish, or painting, something. No more than two and they must leave now.'

Lin went without a word and less than a minute later a car drove away.

'The sea way will be harder,' Ng said to Cheng.

'Perhaps not,' said the old man, pointing to the map. The cove that was Hebe Haven was about two kilometres long and one kilometre wide, an impossibly large area of water to patrol, but the gap that led to the open sea was only a few hundred yards across.

'Here,' said Cheng. 'Two boats placed between the headland at Chuk Kok and the tip of Pak Ma Tsui would effectively seal off the whole cove. Assuming he comes in by sea we could let him in and then shut the door behind him. You could hand over the money but there would be nowhere for him to run to.'

'Unless he beached the boat within the cove.'

'Station men on the beaches, it wouldn't take many.'

Lin had returned now. 'It wouldn't be difficult,' he agreed. 'They all have radios. But if we decide to send them they'll have to go now.'

Ng nodded and once again Lin went to brief his men. This time three cars left. Jill, sitting alone on the Chesterfield, felt alone and quite, quite useless.

'So,' said the old man thoughtfully. 'He comes in by boat. We close the gap after him. He takes the money. Does he have the girl with him, that is the question.' He sucked his teeth, nodding his head up and down slowly. 'I think not,' he said eventually. 'I think he will come alone.'

'I don't see that as a problem,' said Ng. 'Once we have him he will tell us where Sophie is. I have no doubt about that. No doubt at all.'

The chilling conviction in his voice shocked Jill. It wasn't something she'd heard from her husband before, and for the first time she became aware of the power he commanded, the power of life and death, and pain.

Lin came back into the room, baring his teeth at Ng's words. 'He'll talk all right. We'll make him sing as sweetly as one of your songbirds, Master Cheng.'

'The boats will be a problem,' said Ng. 'My launch is berthed at Clearwater Bay. We won't have time to get there and get it to Hebe Haven.' He jabbed a finger at the map, an inch or so above the cove. 'Sai Kung,' he said. 'We can beg, borrow or steal boats from there. Send six men to Sai Kung – they are to choose the fastest boats they can find. And tell them to be discreet about it. We don't know where he's coming from.' Yet again Lin left the study. 'What do you think, Cheng Bak-bak?'

'If he comes from the sea we will have him,' said Cheng. 'But he would also be aware of the danger involved. And we should not assume that merely because he mentioned the pier he intends to come by water. You must also guard the road.'

'There is only one road,' said Ng, 'Hiram's Highway, the one that leads to the Clearwater Bay Road. The road to the pier comes off Hiram's Highway, and if we put one car on either side of it we can seal it completely. There is nowhere else to go. There is a hill behind the road, we can put a man there and he'll be able to see the whole area, from the main road to the pier.'

'I'll be there,' said Lin, who had returned to the room.

'You'd better go now,' said Ng. 'And make sure the cars are inconspicuous, whatever you do. You'll be able to put a few of our men in the boatyards disguised as workmen, but get them in place right away.'

Lin nodded curtly and left.

Cheng and Ng stood together at the map. Jill wanted to join them but she could tell from the strained silence that the two men were deep in concentration and that she would be in the way. She sat on the sofa, legs pressed tightly together, her stomach a mass of nerves. She knew there was no point in even asking Simon if she could go with him.

'Well, Bak-bak, what do you think?' asked Ng.

The old man rocked back on his heels, his hands clasped behind his back. 'If he comes by sea, he will surely be trapped,' he said quietly. 'If he comes by the road he will

177

also be trapped. He surely cannot come by air, unless he can fly like a bird.'

'A helicopter isn't impossible, but air traffic control at Kai Tak would be on his back right away,' added Ng. 'What we must be careful of is a combination, arriving by sea and leaving on land, or vice versa.'

'But even so, once he is at the pier he will be trapped on all sides,' said Cheng, sounding unconvinced.

'You seem worried, Bak-bak.'

'If you and I can so easily see that it is a trap, why did the gweilo arrange to meet you there?'

Ng nodded. 'Presumably because he assumes that he can just as easily get away? But how?'

'I would assume that when you see him, he will not have your daughter with him. He will think that so long as he has her he will be safe. He will want to take the money and release her later, when he is out of harm's way. Sophie will be his way out.'

'But as Elder Brother said, once you have trapped your bird, it is easy to make it sing.'

'But if the bird is not alone, if he has friends, and if the bird does not return to its nest . . .' The old man left the sentence unfinished, hanging in the air.

'We have no choice,' said Ng. 'If we let him escape with the money, there is no incentive for him to release her. Especially as she can identify him.'

'Identification is not such a problem,' said Cheng. 'Do not forget that the headmistress also saw him. I do not think that he will kill your daughter merely because she has seen his face.'

'We cannot take the risk,' said Ng. 'We must hope that he brings Sophie with him, and if he does not then we will force him to tell us where she is. It will not take long.'

'Oh my God,' gasped Jill. 'Please, please be careful, Simon. I just want her back, I just want Sophie back.'

Ng turned round as Jill got up, and took a step towards her and held her close, her head on his shoulder, nuzzling his neck.

'You will have her back,' he said. 'I promise.' Over her shoulder he could see Lin driving through the gates in the Mercedes, leaving the Daimler for him. He looked at his watch. It was 6.25 a.m. 'Time to go,' he said, releasing himself from her clinging grip and holding her shoulders at arm's length. 'You'd better get her room ready, when she gets back she'll be tired and hungry.' He kissed her tear-stained cheek and picked up the briefcase on the desk. He left the house without looking back but knew that she watched him go from the study.

Howells watched them come from his hiding-place below the pier. The water around the supporting legs of the structure was shoulder-deep so he stood next to one, back bowed forward so that he was submerged from the chin down. After making the phone call exactly at 6 a.m., he'd taken the dinghy back to the junk and put on all his diving equipment. He used the snorkel for the first quarter of a mile to save air and only submerged when he got close enough to shore to be seen. As soon as he reached the safety of the pier he switched back to the snorkel as he swayed gently backwards and forwards with the rhythm of the waves. He could see a good chunk of the shoreline and had a clear view of the approach road in the distance, and if he turned round he could see most of the bay, and his junk bobbing up and down in the water.

The first two arrived just after 6.30, a young man in jeans and T-shirt carrying a fishing basket, and an older man with a couple of cans of paint and a tattered holdall. They came one at a time, on opposite sides of the road, but Howells had no doubt that they were together.

The fisherman came first. Howells lost sight of him as he passed through the metal bollards that marked the end of the road, but a minute or so later he heard him walk overhead to the end of the pier. The older man stood by the bollards, pulled out a pack of cigarettes and lit one, leaning back his head and blowing smoke up at the sky. He began to unpack brushes and cloths and after opening one of the tins of paint started to apply unprofessional strokes of red to a bollard.

Five minutes later a white van drove down the road and turned in to one of the boatyards and three men in dark blue overalls climbed out. One of them knocked on the door to the yard's office, and on getting no answer all three moved between the boats until they were out of his sight. Even at this early hour the main road seemed busy, but not so busy that he didn't notice the two big Mercs driving past or see one of them go in the opposite direction a few minutes later. He'd expected them to seal off the road, and knew that the way out to the open sea would be closed off as well.

Howells checked his watch. Ten minutes to go. He shivered, but it was the cold, not fear. The water was colder than he'd anticipated, yet to be warmed by the early morning sun. The harness was starting to chafe against his skin but he knew it would be a mistake to take it off so he ignored the pain. The emergency cylinder was hanging from the harness, occasionally banging against his leg. A plastic bag drifted past, followed closely by a scattering of green leaves from some sort of Chinese vegetable. One piece washed up against his mask and he ducked his head down under the water to clear it. When he surfaced he saw Ng, standing at the top of the stairs, briefcase in hand, shading his eyes as he looked out to sea.

Lin had left his three Red Pole fighters looking under the bonnet of his car, the engine running so they could move quickly if needed, while he climbed up the hill, moving effortlessly through the bushes and spindly trees. He stopped halfway up, not even breathing heavily, and then cut across to give him the best possible view of the pier. He had a pair of powerful binoculars and a walkie-talkie with which he could contact his men who were now scattered around the bay and on two launches just beyond the headland. He spoke to them one by one: the men in the cars on the main road, the team in the boatyard, the man and woman walking their dog along the housing development at Marina Cove on the southern rim of the bay, which overlooked the pier, and the men on the boats. Like Lin they were all armed. His pistol in its leather holster felt heavy under his left armpit.

He put the binoculars to his eyes and scanned the bay. Nothing. He spoke into his walkie-talkie again, asking the men in the launches if there was anything approaching. Nothing. He heard Ng's Daimler tearing up the road before he saw it, then it rounded the bend and indicated it was turning right. Ng accelerated down towards the pier and stopped with a screech of brakes in one of the white-painted parking spaces. The painter looked up, then put his head down and got on with his work.

'Easy, easy,' said Lin through clenched teeth. A flying insect buzzed close to his ear but he ignored it. Ng opened the car door and stepped out, black shoes gleaming in the sunlight. Lin heard the door clunk shut and watched as Ng walked past the painter, briefcase swinging, and headed for the stone steps. Lin knew that Ng's gun was in a holster in the small of his back, under the Italian jacket, and that he had a wicked hunting knife taped to the calf of his right leg. In his inside jacket pocket he had a small walkie-talkie but it was switched off. A blast of static or a careless broadcast could spoil the whole thing. The painter and the fisherman were also under orders to keep theirs switched off. They were too close to the action.

Lin looked at his watch for the hundredth time that morning. Five minutes to go. That surely ruled out a boat, for there was no sign of activity in the bay at all. Lin radioed to the men at the roadside telling them to get ready, that it looked as if the gweilo would be coming by road.

He steadied his binoculars and checked Ng. He was still standing at the top of the steps, looking out to sea.

Howells bit on to the rubber flanges of the mouthpiece and ducked down under the water, the taste of salt on his tongue. He kicked his flippers and hugged the seabed as he headed towards the base of the stone steps. As he covered the fifty yards or so from the pier he unclipped the handcuffs from his belt. The water got shallower and shallower and once or twice his knees banged into sand as he swam, scraping his skin. Then he saw the steps ahead and he slowed to a halt. The water was about five feet deep so he kept his knees bent as he surfaced so that only his head was in the air. Ng was still at the top of the steps and hadn't seen him. Howells removed the mouthpiece and took a deep breath.

'Stay exactly where you are,' he said, firing the words in sharp staccato fashion, like bullets from a machine-gun, knowing that Ng was more likely to obey the authority in a strong voice than a weak-willed whisper. 'Don't look down. Put the briefcase down on the floor.' Ng did as he was told, then stood still with his hands at his sides. 'Now do the same with your gun.'

Ng hesitated. Howells was sure he would be armed, and wired. Neither the gun nor the communications equipment was likely to function under water but it would be safer to get rid of them straight away.

'Do it or she dies,' said Howells, and he saw the fight drain out of Ng. The triad leader reached behind his back and removed the gun, then bent down and placed it next to the briefcase.

'Now the radio.'

Ng took out the walkie-talkie and dropped it on to the concrete steps, where it clattered down and plopped into the dark water.

'Now, walk down the steps towards me,' said Howells.

Lin caught his breath as Ng put the gun on the floor. 'What are you doing, Lung Tau?' he said to himself. Ng straightened up and a few seconds later he took something from inside his jacket and threw it down the steps. Even through the binoculars, Lin could not see what it was. He checked the pier. Nothing – and the road was clear. What the hell was going on? He called up the launches on the radio. No, they hadn't seen anything. There were no boats on the way to Hebe Haven. Ng began to walk down the steps, slowly. Suddenly Lin understood, like a bolt of lightning streaking through his consciousness. He pressed the radio to his lips.

'He's in the water,' he barked. 'He's in the fucking water. Get those boats in now.'

Lin began to run down the hill, slipping and sliding through the undergrowth, not caring about the branches and thorns that tore into his trousers. As he ran he called up the teams by the cars, ordering them to get to the pier, and then he shouted instructions to the men in the boatyard. He didn't wait to hear their acknowledgements, he concentrated on running, on covering the quarter mile to the pier in the shortest time possible. The hillside levelled out and he burst through the trees, vaulted over

a wall and crossed the road in three strides, his arms
pumping up and down as his feet slapped on the tarmac.
As he hurtled down the approach road to the pier he heard
the Red Poles hard on his heels.

Ng was confused. He took four steps down and then
stopped.

'What about the money?' he asked.

'Keep moving,' said the gweilo. 'Keep moving or
she dies.'

Ng took another couple of steps, his mind whirling. The
whole point of this was the money, yet the gweilo wanted
it left behind. It didn't make sense.

'Where is Sophie?'

The man gestured with his hands; something metallic, a
chain perhaps, glinted wetly between his fingers. 'Faster,'
he said. 'Keep moving.'

Ng walked down to the water's edge. The frogman
stood up, his shoulders rising above the water. 'I'll take
you to see your daughter,' said the gweilo. The voice was
powerful but controlled, each word carefully enunciated
and projected.

Ng was still unsure. Behind him he could hear shouts
and the sound of men running. He turned to look up the
flight of steps and then he felt a hand close around his
ankle and pull. He fought to regain his balance but the pull
was too strong and he toppled forward, arms flailing. He
hit the water, the shock forcing all the air from his lungs,
and as he gasped for air he took in salt water and fought

back the urge to retch. The gweilo's arm was round his neck, his face pressed close to his ear.

'We're going under the water,' the gweilo said. 'Put this in your mouth and breathe slowly. The water will sting your eyes so keep them closed.'

Ng saw a silver cylinder with a black mouthpiece thrust towards his face. He didn't want to obey but in his confusion he did as he was told. As soon as his teeth were closed on the mouthpiece the gweilo pulled him under the water and his ears were filled with a roaring noise. The salt water stung his nostrils and Ng reached up to hold his nose. He could feel the gweilo kicking his legs and the sensation of water passing over his body. He opened his eyes, but the salt water burned so he clamped them shut and concentrated on breathing. He felt something hard lock around the wrist of his left hand and then his ears popped as the gweilo continued to drag him down to the seabed.

Lin bellowed like a bull as he ran. The walkie-talkie slipped from his sweating fingers and he ignored it as it smashed on to the tarmac and broke into plastic pieces. One of the Red Poles, Kenny Suen, caught up with him and it gave Lin the adrenalin boost he needed to speed up. The two ran together, chests heaving and arms pounding. The painter looked up and saw the men running towards him, stopped painting and straightened his back. The fisherman at the end of the pier stood up, his line forgotten.

'The water!' yelled Lin. 'The water!' He pointed at the stairs but both men just continued to look at him, totally confused. Suen had pulled ahead and was certain to get to the steps first so Lin stopped and cupped his hands around his mouth. 'Get Lung Tau. He's in the water,' he roared. The painter realized first and he dropped his brush on to the floor and sprinted to the top of the steps. Once he started to move the fisherman followed, running at full pelt down the pier. Lin started running again, and as he passed the bollards he pulled his gun out of the holster. Suen reached the steps first, closely followed by the painter, and both had guns in their hands and were looking down at the water by the time Lin got there.

Lin pushed them apart and looked left and right before he realized they were alone. He opened his mouth to speak but could see that the two men were as baffled as he was. He'd expected the gweilo to be in the water, probably with diving equipment, but there was no way Ng could be under the water. There was no blood, there had been no gunshot, no sign of violence. Nothing.

Suen picked up the briefcase and flicked the catches open. He showed the money to Lin.

'What is happening, Elder Brother?' he asked. Franc Tse and Ricky Lam arrived then, followed by more of the Red Poles in ones and twos until there were a dozen men standing together, all of them armed with nothing to shoot at. They looked at Lin for guidance and he knew with a sickening surety that he had no idea what to tell them.

Ng struggled at first, making it difficult for Howells to make any progress through the murky water. He kept low and kicked the flippers hard, wide scissor-kicks that made his calf muscles ache. Ng's free hand, the one that Howells hadn't handcuffed, groped around, throwing them both off balance, then his head jerked from side to side in panic. But soon he began to calm down, and reached up to hold his nose shut against the water. Howells let go of the small cylinder and allowed Ng to hold it at the same time as pinching his nostrils. At least that way Howells knew that both of Ng's hands were occupied. He rolled Ng over so that he was underneath him, which made it easier for him to swim in a straight line, though it meant that Ng was continually banging against the sea bed. Howells' ears began to hurt and he squeezed the soft rubber either side of his nose and blew gently to equalize the pressure until the pain eased. If Ng was smart he'd do the same, or burst an eardrum. Ng's feet dragged along the sand, clouding the water even more, and first one shoe slipped off, then the other. They were about twenty feet below the surface now so Howells began to level off and the sea bed gradually fell away. The visibility began to improve as they stirred up less sand and in the distance Howells could see the hull of a yacht. He steered Ng towards it.

'Give me your radio,' Lin told Suen. The two launches came round the headland a mile away in a shower of spray. Lin called them up but couldn't make out what they were saying.

'Don't talk, just listen,' he said. 'Head for the pier. Head for the pier now. He's wearing scuba gear, he's under the water. I repeat, he's under the water and he has Lung Tau.'

Tse and Lam were kneeling at the bottom of the steps, shading their eyes and trying to peer through the water but the light reflecting off the surface obscured everything. Lin handed the binoculars to Suen and told him to stand at the end of the pier and watch out for tell-tale bubbles.

'The rest of you come with me,' he said, and he led them towards the boatyards and one of the small wooden piers where there were several dinghies tethered together like goats.

As they got close to the yacht Howells began to dive down, clearing the pressure from his ears again. The anchor was lying on its side, a thick chain leading up from it to the white hull above. He moved towards it, the two men scuttling along the seabed like a crippled starfish. Ng's eyes had become more used to the salt water and he was looking around, his right hand still pinching his nostrils closed and holding the small cylinder. His suit was floating grotesquely around him and his tie had come loose and was drifting over his shoulder. Howells pulled him down hard, closer to the heavy anchor. The motion turned Ng on to his back and his legs rose above his head. He kicked in an attempt to right himself and then Howells tugged him again and locked the handcuffs to the metal ring at the top of the anchor. Howells let go of the cuffs and drifted away from Ng, using his arms and slow kicks of his fins to keep himself standing virtually upright a few feet above the sand. Ng saw him and began trying to swim up to the surface, but realized he was fixed to the anchor. He pulled himself down to it and tried to get free, panic obvious in his movements. He began to breathe faster, his head shrouded in bubbles. Howells doubted if there could be much air left in the cylinder now. There was hate in Ng's eyes, and fear. He put his shoeless feet either side of the anchor and grabbed it with his hands, then heaved up. He managed to get it up to his waist and then tried to push himself up to the surface and its life-giving air. It was too heavy, and dropped back to the side, plumes of sediment scattering around his feet like escaping snakes, while the cylinder swung to and fro from his mouth.

Howells watched, and waited. Getting a gun in Hong Kong would have been difficult, and he hadn't been certain of getting close enough to kill the triad leader with a knife. But here, thirty feet under the waves, he'd know for sure that the man was dead. That's what he told himself, anyway. But in his heart of hearts, in the dark place in his mind where even he was frightened to dwell too long, Howells knew that he wanted to watch, to see the man run short of air, to see water rush into his gasping lungs and to see the eyes milk over as he died.

Ng's chest heaved and Howells knew it would soon be over. He steadied himself with small circular movements of his hands, eyes fixed on Ng's face. Ng bent double, his hand going for the knife strapped beneath his trouser leg. On dry land maybe, just maybe, he'd have managed to do it, to have grabbed the knife and slashed and cut before Howells could have reacted, but with Howells' reactions it would have been a million-to-one shot. Under water it was a non-starter. Howells had all the time in the world to watch as Ng brought out the knife and tried to slash him across the stomach. Howells drifted back in the water, kicked once lazily to move out of range, and then righted himself.

It was better when they fought. Sometimes, when they knew death was inevitable, they gave up, they relaxed and just let it happen. Sometimes they closed their eyes and pretended it was a bad dream and that by wishing hard Howells would go away. Sometimes they called on God for help. Sometimes they called for their mothers. And sometimes they fought to the very end – they were the best. Animal against animal, eyes bright with the fire of life and teeth snarling, one on one. To the victor the spoils, and life. Howells knew how the gladiators of ancient Rome must have felt in the arena, and he knew too why those who were prepared to die gloriously often had their lives spared, while cowards always got the thumbs-down. There was a nobility in dying well that deserved to be rewarded.

Ng tried hacking at the chain with his knife but it was useless. His whole body was heaving as his lungs fought for air, his cheeks blowing in and out as he tried to breathe. He lunged again but the anchor held him back. He turned away from Howells, knowing that it was futile, knowing that it was important to conserve what little air was still in his lungs. His shoulders sagged and then he looked at Howells, straight in the eye. It was impossible to see the look on Ng's face because of the mouthpiece and the cylinder that hung from his face like an elephant's trunk, but it seemed to Howells that the man was smiling. Then the contact was broken as Ng sank to his knees on the sand, as if in prayer.

Even before the knife rose in the water in Ng's fist, Howells knew with a tremor of anticipation what was going to happen, and he moved closer. The knife fell again and again as Ng hacked away at the wrist that was keeping him prisoner, until the water was cloudy with his blood. Howells groaned to himself as he watched.

'Can you see anything?' asked Lin. The men all shook their heads. There were four of them in the wooden dinghy, two rowing while Lin and Kenny Suen knelt at the prow looking down into the water. There were two other rowing boats moving clumsily and noisily through the water in a 'V' formation, gradually moving further and further apart as they splashed away from the ramshackle wooden pier. Out in the bay the two motor launches carved lines through the water, but Lin could see that they were going too fast to be of any use. He called them up on his radio and told them to shut off their engines and drift with the tide.

'How long have they been under?' Lin asked.

Suen checked his watch. 'Fifteen minutes,' he said.

'Anyone know how long a cylinder of air lasts?' said Lin.

Nobody did, and Lin knew it didn't matter anyway. Nobody had seen the diver so they didn't know how many tanks he had or how many more he'd stashed away on the sea bed. One thing was for sure, fifteen minutes was a long time. More than enough time to cover half a mile at a slow walking pace, and a diver with decent flippers and equipment would move a lot faster. But calling off the search would be as good as admitting that the Dragon Head was dead and Lin wasn't prepared to take that responsibility.

Howells watched the triads as they searched, safe inside the main cabin of the junk. Once he was sure that Ng was dead he had swum quickly away, keeping low, hugging the contours of the sea bed, shallow breathing to keep the bubbles to a minimum. Without Ng to slow him down he coursed through the water like a shark, arms loose against his sides, head moving from side to side, all the power coming from his thigh muscles. He'd only slowed once, to check the gauge that told him how much air he had left. He'd made it with plenty to spare.

When he surfaced close to the junk he spent a full minute using the dinghy as cover while he checked that he was in the clear before he slid out of the water and on to the wooden platform at the rear of the junk. He stowed all the gear in the engine-room and wrapped himself in a bathrobe before kneeling down on one of the seats in the dining area and scanning the bay with a pair of binoculars. The men who had been on land were rowing their boats about half a mile away, and there were two powerful launches bobbing in the water a few hundred yards in from the entrance to the bay. Howells knew they'd call off the search before too long. They wouldn't know if he'd swum to a boat, or simply gone ashore at any one of a hundred places around the circumference of the bay and made off in a car. And even if they decided that a boat was the most likely hiding-place, there were still more than a thousand in the bay. Marina Cove alone had spaces for 300 vessels. It would take weeks to search every one, and as it was midweek most of them would be securely locked. All Howells had to do was wait.

'It's ten o'clock, Elder Brother,' said Suen.

'I know,' snapped Lin. 'What do you think we should do? Abandon him? Do you want to explain to his father and his brothers that we left him to die beneath the waves? Do you want to do that?'

Suen lowered his eyes, shamed by Lin's outburst, but knowing that he was right and that he spoke for others. They had been rowing round and round in circles for almost two hours and seen nothing but rotting vegetation, mouldly driftwood and plastic bags. If they were still under water then they were surely dead. If they had left the water then they had done so unnoticed. Either way they were wasting their time.

Lin used his walkie-talkie to talk to the men in the launches and his teams on land. Nothing. He stood at the prow of the boat, his hands on his hips, his chin up defiantly as if daring the frogman to come up and fight him, man to man.

Dugan was reading the *Standard* with his third cup of coffee when the phone rang.

'Good morning, Patrick Dugan.'

'Hiya kid. What's new?'

'Nothing much. Business as usual,' said Petal.

'What's the view like from the tallest building in Hong Kong?' he asked.

'I wish I had a view,' she said. 'I'm nowhere near important enough to warrant an office with a view. Or a high floor. You'd laugh if you saw my cubby-hole. How are you this glorious morning?'

'Knackered,' he said. 'You'll be the death of me.'

'I don't know what you mean, Patrick Dugan. I hope this isn't going to turn into an obscene phone call.'

He laughed, and spilt his plastic cup of coffee across the paper.

'Fuck,' he said angrily, and leapt to his feet.

'I was wrong,' Petal giggled. 'It *is* an obscene phone call. I suppose you want to know what colour underwear I'm wearing?'

'I spilt my coffee, all over my God-forsaken desk,' he said. 'Why does this always happen to me?' He lifted one corner of the paper and carefully poured the brown liquid off and into the waste-paper bin. Luckily it hadn't soaked through to the two files underneath it.

'It's not my day,' he said.

'Cheer up,' said Petal. 'It can only get better.'

'Are you free tonight?' asked Dugan. 'Some of the guys

in the anti-triad squad are having a party at Hot Gossip to celebrate a big drugs bust. You can read all about it on page three of the *Standard*.'

'Sounds great. What time?'

'Fairly late, I've got a stack of paperwork to get through. Say about eleven o'clock. We can eat in the restaurant there, they serve food practically through the night.'

'OK, I'll see you there at eleven.'

'Hey, before you go, can you give me your number at the bank? I've tried to get you a couple of times but the switchboard girls never seem to know where to get you.' Dugan felt that she hesitated, but after a second or two she brightly gave him the number. He wrote it down on the first page of his desk diary. 'One more thing,' he said.

'What's that?'

'Just what colour is your underwear?'

'That is for me to know, and for you to find out,' she laughed sexily, and hung up on him. God, thought Dugan, the night felt like a lifetime away.

Lin eventually called off the search at one o'clock. He radioed the launches and told them to wait at the entrance to the bay and check any boats that left. Wherever possible they were to search the vessels, but if that proved impossible they were to make a note of the name and identification number. He left two Red Poles at Marina Cove and a handful of men scattered around the circumference of the bay, but in his heart of hearts he knew it was too late. The gweilo had been well prepared. He was either safely on board a boat or he'd long since swum to the shore and escaped.

They left the three dinghies tied where they'd found them and walked in disconsolate silence back to the cars. Howells watched them go before allowing the girl out of the toilet.

'I'm hungry,' she pouted.

'Me too,' he said. 'Ravenous. What do you want?'

'I want to go home.' She stamped her foot as she spoke and Howells smiled. Any man who got stuck with this young lady was going to have a hard life.

'To eat,' he said. 'What do you want to eat?'

The look of deviousness that flashed across her face was so transparent that Howells laughed out loud.

'Can I have a look in the galley to see what there is?' she asked as if butter wouldn't melt in her mouth. This was obviously a girl who was used to getting exactly what she wanted from her doting parents.

'No,' said Howells patiently. 'You stay here.'

'A woman's place is in the kitchen,' said Sophie, toying with a strand of her blonde hair. Howells gave her a mock growl and she glared at him. 'You're going to be sorry when my father catches you,' she threatened. Howells said nothing.

The convoy of cars moved slowly up the approach road to the compound like a funeral procession. Lin and Suen were in the lead car, Ng's Daimler. They saw

Jill standing at the front door as they crackled to a halt on the gravelled drive.

'Shit, Elder Brother. Who's going to tell the gweipor?'

'You want to do it?' asked Lin, savagely, and snorted as Suen shook his head. 'I'll tell her. And then I'll speak to Master Cheng. Keep the men by the guardhouse. I'll come and talk to them soon.'

He stepped out of the plush interior of the car and walked towards Jill, his arms out to the side, shoulders low. He found it impossible to meet her eyes as he got close. He had little respect for the white woman, she shared the Dragon Head's bed but not his office and he tried wherever possible to have nothing to do with her. He was certainly not afraid of her, but now she was a stark reminder of his failure, of his failure to protect his boss, her husband.

It seemed to Lin that the closer he got to her, the more his guilt grew, until he could feel it as a heavy weight pressing down on the back of his neck, compressing his spine and making his legs buckle. He tried to straighten his back, to thrust back his shoulders but the pressure just intensified. He stopped, some ten feet in front of her, and looked at her shoes, bright red, the colour of blood.

'Where are they?' she asked quietly. 'What has happened?'

She spoke to him in Cantonese, and as always Lin marvelled at how well she spoke the language that defeated so many gweilos. But when he answered it was in halting English. She was a gweipor and there was no way he could bring himself to speak to a gweipor in his own language. The difference would always be there and in Lin's mind it was a difference that had to be highlighted.

'I am sorry, Mrs Ng,' he said. He forced himself to look at her face. 'The man grabbed your husband and took him into the water. He was wearing diving equipment. We do not know what has happened to him.'

Jill sagged on the doorstep as if Lin had punched her in the stomach. She wrapped her arms around her middle and bent forward, making a low moaning noise like a wounded animal.

'And my daughter?' she asked, still in Cantonese.

Lin shook his head. 'I am sorry,' he said. 'There was no sign of her.'

Jill collapsed in a heap, legs splayed as she slid down the door frame, hugging herself. Lin didn't know what to do; he took an uncertain step forward and then stopped, embarrassed by her show of grief. He was saved by the amah who ran down the corridor and crouched next to her mistress, talking to her softly before helping her to her feet and into the shadows of the house. Lin sighed with relief and turned his back on them. Telling Master Cheng would be no easier, but at least he would take the news better, and he would know what they should do next. He walked around the right-hand side of the house, his feet crunching on the stones. The right-hand wing of the H-shaped house contained the bedrooms, and though it was early afternoon the curtains were drawn. It looked like a house in mourning. The path narrowed and then forked into two, one winding to the left around the back of the house, the other curving away to the right, through a sprinkling of fruit trees and past a small goldfish pool to Cheng's small one-storey house surrounded by its shady palm trees. It was cleverly landscaped so that there was no sign of it from the main house, and Lin heard the songbirds long before he got there. Cheng was sitting on his front doorstep holding a wicker cage in his lap, head on one side as he listened to the deep-throated warble of the yellow and brown bird within.

Lin stood for a moment in front of the old man looking down on his bald head, and then he squatted down, resting his arms on his knees, his backside just a couple of inches from the ground. It put his head lower than Cheng's, and accorded him the respect his age and his position warranted. Lin hadn't adopted such a position for many years; it was a youngster's way of resting, and his knees shrieked with pain and his calf muscles ached but his face remained impassive.

Cheng kept his eyes on the caged bird as he spoke. 'What happened, Wah-tsai?'

The old man spoke to him the same way now that he had more than twenty years ago, using the diminutive of his name. Cheng didn't do it to belittle Lin, or to humiliate him; it reflected the length of time they'd known each other and that theirs was still very much a teacher–pupil relationship. There was a lot Lin still had to learn from Master Cheng if he was ever to get the chance of taking on the mantle of Lung Tau.

'I have failed, Master Cheng,' Lin said softly.

'Tell me what happened,' replied Cheng, his eyes still on the bird. Lin told him in a gentle voice that belied his strength and size.

When he finished the old man carefully placed the cage on a small rosewood table at the side of the door, in the shade of one of the palm trees. He took a small brass watering can and poured a trickle of water into the bird's drinking dish, a reward for a song well sung. The bird dipped its beak into the fresh water then threw back its head and swallowed, shaking with pleasure.

'I shall tell his father,' Cheng said finally. 'You must tell his brother. His brother must come back.'

'He will take charge?' asked Lin. He wanted to lead the triad so badly that he could taste it, but he knew that it was not his time yet. And he also knew that the worst possible thing would be to push himself forward. Such audacity could easily backfire, fatally. He had seen it happen before.

'That will be up to his father. But that does not matter. He must be here. Have you told his wife?'

'I have.'

'How did she take it?'

Lin was going to say 'like a gweipor' but he bit back the words. The bond between Master Cheng and Simon Ng was almost as strong as that between parent and child and unlike Lin the old man's respect and affection included Ng's wife and child. 'Not very well, Master Cheng.'

Cheng nodded thoughtfully. 'She must be watched, Wah-tsai. Her brother is a policeman and she may be tempted to seek his help.'

'It will be done, Master Cheng.'

'We must look for the gweilo. Start with the boats in Hebe Haven, though I do not believe he will be stupid enough to remain there. And send one of your more tactful Grass Sandals around to speak to the headmistress at the girl's school. She saw the gweilo and we need a description. Once we know what he looks like we should begin to check all the hotels. At the moment that is all we can do.'

'Yes, Master Cheng.' Lin straightened his legs with a

grunt and backed away from the old man, taking two steps before turning away. As he walked down the path he could hear the old man talking quietly, either to himself or to one of his beloved birds. Lin couldn't tell which, and he knew it would be impolite to turn and look. He went back to the house to use the phone.

Howells waited until the evening sky darkened before he left the junk. Sophie had demanded that she be allowed to shower and Howells stood guard outside the door to the small shower cubicle until she'd finished. Twice she accused him of peeping and she stayed there until she'd dried herself and dressed again. She wanted to know if he'd get her some clean clothes and he told her that she wouldn't be needing them because she'd soon be going home. He made the girl a cheese sandwich and gave it to her as he locked her in the toilet.

'How long are you going to be?' she asked.

'I don't know,' he said. 'But you'll be going home soon, I promise. I'll call your mother and she'll come and get you. Keep quiet, OK?'

'OK,' she said, taking the sandwich. 'Are you a kidnapper?' she asked, her eyes wide.

'I suppose so,' he said.

'So if you're a kidnapper, what am I?' she asked seriously.

'What do you mean?'

'I mean, what do you call someone who has been kidnapped?'

'A victim,' said Howells, trying to close the door. She put up her small hand and held it open, looking up at him.

'I'm tired of being a victim,' she said quietly. 'I want to go home.'

'I know,' said Howells. 'You're not going to be a victim for much longer. Trust me.'

'OK, I will,' she said, letting go of the door and allowing him to close and lock it.

Howells hadn't decided what he'd do with Sophie when it was over. It would be a simple matter to phone Ng's house and tell them where she was. Or it would be just as easy to kill her. He didn't really care, either way.

He picked up an empty shopping bag from the galley, carried it to the back of the junk and lowered himself down into the boat. It was so dark that he couldn't see the pier or the beach, so he knew that he couldn't be seen from the shore, but even so he rowed the boat across to Marina Cove rather than using the outboard, slowly and taking care not to splash.

He guided the boat in among the luxury yachts moored at the marina and tied it up. Once on land he walked slowly, swinging the bag and whistling to himself. The triads would be there, he was sure, and there was no point in trying to sneak past. His best bet was to be out in the open, just a gweilo sailor going out for provisions. There were several dozen people walking along the marina, and many more sitting on their boats; the triads couldn't stop everyone. He'd left the car at the marina's car park where there were at least fifty others, and he headed towards it. A young man in a faded T-shirt and cut off jeans was filming his pretty, bra-less girlfriend with a small, hand-held video camera as she leaned on a railing at the water's edge. Howells turned to look at her as he walked past, partly to shield his face from the lens but also because he got a good feeling seeing her breasts bouncing under her thin cotton top. She smiled at him as she realized he was looking at her and he grinned back.

The couple with the dog were still there, walking slowly by the moored yachts, occasionally stopping to peer through the portholes. God knows what they thought they were looking for, thought Howells. Wet air tanks and a schoolgirl tied to the bed, no doubt. He reached the car and threw the shopping bag on to the back seat before driving off.

As he drove off he noticed two men in a dirty white Honda Civic, both wearing dark glasses. One of them had a notebook and he started scribbling as Howells turned onto the main road and headed back to Tsim Sha Tsui. They were obviously clocking all the cars that left, and that meant they'd probably be tracing them too. It wouldn't be too long before they tracked down the hire company and it was a short step from there to the Holiday Inn and room 426. No sweat, he was checking out anyway.

Jill Ng sat on the small brass-framed bed with the floppy grey and white Old English Sheepdog on her lap and used one of its ears to wipe her tears. She was in Sophie's bedroom, surrounded by her things, her clothes, her toys, her books. Her Garfield telephone crouched on the bedside table, ready to spring. A poster of a bare-chested rock band that her father had said was too revealing for a girl her age but which she'd begged and pleaded to be allowed to pin on her wall. Her school books piled high, unopened, on her child's size desk. Jill's mind was in turmoil, a jumble of thoughts of her husband and daughter, flashes of the good times, the holidays, the Christmas present openings, the birthdays, the rows, the arguments, the tears.

There was a bottle of tablets next to Garfield, green ones that the doctor had given her to treat the depression that had hit her like a tidal wave during the weeks after Sophie's birth. She'd kept them hidden at the back of the bathroom cabinet like an unsavoury secret, a memory that she was ashamed of but which couldn't be banished. Next to the tablets was a glass of brandy, half finished. She'd used the alcohol to wash down two of the tablets and now she sat and waited for the combination of alcohol and chemicals to numb the pain and allow her to fall into the oblivion of sleep.

Outside the bedroom door sat Rose, squatting on the floor with her back against the wall. She too was crying.

Howells delivered the car back to the hotel and checked out, settling his account in cash. He had no fear at all of being traced as he'd given Donaldson's name and passport details. The trail stopped dead at the Holiday Inn. He walked along Salisbury Road past the Regent Hotel on his left, the grand old Peninsula on his right, to the Star

Ferry terminal. An old man wearing blue and white striped pyjamas and a baggy green pullover was selling English newspapers and he stopped to buy a *Times*. It was only one day old. He paid the man and dropped a dollar coin into the turnstile at the entrance to the ferry terminal and didn't bother collecting his change. The old lady in a blue patterned trouser suit behind him pocketed the unwanted cents without a thought.

He sat in the middle of the ageing ferry on a hard wooden bench seat, listening to the comforting throb of the engines below. Most of the skyscrapers in the island's business district had huge neon advertising signs on the top. Even the futuristic HongKong and Shanghai Bank building, looking for all the world like a Ford Cortina radiator, had the bank's red and white hexagonal logo at its summit. Not one of them was flashing as Kai Tak airport was just across the harbour and it was a difficult enough approach without the hassle of competition for the landing lights.

A ferryman in a dark blue sailor suit and black plastic sandals stood by the upraised ramp that allowed passengers on and off, idly running a thick, hemp rope through his grubby hands. He cleared his throat loudly and spat noisily into the waves.

Howells flicked through the paper. It was the first English newspaper he'd read in more than two years, but there was nothing in it that interested him. The names of the politicians were the same, so were the policies and the rhetoric. Inflation was under control, the pound was strong, the peasants weren't revolting, all was well with the world. None of it mattered to Howells any more. All he cared about was working again, to be given the chance to show what he could do, what he'd been trained for.

He left the paper, half-read, on the bench when he left the ferry. The sailor took it and put it with his collection in his locker. Later that night they would be back on sale.

Howells caught a taxi to the Hilton, where he booked in under his own name. The young man behind the reception desk gave him a big toothy smile and asked how Mr Howells would be settling his account and when Mr Howells said it would be cash the smile tightened a smidgen and he asked for a deposit. The Hilton was used to businessmen and plastic cards, but Howells had plenty of yellow thousand dollar notes left, more than enough to win another gleaming smile.

Howells turned down the offer of a bellboy to show him up to his room. It was on the tenth floor, and not much different from the one he had just checked out of with a colour television, minibar, a big double bed and an uninspiring painting on the wall. It could have been a hotel room anywhere in the world, Hilton circa late 1980s.

It was nine o'clock at night, which meant it was one o'clock in London, lunchtime for the hundreds of thousands of the capital's bureaucrats – not that it would matter. Grey never answered the phone number he gave his agents, or associates as he preferred to call them. Their calls were always routed through to an answering machine which he religiously checked every hour, either manually or with a small coded bleeper that he carried which allowed him to listen to the machine's tape from a phone anywhere in the world. Howells rang through and the machine clicked on after the fourth ring. He heard Grey's sombre voice repeat the number and then there was a high-pitched tone, the signal to talk.

Howells gave his name, the date and time, and said simply that the contract had been signed and that he was now at the Hilton Hotel awaiting further instructions, and then rang off. All that was left to do now was to wait. He thought of calling Mrs Ng and telling her where her daughter was, but decided against it. It would do the girl no harm to spend another night on board the junk, and it would keep the triads doubly occupied, if nothing else. He poured himself a lager from the bar and lay on the bed watching television. He chuckled through an old episode of *The Man from Uncle*, a boyish Ilya Kuryakin and an earnest Napoleon Solo blowing away THRUSH agents with no blood and no recoil from the guns.

Grey was in his office on the ninth floor of Century House when the phone rang, but he made no move to answer it. He sat in his big, black leather swivel chair, his fingers steepled under his chin and listened carefully as Howells dictated his message. When the machine clicked off, he reached for the black push-button phone that squatted next to the brass-framed photograph of his wife, standing in the garden with a basket full of cut roses, the dogs at her heels. He had the number ready on a slip of paper and he punched out the digits that would connect him to Hong Kong.

He waited for the electronic impulses to travel up to the satellite way out in space and back to the few square miles of British soil on the rump of Southern China where it was relayed to an office in the Central business district, to an office with cheap teak-veneered furniture and an answering machine not unlike his own.

A man's voice, guttural with a heavy Chinese accent, carefully repeated the number in English and then the tone signalled that it was time to leave a message.

Grey took a deep breath and in a level voice passed what he knew would be the death sentence for the man he had sent to Hong Kong. 'Geoff Howells,' he said. 'Hilton Hotel.' Then he slowly spelled out the name and hung up.

He had never met the assassin who would get the message, and he hoped he never would. All he knew was that the assassin was called Hua-fan, that Hua-fan had a one hundred per cent success rate and that when Hua-fan's work was done and Howells was dead then the circle would be closed. Strange name for an assassin, he thought. Hua-fan. Chinese for flower petal.

Petal had dressed all in black, and she looked very, very sexy. She had on a pair of cotton trousers that ballooned out over her hips and tapered down to her ankles, like something out of the Arabian Nights. Her top was a close-fitting silk shirt that clung to her like a second skin, the collar buttoned up tight and held in place with a man's black bow tie. Round her waist hung a loose, thick leather belt. The outfit effectively covered every inch of skin below her neck, except for her tiny hands, and what made it all the more sexy was that Dugan knew every inch of her body underneath the clothing – it was as if her body was a secret that she allowed him alone to share. As she walked across the bar to where he was standing, he could see heads turning to watch, attracted by the sway of her hips, the glossy hair and the achingly pretty face, but it was Dugan she slept with, Dugan that she undressed for.

He could see some of the heads looking to see who she was there to meet, and Dugan stood taller and sucked in his gut. Without thinking, he raised his hand to smooth down his hair.

'Hi,' she said, standing on tiptoe to kiss him on the cheek. 'Been waiting long?'

'A lifetime,' he said, and he was only half joking. 'What do you feel like?'

'Just a Perrier water,' she said. 'I've got the beginnings of a headache.'

Dugan ordered her drink and then led her over to the table he'd booked earlier. He pulled the chair out for her and pushed it in as she sat down. Dugan marvelled at the way she brought out the gentleman in him when they were in public, and brought out the animal in him when they were in bed. A waiter came over with two large glossy cardboard menus. Petal ordered a cheeseburger with French fries and Dugan asked for Hainan Chicken – pieces of cold chicken with a selection of spicy sauces, rice and soup. There was nothing unusual in the gweilo choosing from the Chinese menu while the local girl opted for Western food, it happened all the time to Dugan. The girls were trying to prove how modern, how westernized they were, while Dugan simply preferred to eat eastern food.

'Why so late in the office?' she asked, both hands

clasped around the glass of sparkling water. She looked nervous, thought Dugan. Probably the headache.

'A couple of cases that need tidying up, nothing much. One of them comes to court next week so I had to get all the paperwork out of the way. Really boring stuff, but it has to be done.'

'You don't like your job, do you?'

Dugan shrugged. 'It's OK. But I'd rather be doing real policework, rather than just shuffling papers. Life is funny, isn't it? We spend almost one third of our lives doing jobs we don't particularly like, and another one third asleep. That means we only do what we really want to do for one third of our lives, and into that time we have to cram eating, washing, shopping, cleaning the house. Life is so short, Petal. Too short to fill with things we don't enjoy. Don't you think?'

'At least you can change your life, Pat. You can switch jobs, or you can always go back to England.'

'Sure, but I still have to work. But what can I do? No work, no money. And Hong Kong is the last place in the world to be without money. That's what makes the place tick. I wish I'd been born rich.'

'You're not poor, not by any means.' She reached up and touched his cheek. 'Stop feeling sorry for yourself.' She pinched the lobe of his ear, hard.

'Ouch,' he said, surprised at the pain, but at the same time excited by it.

'Well,' she said, 'you need jogging out of your misery. Stop being so morose.'

'Yeah, you're right,' he said grudgingly. The waiter returned, a plate in each hand. 'Do you feel like wine?'

'No, I'm fine with Perrier,' she said. Dugan ordered a

lager for himself, and another Perrier for Petal. She toyed with her food, pecking at it with her fork.

'Not hungry?' he asked.

'I'm OK,' she said brightly. 'I'm just feeling a bit, how do you say it, out of sorts.'

'I'm sorry. Can I help?'

'Just being here helps,' she said. She put her knife and fork down. 'You don't know how lucky you are,' she said earnestly.

'What do you mean?'

'You have so much freedom. You can go anywhere. Do anything. I envy you, and all you do is complain.' Dugan realized he had touched a nerve and reached over to hold her hand. 'Imagine living in a world where you are told what to do all the time: what to study, where to work, what to eat, where to live, what to think. To have no freedom at all. To be taken away from your family, to be made to work on a farm, to be forced into a job you don't want to do just because you show a talent for it. You have so much freedom, Pat, and you fritter it away and moan about what a tough life you have.'

Tears were welling up in her eyes and the couple at the next table glanced over to look at the big, awkward gweilo bullying the small Chinese girl. Dugan hunched forward over his plate, wanting to get closer to her, wanting to comfort her but not knowing the magic words that would make it all right.

'Do you have any idea what life is like in China, Pat Dugan? Have you any idea at all?'

He shook his head. He wanted to tell her that it was OK, that he understood, except that he didn't think he did.

'I'll tell you a story,' she said slowly. 'And maybe

when I've finished you'll count your blessings and stop feeling so sorry for yourself.' She sniffed and groped in her bag for a packet of paper handkerchiefs. 'I was born in Shanghai,' she said. 'My mother was a singer, a very famous singer. She could sing Chinese opera, but preferred western music and jazz, and in Shanghai during the fifties and early sixties she was as famous as Anita Mui is in Hong Kong today. Her concerts were packed out, and she was courted by all the rich and famous people, invited to all the best parties. She was a star, a real star, not one of the manufactured Cantonese pop idols of today. She had the pick of all the eligible men in Shanghai, but chose my father, a doctor. One of those crazy things; she sprained her ankle horse-riding, he was there when she fell, he treated her, they fell in love. In any normal, sane world they would have been happy ever after. But not in China.'

'What happened?' Dugan asked quietly, conscious that, for whatever reason, Petal was allowing him inside her shell for the first time.

'They married, they had me, and three years later my brother was born. That was before the days of the one-couple, one-child craziness. For a time we were the happiest family you could imagine; we were rich, life in Shanghai was so good. It was a thriving, bustling city, lots to do, lots of places for children to play. We lived in a big house, with servants, and horses. I had my own pony. You can't imagine how perfect it was.'

Her voice was dropping in volume and Dugan had to strain to hear her over the noise of the videos.

'And then?' he said, gently urging her on.

'The Cultural Revolution,' she said. 'The country went

213

mad. Anything artistic, anybody with money, anybody who was not prepared to swear total and complete allegiance to the Communists, was treated with such contempt, such bitterness, such savagery. The Red Guards stormed our house one day. Actually that's not true, the servants let them in. The servants joined them. They smashed up everything we had. I have no pictures of my parents, none of my mother's records. They even killed my pony, can you think of anything so horrible, so vindictive? They slit its throat in front of me, screaming that animals were for food or for work, not for pleasure. Patrick, they killed my pony.'

She was crying out loud now, small sobs that she tried to stifle with her handkerchief. Dugan felt totally lost. He had no idea what had brought this on, and had no idea what to say. She blew her nose, pocketed the screwed-up ball of tissue and picked up her knife and fork. She had her head down over her plate as she hacked at her burger, her hair hanging forward like a veil. She looked up with a forkful of meat halfway to her mouth and tried to smile.

'I'm sorry,' she said. 'I didn't mean to sound so upset. I've just had a hard day, that's all. I'll be all right, honest.'

Her eyes looked different, as if a bullet-proof screen had come down behind her pupils, locking her emotions in and Dugan out. He felt cheated; for one blinding moment he had glimpsed the pearl within the shell, and then it had closed. He didn't know how long it would be before she opened up to him again, or if she ever would. He began to eat again, but the chicken had no taste.

Both English-language television channels closed down at about one o'clock in the morning. Howells flicked through the buttons on the remote control. He found a black-and-white Chinese historical drama where the men had pigtails and the women looked like porcelain dolls, and a horse-racing programme presented by two young Chinese men in matching blazers. He switched off the set and got undressed. He'd wake up soon enough when Grey rang. For the moment he was tired, dog-tired. His calf muscles ached from the exertions of the morning, and his knees were grazed where he'd scraped against rocks on the sea bed. He slipped quickly and easily into sleep.

Whatever had upset Petal, it didn't get any better as the evening progressed. She seemed lifeless and withdrawn, almost a stranger. Dugan tried to make light of it, told her a few jokes which were rewarded with a weak smile and did everything short of standing on his head to win her round.

'I'm sorry, Pat, I'm terrible company tonight,' she said, half-way through her third Perrier water.

'No you're not,' he said. 'Perhaps you'd feel better after a drink.' He raised his glass of lager. 'Drown your sorrows.'

She shook her head. 'Drink won't help,' she said.

'Anyway, I've got a headache. A drink is the last thing I need.'

Dugan waved at a waiter and asked for the bill. It arrived on a stainless steel tray and he paid with a handful of red notes.

'I'll take you home,' offered Dugan, pulling out her chair for her.

'No, no need,' she said. 'I just don't feel very well, that's all. I'll just go home and rest. You stay here; your friends will be downstairs, won't they?'

'Of course,' he laughed. 'They never go anywhere else.'

'Well, you stay here with them. You can walk me to a taxi.' She held his arm as they walked out of the door and down the steps to the road. A cab was waiting there with its light on but with a red card with the Chinese characters for Hong Kong covering its 'For Hire' sign. Dugan held the door for her. She stood in front of him, her breasts against his chest, her head tilted back so that she could look at his face. 'Thank you for a lovely evening,' she said. Dugan snorted, but he smiled as he did it. 'I'm serious,' she said. 'I'll be OK tomorrow, I'm sure.'

'I hope so,' said Dugan. He kissed her on the forehead. 'Petal?'

'Hmm?'

'Is there anything I can do to help?'

'Don't be so silly,' she said. She reached up, linking her arms around his neck and pulling herself up on tiptoe to kiss him full on the lips. 'Good night,' she said, and slid into the taxi.

Dugan closed the door and stood on the pavement to watch it drive towards the harbour. He could see the dark shape of her head in the middle of the back seat. She didn't turn round and Dugan felt cold and empty inside. He turned and went back to the lights and noise of the disco.

There were three of them, two men and a girl. One of the men bent down over the lock and inserted two thin pieces of wire, one hard, the other curved and springy with a hook on one end. While he worked, silently pushing the tumblers back one by one, the girl and the second man stood at either end of the corridor, keeping watch. It took him less than a minute, and then he rested back on his heels and nodded to his colleagues. They walked carefully, placing each foot flat on the carpet, heel then toe, arms slightly away from their body so that they didn't even disturb the night air with the rustle of clothing.

There was no need to speak; the three had worked together for many years. They worked as one. The lock-picker slowly rose to his feet and rested his palm against the wooden door. He put his tools in the inside pocket of his poorly fitting suit and slowly opened the door. All three were tidal breathing, their lungs taking in just enough air to breathe, no exertion, mouths slightly open.

The two men entered first, moving as if in slow motion, past the bathroom and the minibar, stopping as the girl gently pushed the door closed, turning the handle in fractions of degrees so that it locked with no noise. She carried a small leather bag in one hand. The room was very dark, the thick curtains blocking any outside light, and the trio stood for a while until their eyes grew used to the room. They could make out the dressing-table, the wardrobes, the television, the bedside table and Howells, lying on his back, one arm across the pillows, the other under the single sheet that covered the lower half of his body. It was hot and airless in the room because he'd switched off the air-conditioning.

They moved quickly then, the two men up on the balls of their feet crossing quickly to opposite sides of the bed, grabbing an arm each. Howells woke as the man on his left grabbed hold of his arm, the nails biting into his flesh. He rolled towards him, freeing his right arm from under the sheet and preparing to slash out, fingers curled to strike when it too was seized and thrust down on to the bed. Howells made no sound, he knew there was no reason to cry out, there would be no one to help him. He tried to lift his shoulders off the bed but a bitter-smelling hand hit him in the face and pushed him back on to the pillow, the palm firmly under his chin, clamping his jaw together and making breathing difficult. The fingers of the hand moved to either side of his nostrils and he was forced to breathe through clenched teeth like a muzzled dog.

He tensed, waiting for the knife or the gun or whatever else they were going to use, testing their strength by pulling his arms in towards him. There were two hands holding his left arm, one holding the right, because it was the man on his right who was holding down his head. That was a mistake; Howells was right-handed and when he moved that would be the way he'd go. He kicked out with his legs, pushing the sheet off the bottom of the bed so that he'd be able to lash out with his legs. He saw the girl then. She was standing at the dressing-table with her back towards him. She was dressed in black and seemed little more than a shadow, and when she turned her face and hands were all he could see, everything else faded into the dark. Even her face was partly obscured by her black hair. She was pretty, very pretty, and Howells had the feeling that he'd seen her somewhere before but he couldn't place it, there was just a niggling feeling at the back of his mind. She had something in her right hand, and as she stepped forward to the foot of the bed he could see it was a hypodermic, the needle pointed to the ceiling. She held it in both hands, pushing the plunger up slowly and expelling a small amount of the liquid. It dripped slowly down the needle and she tilted it so that it wouldn't run down her hands.

She moved to the left side of the bed, stepping on the sheet that he'd kicked on to the floor. Howells moved his legs up the bed, crossing his left thigh across his groin, and she smiled at his attempt to cover himself. She knelt on the bed, slowly, handling the hypodermic carefully as she prepared to mount him. Howells flinched, drawing his legs up to his left side, and her smile grew wider. She flicked her head to one side, throwing the black sheet of hair away from her face and she was still smiling when Howells threw all his weight to the left and swung his right leg round and kicked her full on the side of the face with the ball of his right foot, the toes pulled back, the ankle tense, hard enough to kill if he hadn't been held flat on his back and only able to use the lower half of his body.

Her head snapped away and she crashed off the bed, the hypodermic spinning through the air and hitting the curtains. Howells pulled in with both arms, breathing hard with the exertion, then quickly thrust his right arm to the side, slipping through the man's hand just enough so that he could twist it round. He kicked across with the left leg, missing the head but making the man relax his grip again. He released Howells' head but before he could get both hands to hold the arm Howells twisted again and grabbed the man's index finger. He bent it back savagely, hearing the bone crack. The man screamed involuntarily but then bit back the pain as Howells released him. The man on his left hadn't moved, he'd concentrated on holding the left arm firmly on the bed, and he looked across in surprise as Howells' right arm whipped across, fingers rock-hard, the cutting edge of the hand curving through the air and then arcing up and thrusting hard into his temple. His head jerked back and both hands let go. Howells was on his feet immediately, crouched low on the bed. The man shook his head and his eyes focused just in time to see the second strike coming, a clenched fist that smashed into his windpipe and shattered the cartilage. He collapsed on top of the girl, his eyes wide with panic as he fought for breath, air bubbling through the blood that ran thickly down into his aching lungs.

Howells whirled around, dropping down into his fighting crouch again, but as he did his ears roared with a deafening explosion that stunned him and he felt a crashing blow on his right shoulder that knocked him backwards into the modernistic painting on the wall behind the headboard. He rolled along the wall, smearing blood against the painting, and staggered off the bed. The pain hit him then, a red wave that flashed from his shoulder and made him grit his teeth, swallowing the roar of rage that wanted to erupt from his mouth. He dropped low, forward hand up to block any attack, rear hand clenched at waist height, ready to punch despite the searing pain. It was a reflex action because the strength had deserted his right arm, it ached fiercely and he could feel wetness spreading around the wound. The man with the broken finger was standing with a wicked-looking gun in hand, a wisp of smoke oozing from the barrel. Howells realized that if he hadn't been turning the bullet would have struck him in the middle of the back, instead of hitting him in the shoulder. He knew also that he had to move immediately because he could see the man's finger tightening on the trigger. He was perfectly calm, despite being stark naked and facing a man with a gun. All fear, all hesitation, had long ago been trained out of Howells. The gun was in the man's left hand, the right hand out for balance with the index finger awkwardly crooked, and Howells knew instinctively that the man was right-handed. He ducked to the left, a feinting movement that moved the gun just a fraction, and then dropped his weight back on his right leg and flicked his forward leg out and up, so fast the movement was a blur. It wasn't a killing kick, there was little or no focus, but it moved so quickly that before the man's finger could generate enough force to pull the trigger the foot had reached its target, knocking the gun upwards. Only then did the trigger kick, the explosion making Howells flinch as the bullet ripped over his head and buried itself into the plaster ceiling. Howells dropped his kicking leg to the floor and moved forward, bringing his right knee up and then powering forward, focusing the kick a good nine inches behind the man's sternum, kicking through him rather than at him. As the ball of his foot connected with the chest, Howells twisted his hip into the kick, tightening all the muscles in his legs, the whole weight of his body behind the blow. A killing blow. The sternum disintegrated and the diaphragm collapsed as Howells followed through until the man slammed into the wall, blood frothing from his lips as he grunted and died.

Howells stood over the man as he slumped to the floor, watched as his eyes filmed over and only then did he walk over to the mirror above the dressing-table, to check the damage to his shoulder. The man's gun had been a small calibre, a .22 maybe, not a professional's gun. There was no exit wound, the bullet was still in there; he couldn't feel it, but he knew he would once his body's adrenalin and enkephalin had dropped to normal.

He was lucky, lucky that the man hadn't had a .357, lucky that he'd ducked as he turned, lucky that he'd hurt the man's shooting hand. Lucky that they'd planned to kill him with some sort of an injection and not a bullet. But luck was often all that separated the living from the dead. Luck and training.

He dressed as quickly as he could, knowing that someone was sure to have reported the shot. He pulled on his trousers and his socks and shoes, using only his left hand. He could feel blood dripping down his shoulder, so he shook a pillow out of its case and wrapped the white linen across the wound before gingerly putting on a rust-coloured shirt. It wouldn't stop all the bleeding but at least it wouldn't show if it soaked into the shirt.

He looked at himself in the mirror. The bulky pillow-case was bulging under the shirt, it was as obvious as hell.

He had a black cotton bomber jacket so he put that on, too. That looked better. His wallet was on the dressing-table and he put it in his jacket pocket, using his left hand, and then slotted his passport and Donaldson's into the back pocket of his jeans.

The shock was beginning to wear off and shafts of pain shot through his shoulder, making him wince. He stood with his eyes closed, breathing deeply and willing the pain to go away, then he moved quickly to the door. He couldn't risk taking his bag or belongings in case the front desk stopped him. He checked the corridor, both sides, and then slipped out, locking the door behind him.

Pat Dugan was pissed. Well pissed. He'd stayed in Hot Gossip with Burr and a handful of the anti-triad boys, drinking hard and fast. He was angry at Petal for leaving him, angry with himself for not knowing how to handle the situation, and angry at the world in general. He laughed too loud and drank too much until even Burr told him he'd had enough.

'Fuck you,' Dugan told him.

'Fuck you, too,' said Burr. 'Go home.' He walked off, leaving Dugan standing by himself at the bar.

'Time to go, Pat,' he told himself and then headed unsteadily to the exit, bumping into one of the dinner-jacketed bouncers on the way out.

A cab pulled up in front of a young Chinese couple standing at the kerbside and Dugan grabbed at the handle, getting hold of it a fraction of a second before they did. He yanked open the door and glared drunkenly at them, daring them to argue. They moved away, embarrassed by the open show of hostility, and Dugan tumbled on to the back seat. The driver leant over and pulled the door shut. Dugan lay where he was, face down, and shouted his address in Cantonese. The driver grunted and drove off.

Howells had to stand in a queue outside the Hilton Hotel while a tall, bulky Indian with a gleaming white turban, black and yellow tunic and white breeches went down to Queen's Road and flagged down taxis, directing them up the slip road. As he stood in line he felt faint, his head filled with the throbbing sound of his own heartbeat. He gasped for breath and rubbed his forehead with his sweating left hand. His right arm and shoulder ached horribly. His legs began to tremble and he had to lock his knees rigid to stop himself falling over. Two cabs arrived, then a third, and then thankfully it was his turn. The Indian asked, in impeccable English, where he was going, and only then did he realize that he had no idea, simply that he had to get away from the hotel before the bodies were discovered. He heard himself say 'Wan Chai' before he carefully got into the cab.

The Indian nodded and told the driver, and the driver grinned at him. 'Another fucking gweilo about to get fleeced,' he said in rapid Cantonese.

'They never learn,' agreed the Indian.

'Fuck his mother,' said the driver, slamming the car into gear and lurching back to the road. Howells groaned and kept his eyes shut.

There were certain preparations that had to be made if Dugan was to make it through the night, what was left of it. He made sure the aircon was switched on, and pulled a plastic bottle of distilled water out of the fridge and drank as much of it as he could force down before placing it next to his bed. He took a bottle of orange-flavoured Eno fruit salts and tipped a spoonful into a glass and put that down next to the water. He did it all on automatic pilot, humming quietly to himself, and then he sat down on the bed and undressed, dropping the clothes on the floor before flopping back and passing out. He'd left the light on, but he didn't notice.

The taxi stopped outside the Washington Club and Howells fumbled with his wallet. He handed over two green notes and didn't wait for the change. The driver grinned and used a lever under the dashboard to pull the door closed after him.

The aged doorman heaved himself off his wooden stool and opened the door for him, allowing out the pulsing beat of a Cantonese pop song. Howells caught sight of his reflection in the fish tank as he walked into the bar. He looked terrible. Big deal. He felt terrible. He felt like his shoulder had been put between the jaws of a red-hot vice and was being squeezed, hard. The bar was busy but there were a couple of empty seats side by side and he walked to one, being careful not to bump his arm. On the seat to his left was a small man in a crumpled beige suit with sweat stains under the armpits drinking Foster's lager from a can. He raised it to Howells. 'How's it going, digger?' he asked in a broad Australian accent.

'Great,' said Howells. The Australian had blank eyes, a film of sweat over his skin, and a stupid grin on his face. He was well gone.

Howells looked around for Amy. He missed her at first because she was standing on the opposite side of the bar with her back to him, caught between two men in dark business suits, drinking champagne. One of them had his hand on her hip, the other was looming over her, teeth bared like a vampire about to take a piece out of her neck. She laughed out loud and he thought it sounded forced. Wishful thinking, maybe.

She turned to pick up the bottle of champagne out of a battered stainless steel ice bucket and pour the last drop into her glass. She saw Howells then and instantly smiled at him, then followed it by pulling a face and nodding her head towards the man on her left. He grimaced back and she smiled again. She held her hand up, fingers splayed and mouthed 'five minutes'. She was wearing a lemon-coloured evening dress with white frothy lace arms. Howells nodded and told the barhag in front of him that he wanted to see the wine list.

'Huh?' she barked at him.

'Lager,' he said.

She screamed the order over the top of his head at one of the waiters behind him.

'What's your name?' she asked him, leaning her elbows on the bar and breathing garlic fumes into his face.

'Fuck off,' he said. She glanced at him and cursed in Cantonese. 'Fuck off,' he repeated, quietly this time, and she read the menace in his eyes. She backed away, saying nothing.

The Australian was impressed. 'Jesus, digger, you sure know how to treat a girl.' Howells ignored him.

He left his right hand on the bar, trying to keep the weight off his throbbing shoulder. Occasionally he lifted the glass of lager to his lips but he only sipped at it. His mouth felt dry but he knew alcohol would only dehydrate him and that would make him feel worse.

It took Amy more than fifteen minutes to drag herself away from the three-piece-suited barracudas, during which she drank two more glasses of champagne and allowed them to fondle her breasts, albeit briefly.

She stroked the back of his neck as she passed behind him, then allowed her hand to move across his right shoulder. Howells nearly screamed and he had to clamp his teeth together to keep the noise in. It felt as if she'd stuck a red-hot poker into his flesh and then twisted it round, deeper and deeper. She pulled back her hand as if he'd bit it.

'What's wrong?' she said.

Howells kept his eyes closed but he could still see a red mist punctuated with flashes of bright yellow light. He waited until the waves of pain subsided before he risked opening them. He saw Amy sitting on the stool next to him, one hand covering her wall of teeth.

'Tom, what's the matter?'

Howells kept his voice low so that the Australian wouldn't hear him. 'I need your help, Amy.' The dimpled barhag appeared next to him and demanded that he buy Amy a drink. He agreed and she walked off, a satisfied smirk on her face.

'What do you mean?' Amy asked.

'Can I pay your bar fine?' he asked urgently. 'Can I take you out?'

'Of course. But it is expensive. Are you sure you want to?'

'Yes,' he hissed, the pain returning.

'I'll speak to the mamasan,' she said. She slipped off the stool in a rustle of silk and went over to a wrinkled old woman who was wearing an ill-fitting wig and an equally ill-fitting navy blue dress. She had a lousy dress sense, but Howells could see she was wearing a solid gold Rolex and he doubted that it was a fake.

The old woman looked at Howells and he felt as if he was a side of beef being weighed up by a butcher. Then she nodded and Amy smiled and came back over, her hands clasped together across her stomach.

'Mamasan says it's OK. How will you pay?'

Very romantic, thought Howells, but he knew it wasn't romance he needed. It was help, a place to hide and someone who knew what they were doing to take the bullet out.

Howells gingerly took his wallet out and handed it to Amy. 'Take out what you want,' he said. She looked through it and pulled out a handful of notes before giving it back.

'You stay here while I change,' she said.

'Don't worry,' said Howells. 'I won't run away.'

Thomas Ng couldn't remember exactly when it had happened, but somewhere along the line he'd begun to develop a fear of flying. He could remember the time when he thought no more of making the trip from San Francisco to Hong Kong than he did of driving through the Cross Harbour Tunnel or over the Golden Gate Bridge. The first few times he'd actually enjoyed the flight, relishing time to relax away from ever-ringing phones and the demands of others, time to watch a movie and catch up on some work. Then the trip became a regular chore, something that had to be done to keep the family business running, painless but boring. Not something he gave any thought to. But recently he had started to dread the flight, lying awake the night before, tossing and turning, trying wherever possible to postpone the time when he'd be sitting in an aluminium tube thousands of feet above the earth. He'd begun asking for aisle seats so that he couldn't see the wings flexing, he'd started taking a couple of Valiums an hour or so before checking in at the airport. And whereas in the old days he'd have sipped a tonic water with his meal, now he'd put away a couple of Martinis. Or more. None of it helped; he could still feel his heart beating, the sweat beading on his forehead, the physiological symptoms of his apprehension. To make it worse, this time he'd had to fly United Airlines, all the Asian airlines had been fully booked. So instead of being waited on by the girls of Cathay Pacific he had to suffer overweight gweipors with fat arses, plastic smiles and too much make-up.

First had been full and half the plane seemed to have been given over to Business Class and the treatment he was receiving was worse than he'd ever got in Economy with Cathay or Singapore or Thai. He'd held out his jacket to a blonde with scarlet-smeared lips and over-plucked eyebrows but she just looked at him with contempt and suggested he put it in one of the overhead lockers. He'd asked for a Martini and been told he'd have to wait. He asked for headphones and was told they'd be issued after they'd taken off. Ng supposed it was to be expected with a Western airline, but he'd had no choice, he had to get to Hong Kong immediately.

One of the ways he tried to dampen his newly acquired fear of flying was to concentrate on work for as long as possible during the flight, and he sat with a Toshiba laptop computer in front of him, checking and cross-checking his accounts. At first he'd had great doubts about trusting the micro-computer with information about the family business, the drugs, the extortion, the money laundering, the dummy corporations and bank accounts that now spanned the world. He dreaded to think what would happen if it ever fell into the wrong hands. But one of his programmers had devised a foolproof security system that would immediately delete all the information it contained if the correct password was not keyed in. And at regular intervals the machine would ask questions that only Ng could know the answers to. A wrong answer, or a delay in keying in the information, would also delete the on-board memory and clear the disk. And one of the control keys had been reprogrammed so that if Ng was ever surprised while using the machine he could press it and render it useless. Ng made regular copies of the files on floppy disks which were stored in safety deposit boxes in banks in Hong Kong and San Francisco. It was an empire that Thomas Ng was proud of, one that he'd created. If it hadn't been for him the Ng fortune would still be nothing more than money from vice, confined to Hong Kong, and with little or no future after 1997. His father had given no thought to the future other than to ensure that his three sons were well educated at overseas universities. Thomas had studied accountancy at Columbia University and had spent a year at Harvard, and he'd been keen to put his knowledge to good use. Over seemingly endless cups of insipid tea he'd managed to persuade his father that the way ahead lay overseas – overseas property, overseas investments, preparing for the day when the Communists took back Hong Kong. As far as cash flow went, Thomas had realized that it was the drugs business that was the crux of the whole operation, master-minding the export of heroin from the Golden Triangle and distributing it in Hong Kong. Without too much effort that distribution could be extended to the West Coast of America, especially in cities like San Francisco which had bent over backwards to welcome Chinese immigrants. The growth of Chinatowns also allowed the triad to expand its prostitution and extortion activities overseas, and they, too, were good revenue generators. In fact, it was the huge amounts of money generated in the United States that had led to the legitimate side of the Ng business empire.

Whereas Hong Kong banks and deposit-taking companies were quite accustomed, and happy, to handle cash, the US institutions were bound by law to report all cash transactions of over $10,000. But $10,000 didn't buy much of the white powder, and a half-decent hooker could pull in that amount in one day.

There were a number of ways the cash could have been laundered, and in the early days Thomas Ng had simply used his triad soldiers to pay the money into various accounts in small amounts, but as the criminal empire grew that became too time-consuming. He'd had a team of twelve working throughout the day but it still wasn't enough.

He put money, again always less than $10,000 at any one time, into tax-free bonds through a number of stockbrokers, and then once he'd amassed a sizeable mountain of cash he had the brokers transfer the balance to their bank account. The bank then cashed the bonds and passed the money through to an account in one of several tax havens the Ng family used. But before long that, too, became time-consuming and involved too many people.

Thomas Ng hit on the idea of setting up legitimate businesses with a high cash flow and pumping the dirty money into them. He started off with video rental shops, big operations with thousands of videos in stock. Nobody ever checked on how many of the videos were actually rented out, and nobody cared, but each year the carefully tended accounts of each shop processed hundreds of thousands of dollars. Then he set up a chain of quality car rental outlets, offering Porsches, Rolls-Royces and Ferraris. Nobody knew how many of the cars were actually being driven around by customers and how many were simply parked in garages. Nobody cared, but the books showed a very healthy profit curve. High class bakeries were next, shops selling overpriced speciality breads and cookies at exorbitant prices.

When Thomas set the businesses up, their main role was to act as a conduit for money pulled in from the illegal sources, but before long they were thriving in their own right. The money, legal and illegal, was funnelled through a daisy chain of companies that spanned the world, from bank accounts in Switzerland to a shell corporation in the Cayman Islands to a discretionary trust in Vanuatu, most of them little more than brass plaques on a wall. Thomas moved into property then, first buying the leases on his shops, but soon moving into hotels and residential blocks. And he'd now got to the stage where the legitimate side of the operation was on a par with the vice activities. In fact, Thomas was now giving serious consideration to pulling out of drugs and prostitution altogether. What he really wanted to do was to move into banking and financial services, maybe insurance, that was where the really big money lay – big and legal. But how to persuade his father that that was the way to go? He was a man who was devoted to tradition, to his ancestors, and to his family. A man who humoured his Number Two son by letting him run his own business in America – except that the Number Two son was now Number One son, as of eighteen hours ago.

Thomas Ng sat in the aeroplane and scanned the columns of figures on the screen in front of him, but his thoughts were miles, and years, away. His thoughts were of his older brother, the man who'd stayed behind in Hong Kong while Thomas made his way in the world with the sanctuary of a United States passport. Simon Ng, who had been unable to get US citizenship, or citizenship anywhere outside Hong Kong, because of a criminal record acquired when he was nineteen years old and Thomas had been fifteen. Simon, who'd stood in the dock in front of a gweilo magistrate and confessed to slashing an 18K Red Pole with a machete and Simon who'd paid the fine, in cash. Except that it hadn't been older brother who'd lost his temper and pulled out the knife, it had been younger brother. And it had been younger brother who'd drawn blood and dropped the weapon and run away, and older brother who'd picked it up and been caught by the police trying to wipe off the fingerprints. Simon Ng who'd taken the blame and Thomas Ng who'd got the passport. It was a debt that Thomas had never been able to repay, and now he would not have the chance. His older brother would be avenged, that much Thomas Ng could promise.

Howells had nearly passed out when he bent down to get into the cab outside the Washington Club. His knees sagged and Amy had moved forward to support him; thank God she'd grabbed his left arm. She moved on to the back seat next to him.

'Are you OK?' she asked. Howells nodded. 'Are you still at the Mandarin Hotel?'

Christ, she had a good memory, even he'd forgotten he'd told her he was staying there.

'No,' he said. 'Look, Amy, I really do need your help. Can we go to your house?'

'No,' she said, shocked. 'Of course not. You are gweilo, you cannot come to my home. What would my neighbours think? Aieee yaaa! You are crazy.'

'I'm hurt, Amy. I've been shot. I can't go back to the hotel and I can't go to hospital.'

She looked confused, and frightened, and before he could stop her she put her hand forward and grabbed his right arm to shake him. The pain was excruciating but before he could scream he passed out, his face white. His head pitched forward and banged into her shoulder. She put her arm around him and cradled him. His right hand lay in her lap and for the first time she saw the trickle of blood crawling over his wrist. She wiped it with her handkerchief.

The driver impatiently asked her where she wanted to go.

Amy sighed and told him her address.

Dugan was having a hell of a time, flat on his back with a Filipina each side, one with a mug of warm tea, the other with a glass of cold water. They were doing terrible things to him below the waist, and the alternation between hot and cold was driving him wild, until the jangling bell of the telephone dived down into his subconscious and dragged him kicking and screaming out of his dream.

He opened his eyes a fraction and squinted at his watch. It was six o'clock in the morning. It had to be a wrong number and he was sure that when he picked up the receiver a voice would go 'Waai?' and then hang up.

Phone etiquette was not something they went a bundle on in Hong Kong, where good manners were not one of life's priorities. He tried burying his head under the pillow but the phone was insistent. He groaned and rolled over on to his stomach and groped for the receiver. It was Bellamy.

'Dugan?'

'Yeah. Do you know what time it is?' he moaned.

'Pull yourself together, you drunken bum. Petal's been hurt.'

'What?' The mention of Petal cleared his head a little. He pushed himself up and sat on the bed, his feet on the wooden floor. His stomach heaved but he managed to stop himself from throwing up.

'She's been beaten up, badly,' said Bellamy. 'She's in Queen Elizabeth's Hospital, room 241.'

'What happened?'

'We're not sure, Pat. It's a complete fucking mystery at the moment. She was found in a room at the Hilton, along with two bodies.'

'Bodies?'

'Two Chinese. They'd been killed by some sort of kung fu expert by the look of it, a real professional job.'

'Some sort of triad thing?'

'Fuck, we just don't know. The room was booked in the name of a gweilo, and he's disappeared. At the moment he's our prime suspect, or another victim. At the moment it looks as if they were trying to inject the gweilo with something; the lab is checking it out, but it sure as hell isn't distilled water. Look, I've got things to do, Pat. I just called to let you know where she was. If I were you I'd get down there straight away.

I'll call you later this morning. See if you can find out what happened to her.'

'Sure, sure. Will do.'

He hung up and sat with his shoulders on his knees, taking deep breaths to quell his queasy stomach. If he had the choice between two sexy young Filipinas or the glass of iced water it would be no contest. His mouth felt like a ferret's den. He opened the bottle of water and poured it on to the orange crystals. They bubbled and fizzed and frothed and he drank it in one go before groping his way to the bathroom, a thousand questions fluttering around his skull like trapped butterflies.

The doorman who was supposed to be standing guard over the entrance to Amy's block was asleep as usual, slumped on a rickety wooden chair, his head back, mouth open showing rotten teeth as he snored. She led Howells down a corridor, cracked tiles of dirty-white with a brightly coloured motif composed of bowls of grapes, towards the stairs. At the bottom of the concrete steps she held him against the wall and whispered urgently: 'There's no lift, Tom, and it's four floors up. Lean on me.'

Howells had kept his eyes shut ever since he'd fallen against her in the cab. He was so white, Amy thought, as white as freshly boiled rice, as if all the blood had oozed out of his head and down his arm. His sleeve was wet with blood and it was staining her own clothes. She hoped to all the gods in heaven that her neighbours were sleeping as deeply as the old doorman.

Howells nodded and grunted and put his good arm, the left one, around her shoulders. Together they scaled the stairs, Howells putting first his right foot on a step, then his left, shuffling up one step at a time. At the top of each flight Amy let him rest, encouraging him to take deep breaths to clear his head, but he seemed to get weaker the higher they climbed.

Eventually they were outside her door, and Amy made him stand by the wall as she went through her bag for her keys. She opened the door and switched on the light before helping him in. The living-room was small and square, a tiny kitchen to the left and a bathroom to the right. It took only a dozen of Howells' small steps to cross the room to the bedroom door, which Amy nudged open. His legs began to buckle and she barely managed to support his weight until they reached the bed. It was a single bed with one pillow and a thin quilt. Amy did not bring customers home – ever. She would go to a hotel, or if they were local she would go to their flat. That was all. Howells was the first man she had ever allowed through the door, except for the plumber who once fixed a leaking tap for her.

Howells pitched forward and lay face down on the bed, head turned towards the wall. She felt his forehead. He was very hot, the flesh damp with perspiration. Her small flat did not have an air-conditioner but there was a floor-mounted fan under the window. She switched it on and directed the cooling breeze at the injured man.

Amy went back into the lounge, dropping her bag on the one small sofa there. She closed and locked her front door and slipped off her shoes. In the kitchen she filled a blue plastic washing-up bowl with warm water and took it along with a small bottle of disinfectant and a roll of paper kitchen towel into the bedroom. She tried to get the cotton jacket off Howells but as soon as she moved his right arm he screamed involuntarily. She took a large pair of kitchen scissors from a drawer under the sink and used it to cut off the jacket, piece by piece, and she placed the bits gingerly on to a newspaper on the floor. The shirt was rust-coloured, but the area around his right shoulder was darker than the rest, and when she touched it her hand came away stained red. She cut the shirt along the back, up through the collar, and then down along the seam to the cuff. She gently pulled it away and gasped as she saw the blood-soaked material wrapped around his shoulder. She removed it and put it on the newspaper. Blood seeped out and was absorbed by the newsprint. She used pieces of the kitchen roll to clean up his torso, starting from the waist and working up. She was amazed to find that all the blood had come from one small hole just below his shoulder, about the size of a one dollar coin.

She dipped a fresh piece of paper into the disinfectant and dabbed at the wound. She could tell that it wouldn't heal on its own, Tom would need a doctor. She eased her hand under the front of his shoulder and felt around, but there was no wound there. Tom had said that he'd been shot so that meant the bullet was still inside. She carried the bloodstained paper and cloth through to the kitchen and put it in a black plastic rubbish bag, carefully tying it at the top. She put it in a bucket in the cupboard below the sink.

Back in the bedroom she removed his shoes and socks, his jeans and his underpants, putting them on a small wicker chair at the bottom of the bed. She checked the pockets, finding the wallet and the two passports. Both were British, but only one contained his picture. Howells, the passport said his name was. Geoffrey Howells. The other belonged to a much softer-looking man, a man who looked as if he sweated a lot. His name was Donaldson. Neither of the men was called Tom.

She went through the pockets of the wallet. A few thousand dollars, and a handful of credit cards. Some of them were in the name of Howells, and some of them were Donaldson's.

She took the cash out of the wallet, and put the passports into the top drawer of her dressing-table. From the bottom drawer she took a white sheet and draped it over the unconscious man, careful to keep it off the shoulder. There was a telephone on the wall, next to the kitchen door. She went to it and dialled a number as she rubbed the notes between her fingers.

At first Dugan thought that maybe the nurse at the reception desk had sent him to the wrong ward. There were two beds in the semi-private room, separated by a green curtain. The bed nearest the door was empty and the girl in the bed by the window looked nothing like Petal; the face round and puffy, the lips cracked and bleeding, the nose flat against the face. As he got closer to the small figure on the bed he could see that her head was circled with a bandage and that there was some sort of padding on her left cheek. Around her neck was a plastic surgical collar. Her eyes were closed. It was Petal, all right.

He sat on the edge of the bed and took her hand in his.

Her eyes fluttered open and between clenched teeth she whispered, 'Hello.'

'Hello yourself,' he said.

A nurse appeared at his shoulder, a tall, thin woman with buck teeth and lank hair. 'Her jaw is badly bruised, so she can't talk much,' the nurse said.

'Not broken?' asked Dugan.

The nurse shook her head. 'No, but she has lost two teeth, her neck is badly sprained and her cheekbone is cracked. She shouldn't be talking at all.' There was a look of disapproval on her face and Dugan could see that she was gearing up to ask him to leave.

He opened his wallet and showed her his warrant card. 'I won't be long,' he said. The nurse nodded curtly and left the room, closing the door behind her. Petal squeezed his hand and Dugan leant over and kissed her on the forehead.

'You don't look too bad,' he said and she smiled with her eyes. 'Does it hurt?'

'They've given me something,' she said, keeping her lips still as she spoke. 'I just feel sleepy.'

'Can you tell me what happened?'

She closed her eyes.

'What were you doing in the Hilton Hotel? Who hit you? Who were the men in the room? What is going on?' The questions tumbled over each other, even though he knew she'd have to take it slowly and that talking was an effort for her. But he had to know. Part of it was the copper in him, but it went deeper than that. He was falling in love with this pretty little Chinese girl and he didn't want to be locked out of her life. He wanted to know everything, to knock down the wall of secrets and silences between them. And this she couldn't shrug off with a joke or a deft change of subject.

'You won't like it,' she said, still with her eyes firmly shut. He moved up the bed to get closer to her, so that he could catch the whispered words.

'Try me,' he said.

'I have to trust you, Pat,' she said. 'They'll be coming to take me away soon, so when I've told you you'll have to go. You have a right to know, but you must keep what I tell you to yourself.' She opened her eyes and studied his face. 'Do you promise?'

Dugan nodded. He would promise her anything.

'I was there to kill him,' she said simply.

The confusion showed on his face and he shook his head wordlessly.

'It's true,' she said. 'I work for the Chinese, for their equivalent of a secret service. The two men with me were part of my team. The man we were to kill was a guest in the hotel, Howells was his name. It went wrong – he was so fast, so vicious. I have never seen such a man.' There was admiration in her voice and Dugan was simultaneously hit with anger and jealousy, that she could admire the qualities of the man who had beaten her so badly.

'Why?' he asked. 'Why were you trying to kill him?'

'It's my job,' she said flatly.

'You kill for money?'

'No, Pat. I kill for my country.'

Dugan was totally lost, unable to comprehend what she was saying. All he could think of saying was: 'Why?'

'I have no choice,' she said, her voice faltering. 'They tell me what to do. They tell me where to live. They control everything I do.'

'Not in Hong Kong,' said Dugan. 'And who are they?'

'Beijing. The Government. Oh, you don't understand.'

She'd got that right at least, thought Dugan. He ran his hands through his hair and wiped his eyes with the backs of his fingers. To Petal he looked like a small child, trying to be brave.

'Why do it?' he asked. 'You can get away from them here. This is Hong Kong. I can help you. You can get asylum or something.'

'It's not as simple as that,' she said. Her voice was getting quieter and Dugan leant forward, putting his hands on either side of the pillow and lowering his head so that he could hear better. 'I told you about what happened during the Cultural Revolution. Remember?'

Dugan nodded. 'They killed your pony.'

'They did more than that, Pat. Much more. They took everything we had, they paraded us through the streets. They made us wear placards and stupid paper hats. Then they took me and my brother away from our parents, for re-education they said. I was sent to a farm in northern China. My brother was sent to a village in Manchuria. I never heard from my father again, he was sent away to a commune in the middle of nowhere to work as a barefoot doctor. He's dead now.'

'And your mother?'

'She died, Pat. In prison. They put her in prison for being a singer. They persecuted her for being talented. They made me work in rice fields until I was fifteen and then they put me in the army. I served for three years on the Sino–Russian border and then I was sent to Beijing for what they called special training. Now I do what I do.'

She slowly closed her eyes, either from exhaustion or from the medication.

'Let me tell the police. We can get you away, get you to Canada or Australia where they can't get you.'

'Defect, you mean?' she whispered. 'I can't. My brother is still alive. They let me see him every Christmas. He's a soldier, now. He's about to get married. So long as he is in China I must do exactly as they say. He is insurance that I do not run away. But if I do well, he gets a good salary, his children will go to the best universities, he will have an easy life. And so will I.'

'All you have to do is kill for them?'

'Yes, that's all I have to do,' she said bitterly.

'Is there nothing I can do?'

'Nothing,' she said. She lifted up her right arm and gripped his shoulder. 'Pat, they'll come for me soon, to take me back. They'll say they're from Bank of China or the New China News Agency but they'll be from Beijing and they'll put me on the first CAAC jet out of Hong Kong.'

'And then?'

'I don't know,' she said. 'I've never failed before. I don't know if they'll punish me or retire me or just rap me on the knuckles and send me on another mission. You can never tell.'

'Do me one thing,' said Dugan. 'If you can, get in touch with me. Let me know that you're OK. Tell me where you are, anywhere in the world. I'll come and see you.'

'I will,' she said. 'I promise. And if I can get my brother out of China, who knows . . .' Her voice tailed off again.

There was something niggling at the back of Dugan's

mind, something worrying him but he couldn't pin it down. It kept drifting just out of range. He released her grip from his shoulder and put her hand under the sheet. 'I don't want to lose you,' he said quietly. 'I've known you for such a short time, but . . .' It was there again, a shadowy thought floating around a corner of his mind. He tried to grasp it but it shied away like a nervous animal.

'I feel the same,' she said, through unmoving lips. 'I never thought I would, but I fell for you, Patrick Dugan, in a big way.'

It hit Dugan then, like a wave crashing over his head, drenching him with the horrible realization that it hadn't been an accident, meeting Petal. He'd been pushing to one side the fact that never before had such a pretty and intelligent girl been so keen to go out with him, to be with him, to sleep with him. He'd been frightened to look a gift horse in the mouth, to wonder why a girl like Petal would go out with a balding policeman with no prospects.

She saw the frown on his face and her eyes narrowed. 'Don't think about it, Pat,' she said.

'Why did you go out with me?' he asked, his heart filled with dread, wanting to know the answer but at the same time frightened that he wouldn't be able to handle the truth.

'Don't think about it,' she repeated. 'Don't look back. I love you now, that's all that matters. Why it happened isn't important.'

'I know, I know,' he said, sitting up straight. He began biting the thumbnail on his right hand, a nervous habit he'd had since he was a kid. 'I have to know why,' he said. 'It's the policeman in me.'

She sighed, deeply and sadly. 'Your brother-in-law. I was supposed to get close to him.'

'To kill him?'

'I was a back-up,' she said. 'Somebody else was to kill him. I don't know who. But if he failed then I was to do it.'

'When?'

'The barbecue would have been soon enough. But I was only the back-up.'

'But you would have done it if they'd told you to.' He couldn't hide the anger in his voice.

'I'm a soldier, Pat. I obey orders.'

She made it sound so matter-of-fact, so cold, that Dugan began to wonder if he was dreaming. He couldn't believe it was possible that a girl he'd grown to love could so easily talk about killing the husband of his sister, someone she'd met and seemed to have befriended.

'And this man Howells?'

'They didn't say why, they never do. But they said it had to be done immediately.' She fell silent.

'Why?' he pounced. 'What do you think?'

'I think that maybe he was the one that was supposed to kill Simon Ng.'

'So why were you ordered to kill him?'

'Perhaps he refused. Perhaps he changed his mind.'

'And why would the Chinese use a gweilo to kill a Hong Kong triad leader? It doesn't make sense.'

'It never does,' she said.

The nurse came back into the room and told Dugan he'd have to go. Behind her were two shortish Chinese men in dark suits and behind them was the uniformed constable who'd been posted outside the door. He hadn't seen the two men before but they had the look of policemen the whole world over, hard eyes that had seen too much of the dark side of human nature, faces that looked as if nothing would surprise them any more.

'Don't make it difficult for me, Pat,' said Petal.

He leant forward and kissed her on the forehead. 'Remember what I said,' he whispered. 'Whenever, wherever.'

'I promise,' she said.

As he left the room the two men walked in and closed the door behind them.

Amy was sitting on a straight-backed wooden chair with her hands in her lap listening to Howells snoring when the doorbell buzzed. The sound, even though expected, made her jump. She tiptoed across the floor and looked through the peep-hole in the door. She recognized the distorted features of the man on the other side of the door and she unlocked it and let him in. He was carrying a brown leather bag with a brass clasp.

'*Lam Siu Fe. Neih ho ma?*'

'I am fine, Dr Wu. And you?'

'Getting by, getting by. Where is the patient?'

Wu was not a man who wasted any time, which was probably best considering he charged by the minute. He was called Dr Wu by everyone who knew him, and by everyone he treated, but he had no medical qualification that would be recognized by any decent hospital. Medical knowledge he had, in abundance, but he had learned his trade within the Walled City, the enclosed slum close to Kai Tak airport where the police were frightened to go. The city had been demolished but it left hundreds of doctors and dentists without a livelihood. At sixty, Dr Wu was too old to study for a recognized qualification, and too old to find any other sort of work, so he continued to practise, but illegally. His patients now were those who didn't want to go to private or government hospitals for whatever reason. He treated hookers, junkies and triads, and the treatment they got was as good as in the best hospitals in Hong Kong. He had performed an abortion on Amy two years ago with the minimum of fuss and pain. Amy had always been grateful for the gentle way he had treated her, even coming back to check up on her twice, drinking tea and eating a sweet cake she had baked.

'He is in the bedroom,' she said, and took him through. She moved the chair closer to the bed so that he could sit while examining Howells. She stood at the door, feeling useless, as Dr Wu pulled back the sheet and looked at the shoulder wound.

He looked back at Amy over the top of his gold-rimmed glasses. '*Lam Siu Fe*, this is a bullet wound. This man has been shot.'

'I know, Dr Wu,' she said. 'He came to me for help. He said not to call the police.'

'A gweilo frightened of the police?' said Dr Wu. 'Very strange. He is a friend of yours?'

'No Dr Wu, he is not. I only met him a short time ago.'

'No matter, no matter. First we shall make him well, then we shall discuss what must be done.' He did as Amy had done earlier and checked the front of the shoulder for an exit wound. 'The bullet is still in the shoulder,' he said, and Amy nodded. Wu peered at the bullet hole and gently brushed it with his fingertips. 'A small calibre, I think, possibly a .22. He is a very lucky young man.'

'He will be all right?'

Dr Wu looked over his glasses, this time pushing them up the bridge of his nose. 'He is lucky that you called me so quickly. He has lost some blood, but not so much that his life is in danger. And while the damage appears bad the bullet did not destroy any major blood vessels. Once the bullet is out and I have tidied up the wound, he will recover. He will be in considerable pain for a while, but I can give him something for that. Now, I have everything I need except for clean towels and hot water. And you can get that for me, and quickly please.' He put his bag on the bedside table and opened it. A gweilo who has been shot and who does not want to go to the police, he mused. Very curious.

Dugan waited until he was in his own office before ringing Jill. His stomach was still queasy from the previous night's aggressive drinking spree and he forced down a couple of aspirins with a cup of machine coffee. So much of what Petal had told him didn't make sense, and the bits that did make sense made his head spin.

That she had tried to kill a gweilo in the Hilton Hotel seemed to be beyond doubt, that she was a Chinese agent he could just about accept. But he could think of no possible reason that the Chinese would have for wanting to kill his brother-in-law, or to get involved in any sort of violent action in Hong Kong during the run up to 1997. The colony's six million population was so jittery about being handed over to Communist China that such direct action could easily spark off a violent reaction. Hong Kong was no stranger to riots in the streets and it would only need one more heavy-handed example of a Beijing clampdown to ignite a powder keg of resentment.

He could also think of no reason why the Chinese would kill an assassin who was supposed to do their dirty work, unless, as Petal had suggested, he had backed out. Maybe he'd been paid in advance and had refused to pay back the money. But killing the guy seemed to be a massive over-reaction.

The method that Petal and her two assistants used, or had tried to use, also didn't make sense. Killings over money were usually violent and bloody, a warning to others. Using an injection sounded more like they wanted it to look like natural causes. He'd meant to ask Petal what it was she had been trying to inject into the gweilo but he'd been so upset it had slipped his mind. He'd have to wait until the lab had finished its investigation. For now he wanted to speak to Jill, to check that her husband was all right and to warn him to stay out of harm's way.

He tapped out the number and it was answered on the third ring by a guttural Chinese voice. In English he asked for Jill and was told she wasn't in. He asked for Simon and got the same answer.

'Do you know where they are?' he asked.

'They are out,' replied the voice. Probably one of the bodyguards; he couldn't place the voice, but he recognized the attitude. That was odd; usually Jill got the phone herself and if she was out one of the maids would answer. Jill didn't like Ng's men in the house.

He switched to Cantonese. 'When will they get back?'

'Who's calling?'

'Dugan. Pat Dugan. Mrs Ng's brother.'

'I'll tell her you called,' the voice growled and hung up.

At least they were OK, thought Dugan. He picked up one of the files on his desk and began to read it. He was beginning to feel better.

Thomas Ng stood in front of the immigration officer, tapping his foot impatiently. The man in the uniform looked as if he'd barely left school. He flicked through the pages of the US passport for no other reason than to see how many countries Ng had visited. There were a lot.

'American, huh?' grunted the youngster, and he looked up at Ng. Ng had seen the look before when presenting his travel documents at Hong Kong immigration. It was the sort of look bestowed on the passenger of a jumbo jet with engine trouble, a passenger with a parachute strapped to his back. No one knew for sure what would happen when the colony and its six million inhabitants were handed back to the Communists, but there was always an unspoken envious resentment directed at those who had a safety route already mapped out by those who feared they would be left behind. The rush to emigrate had been frantic enough before the killings in Tiananmen Square. Now it bordered on hysteria.

'Yeah, American,' said Ng, using his very best San Francisco accent.

The boy stamped the passport as if he was burying a hatchet into Ng's neck.

Ng walked past the desk and when he had collected his single suitcase walked unheeded through customs, turning left towards the greeting area. The electric doors swished open and the babble of three hundred voices washed over him, Cantonese, Filipino, English, Indian, an international potpourri that reflected the racial mix of Hong Kong. He walked slowly down the ramp, looking right and left for a glimpse of a face he recognized.

He heard his name called and saw Lin Wing-wah waving at him. Standing either side of him were Franc Tse and Ricky Lam, looking grim. So they fucking well should be, thought Ng. Their job, their sole *raison d'être*, was to protect Simon and their failure was written all over their faces. He nodded at them, masking his anger, but Lin's was the only hand he shook.

'Elder Brother, you look fit and well,' said Ng. Like all triad members he referred to Lin as Elder Brother, rather than by his rank or his given name.

Lin's grip was strong and dry. '*Ho noy mouh gin*. America has been good to you, Mister Ng.'

'What is this, Elder Brother. You have forgotten my name?'

Lin looked awkward. 'Now you are Lung Tau, the Dragon Head. You are to be accorded the respect that is due.'

Ng looked at him levelly. 'Have you found my brother's body?' he asked.

'No,' said Lin.

'Then my brother is still Lung Tau. Come, tell me everything that has happened.'

Lin walked by Ng's side as they headed towards the waiting Mercedes, talking quietly, while Tse and Franc walked behind, nervously checking faces. They had lost one Dragon Head – they would not be caught wanting again.

Ng didn't recognize the driver but nodded to him as he climbed into the back seat after Lin. Lam moved in after him while Tse took the front passenger seat. As the car pulled away from the pavement Lin told him about the handover of the money, how his brother had disappeared under the water, how they had searched for hours but found nothing.

'We have no idea what the gweilo looks like, or who he is?' Ng asked.

'We do not know his name. And the only person who has seen his face is the headmistress at Sophie's school.'

'So we can get a description from her?'

'We should be able to do better than that,' said Lin. 'Once it became clear that we had lost your brother I arranged for men with video cameras to cover the whole area, filming everyone around Hebe Haven for hours afterwards. We might have him on film.'

'How many cameras?'

'Three,' said Lin. 'And they filmed for about ten hours. So we've got about thirty hours of tape. If he left the area that day we should have his picture.'

'A big if,' said Ng. 'But a good idea.'

Lin smiled broadly, but in the front seat Franc Tse glowered. It had been his idea but he could see that Elder Brother was going to take the credit. Fuck his mother.

'So now you will show the tapes to the headmistress?'

'That is the idea.'

'Good. She a gweipor or Chinese?'

'Gweipor.'

'Best to pick her up and take her to the house. She'll be able to concentrate there. And it'll cause less fuss.'

'It shall be done, Mister Ng. But what if she refuses?'

'I shall come with you and explain to her how important it is she helps us. If that fails I shall offer to buy her school the latest computer. And if she still doesn't help us you can hold her down and I will break every bone in her body until she changes her mind.'

Lin nodded. He could tell from the man's voice that he was serious. He had not gone soft in the United States.

'We'll go to the school first, drop the gweipor off at the house, and then I must go and see my father. He has been told?'

'Yes,' said Lin. 'Master Cheng visited him yesterday.'

'How did he take it?'

'Not well, Mister Ng. Not well at all.'

Howells dragged himself out of a dreamless sleep. He was lying on his front, his head to one side, the pillow beneath his cheek damp with saliva that had dribbled from his mouth. The room swam in and out of focus, but even when his vision had cleared he did not recognize the place. He tried to lift his head but winced and dropped back. The pain passed quickly and he realized he'd been drugged, and so long as he didn't try to move the injured

arm he felt relaxed and slightly light-headed. There was
a bandage around his shoulder, too, but he wasn't in a
hospital bed. From where he was lying he could see a
bookcase filled with toy animals, a fluffy white cat, a
green crocodile with gaping jaws and a long red tongue,
a monkey with cross-eyes, an elephant with floppy tusks,
and on one wall was a framed cinema poster advertising
some sort of Cantonese gangster movie.

He remembered the fight in the hotel, and the shooting,
he remembered the pretty Chinese girl and the hypodermic
and the way she smiled as she moved on top of him,
and he remembered getting into a cab, but that was
all. Amy walked through the door then and it all came
back to him.

'Thank you,' he said.

She smiled, and quickly moved her hand up to hide her
teeth. 'I thought you would never wake up,' she said.

'What time is it?' he asked.

'Midday.'

'Where am I?'

'My home,' she said. 'You said you didn't want to go
to hospital so I brought you here.' She held up a white
carrier bag. 'I bought you a new shirt. Your old one was
ruined,' she said.

'Thank you,' he said again.

'No need,' she said.

'Who put the bandage on? You?'

'No,' she laughed. 'A doctor friend of mine. He took
the bullet out, too.'

'You can keep it as a souvenir,' smiled Howells. 'How
good a friend is the doctor?'

'I don't think he will tell anyone,' she said. 'He is used

255

to dealing with patients who can't go to hospital. Besides, I have only paid him half his fee. I promised him the rest later, once you are on your legs.'

'Feet,' said Howells. 'On my feet.'

'On your feet,' she repeated. 'Thank you for English lesson, Geoff.'

'No need,' he said, before he spotted the trap. 'How did you find out my name?' he said quietly, but smiling. She'd already demonstrated her loyalty; if she was going to betray him she'd had plenty of chance while he was unconscious.

'Your wallet,' she said. 'And the passports. Don't worry, many men not give me real names.'

'I'm sorry, Amy. My name is Geoff Howells.'

She nodded. 'Pleased to meet you. You buy me drink?'

They laughed together, Howells ignoring the pain in his shoulder as it moved.

'Howells,' she repeated. 'Like a wolf.'

'Yeah,' he said. 'Like a wolf. But a different Howells – not the same spelling.'

'Do you want water?'

'I'd rather have coffee.'

'Doctor said only water.'

'What does he know?' said Howells. 'Coffee, black with no sugar. It'll give me strength, I promise.'

'OK,' said Amy, and she went to the kitchen to boil the kettle. The smile faded as she left the bedroom. She liked this man, this Geoff Howells who smiled so easily but whose eyes seemed to belong to a long dead animal, but she could sense that he would bring trouble to her ordered life.

Behind her Howells closed his eyes and let himself be sucked back into the black clouds of sleep.

Rosemary Quinlan was worried, more worried than she had ever been in all her fifty-four years, and if the truth were to be told it was her own future that preyed most on her mind. To be sure, she was frightened for Sophie, but in the scales of her mind it was her own career and pension and reputation, and the loss of it, that were tipping the balance. She sat behind her large oak desk and polished her glasses as Thomas Ng followed her secretary into the office.

'Mr Ng,' she said, and offered her hand limply. Ng shook it and nodded.

He quickly explained what had happened to his brother, and to Sophie. She interrupted once to say that Simon Ng had called her to explain that it was all a misunderstanding, but Ng told her that things had changed. His brother had not told the truth because he hadn't wanted to alarm her. Now they needed her help.

The headmistress looked at him gratefully. It wasn't going to be as bad as she had feared, he wasn't angry, and she thanked God he hadn't arrived with the police. Or worse, a lawyer. God knows what would happen if it became known that she had handed one of her charges over to a man claiming to be a policeman. Why, oh why, hadn't she checked with the police station? Why hadn't she examined his identification? Why hadn't she spoken to Mrs Ng first?

'Miss Quinlan, I need your help.'

'Of course; I will do everything I can to help,' she said, the words coming out in a rush. 'Anything, absolutely anything. Have the police been . . .'

Ng held up his hand to quieten her, shaking his head. 'No, the police have not been notified. And, Miss Quinlan, I must have your assurance that you will not call the police, or tell anyone what has taken place. It is very important that the authorities are not notified, and I am sure that you would prefer that the authorities do not find out what has occurred. Do we understand each other?'

The headmistress took a deep breath and replaced the glasses on her nose. The man's threat was veiled, but it was a threat nevertheless, and her stomach churned. She looked at him steadily and nodded. She picked up the brass paperknife and rubbed the blade slowly back and forth.

'I understand completely, Mr Ng. And I repeat that I will do everything I can to help put this right.'

Ng smiled, and he tried to put some warmth into it. It wasn't the old gweipor's fault and there was no point in being unduly hard on her. And at the moment she was the only one who could identify the gweilo. He explained about the video cameras, and that he wanted her to go back to the Ng compound to watch the videos and identify the man.

'Now?' she said.

'I am afraid so. It is important that we act quickly. If we can identify the man we might be able to get to him before he can hurt Sophie.'

The headmistress hesitated for less than a second. She reached for the intercom and called in her secretary, explained that she had to go out and that she would phone later that afternoon to say when she would be back. She collected her coat from a rack next to the door and went with Ng to the Mercedes outside the school gates, engine purring.

The phone on Dugan's desk rang and he grabbed at it, his heart soaring with the thought that it might be Petal, but even as he put the receiver to his ear he knew it couldn't be her. It was Bellamy.

'What the fuck's going on, Pat?'

'What do you mean?'

'What did she tell you?'

Dugan knew he'd have to be very careful from now on. He was in unchartered waters, not knowing exactly how much Bellamy knew, not even sure how much of what Petal had told him was the truth. He didn't want to lie to Bellamy, but there was a bond between him and Petal that he didn't want to break, a trust he didn't want to betray.

'She said she was kicked by a gweilo in the hotel room, and that he attacked the two men she was with.'

'And?'

'And what?'

Bellamy's voice hardened and Dugan was glad that he was at the other end of a phone and not across the desk in an interrogation room. 'Don't fuck me about, Dugan, what was she doing in the hotel room? And who were the two heavyweights with her? And why were they trying to inject a stimulant into him

259

that was powerful enough to give a carthorse a heart attack?'

'You've got the results from the lab?'

'What do you fucking well think? Look Dugan, you've had a rough ride as it is in the force. But it's nothing compared to the shit that's about to hit the fan over this one.'

'She told me nothing, Jeff. Honest. She's doped up to the eyeballs and in deep shock. She's in no fit state for anything.'

'That's not what the nurse said. She said you spent a good fifteen minutes talking to her.'

'She was rambling,' whined Dugan. 'Delirious. She wasn't making any sense. The best thing would be to leave her for a day or two until she's more coherent.'

'It's too late for that,' said Bellamy and a cold fist grabbed Dugan's heart and squeezed.

'Oh God,' he moaned, 'she's not . . .'

'No, you daft bastard, she's not dead. But she's not in hospital anymore. A group of Xinhua spooks turned up and took her to the airport and a CAAC jet left thirty minutes ahead of schedule with her on board. There's something bloody funny going on, and I've got a feeling you hold the key, Dugan.'

'I'm as confused as you are, Jeff.'

'You better had be, old lad.'

'Is that a threat?'

'Take it any way you want. But I'd forget any ideas you have about a long-term career with Hong Kong's finest.' The line clicked quietly but Dugan could tell that Bellamy had slammed the phone down.

Lin and Tse waited in the car while Ng took Miss Quinlan into the house. The television and video recorder had been moved out of the lounge and placed on the desk in the study. On the couch were a handful of videocassettes and Ng slotted one into the recorder.

'Would you like to sit on the couch, Miss Quinlan, or would you like me to bring in an easy chair?' he asked the headmistress.

'This will be fine, thank you,' said Miss Quinlan.

The maid came into the study and asked for her coat and she handed it over with a murmur of thanks.

'Can I get you a cup of tea?' Ng asked, wanting to put the woman at ease. If she was tense she might miss something.

'Thank you, no.'

She took her glasses off and began polishing them. Cheng walked in and Ng introduced him to the headmistress.

'Mr Cheng will stay here with you,' explained Ng. 'If you recognize anyone on the tapes then please tell him.'

Cheng picked up a wooden chair, removed its red cushion and put it down next to the Chesterfield. He sat down with his hands in his lap, smiling at Miss Quinlan.

'Ready?' asked Ng.

The woman nodded and Ng pressed the 'Play' button. The recorder whirred and after a few seconds a view of the pier jerked across the screen, scanning right and left, homing in on faces, seemingly at random, pulling in and out of focus before moving on. Watching the screen made Ng feel nauseous, like riding a big dipper, and he didn't envy the headmistress the hours ahead.

In Cantonese Ng told Cheng to make sure that she concentrated – any lapse and he was to rewind the tape. And if after viewing all the tapes she recognized no one, then she was to sit through them all again. As he turned to go Ng almost bumped into Jill, who had appeared at the doorway. She looked rough, her face pinched and drawn, dark rings around her eyes, her hair lifeless, her eyes dull.

Her lips drew back in an animal snarl. 'What the fuck is that old bag doing in my house?' she hissed. 'Get her out. I want her out of my house now.'

Ng reached for her, holding her shoulders. 'She's here to help.'

Jill glared at him wildly. She threw up her arms and knocked his hands away, then pushed him savagely in the chest so that he had to take a step backwards.

'Get her out of my house,' she screamed. Ng tried to grab her again but Jill's hands lashed out, fingers curled, and one of them caught Ng on his cheek, tearing the skin. She kicked him on the shins and pushed him again and then he lost his temper and slapped her hard across the face, left and right. She collapsed then, keeling against the door-frame and holding it for support, her body convulsed with sobbing.

'She gave away my daughter,' she gasped.

'I know, I know,' soothed Ng, stepping forward and taking her in his arms. She reached around his waist and held him tightly, like a lover, her wet cheek against his as she cried. He led her out of the room and across the hall to the lounge. Cheng looked across at the headmistress, his face a mask.

'Mrs Ng is under a lot of strain,' he said quietly. 'Please forgive her.'

'I understand,' said Miss Quinlan. 'I wish there was something I could say to her to show her how sorry I am.'

'Identifying the man will be help enough,' said Cheng. He stood up and walked over to the recorder to rewind the tape back to where it had been before Jill's outburst.

'And I will concentrate, I promise,' she said. 'I have no desire to go through the tapes twice.'

Cheng nodded. The gweipor spoke Cantonese – he would not forget.

Ng closed the lounge door and helped Jill on to one of the settees.

'Do you want a drink?' he asked, though he could already smell alcohol on her breath.

'Brandy,' she said.

He splashed some into a balloon glass and handed it to her. She gulped it down and handed it back, empty. Ng didn't refill it. He put the empty glass down on the drinks cabinet and went to sit down next to her.

'What's going to happen?' she asked.

'Miss Quinlan is looking at some videotapes that were recorded soon after Simon disappeared. We hope that the man who took him might be on one of them. She saw the man when he took Sophie. If we can find out what he looked like we should be able to catch him.'

'Unless he's already left Hong Kong.'

'That is a possibility,' admitted Ng. 'We are hoping that isn't the case. But we have already made arrangements to identify all gweilos who fly out as of today. We have a number of our own men in the immigration department, and while we cannot prevent anyone flying out we will at least have a record of anyone who leaves. Once we have a picture it will not be too difficult to track him down. But we are assuming he is still in Hong Kong. For one thing, he still has Sophie, and there is no reason why he would want to hurt her.'

At the mention of her daughter's name, Jill began to cry again, and she pressed the palms of her hands against her temples as if she had a migraine.

'We will get her back, I promise that,' Ng said, but even as he said it he knew it was not a promise that he was in a position to make.

'And what about Simon? What about my husband?'

Ng didn't know how to answer that. He went into the kitchen to get the maid and told her to take Jill to her bedroom, and to give her some hot milk and make sure she took one of her Libriums. She'd be less of a liability sedated than drunk. 'Anyone who calls is to be referred to Master Cheng,' he said to the maid. 'Anyone. Once you have put Mrs Ng to bed I want you to remove the phone from her bedroom so that she is not disturbed. Do you understand?'

The maid nodded, her eyes wide. She understood; Mrs Ng wasn't to speak to anyone outside the house. The maid didn't know what had happened, but she knew it was bad and she knew enough about the Ng family to know that it was best not to ask any questions. Ng watched as she led Jill upstairs, before going out to rejoin Lin and Tse at the car.

'OK,' said Ng, more relaxed now that he was away from Jill. 'Let us go and see my father.'

Golden Dragon Lodge was an anachronism, every bit as out of date as the old triads were in today's hi-tech society, and Thomas Ng hated it. It was two-thirds up the Peak, some distance below the palatial mansion called Sky High which belonged to the chairman of the HongKong and Shanghai Bank, at the end of a small private road. The grounds were surrounded by a stone wall built without mortar, three times the height of a man, and the only way in was through two huge wooden doors, painted scarlet and peppered with black metal studs as if someone had fired them from a giant sawn-off shotgun.

The wall surrounded six or seven acres of prime residential land that Ng knew could be redeveloped into a huge tower block worth millions upon millions of dollars. He'd made enquiries some years ago and found that planning permission would not be a problem and that the site had a plot ratio that would allow them to build more than twenty storeys high. He had broached the subject with his father, but only once. He made it clear in no uncertain terms that Golden Dragon Lodge was not to be touched and the matter was not to be raised again.

The grounds sloped at a twenty-degree angle, with the house somewhere in the middle, with breathtaking views of Victoria Harbour and the skyscrapers of Central and Admiralty, and beyond to Tsim Sha Tsui. In the distance, shrouded in mist, were the eight hills that hemmed in Kowloon.

Two guards opened the huge doors to allow the Mercedes in, and it drove slowly along the gravelled track which twisted along the contours of the hill until it ended in front of a double garage with a circular turning area. Although the house itself was built on foundations which cut into the hill, much of the grounds sloped and the site was criss-crossed with wandering paths and stepped walkways. Getting from the garage to the house involved walking up a dozen stone steps and then along a wooden bridge that curved over a man-made pool in which the humps of a stone dragon, twenty yards long at least, rose and fell in the water, leading to a massive head with gaping jaws and staring eyes that glared over at the Bank of China building. In the waters swam huge goldfish which his father fed every morning. Ng stopped on the bridge and looked at the dragon's head, remembering how he had played around the water with his brothers when they were children. Lin and Tse stopped behind him, fidgeting, not wanting to intrude.

The grounds were tailor-made for games of hide and seek, full of secret places: caves made from concrete with hidden shrines inside, groves of exotic plants that his father had imported from all over Asia, walkways that led to small pagodas with stone seats and tables, there for no other reason than for you to sit and admire the view. There were statues of giant birds and animals, objects that his father had bought on a whim and spent hours deciding where to place in the wonderland of a garden. There was a Japanese rock garden, dotted with tiny stunted trees, a banana plantation, an orange grove, a waterfall that was powered by a giant pump which cascaded over a secret place where Simon, Thomas and Charles used to sit and eat rice cakes and drink lemonade when they wanted to get away from their young sister. At the bottom of the site, screened from the house, was a swimming pool with its own changing-rooms, tiled like a school's pool with the depth marked off at intervals and lanes marked in blue tiles on the bottom, with a high-diving board and a springboard. There was another man-made pool to the left, behind a clump of pine trees in which their father had built a stone junk that could only be reached by walking along a stout plank. They used to play pirates there with wooden cutlasses, fighting for possession of the ship for all they were worth, sometimes allowing Catherine and her dolls to play the part of hostages.

Ng began walking again, over the bridge and up the path that zig-zagged to the front of the building. It was a traditional three-storey Chinese house, but so traditional that it looked like a mockery of what a Chinese house should be. It looked as if it belonged to one of the Cantonese soap operas where warriors with pigtails flew through the air and wizards disappeared in puffs of purple smoke. The roof was pagoda-shaped, with orange tiles that curled up at the edges, and at the four corners were dragon-heads with flaring nostrils and forked tongues. The windows were small and all had shutters. The house had no air-conditioning; it never had and it never would, not so long as his father lived there. The shutters were closed in summer to keep out the searing heat, and closed in winter to keep out the cold, and as a result the house was dark and gloomy all year round, except for a few glorious weeks in spring and autumn.

There was a flagstoned area in front of the main doors to the house where his father waited for him, hands locked behind his back as he looked out across the harbour.

Tse and Lin stopped at the end of the path, leaving Ng to walk alone across the flagstones to his father. Only at the last minute did the old man take his eyes off the ships in the harbour below and smile at his son.

'You look well, Kin-ming.'

'And you, Father.' The old man steadfastly refused to use his sons' English names, and they had given up trying to persuade him otherwise.

The old man had reached the age where the passing of the years seemed to have no effect on him. His hair had all but disappeared and his skin was mottled with dark brown liver spots, but there were few wrinkles on his face. He was a small man, with round shoulders and slightly bowed legs, the sort of man who always received poor service in shops and hotels until people discovered who he was. It was partly the old man's fault; he had never been one to wear his wealth. His clothes were always cheap and off-the-peg, his watch was a simple wind-up steel model that was at least thirty years old, and he preferred sandals to shoes. The only jewellery he wore was a thin gold wedding ring. At a conservative estimate his father was worth US$250 million, but he looked like a hawker, spoke guttural Cantonese with a thick mainland accent and could only manage broken English.

The old man kept his hands clasped behind his back and made no move to touch Thomas. That was his way. He could barely remember the last time they had touched, let alone hugged each other. His father was not a physical man, not a toucher, and he always hid his emotions. Even now he seemed placid and at ease, despite the reason for the visit. He had looked the same way at his wife's funeral some ten years earlier and had looked scornfully at the tears in the eyes of his sons. Thomas had heard him later that night though, alone in his bedroom on the top floor of the house, crying softly and repeating his wife's name over and over again. Thomas had felt more love for him then than he had ever done before, but he stayed where he was at the bedroom door, unable to walk in and hold his father. He knew that if he had, the old man would never have forgiven him, and he had crept silently back down the stairs.

'Walk with me,' his father said, and turned along the path that ran by the side of the house. The path was narrow and it wasn't until it reached a flight of steps set into the hillside and reinforced with slats of wood that they could walk side by side. The steps led to a wide strip of grass surrounded by ornate flower beds. In front of one knelt one of the six old gardeners who toiled to keep the estate in pristine condition. They were paid a pittance, and were now at the age where they worked out of loyalty to the old man and love of the gardens. They lived in a small row of huts behind the pool changing-rooms, along with the three Filipina maids who looked after the house. There were also half a dozen Red Poles assigned to look after the old man. Ng had only seen the two at the gate but he knew that at least two more would be close by, shadowing them as they walked.

They moved in silence through a circle of alternating stone herons and turtles, all looking up at the sky, and clumps of bushes that gave off a heady perfume that made Ng's head swim.

The path led to the two flights of steps, one meandering down to a tarmac tennis court at the far side of the house, the other angling sharply up. The old man gripped the wooden rail of the steps that went up and began to climb, rolling slightly from side to side like a sailor unused to dry land. Ng followed behind, out of breath.

'Not tired, are we, Kin-ming?'

'No Father,' said Ng. The old bastard was doing it deliberately, to show how fit and strong he was.

There were eighty-eight steps, a lucky number – unless you were out of breath and had a rapidly expanding waistline. At the top were two red and gold pagodas, left and right, each containing a large circular stone table surrounded by four stools. Beyond the pagodas were two long single-storey buildings, red-painted wood with tiled roofs, where the old man would play mah jong or cards late into the night with his cronies, or table tennis with Thomas, Simon and Charles when they were young. The buildings were either side of a courtyard the size of a basketball court where the old man practised t'ai chi every morning, and where the boys had learnt kung fu with a succession of teachers. It was a play area, a training area; and a place to come and enjoy the view. It was the highest point of the estate, bar a few yards of sloping hillside which ended at the boundary wall, and it had been Thomas' favourite spot, until their mother had died, and his father had decided to put her grave on the edge of the courtyard, facing the steps. And not just a grave; the edifice he had built was a monument to her, a huge stone dome inscribed with gold Chinese characters standing on a metre-high podium. It dominated the area, and while it could not be seen from the house below, Ng was constantly aware that his mother was buried there. What made it worse was that his father had decided that he also wanted to be buried there, next to her in the tomb. His father had stipulated so in his will, but Thomas knew that once the old man had died the site would be redeveloped as soon as possible if he had his way.

The old man ambled over to the right-hand pagoda and sat on one of the stools, motioning for Thomas to take the seat next to him. They were both facing the harbour and they sat in silence watching the ships, junks and ferries criss-crossing the blue waters and the stream of planes landing and taking off from Kai Tak.

'You are watching the airport,' the old man said eventually, and it was not a question.

'And the ports,' said Thomas. 'We are photographing every gweilo who leaves. Once we know what he looks like we will check all the pictures, and we will know whether or not he has left. If he has left there is nowhere in the world where he can hide.'

The old man nodded. 'But you think he is still here?'

'Yes.'

'Because of Sophie?'

'Whatever has happened to Simon, and we are still not sure exactly what has happened, it is the work of a professional. And professionals do not kill children.'

'In the past, maybe. But the world is different now. They blow up planes, they plant bombs in shops.'

'Terrorists, Father, they are terrorists. What has happened to Simon is different. The man who attacked him was a professional. That is another reason we think he will still be in Hong Kong.'

'The fee?'

Ng nodded. 'He is a gweilo so it cannot be personal. He must have been paid to do the job, and killers are not usually paid in full in advance.'

They lapsed into silence again, and despite the unlined and unworried features of his father's face Ng knew that he was deeply troubled. Once more he wanted to reach out and hold him, to offer comfort, but the fear of rejection preyed on his mind and he held himself back. In the gardens below a peacock screamed, the sudden noise making the old man jump.

'Are we sure the gweipor will be able to identify the gweilo?' he asked.

Ng shrugged and admitted that there was no way they could be certain that the man had been captured on videotape or that Miss Quinlan would be able to spot him. 'But it is our best hope,' he said.

'And when we know what he looks like, how do we find him?'

'We search for him, Father. We search every house, every hotel, every boat, every single place where he could hide. There are only 50,000 or so gweilos in Hong Kong, plus tourists. It will take time, but it will not be impossible.'

'There is one thing you seem to have overlooked, though. It will mean moving into territories controlled by other triads, areas where we are not allowed to operate. You must move carefully, Kin-ming. Large numbers of our men in other triad territories could start a war.'

'Unless we tell them first.'

'That is what I was thinking,' said the old man, smiling for the first time. 'I have arranged for the triad Dragon Heads to come here tonight, to Golden Dragon Lodge. I will have to explain what has happened, and ask for their understanding.'

'And will you get it?'

'We will have to,' said his father. 'Tonight I will ask them to take part in the ceremony of Burning The Yellow Paper. I do not think they will refuse.'

A cat stalked out of the undergrowth behind the pagoda and began rubbing its back against the old man's legs. There were dozens of cats roaming virtually wild on the estate. All were fed each morning, but were not allowed inside the house. Ng's father reached down and picked it up and placed it in his lap where he stroked its head. The cat purred loudly and closed its eyes, pushing up against the hand and arching its back, tail upright.

'Father, do you have any idea why anyone would want to kill Simon? Is the triad in any sort of conflict here in Hong Kong?'

The old man kept his eyes on the cat and said no, each triad was now concentrating on its own dominion, and apart from the occasional power struggle or territorial dispute, most were simply getting on with making as much money as possible before 1997.

'At first it looked like a straightforward kidnapping,' said Ng. 'But the gweilo made no attempt to take the money. I think we must assume that it was Simon he wanted.'

The old man sighed deeply through his nostrils. 'Your brother did not tell me everything he was doing. He still had the impetuosity of youth, and there were some things I had to find out for myself.'

'Such as?'

'Things that were outside the normal business of the triad.'

There were times when the old man could be infuriatingly obtuse, but Ng kept a tight grip on his impatience. He resisted the urge to keep asking questions and waited for his father to tell him in his own time.

The cat had tired of being stroked and it jumped to the ground and disappeared into the bushes.

'It used to be so much simpler,' the old man said. 'So uncomplicated. You took what you could, you defended what you had, and you made money. Now everything is political: the Government, China, you and your businesses overseas. The British should never have given Hong Kong back to China. A benign dictatorship it might have been, but it was a system under which everyone prospered.'

'The British have been good, that is true,' agreed Ng. 'They even introduced us to the opium on which our fortunes are based,' he added with more than a touch of irony.

'And they have given it all away. A curse on them.'

'They had no choice, Father. The lease ran out in 1997.'

The old man snorted. 'Only the lease on the New Territories. The island was theirs for ever. The Chinese could never have taken it back. It belonged to the British legally, by treaty.'

Ng couldn't see where this Form Five history lesson was heading, but he played along with his father anyway. 'Hong Kong island cannot survive without the New Territories, it is too small; all it has are houses for the gweilos and office towers. The British got the best deal they could. Fifty years of stability after 1997.'

'That is what your brother said. And look what happened to him.'

Ng was confused now, he could see no connection between 1997 and his brother. Simon had never been one to get involved in politics, he was a triad leader pure and simple.

'Your brother kept telling me that there was only one way for us to survive after 1997, and that was for us to forge links with Beijing now, to gain favours from the Communists that would be repaid after they took control of Hong Kong.'

'The Communists are not to be trusted,' said Ng flatly. 'They make easy promises but rarely keep them.'

'I told your brother that, but he would not listen. Even after what the madmen did in Tiananmen Square. Even after the children were butchered. He had begun travelling regularly to Beijing, meeting highly placed cadres, and he entertained them when they came to Hong Kong – entertained them like kings; the best food, the best wine, the best of our girls. But that wasn't enough for them.'

'What did they want from him? From the triad?'

'Information. Intelligence. On the police, on the triads, on Special Branch. On the drugs business, the protection rackets, everything. The Chinese want to know how Hong Kong operates, the good points and the bad.'

'And Simon told them?'

'Not everything, of course. He was playing a dangerous game, telling them enough to win their trust but trying not to give away our secrets. He argued that someone would give them the information, so it might as well be us.'

'He had struck a deal with them?'

The old man cleared his throat noisily and spat on to the grass. 'Not a deal. "An understanding" was how he described it. He understood that if he helped them now and co-operated with them after 1997, the triad would be allowed to prosper.'

Ng snorted. 'And he believed them? He is so naïve.'

'He was doing what he thought was best for the triad and for the family.'

'How many times have I told you, the way to go is into legitimate businesses, to turn our backs on the old ways. We should be moving into retailing, to transport, to property. At least property developers do not have each other killed.'

His father turned to look at him with cold brown eyes. 'Now who is being naïve, Kin-ming,' he said softly. Ng flushed, he was not used to being spoken to as if he were a child. He waved his hand in front of his face as if to brush away an annoying insect.

'You know what I mean, Father.'

The old man's face softened into a smile. 'I know what you mean. You must forgive an old man's tongue. Today has not been a good day.' That was the nearest he would come to admitting the pain he was feeling, Ng knew. He reached out and put his hand on top of his father's; the skin felt wrinkled but soft and cold, like a piece of tripe. Ng squeezed his father's fingers gently, then withdrew his hand before the old man had the chance to show disapproval or otherwise at the show of affection.

'You think that Simon might have been killed because he was passing information to the Communists?'

'It is a possibility.'

'But what could he possibly know that would make somebody want to kill him?'

'There is much happening in Hong Kong at the moment that people would not want the Communists to know about. Business deals that are not in the mainland's interest, smuggling of antiquities from China, illegal immigrants crossing the border, agents of foreign governments who are acting against China. There are a host of possibilities.'

'And the most probable?'

'I do not know, Kin-ming. Your brother was being very secretive about the ways in which he was helping the Communists. I do not think we will get anywhere by pondering the reasons why he was killed. Find the killer and we will solve the puzzle.'

It seemed that the old man had already decided that Simon was dead, despite the absence of a corpse. Ng had been constantly reminding himself that there was a chance that his brother had simply been kidnapped, but in his heart of hearts he knew that he was fooling himself. The gweilo already had Sophie, and there were easier ways of kidnapping a man than taking him under water.

'You are right, of course,' said Ng. 'I must go.'

His father nodded. 'You will be here tonight for the ceremony? I suggest nine o'clock.'

'I will be here.'

The old man remained seated while Ng got up and walked back down the steps towards Lin and Tse. He heard a cry somewhere behind him, but it could have been one of the peacocks.

Dugan was swallowing another couple of aspirins when Tomkins appeared at the door.

'How's the brain tumour?' he asked, and Dugan grimaced.

'This one is drink-induced,' he said.

'You have my sympathy then.' He walked over to the desk, buttocks clenched, and looked over Dugan's papers. 'Was it any use to you?'

'What?' said Dugan, his mind a blank.

'Lee Ling-ling's futures dealing. The papers I gave you.'

'Oh shit, I'm sorry. I forgot all about them.' Dugan didn't like the look that flashed across Tomkins' face. It was a look that said 'amateur' and 'incompetent' and 'why the fuck did I bother?' Dugan opened his desk drawer and took out the papers.

'I was just about to go through them,' he said.

'Perhaps you'd better just photocopy them,' said Tomkins. 'Then you can read them at your leisure.'

Dugan was too tired to argue, so he walked with Tomkins along the corridor to the photocopying room. Tomkins stood with his arms folded across his chest like an impatient executioner as Dugan copied each sheet, and then took the original version off him when he'd finished.

'Are you OK?' he asked Dugan. 'You look as if you've got something on your mind.'

'I'm OK,' said Dugan. 'Just a hangover.'

He didn't want to tell Tomkins about Petal, but there was no point in lying because Commercial Crime was a close-knit family and he'd find out before long anyway. 'And I think I need glasses,' he added lamely.

'I've always said you needed your head examined,' agreed Tomkins and tottered stiff-legged down the corridor to his office.

Dugan kept his head down as he walked back to his own desk, deep in thought. He rang Jill again. This time the phone was answered by a Filipina, obviously one of the maids. She said the same as the bodyguard who'd answered earlier, that Jill was not home but was expected back. Dugan asked if Mr Ng was at home.

'Which Mr Ng is it you want, sir?' the maid asked.

'Why?' asked Dugan. 'Is Simon's father there?'

'No, sir, but his brother has returned today from America.'

'Thomas?'

'Yes, sir, Mr Thomas Ng.'

'Can I speak to him?'

'No sir, he is not here right now.'

Despite all his years in Hong Kong, Dugan could still get annoyed by the way Asians could be polite, precise, and at the same time so infuriating that he could quite happily bang their heads against a wall. Secretaries would insist on him spelling his name three times and asking him for a detailed explanation of his enquiry before politely telling him that the person he wanted wasn't in the office. Or they'd tell him four or five times that the person he wanted was not in the office, but not mention the fact that he was on long leave and wouldn't be back for a month. They weren't being deliberately unhelpful, just unimaginative. He thanked the maid and said he'd call back.

The fact that Thomas Ng was back in Hong Kong was a surprise, and a worry. His visits were few and far between, and planned well in advance. According to Jill he was frightened of flying and as a result it was usually Simon who flew over to see his brother. It was too much of a coincidence that he was back in town at the same time that somebody in China was trying to kill Simon.

'Jill, where the fuck are you?' he said under his breath, glaring at the phone. He picked up Tomkins' papers and read them, but his eyes only passed over the typewritten words, they didn't penetrate and he had no idea of the content. He was too busy thinking about Petal and when he'd see her again. Or if he would see her again.

The headmistress saw Howells on the second tape. She leant forward like a retriever that had spotted a downed bird, blinking her eyes. Cheng stood up and walked over to the video recorder.

'You have seen something?' he said.

'Him,' she said, and pointed to a casually dressed gweilo, white cotton trousers, sandals and a red sweatshirt, swinging a shopping bag. He looked directly into the camera for a fraction of a second and then turned sharply to look at a young Chinese girl, then the camera was focused on a family heading towards the pier.

'Let me play it back for you,' said Cheng, and he rewound the tape. 'Watch very carefully.' Miss Quinlan stood up and walked closer to the television screen, and peered at it as Cheng pressed the play button.

'It is him,' she said, after watching the few seconds of film.

'Are you sure?' asked Cheng. 'Let me play it for you one more time. Don't just look at the face, look at the way he moves, the way he holds himself. Look at the whole man, not just the face.'

After the third viewing Miss Quinlan was just as certain, and Cheng allowed a smile to pass over his lined face. The headmistress smiled back, relief flooding over her like a warm tropical rain. At least she'd been able to do something to put right the damage she'd done.

A car pulled up outside, and Cheng and Miss Quinlan heard doors open and close and footsteps crunch along the gravel to the front door. It was Ng. As he walked into the study he could see the triumphant look on Miss Quinlan's face and he raised his eyebrows.

'You have recognized him? Already?'

The headmistress nodded quickly. 'I am sure it's him. Look.'

Cheng had frozen the film at the point just before Howells turned his head. It was a thin face with deep-set eyes, clean-shaven, and with a longish neck. Cheng pressed the advance button and Ng watched the man jerk his head around and walk past the camera. He moved well; there was a fluidity in his walk that suggested he was a man used to sport, or physical exercise. Ng had trained in many dojos in Hong Kong and America, and the gweilo moved like a martial arts expert, relaxed but ready to move fast and hard at the merest hint of aggression or danger.

'We need photographs, close-ups,' Ng said to Cheng.

'I will arrange it. We have a brother who is an editor at one of the local television stations. He will be able to enhance the picture and make prints for us.' Cheng spoke to Ng in rapid Cantonese but he noticed that the gweipor was listening. He turned to her and said: 'Would you do me a great service, Miss Quinlan?' He ejected the cassette and slotted in another. 'Could you watch this third tape, just in case the man returned, or you recognize anyone else?'

What Miss Quinlan really wanted to do was to get back to her school, her office, and her desk, but she knew she could refuse them nothing. She meekly said yes and sat down again and watched the dizzying images on the television set while Cheng ushered Ng across the corridor and into the lounge.

'The gweipor speaks Cantonese,' he explained to Ng.

'A rarity,' said Ng. 'So few of them bother.'

'A teacher. It would be useful in her job. But a rarity nonetheless. I will arrange for the tape to be delivered to our man. What shall we do with the prints?'

'First we must rush copies out to our men at the ports and the airport. We must know whether or not he has left Hong Kong. If he has left, then we must go after him. But for the moment we will assume he is still here. Distribute copies to our men, all of them. Then they are to begin checking all the hotels and guest houses in the territory.'

'There are many.'

'I know there are many, but we must start somewhere. He is a gweilo and he must be staying somewhere. I also want some prints sent up to Golden Dragon Lodge.'

'How many in total?' asked Cheng.

Ng thought for a while. 'One thousand,' he said eventually. 'I think one thousand will be sufficient.'

The normally inscrutable Cheng could not prevent his surprise showing on his face. 'One thousand?' he snorted.

Ng laughed and put his hand on the old man's shoulder. 'My father is going to ask the other triads for their help. And I do not think they will refuse him. It will save time if we have photographs ready to distribute this evening.'

'Asking for favours can be a double-edged sword,' warned Cheng.

'He is aware of that, Master Cheng. But we have to find the gweilo, and to do that we will have to search more than our own territory. Better to ask for their co-operation than to be caught unexpectedly in areas we do not control.'

'Your father knows best,' said Cheng quietly, but it was obvious from his tone that he was far from happy. Ng made a mental note to mention to his father to have a talk with Cheng, to smooth his ruffled feathers. Cheng was too valuable an adviser to upset. He had to be treated with kid gloves, and Ng was out of the habit of being delicate with people's feelings.

'You want to leave the gweipor in there watching the tapes?' he asked Cheng.

'I think it best to keep her here,' he answered. 'I doubt he will be filmed more than once. The shopping bag will have been to confuse any watchers. But better we know where she is. And while she is here she cannot talk to anyone else about what has happened.'

'I doubt that she will tell anyone. She values her job too much,' said Ng.

Cheng inclined his head slightly, a half nod that let

Ng know that he had once again offended the old man. Shit, he thought, and before he could stop himself the thought that Chinese were always so fucking easy to upset flashed through his mind. There were times when he no longer thought of himself as Chinese, he thought like an American, he talked like an American, and in most things he acted like an American, and he now found the Asian sensitivity, 'face' as they called it, infuriating at times. Patience was one of the virtues he had left behind him when he moved to San Francisco.

'But best we do not give her the opportunity,' he added, hoping that would mollify Cheng. He patted the old man on the back and watched as he went back into the study.

He called Lin and Tse in from the outside and went with them back into the lounge. He explained to them about the photographs and told Lin to speak to Cheng about the tape and the prints and to handle it. The phone rang as he was talking and Tse picked it up, listened, and then cursed loudly. He banged down the receiver hard enough to jolt the table and his eyes were glaring as he turned back to face Ng.

'Some prick reporter from the *South China Morning Post* saying he'd heard a rumour that Lung Tau had been killed.'

'Tell him to go fuck his mother.'

Tse grinned. 'Already done,' he said.

Ng pointed his finger at Tse, stabbing the air as he spoke. 'And tell everyone to keep their mouths shut. There's only one way a reporter could have found out what's happening and that's if one of our brothers spoke out of turn. No one, repeat no one, is to discuss this outside the triad. Spread the word round.'

The grin vanished from Tse's face and he nodded and grunted, avoiding Ng's glare.

'About the pictures, Mister Ng,' said Lin.

'What?'

'How do we get so many printed so quickly?'

'Make sure we get several negatives, and then take them to the developing shops that we control. They have machines for such things. Give five hundred to the Red Poles and have them show them at all the hotels and guest houses. Take five hundred to my father's house.' He couldn't bother explaining why and dismissed Lin with a wave of his hand. He hadn't forgotten that it was Lin who was supposed to be guarding his brother when he was taken. Tse stood by the door, shifting his weight from foot to foot, before deciding to go with Lin.

Ng called for the maid and she practically ran out of the kitchen, nervous hands clutching at her white apron.

'Get me a martini,' he said.

'I'm sorry, sir?' she said, looking close to tears.

'A martini. Make me a martini, please. A very dry one.'

Now there were tears in her big, brown eyes. 'I'm sorry, sir,' she said in a small voice. 'I don't know what a martini is.'

'For God's sake, can't anyone do anything here!' Ng yelled. 'I'll make it myself then.'

The girl backed away from him and Ng suddenly felt sorry for her. She was a pretty young thing, nineteen years old or so, long lean legs, firm breasts that moved under her blue uniform as she breathed and skin that matched the colour of the parquet flooring. Her lips were full and red even without lipstick, and her eyelashes had no need of mascara.

'I'm sorry,' he said, smiling. 'I did not mean to shout.'

'I'm sorry, sir, I'm sorry,' she repeated, and continued to back away until she reached the kitchen door, then she whirled around and was gone in a flurry of brown, white and blue.

Filipinas were every bit as sensitive as Chinese, he thought ruefully. He was going to have to get used to operating under Hong Kong rules again.

Sophie sat on the toilet, the lid down, her knees up against her chest, rocking slowly from side to side. Her throat was aching, and she felt hot all over. She'd waited until she was sure that the man had left the junk and then she'd screamed for all she was worth, but no one had come and eventually she'd given up. She'd kicked the door until her feet hurt and she'd tried rattling it to see if she could loosen the lock but it had been no good. She drank a little water from the tap above the tiny triangular washbasin but her throat still hurt. There was no airconditioning and the air in the confined space was hot and stuffy. There was a pink flannel on the side of the washbasin and she ran cold water over it and then used it to wipe her face.

For the hundredth time she looked around for a way out, but with the door firmly locked and no porthole she could see that she was trapped. She was hungry. She'd eaten the cheese sandwich an hour after he'd left. Surely the fact that he'd given her so little food meant he was coming back soon? Or perhaps it meant that he'd left her to starve. She sobbed but no tears came; she was all cried out.

Howells opened his eyes to see the huge tongue of the crocodile, spilling out of its mouth between padded teeth. He knew exactly how the beast felt, his own tongue felt furred and far too big for his own mouth. There was a mug of coffee on a small table by the side of the bed. He raised himself up and reached for it with his left hand, ignoring the burning sensation in his right shoulder. It was cold but he drank it, swilling it around his mouth before swallowing to get rid of the bitter taste that made him think of chewed aspirins. He moved to put the empty mug back but the strength failed him and it clattered down on the table and fell to the floor.

Amy came running into the bedroom. 'What's wrong?' she asked, kneeling by his side.

'Nothing,' he grinned sheepishly. 'I dropped the cup, that's all. I'm sorry.'

'The doctor say you will be weak for some time, Geoff. You must relax until your strength comes back.'

'I'll be OK,' he said. 'I heal fast.'

She ran her hand along the back of his neck, rubbing the small, curly hairs there.

'He said someone shot you before. Many times. He saw the scars. And a knife scar on your leg.'

'Old ones,' Howells laughed. 'I'm faster now.'

'Not so fast,' she said. 'Or you not be lying in my bed.'

'I can't argue with you there, Amy. I think the doctor was right.'

'What do you mean?'

'About water being a good idea. Could you get me a glass?'

'Of course.' She walked behind him, out of vision, and he heard a door open and the sound of running water. She came back and lifted a glass to his lips and held it there until he'd emptied it.

'More?' she asked.

'No thanks, that's fine. What time is it?'

'About seven o'clock.'

'At night?' The curtains were drawn and the window was behind him, so he had no idea if it was day or night.

'Yes,' she said. 'Listen, Geoff. I have to go work.'

'Work?'

'The Washington Club. I have to be there at eight o'clock or big trouble for me.'

'Tell them you're sick.'

'I can't.'

'You can.'

'You don't understand. If I don't go to work they will fine me double my bar fine. And mamasan fine me for every hour I am late. It is a rule.'

'Even if you're sick.'

She nodded. 'Unless I have a letter from the doctor. And anyway, they saw me leave with you last night. They will not believe me. They will think I am with you and not charging you bar fine. It will mean big trouble for me. Better for me to go.'

Howells didn't want her to go – not that he was worried about being left alone; he was worried that while away from him she might have second thoughts, and he was in no fit state to take care of himself, just yet. He healed fast, but not that fast. 'Can't I pay your bar fine?' he asked.

'You do not have much money left, Geoff,' she said quietly.

'You checked,' said Howells, allowing the bitterness into his voice.

She looked crestfallen, and bit her lower lip. 'No,' she said. 'You gave me your wallet to pay bar fine last night. There was not a lot left after I paid. I did not check on you.'

'I'm sorry,' he said. 'I take that back.' The last thing he needed now was to get her angry at him. He reached over and held her hand. 'I really am grateful to you,' he said. 'When I'm well I'll make it up to you, I promise.'

She stood up, and smoothed down her jeans. In casual clothes she looked an unlikely hooker, more like a student or playgroup leader, a cheerful, bouncy girl, in faded denims and white training shoes. She walked behind him again and refilled the glass with water. This time she sat on the bed, and ran her long fingernails down his back, gently scraping the flesh, and being careful to keep away from the injured shoulder.

'I won't be long, Geoff. The doctor will be back early tomorrow. I will be here before then.' Howells sighed, too tired to argue. 'No need to worry,' she said. 'I not tell anyone.'

Grey thought long and hard before ringing the American. Like a grandmaster considering all the options to the nth degree, he replayed countless scenarios in his mind: coming clean and telling his superiors what he'd done; early retirement under a cloud; relying on the notoriously inefficient Chinese to track Howells down and try again; recruiting another freelance and buying his way out. Unpalatable as it was, asking Greg Hamilton for help seemed to be the only way of salvaging the situation, and his career.

Hamilton was his opposite number in the CIA, equivalent rank and status and three times the salary with a former model for a wife and a lawyer for a son. They arranged to meet in Hyde Park on a day when the wind was cold enough to keep the Trafalgar Square pigeons huddled on ledges with their heads tucked under their wings for warmth, but not harsh enough to deter the scavenging ducks on the Serpentine. So much for summer. Grey had a perfectly adequate office halfway up Century House but he rarely used it to meet contacts from outside the Service. He preferred to meet people on their own territory, or on neutral ground, and he made it a rule never to brief his operatives in his office. Both men wore overcoats, Grey in a dark blue Savile Row wool overcoat and Hamilton in standard CIA issue Burberry. Hamilton was six or seven years younger than Grey, but the age difference seemed wider thanks to the American's all-year-round tan and snappy dress sense.

Grey kept his head down as he walked, his chin thrust hard against his chest. He looked to be deep in thought but Hamilton knew that all the thinking had been done long before he'd got to this stage. Grey wanted something, something that couldn't be discussed in his office, something that embarrassed the man. Grey wanted a boon, a favour that at some point Hamilton would be able to call in, so he waited patiently as they walked along the side of the lake. A handful of inquisitive ducks paddled over, backsides twitching furiously, eyes alert for food as they kept pace with the walking men.

'I have a problem,' said Grey eventually, talking to his tie. For a moment Hamilton wondered if the man might be wired, but disregarded the thought. If Grey had wanted to record the conversation he could simply have arranged it to have taken place in his office. He kept silent. The ducks gave up and paddled over to a couple of secretaries sitting on a wooden bench and eating sandwiches.

'Do you remember an operative of ours called Howells?'

'The psychopath?'

Grey sighed into his jacket. 'I do wish people would stop calling him that. The psychologists labelled him a sociopath.'

'With homicidal tendencies.'

Grey looked up and smiled thinly. 'Whatever.'

'Howells is your problem? I thought our headshrinkers had solved that one for you.'

'They did. They did a first-class job, too. He was as docile as a lamb by the time they'd finished with him. We put him out to grass.'

'So what's the problem?'

Grey took a deep breath. 'He's back.'

'Back?'

'In action.'

'That couldn't happen.'

The two men walked in silence again. Hamilton didn't

want to press Grey, it had to come in his own time. Any pressure and he'd be frightened off.

'We brought him back. And now it's gone wrong.'

'He's dead?'

'No, no. Quite the opposite in fact. He's the one doing the killing.'

'But I thought our boys had put a stop to that. They neutered him, no?'

'Yes, they did. But we needed him for a job. In Hong Kong.'

'Jesus Christ. You started him killing again? Howells?' Anger flared in Hamilton's eyes but he dampened it quickly. He'd never seen Grey like this before, and if he played it right it would give him an edge over the Brits that he'd be able to use to full advantage.

'One of our own psychologists was on the team that treated him and he'd left a trapdoor in their programming, a way of reactivating the Howells of old. And we used it. We turned him back into a killer.'

'But to kill who?'

'A triad leader in Hong Kong.'

Hamilton didn't need to mention the fact that the colony was outside Grey's normal jurisdiction. The Brits' activities were supposedly confined to internal security, the British Isles, and, on one occasion, Gibraltar, but that had required special authorization from the PM. In fact, the more Hamilton heard of this story the more he was sure that when Grey said 'we' he actually meant 'I'. Grey had been running some sort of maverick operation which had come unstuck. And whatever it was, it was serious enough for him not to be able to use his own people to put it right. He could feel the excitement mounting inside as he realized that if he played his cards right he was going to end up with his own man inside British Intelligence. A man who owed him.

'Did he do the job?'

'Perfectly. As usual.'

'So what's the problem?'

Grey lifted his chin off his chest and turned to look at the American. They stood stock-still, facing each other like gunfighters about to draw their six-guns.

'Let's sit down,' said Grey, and he waved Hamilton towards an empty bench. A young girl with long blonde hair wearing a scruffy sheepskin jacket and faded jeans ran past with an unkempt spaniel tugging at a lead. Grey wished he had his dogs with him. You could rely on dogs, they wore their loyalty and their trust on their faces. Dogs couldn't disguise their emotions; if they were happy their tails wagged and their eyes sparkled, if they were sad or guilty they wouldn't meet your gaze and they'd slink around. A dog couldn't lie even if it wanted to.

He sat with his legs pressed together, his hands resting in his lap. Hamilton crossed his legs and reached into his inside jacket pocket for a pack of Silk Cut.

'Do you mind?' he asked. Grey lied and said no, he didn't. The American's lighter was gunmetal grey, one of the old-fashioned type where the top of it opened and flicked into life with hard downward jabs of the thumb. A Zippo. Grey looked at it and wondered if the CIA man was bugged – the lighter looked big enough to hold a full stereo system. Not that it mattered. The American was Grey's last hope and to enlist his help meant putting himself completely in his power. Grey had resigned himself to that and to all its implications, and having it on tape wouldn't make a blind bit of difference.

Hamilton drew deeply on his cigarette. Smoke blew across Grey's face and he stifled the urge to cough with a gloved hand. It was time to take control, Hamilton realized. 'Tell me what happened,' he said quietly. Grey told him. Everything. About Donaldson. About the mission. About Howells' phone call from Hong Kong. About the attempt to kill Howells and how it had all gone wrong.

'And now he's going to be after you?' The question was obviously rhetorical but Grey nodded.

'And what is it you want? Protection?'

'More than that. I want him taken care of.' Grey looked down at his gloves. 'You understand why I can't do anything myself?'

'Sure.' Hamilton blew a plume of smoke through clenched teeth and it formed a veil in front of his face. 'I can't get over the way you used Donaldson like that.'

'He was a paedophile. A grade A security risk just waiting to be uncovered by someone. And don't tell me you haven't done the same in the past.'

'I can't argue with that,' said the American. 'It's becoming a shitty business.'

'It's always been a shitty business, as you so eloquently put it.'

'Yeah, but it seems to be getting worse. Dirtier.'

'Don't delude yourself,' said Grey. 'It's always been this way. Have you ever read *The Art of War* by Sun Tzu?'

'I'm waiting for the video to come out,' said Hamilton, but his attempt at humour was lost on Grey.

'He was one of the world's greatest military strategists.

He wrote his book in China in 500 BC, almost two and a half thousand years ago. Just think about that. Two and a half thousand years. His book is a classic on the subject of warfare, and the use of secret agents.' He was warming to the subject now, his gloved hands clenching into fists in his lap. 'He realized that any army's main purpose was to administer the *coup de grâce*, to go in for the kill when the enemy has been weakened. That still applies today. There's nothing more futile than a battle between two equally matched forces. It's only worth fighting if you are sure to win.'

Hamilton let the Brit talk, calm on the outside as he drew on his cigarette, but inside he was in turmoil, as excited as the yapping spaniel.

'He defined secret agents as being in five classes: native, inside, double, expendable and living. And he tells a story of an expendable agent, a condemned man who was taken on to the payroll, disguised as a monk and given a ball of wax containing a secret message to swallow before being sent into an enemy stronghold. He was captured and told them everything as soon as they started to interrogate him. They waited for the wax ball to make its appearance and opened it to find a message from the monk's spy master to one of their generals. It was fake, of course. The completely innocent general and the expendable monk spy were both executed. And that was two and a half thousand years ago.'

Hamilton nodded and dropped the butt of his cigarette on to the path, grinding it with the heel of a highly polished shoe. No laces, Grey noticed.

'Sounds like a smart guy. What was his name?'

'Sun Tzu. I'll send you a copy.'

'I'd appreciate it. How did you come across it?'

'I studied Oriental languages at Oxford. And I was in our Beijing embassy for four years during the Sixties.'

'We were practically neighbours,' said the American.

'I don't follow,' said Grey, annoyed by Hamilton's tendency to go off at a tangent.

'I was in Vietnam.'

'Of course,' said Grey, dryly. He would have been – probably enjoyed it, too.

'You've thought through the ramifications of this?' said Hamilton.

'Of course I have. There is no need to rub my nose in this. I need your help and I'll pay you back. You'll get your pound of flesh, don't worry.'

'Just so we understand each other,' replied Hamilton. 'What you are asking me to do is every bit as wrong as what you did. It's my head on the block, too. Even the CIA doesn't go around killing at random.' Grey chuckled like a contented grandfather and Hamilton laughed along with him. 'Not recently, anyway,' said the American.

They watched the teenager unleash the enthusiastic dog. It barked happily and jumped up, pawing at her crotch and she pushed it away giggling. It was getting over-excited, running backwards and forwards, barking at her, barking at the ducks, the trees, the sky, at life.

'You've told me the what, when, how and who,' said Hamilton, 'but what you haven't told me is why. Why you wanted this triad leader killed and why you didn't do it through the normal channels.'

Grey folded his arms across his chest defensively. 'I had to protect an agent. As Sun Tzu would have said, an agent in place.'

'In Beijing?'

'In Beijing.'

'Highly placed?'

'The top.'

'Jesus H. Christ. You've had a mole in Beijing since the Sixties?' Grey nodded. 'All through the negotiations over Hong Kong's future, the talks between China and Russia, the Sino-Israeli arms deals, Tiananmen Square, you've had your own man there. Jesus H. Christ.'

'I recruited him after I'd been in Beijing for a year. That's why I stayed so long. He was nervous, kept saying he'd deal only with me. It took a lot of time and work to reassure him, before I could leave, but still he'd deal only with me. Not often, but it was always gold. Top grade. And one hundred per cent accurate. But always insisting that I remained his handler.'

'It would have been nice if you'd shared some of the gold with your friends,' said the American.

'You must allow us some secrets,' said Grey. 'But we did share much of it, but in such a way that you'd never know where it had come from.'

I bet, thought Hamilton. I just bet. But he smiled and nodded. 'And where did Howells come in?'

'A month or so ago my man got in touch with me; he was frantic. He was already in a state of near-panic following the 1989 purges. He'd survived by distancing himself from Zhao Ziyang early on, and there was a rumour that he'd had a hand in the death of Hu Yaobang. Heart attack, they said. Anyway, he'd managed to stay in favour with Deng Xiaoping and the hard-liners, but this time he said he was sure that he was about to be exposed and that I had to get him out. He wanted me to arrange for his defection, urgently. I calmed him down and went to see him.'

'You?'

'I told you. He was mine. Throughout all the years I was the only one he'd deal with. I was the channel through which all his information passed – it had to be me. So I went and talked him down, and got to the root of his fear.'

'The triad leader?'

'Yes – Simon Ng. Drugs, prostitution, extortion. A nasty piece of work. Married to an English girl of all things.' It seemed to Hamilton that it was the mixed marriage rather than the threat to his agent that caused Grey the most discomfort. 'It seems that this Simon Ng is, or was, also an agent.'

'For whom?'

'Freelance. He worked for the highest bidder. His criminal connections have gained him access to some very useful information. It was information that we were happy to pay for, and I'm sure that if you check you'll find he was on the CIA's books as well.'

'I'm sure. We generally pay better than the British.'

Grey gave him an exasperated look. He was starting to tire of the American's college-boy humour.

'According to my man, Ng had begun to deal with the Chinese. And in a big way, too. But this time it wasn't money he was after, it was political.'

Hamilton looked curious, and lit another cigarette with the Zippo.

'He wanted a guarantee that his triad organization could continue to operate after 1997, when Hong Kong becomes a Special Administrative Zone, part of China.

298

The Chinese refused, of course. They've been cracking down on organized crime in a big way on the mainland. Ng said he could deliver them a deep penetration mole. He'd say nothing more than that, but my man went hysterical. He was sure he was about to be uncovered.'

'How had this Simon Ng found out about your agent?'

Grey shrugged. 'I don't know. Personally I'm not even sure that his cover was in danger of being blown.'

'There was no reason for Ng to lie. Not if he was planning some long-term relationship with the Chinese as you said.'

'It could have been a first offer, just to make them think he had something big, a way of upping the stakes. He might well have been after money when all was said and done, and the agent could have been one of Taiwan's. The mainland is riddled with Taiwanese agents.'

'But your man didn't think so?'

'He was panicking. I could see only one way of keeping him in place.'

'Howells.'

'Yes. Howells.'

'Why not use one of your own men?'

'You can see why. Ng was an agent we used ourselves from time to time. We could hardly be seen killing one of our own. Even a freelance.'

Grey seemed to have conveniently forgotten that Donaldson had been one of his own, mused the American.

'Plus, it wasn't a normal sort of operation. Ng was very well protected, his place was practically a fortress. We needed someone good, someone very good.'

'And you needed someone expendable?'

Grey's upper lip curved up in a smile, a smile without warmth. 'You do understand then?'

The American blew a stream of smoke from his nostrils and a gust of wind blew it across Grey's face.

'I think so. Once Howells had done the job your agent could expose him as the killer. That would do his credibility no end of good. He'd have Howells killed, Howells who was known to be a headcase and no longer used by the British. I suppose they'd assume he'd gone freelance. Maybe they'd even think he was working for us?'

'Hardly,' said Grey.

'But the end result would be the removal of Simon Ng and a pat on the back for your man.'

'Two birds with one stone,' agreed Grey.

'Except the Chinese missed him.'

'They lost two of their best men, and a woman was injured.'

'They'll try again.'

'Of course they'll try again. But now Howells knows they're after him. And he must know by now that I told them where he was. Nobody else knew.'

Caught between a rock and a hard place, thought Hamilton. Grey could hardly use his own people to hunt down Howells, not without answering a lot of very sticky questions. So the Brit needed help, and Hamilton knew the price of his help.

'I'll handle it,' promised Hamilton. 'It won't be a problem. I'll be in touch.'

The two men stood up, shook hands, and walked off in opposite directions. The deal had been struck without even being discussed. Hamilton was elated and was humming quietly to himself as he waited for a cab. It was a good exchange, he reckoned. The life of the psychopath for a share of the Beijing goldmine.

Thomas Ng arrived at Golden Dragon Lodge an hour before the ceremony was about to start. With him in the back of the car was Cheng Yuk-lin, who as well as being the triad's most trusted Double Flower White Paper Fan was also Heung Chu, the Incense Master, guardian of the ceremonies and initiation rites that bound the organization together.

Ng had decided to take the Daimler and he'd given Hui the chauffeur the night off. Lin Wing-wah was driving, and next to him was Kenny Suen, but they were told to remain in the car. The Burning of the Yellow Paper ceremony was only for the triad leaders. Strictly speaking Ng himself should not have been there as, for this meeting at least, his father had once more assumed the role of Dragon Head.

Lin's small pigtail waved from side to side as the car powered up the drive to the garage and stopped smoothly. Without a word Cheng and Ng got out of the car and walked up to the house in the gathering gloom. Cheng carried a green sports bag which he swung backwards and forwards in time with his steps. Suen remained in the car but Lin went back down to the gate to supervise the guards as they admitted the guests. Tonight would not be a night when any mistakes would be tolerated.

Ng Wai-sun was waiting to greet them at the entrance to the house wearing his red robe of office, a white belt loosely around his waist and a red band with several ungainly knots tied around his head. On one of his feet was a plain, black slipper but the other was adorned with a hand-made fibre sandal. He looked ridiculous, a small, balding man about to go to a fancy dress party, but Ng knew better than to smile.

'My son,' said Ng Wai-sun, stepping forward to shake his son's hand. He turned to face Cheng and put both hands on his shoulders. 'Cheng Yuk-lin. My good friend. I will need your help and support tonight.'

'You have it,' said Cheng. He raised the sports bag. 'I have my things here,' he said. 'The ceremony will be in the usual place?'

'It has been a long time, but yes, the usual place.'

Cheng nodded. 'I shall go upstairs and change.'

He walked into the house, the interior of which was lit by small, oil-burning lamps that gave off an orange glow. The house had electricity, but the old triad leader wanted the lamps on.

'It seems an eternity since you were in this house wearing the triad robes,' said the old man to his son.

'Most of our business these days takes place in board-rooms,' admitted Ng.

'The ceremonies have their place,' said his father. 'They are the glue that binds the triad together. They make us a family. Come into the house.' He took Ng by the arm and led him over the threshold, as if it was the son who was the weaker of the two. 'Who came with you?'

'Lin Wing-wah and Kenny Suen, but they will stay with the car.'

'That is good; there must be as little tension as possible in the house tonight.'

It was a warm evening and the lack of air-conditioning and the orange light gave the house a hellish feel, but Ng could never remember being frightened in it. It was an anachronism now, but it still had the friendliness of home, the reassurance that he knew every nook and cranny, every hiding-place. The house had many dark corners but they had all been explored long ago and held no fears for him.

The main room was very formal, with hard chairs and low tables, ornate gilt screens on the walls and two of his father's priceless jade carvings on rosewood tables either side of an antique wooden fireplace. The room was purely a reception area, the family rooms were all upstairs along with the bedrooms and the bulk of Ng's jade collection. To the right of the reception room were a pair of teak doors, dragons carved on to each, rearing back on their hind legs, flames spewing from their mouths and noses. The old man pushed them, one hand on each, and they grated inwards revealing the room beyond. It was a square room, each wall ten paces long, dominated by a huge circular table that could comfortably seat sixteen but which on some hectic family celebrations had seen more than twenty squabbling over laden plates. Tonight there were places for twelve, sheets of notepaper and gold pens spaced evenly around the circumference. There were no name cards; with a circular table there were no feathers to be ruffled by insensitive seating arrangements.

The shutters had been closed and locked and the only illumination came from four brass oil lamps, one in each corner of the room, casting orange orbs that met in the middle of the table and the centre of the ceiling. On the wall to the left of the twin doors was a framed portrait of the Kwan Kung god. The other paraphernalia of the triad, the banners, the sacred objects, the wall hangings, were missing, and Ng realized it was because this was a meeting of many triads and his father did not want to make it appear that his guests were on enemy territory, even though that was the case. The triads rarely indulged in the gang wars of old, but they were still fierce competitors and they would be insecure enough coming to Golden Dragon Lodge, never mind being surrounded by the artefacts of a rival. In front of the portrait was a rough wooden table, the surface notched and hacked like a butcher's block. On it stood a black ceramic bowl.

The room served two functions. It was used for the most important triad ceremonies and initiations, usually those that involved close family members. Thomas, Simon and Charles had all been initiated there, and it was in the room that Thomas had promoted Cheng Yuk-lin to the rank of Double Flower White Paper Fan. But it was also a family room, where Ng Wai-sun held court over the generations, at Christmas, Chinese New Year, and at birthdays and weddings, enjoying the feeling of heading a dynasty, patting heads and passing out red Lai See packets.

The room was also a record of the Ng family. Around the walls, starting on the left of the doors and running along three and a half of the walls was a series of family photographs that spanned two thirds of the life of Ng Wai-sun and all of Thomas Ng's. The first photograph, and one nearest the door, was of Ng Wai-sun and his bride on their wedding day, he in a grey morning coat, holding a top hat, back stiff and face unsmiling, she a radiant young woman in a European-style white wedding dress looking up at him with unashamed adoration.

There followed almost forty pictures, each taken on the anniversary of their wedding day, children starting as small babies, growing into toddlers and then teenagers, and finally men. Walking along the line of photographs was like watching a flickering black-and-white movie, as Ng Wai-sun changed from a whipcord-thin youngster with black straight hair to a balding old man and his wife from a radiant bride to a stooping old lady with clawed hands and parchment skin, the two of them surrounded by three middle-aged men and a woman, and a clutch of small children, including one with blonde hair and pale white skin.

The changes between consecutive pictures were small, other than when babies appeared, but in their totality they made Ng all too well aware of his own mortality. When he was younger it was different; the series of pictures gave him a sense of history, of tradition, and it gave him a feeling of security seeing his parents stretching back across the years. But the fact that his mother had disappeared and no longer took her yearly place at her husband's side made Ng realize that no one lived for ever. And in next year's picture there would be no Simon, standing there with his hands on Thomas' shoulder, and maybe no Sophie either.

He looked at the last picture in the series, taken some three months earlier, the three brothers and sister and a scattering of children, most of them belonging to Catherine, the youngest of Ng Wai-sun's children but by far the most productive. Still in her twenties, she and her banker husband had produced five children, one boy and four girls. Charles and his American-born Chinese wife Sandra had two boys, and Simon and Jill only had

Sophie. Thomas caught his father looking at him as he studied the picture.

'No Father, I have no plans to marry,' he said quietly, without turning his head. Ng had plenty of girlfriends, and no shortage of female company when he was between regular companions, but he had never wanted to marry, and he had no plans to get hitched just to satisfy an old man, especially one who was already a grandfather eight times over. Or seven, if they lost Sophie. Ng Wai-sun tut-tutted, but his eyes were smiling.

'I have had a robe prepared for you in your old room,' he said.

Ng nodded. The robes were just as much an anachronism as the house, but he knew that the other triad leaders, the old ones at least, put as much store by the ceremonies as his father did. The request he was about to make tonight was unusual, unusual enough to warrant them appearing in what, when it came down to it, was little more than fancy dress. Ng went upstairs to change, leaving his father looking wistfully at the last photograph.

The bedroom door was on the first floor, and it was exactly the same as when he'd last seen it some three months earlier, save for the black robe lying on the bed. Ng knew that the room was dusted every day and the bedding changed every week, even though it had been at least ten years since he had actually slept there. It was his room and it would be until he died. There were rooms on the same floor for Simon, Charles and Catherine, though it had also been more than a decade since they had been slept in.

Ng took off his suit and shirt and pulled the robe over his head, draped the scarlet scarf around his neck, the ends reaching past his knees, tied and untied the white belt until it looked right and then he put on the headband with its single knot. At the end of the bed he found a brown shoe and a rope slipper and he put them on over his socks. He checked himself in the large free-standing mirror by the window and couldn't help grinning at his reflection. He looked absurd, and he wondered what his banker friends in San Francisco would say if they saw him in the outlandish outfit, the ceremonial dress of a Pak Tsz official, the adviser.

It was one o'clock in the morning and every girl in the Limelight Club was a virgin. That's what they all told Jack Edmunds, anyway, as he sat on his stool nursing a tumbler of Jack Daniels and watching the dancers sway in time to the music. The Limelight was on the ground floor of Pat Pong One so all the girls were dressed, albeit scantily in bikinis or cutaway swimsuits. You had to go up to one of the first floor bars to watch nude dancers or sex shows but after four days in Bangkok he'd just about seen it all: girls putting safety-pins through their breasts, burning themselves with candles, using their vaginal muscles to shoot darts through blowpipes and to write with large felt-tipped pens. He'd seen full sex and lesbian sex and sex with a German Shepherd dog. Now he was jaded and preferred to sit and drink in the Limelight, where at least there was something left to the imagination. The girls seemed prettier too, though after half a dozen beakers of the amber fluid they all looked good. The bar was a large oval surrounding a raised dance floor on which there were ten or so Thai girls dancing; few moved enthusiastically, but they were all smiling. They were just tired; most of them had been on their feet for the best part of four hours. They danced in twenty-minute shifts, once an hour. The rest of the time they sat around the bar or at the tables around the edge of the room, groping customers' thighs and hustling drinks, much as the girls sitting either side of Edmunds were doing. Small hands, moving inquisitively around his groin. Neither looked much more than seventeen years old but Edmunds knew just how difficult it was to pinpoint accurately the age of an Asian girl. Sure, you could tell the ones that were obviously underage, flat-chested and no pubic hair, and you could spot the old hags, the over-the-hill hookers who still toured the bars looking for a tourist so drunk that he couldn't see the wrinkles and the scars. But in between the two extremes there was no way of telling – they all had the same jet-black hair, smooth brown skin and shining brown eyes.

The one on his right was called Del; her long hair was twisted into a single braid which had been wound around her head like a crown, and she wore a bright green swimsuit. She had two cigarette burns on her left thigh, healing nicely. Edmunds had asked her what had happened but she'd just smiled and shaken her head. There were three cuts on one of her wrists, an inch long and half an inch apart. Not deep enough to be suicide attempts, and obviously done at different times. One was a white scar, the middle was still red and the skin raised, and the third was covered with a thin scab.

The other girl had short, pageboy-style hair and a

rash of acne badly disguised with make-up. She wore
a scarlet bikini that barely restrained her lemon-shaped
breasts between which nestled a small chunk of jade on
a thin gold chain. Her name was Need. Edmunds knew
enough Thai to know that Need was a common name
for girls or boys – it meant small. For the tenth time
that night she looked at Edmunds, stroked his thigh and
said: 'You make love now?' She had the sort of teeth that
would drive a dentist into bankruptcy. Not a single filling.
Edmunds' mouth contained five thousand dollars' worth
of bridgework. The first time she'd asked he'd shaken his
head and said 'not tonight', the fifth time he'd said 'no
money' but now he'd reached the stage where he said
'maybe later'.

'I want now,' she pouted. She pointed to Del. 'Two
girls, good price.' Del nodded enthusiastically and her
hand joined Need's, gently rubbing up and down his
prick. Edmunds took a deep breath and drained his
glass. He waved at a waitress behind the bar and
gestured at his glass and those in front of the two girls.
They were drinking lemonade at twice the price of his
Jack Daniels. That's how the girls earned their money,
commission on the non-alcoholic drinks plus whatever
they could screw out of the customers as tips or payment
for sex.

'I want make love,' insisted Need, bouncing up and
down on her stool. She did have a cute arse, Edmunds
decided. Beautiful firm breasts. And the acne wasn't
that bad.

'I love you,' said Need.

'No shit?' he said.

'No shit,' chorused the girls and they giggled. He was

almost three times their age, he realized, but that didn't make him feel any less aroused.

'Now? I very tired,' said Del, resting her forehead on his shoulder and playing with his zip.

'Soon,' said Edmunds, his mouth dry and his mind made up. He reached for his drink and closed his eyes as he swallowed. He wanted the two girls but he hadn't drunk enough yet to dampen the feelings of revulsion in the pit of his stomach. It happened every time he came into one of the Pat Pong bars. He'd sit by himself, intending only to watch and drink, feeling nothing but scorn and contempt for the middle-aged men who sat in the gloom and fondled girls young enough to be their daughters. He'd look at the girls and chat to them, buy a few drinks and watch the shows, knowing that he wouldn't be tempted, feeling anger at the obscenity of a German businessman with an expense account gut and three chins bouncing a sixteen-year-old Thai girl up and down on his knees and slipping his wrinkled hand down the back of her swimsuit. He'd talk to the girls as best he could, ask them where they were from, how long they'd been in Bangkok, and he'd buy them drinks. It happened every time. The alcohol relaxed him, their hands began to wander, and before long the thought of being in bed with a girl young enough to be his grand-daughter didn't seem too abhorrent.

'How much?' he asked Need and she beamed, knowing that he was hooked. 'How much for you both?'

She told him. About the same as a decent bottle of whisky would cost back in the States. Economic rape, he thought. Del's hand grasped his prick through the material of his trousers.

'Now?' she said, looking into his eyes.

'Not here,' said Edmunds. He'd taken one of the girls into a back room a couple of days ago. 'Short time,' she'd called it, down a corridor and into a small square room big enough only for a double bed and a sink. The bed was covered with a sheet stained with God knows what. No pillows, no blankets. A room designed for one thing and illuminated by a single red light-bulb hanging from the ceiling. The girl had looked young, very young; she said her name was Orr but he'd called her Number 11 all evening. That was the number on the badge pinned to her black and white swimsuit and it was about how old she'd looked. She'd taken the money off him and squatted over the sink and cleaned herself, and then insisted that he did the same. She helped him and as he grew hard she'd opened a foil packet and expertly slipped on a condom and pulled him down on the bed, on top of her and into her. Her legs came up either side of his arse and her heels had hooked behind his thighs as she thrust herself against him, hard and fast and tight. Her face was turned to one side, blank and expressionless and he remembered how cheated he'd felt. He started moving, harder and faster, trying to get some reaction from her, some sign that she was enjoying it, but she just gritted her teeth. 'Look at me,' he'd said but she'd just continued to grind into him, wanting it to be over. Wanting to get back to the bar, to the next customer. He'd begun pounding into her then, wanting to hurt, to make her feel pain if nothing else, wanting her to acknowledge that he was there, inside her. She'd winced and closed her eyes but said nothing, just kept moving her hips until he came. Edmunds had felt disgusted with himself then, ashamed at the violent feelings he'd had towards the girl, the way sex had got mixed up with pain in his head. He'd washed himself in silence and given her another note as he left the room.

'No short time,' he said to Need. 'You come back to hotel with me.' The girls smiled. Back in his room he had a king-size bed and clean sheets and more booze. And he'd have time, time at least to feel he was being treated like a human being. Getting the girls in wouldn't be a problem, the hotels in Bangkok knew which side their bed was buttered. Sure, the girls had to be checked in at reception and have their identity cards recorded, but that wasn't to hassle the guests, it was to make sure that they weren't ripped off. And there'd be no snide, knowing smiles from the staff, just polite acceptance of the way the system worked.

'We go now?' asked Del. 'Me horny.'

Jesus Christ, thought Edmunds, where the fuck do they learn their English? But he knew the answer to that – in bed. On their backs. Their hands were fondling him, probing, rubbing, insisting. Two more hands began massaging his neck, slowly and sensually. He dropped his head forward and sighed.

'Mmm,' he said. 'That's good. So good.'

He closed his eyes and concentrated on the cool, strong hands on his neck. The girl was good, very good. She knew what she was doing, all right, he could feel the tension being pulled from his muscles. God, what could she do to him in bed? He'd be putty in her hands, she'd be able to do anything to him. With him.

The hands slid around his neck, stroking the sides until they found the carotid artery and then they tightened, cutting off the blood supply to his head. His eyes bulged and he gasped for breath and he tried to unclasp the fingers around his throat before he passed out. Then they were gone and he fell forward on to the bar, knocking over his glass which spun on to the floor and shattered. As he gasped for breath a decidedly masculine voice behind him said: 'You want massage, you randy bastard?'

Edmunds didn't have to look round, he could think of only one arsehole who'd behave like that.

'You're a cunt, Feinberg. A grade-A motherfucking cunt.'

'I love it when you talk dirty, Edmunds. It gives me a hard-on.'

Del slid off her stool to make way for the second man and he patted her backside as she moved behind him and then stood between them, her hand finding its way back into Edmunds' lap.

'I suppose you want a fucking drink?'

'Jack, I thought you'd never ask,' said Feinberg, in a drawling imitation of W. C. Fields. 'And what about one for your wife here?'

Feinberg had a puerile sense of humour, but the business with the neck hadn't been funny, thought Edmunds. Feinberg could kill with his concert pianist's hands. And had done. Edmunds massaged his neck muscles.

'What do you want?'

'Rum and Coke, thanks.'

Edmunds ordered a round of drinks, and as he waited he remembered the last time he'd seen Rick Feinberg. It was at CIA headquarters in Virginia, eighteen months ago, at a debriefing following a very messy job in South America, and it had been Feinberg's fault that it had been so messy. A bomb that was to have taken out a general with a nasty line in torture also blew three passing schoolchildren into a million bloody fragments. Strictly speaking the two Americans weren't to blame; the bomb had been set off with a simple electric timer and they were back in their hotel when it went off, but Feinberg had decided how much explosive to use.

'I love a big bang,' he'd said as he slipped the carrier bag containing the bomb under the rear passenger seat of the general's Mercedes. Not that Edmunds had told the investigators that when they got back to Langley. Edmunds was a team player – always had been, ever since he played college ball. Always would be.

The drinks arrived and Feinberg leant forward, sipping from the glass as it stood on the bar, like a lion drinking from a water-hole. Del began to rub Feinberg's thigh and she whispered in his ear.

What the hell was Feinberg doing in Bangkok? It was too much of a coincidence to be drinking in the same bar; Feinberg must have been looking for him, even though he still had more than a week's leave to go. He studied him as he drank. He was tall and stringy enough to be a marathon runner but not enough for basketball, with sharp features, a slightly pointed chin and an angular nose between hooded eyes that forever looked as if they hadn't had enough sleep. Since he'd last seen him Feinberg had grown a Mexican-style moustache that drooped down either side of his thin, bloodless lips. It was wilting in the heat. Feinberg was wearing a white short-sleeved Lacoste shirt with green stripes, and jeans held up with a green and red Gucci belt. Edmunds looked past the younger man to a mirrored wall and saw himself. Christ, he looked old. His paunch was spilling over his trousers and though he still had a full head of hair it was all grey. It had been that way for a good ten years, but whereas before he could tell himself it was prematurely grey, now it was just grey. His face, like his body, was fleshier than Feinberg's, the features all smoothed out by subcutaneous fat, though he had the same world-weary eyes. Edmunds' was a temporary condition, though, the result of too much booze and too many late nights. A few days back in the States and he'd soon be bright-eyed and bushy-tailed.

He sucked in his gut, which seemed to take a good five years off the age of his reflection but it was too much of an effort to hold it in and he exhaled with a mournful sigh. He realized that Feinberg was watching him in the mirror with a knowing grin on his face.

'You're putting on a bit, Jack,' he said. 'Stopped the old morning exercises, have we? Not keeping fit any more?'

'You wanna step outside and find out just how fit I am?' snapped Edmunds. 'I can still take you out, and I don't need a kilo of high explosive to do it.'

Feinberg raised his hands in a gesture of surrender. 'Whoa, touchy, touchy,' he said.

'What do you want, Rick?'

'Enough money to be comfortable, a loving wife, peace on earth. Just the normal sort of shit we all want,' said Feinberg. 'And a couple of hours with this pretty young thing.'

Edmunds felt a flare of irrational jealousy burst somewhere inside him. Del seemed to have forgotten he existed, though Need's fingers were as insistent as ever.

'What are you doing here, Rick?' Edmunds pressed.

'Just passing through,' sighed Feinberg, his eyes on Del.

'From where?' Need's nails bit into his thigh.

'Langley.'

'To where?'

'Hong Kong.'

'And?'

'What do you mean?' he asked. Need sighed deeply and Edmunds felt the warm breath from her nostrils on his neck.

'I get the feeling there's something you're not telling me.'

Feinberg sniggered. 'Oh yeah, I forgot to tell you. You're coming with me.'

'I'm on leave, Rick. Rest and recreation.'

'More recreation than rest, I'd think.'

'I can't argue with that. What's the game plan?' Need slid off her stool, resigned to the fact that she'd lost Edmunds' attention. And his money. But it was still relatively early and there were plenty of customers in the bar. Del saw her go but decided to continue trying her luck with Feinberg.

'A small problem that our masters want taken care of.'

'Anyone we know?'

Feinberg turned to look at him at last. 'Geoff Howells – a Brit. You know him?'

'Doesn't ring a bell. What did he do?'

'Hey man, ours not to reason why, et cetera et cetera. Since when have we been interested in the whys and wherefores?'

'Since I'm getting pulled off my well-earned leave,' Edmunds smiled.

'He killed one of our men in Hong Kong.'

'Who?'

'A chink. I'd never heard of him, a guy called Ng. A freelance.'

'So why would a Brit kill one of our men?'

'There you go, asking why again.' He began toying with Del's young breasts, fingering the nipples to make them hard. 'We make love?' she asked him. Feinberg grinned wolfishly and pinched her until she winced. 'Never in a million years,' he said. He continued to pinch until tears welled up in the girl's eyes but she wouldn't cry out, didn't try to remove his hand.

'Leave her be,' said Edmunds.

'You're getting soft in your old age,' said Feinberg, but he stopped hurting the girl. She rushed off to the toilet and Edmunds knew she would cry there, away from them. His heart went out to her. Maybe Feinberg was right, maybe he was getting soft.

'Seems a bit strange, that's all.'

'Apparently he's gone loopy. History of psychological problems. You sure you've never heard of him? I thought you knew everybody in this business, the length of time you've been around.'

'I'm getting a bit fed up with all the cracks about my age,' said Edmunds.

'Hey, no offence meant.'

'I bet. So, what do we know about this Howells?'

'Full biog, pics, the works. No details of location but Hong Kong is locked up tighter than a frog's arse. He's not going anywhere.'

'Sounds cool.'

'Cool? Hey, nobody says cool anymore. Cool went out with flared trousers.'

Feinberg saw the anger in Edmunds' eyes and immediately held up his hands. 'For fuck's sake, man, don't be so goddamned sensitive.'

Edmunds laughed, finished his drink and got unsteadily to his feet. 'I'm going back to the hotel. What time's our flight?'

'Just before noon. I'll call you. I'm in the Sheraton as well.'

'OK. You staying here?'

'Sure. I'm going to have me that little girl there.' He gestured at one of the dancers, a tall girl in knee-high boots with long hair tied back in a ponytail. 'I'm going to make her do terrible things to me with that hair. I'm going to make her wrap it . . .' Edmunds didn't hear the rest, it was lost in the pounding music as he headed for the door. On the way he passed the toilets and saw Del leaning against the wall. Her eyes were red but she beamed when she saw Edmunds. 'We make love?' she asked hopefully. 'I love you.'

Edmunds felt a wave of sadness wash over him, sadness mixed with guilt in about equal parts. He pulled out his wallet and thrust a couple of brown notes at her. 'I'm sorry,' he said, and walked out into the hot night air, thick with the smell of spices and motor-cycle fumes.

The twelve triad leaders sitting around the circular table controlled the lion's share of drugs, vice and illegal gambling in Hong Kong, as well as a good chunk of the colony's legal business, but to Thomas Ng they looked like a group of pensioners being told about a forthcoming outing. They sat quietly, occasionally nodding or grunting, as Ng Wai-sun stood in front of the framed portrait of the fierce Kwan Kung god and put before them the events of the previous forty-eight hours. He spoke quietly, his voice steady as he looked each of the men in the eyes in turn.

They had all arrived in separate cars with their own bodyguards, but all had walked alone to the entrance of the house to be greeted by Ng Wai-sun. Some had worn expensive suits, some came in designer casual clothes and one, a man who appeared to be even older than Ng's own father, had turned up in a traditional black silk Chinese suit with ivory toggles, and each had carried a small bag containing his robes of office. One by one they had gone upstairs to change and then taken their place at the table. Ng stood to the left side of the double doors, his arms folded across his chest, and Cheng stood at the right.

The old man told the triad leaders about the kidnapping of his grand-daughter by the gweilo, the abduction and assumed murder of his son, and how they now had a photograph of the man they believed was responsible. Then he paused and slowly looked from man to man before speaking again.

'In days gone by triad often fought against triad in the battle for territory, and for profits, but we have put those days behind us. We have only a few years ahead of us before the Communists take over Hong Kong, and we know what that will mean.' The elderly men nodded in unison. One cleared his throat noisily and looked around for somewhere to spit but decided against it. 'In recent years we have learned the benefits of cooperation rather than confrontation, each maximizing the profits from his own territory and not wasting resources in conflict; the Sun Yee On in Tsim Sha Tsui, the 14K in Mong Kok, the Tan Yee in Wan Chai and Causeway Bay.' He nodded to the respective leaders as he mentioned their triads.

'Today I have to ask you for your consideration during this difficult time for me and for my family. We wish to conduct a search for this gweilo, and it is certain that the search will involve my men going into areas over which you have authority. I do not want our actions to be misunderstood, nor do I wish to cause you any offence; therefore I stand before you and ask your permission.'

He clasped his hands over his stomach and waited.

The Dragon Head of the Luen Ying Sh'e was the first to speak after slowly getting to his feet.

'Ng Wai-sun, I offer you my condolences for the tragedy that has befallen your noble family, a tragedy that is all the more insidious coming as it did at the hands of a barbarian. I offer your men safe passage through Luen Ying Sh'e territory until you have found the man you speak of.'

He was followed by the man who had wanted to spit at the thought of the Communists; he too stood up and pledged his support. But Ng knew that the two were small fry, eager to please and to grant a boon to his father because they knew at some time the favour would be returned. Between them they probably controlled less than ten square miles, and most of that in the New Territories. Despite that Ng Wai-sun bowed to each of them and thanked them profusely. There was silence then, and the remaining triad leaders looked at each other, faces carved from stone, wondering who would be next to speak.

It was the Dragon Head of the Tan Yee who rose first, a bull of a man standing a head and a half taller than Ng Wai-sun and double his width. In his youth he had been one of the most feared of Tan Yee's fighters, and had served a sentence for manslaughter in Stanley for hacking off the head of a Red Pole from a rival triad. It should have been a life sentence for murder but the triad had flown in a top London QC and killed two witnesses, one of them a police sergeant. Mok Shih-chieh had mellowed a bit since then, but not much. Despite his seventy years he still had a full head of hair, though every strand was now pure white, and though most of his muscle had long since run to fat, he was still an impressive sight in his red robes. Five years earlier he'd had half a lung removed and his breath rasped in his throat in time with the movement of his huge chest.

'I echo the sentiments of those who have already spoken, Ng Wai-sun. And I agree with what you have said about our organizations, our families, using our resources wisely. No one here can deny that since we devoted ourselves to business and stopped petty squabbling we have all prospered.'

The men at the table grunted and nodded in agreement.

'Despite one or two minor territorial disputes,' – he gave a knowing look at one of the younger Dragon Heads, who bowed his head under the scrutiny, 'we have concentrated on cooperation rather than confrontation.' He paused and took deep wheezing breaths, leaning forward and placing his hands on the table for support. 'I think the time has come for us to show that this co-operation can be extended even further. You are right, Ng Wai-sun, when you say that we have little time left in Hong Kong. Life will be different here in Hong Kong when the Communists take over. It will not be impossible, but it will be difficult. I myself am glad that I will not be here to see it.'

The men shook their heads at that, but it was generally known that the cancer had reappeared and that Mok Shih-chieh was refusing to have another operation.

'You have shown us the advantages of moving into businesses overseas, Ng Wai-sun, though we have not all the benefit of such an able son as you have.' He nodded at Thomas Ng who smiled, pleased and surprised at the recognition. 'As we move out into the world, away from Hong Kong and the Communists, I think we should do so together, as business associates, rather than as competitors. We are, after all, Chinese, despite our differences. It should be us against the world, taking strength from each other. This is something that I am sure will happen the closer we get to 1997. But I wish tonight to take a step in that direction, to forge the bonds of co-operation. What I am offering, Ng Wai-sun, is not just unhindered passage through Tan Yee territory. I am offering help. The Tan Yee triad will help search for this barbarian, and if we find him we will deliver him to you. I make this pledge in the name of friendship, and trust that it will be accepted as such.' He grunted and sat down heavily, his chair scraping along the floor.

Ng's father bowed to the Tan Yee Dragon Head. 'I am grateful for your assistance, Mok Shih-chieh.' He nodded at Cheng who quietly opened the door and slipped out. 'I accept your offer, and the spirit of friendship in which it is made. And I look forward to closer co-operation between our organizations.'

In quick succession the remainder of the Dragon Heads stood and pledged their help to Ng Wai-sun, and Cheng came back into the room as the last one was sitting down. Cheng had twelve bundles of colour photographs and he walked slowly around the table, placing a bundle in front of each of the Dragon Heads.

'These are the best photographs we have of the gweilo,' Ng's father explained. 'We know what he looks like and we know that he has not left Hong Kong, or at least he has not to the best of our knowledge left through the port or the Kai Tak. But we do not know his name, nor do we have any idea where he is. Master Cheng will be co-ordinating the search, and he can be reached here, any time, night or day.'

Cheng left the room and returned with his bag. He carefully closed the double doors and walked to the table behind Ng Wai-sun. 'I ask you now to join me in the ceremony of Burning The Yellow Paper,' the Dragon Head continued. Behind him Cheng unzipped the bag and took from it a piece of yellow paper and placed it next to the cast-iron bowl. From the bag came a soft, clucking sound. Cheng handed the Dragon Head a black writing brush and unscrewed the top of a small bottle of blue ink. With careful, measured strokes Ng Wai-sun began to write on the paper, speaking each character out loud as he finished it, spelling out the oath of allegiance and the agreement the Dragon Heads had reached. The men around the table nodded their heads in agreement as he spoke. When he had finished he walked over to the Tan Yee Dragon Head and gave him the paper and brush.

'If you would do me the honour of signing first, Mok Shih-chieh.'

Mok smiled in acceptance and wrote the three characters of his name below the oath. The paper and brush were then passed clockwise around the table, and when there were twelve signatures Ng Wai-sun added his own before taking it back to the portrait.

Cheng produced a box of matches and a bottle of port from the bag and while the Dragon Head held the paper over the bowl Cheng lit a match and set fire to it. Flames licked at the paper and smoke curled above it, forming a cloud as if it came from the mouth of the Kwan Kung god. The red-faced warrior seemed to glare through the smoke, and his hands appeared to tighten on the war sword he held across his armoured chest. The old man held the burning paper until there was nothing but ash, ignoring the pain, his teeth clenched tightly. The flame flickered and died and he dropped the burnt sheet into the bowl. Cheng uncorked the port and poured it into the bowl, playing the stream of liquid over the ashes. He placed the empty bottle on the table, and from inside his robe took an ivory-handled curved knife, the blade wickedly sharp, which he handed to the Dragon Head. He leant over the bag once more and pulled out a black chicken by its feet. The bird's wings had been tied tight against its body with string, and Cheng held it out towards Ng Wai-sun so that he could cut the bonds and allow the chicken to flap freely. The Dragon Head seized it by the neck with his left hand and drew the blade across its neck with one firm stroke. Blood splattered into the bowl, some of it spilling on to the table, and then it poured out as the chicken thrashed and shook. Cheng waited until the bird was still before dropping the corpse into the bag and taking the bloodstained knife from Ng Wai-sun. The Dragon Head picked up the bowl and held it close to his chin as he swirled the contents around. With his eyes fixed firmly on the men sitting at the table he raised the black bowl to his lips and drank deeply. When he'd finished he handed the bowl to Mok Shih-chieh. The mixture of blood and wine had given him a red line above his lips like a parody of a smile, a hellish clown's grin. Mok took the bowl almost reverently and then he too drank before passing it to the man on his left.

The bowl went round the table, as the yellow paper had done previously, each man drinking from it in turn until it returned to where Ng Wai-sun was standing. He took it and walked back to the table and held it up before the framed portrait.

'Whosoever breaks the oath and betrays the trust of those who signed the yellow paper, may he perish as the chicken has perished,' he said, before turning to face the men at the table. He threw the bowl down and it smashed into small pieces, the rest of the sickly-sweet mixture spilling on to the floor where it lay in slowly spreading pools, unable to soak into the polished wood.

'And may their families be broken as the bowl has been broken,' he said.

The Dragon Heads nodded agreement, as one.

The anchor chain dropped above Dugan's head at dead on six o'clock, and it was followed by the sound of one dollar coins being dropped into a tin bucket from a great height. For once it didn't annoy Dugan, not overmuch anyway, because he hadn't been able to sleep for more than half an hour at a time. Thoughts of Petal kept riding roughshod over his subconscious and he kept playing his last conversation with her over and over in his mind.

The key to what had happened, he was sure, lay with his brother-in-law, but according to the maid he and Jill hadn't been in all day. The last time he'd phoned, at eleven o'clock at night, he'd left his number and asked that Thomas Ng give him a call. The telephone had remained stubbornly silent all night.

He was in the office at half past seven, drinking coffee with his feet on the desk and he waited until eight before ringing Ng's house. The Filipina maid answered. No, Jill and Simon Ng were not at home. No, she didn't know if they had come back last night. No, Thomas Ng was not there. No, she did not know when he would be back.

Some 30,000 feet above Vietnam Feinberg handed a light green file to Edmunds. 'That's our boy,' he said. 'A real pro. I'm looking forward to this job.'

He was too, Edmunds could see it in his eyes, a manic gleam that he'd seen all too often during his days with Special Forces, when he had been down in the jungle below, killing and torturing and serving his country. He'd believed in what he was doing then; even among the blood

and the pain and the shit he knew he was doing the Right
Thing, serving God and Country and the President in the
best way he could. He'd seen the thousand-yard stare
in the eyes of grunts coming to the end of their tours,
short-timers who'd seen too much death and lost too many
friends, young men who would never be the same again.
He'd seen the look and understood it, but he could not
fathom how a man like Feinberg, who'd still have been
in short trousers when the last helicopter lifted off the
roof of the US embassy in Saigon, could have the same
cold fury in his eyes. Somewhere along the line Feinberg
had just stopped caring. Feinberg would never be sorry
for anything he did – no regret, no remorse, no feeling.
In a way Edmunds envied him, not for the thousand-yard
stare or the eagerness for combat, but for the way he had
come to terms so easily with what he did.

Maybe he would change as he got older. Edmunds had.
He didn't have flashbacks or anything the documentary-
makers described when they went to interview the Vets
living rough in the wilderness or locked up in institutions.
He didn't wake up screaming in the middle of the night
and he didn't flinch at loud noises. It was just that he
kept getting overcome with a deep sorrow, a suffocating
sadness for what he'd done in the past that dogged him
even during his happiest moments. It was there, like a
tumour, and like cancer it seemed to grow over the
years until now it had almost filled his whole body and
was now preparing to burst out of his skin and into the
open where everyone would see what he had contained
all these years.

'Are you OK?' asked Feinberg.

Edmunds nodded. 'Yeah, I'm just a bit hung-over.'

Feinberg grinned. 'You should have stayed till the bitter end.'

Edmunds forced a smile. 'Did you get her in the end?'

'Who?'

'The dancer. The girl with the ponytail.'

'Fuck, no. She left just before the bar closed, ran out and jumped on to the back of a motor-bike. Her boyfriend, I suppose. Or more likely her pimp. Bastard. No, I picked up two really young ones; Jesus, they couldn't have been more than fifteen, hardly any hair on them at all, if you know what I mean. God, I was up all night with them. Outstanding.'

Feinberg liked using phrases like 'outstanding', words that he'd picked up from books and films about the Vietnam War. In many ways it was a pity he hadn't had a chance to serve in the early Sixties, thought Edmunds. Perhaps if he had he wouldn't have been so keen to use the jargon.

The two men were sitting in the almost empty Business section of a Thai International Airbus where two Thai stewardesses in long purple dresses were about to serve breakfast from a trolley. Edmunds just took coffee and a plate of fresh fruit, but Feinberg took the works, scrambled eggs, bacon, mushrooms and tomatoes, and three bread rolls spread thickly with butter. Edmunds peeled a banana and began to eat but he had no appetite.

The file lay on the tray in front of him, unopened. It was the same green as the fatigues they'd worn when they went into the jungle at night on the sort of operations that would never get into the history books. Edmunds had killed men, women and children in the name of duty, usually with a knife or his bare hands, often at night, and always with the aim of terrorizing the enemy. Edmunds had been all of twenty-five years old then, not much younger than Feinberg was now, and he had been one of the older ones. They were sent into the tunnels where the North Vietnamese rested up between raids or to the thin jungle trails where they sat for days waiting for a VC patrol. Then they killed. And when they'd finished killing they mutilated the bodies to serve as a warning to the rest. No, not as a warning, there was precious little to warn the VCs about; it was to serve as a lesson. This is what will happen to you if we catch you. So keep away. They gutted children and they castrated the men and defiled the women with their hunting knives. On several occasions they'd been helicoptered into friendly villages that had been attacked by the VCs and told to mutilate the bodies of the civilians, dead but still warm, still bleeding. Then just as quickly they were flown out before the Army took in the Press Corps to show them what it was they were up against.

Edmunds thought now as he thought then, that he had been doing the Right Thing. But whereas then he had gone in hard and cold, now he felt sorry for what he'd done, and he wished he'd just been a grunt fighting cleanly with an M-16 in the mud rather than as an assassin with a knife. He couldn't remember how many he'd killed, but there were some he could picture clearly in his mind, as if etched into metal by acid. There was a teenage boy with a rifle whose throat he'd slit from behind, only to find that it was a girl with a broom, there was a woman he'd disembowelled who turned out to be pregnant, a toddler who crawled out from under a bed while he was on the floor hacking away at its mother, an old man who had smiled when he stuck a knife through his ribcage and into his heart. He could remember all their faces, and he knew he would remember them at the moment of his own death, when it came. He sighed deeply and picked up the file, hoping that reading about the man called Howells would take his mind off the memories.

Inside the file were three faxed sheets, two of them containing lines of type; the third was a photograph. It was of a man in his thirties, with a thinnish face, deep-set eyes and a hard-set mouth. It was a face Edmunds recognized, a face he'd seen once, four years earlier, in the Lebanon.

He looked across at Feinberg but he had his head down over his plate, concentrating on his eggs. He scrutinized the picture, but there was no doubt. Howells had saved his life. Edmunds had been working out of the embassy in Beirut when he'd been kidnapped by one of the militia groups. They'd locked him away in the basement of a whitewashed house in the suburbs and told the embassy that if they didn't pay a ransom of US$100,000 they'd kill him. They'd kept him in the room for three months, blindfolded for most of the time, with nothing stronger than water to drink and food out of tins. He'd almost gone mad from the sheer monotony of it all. The threat of death had been nothing new, that he could deal with, but over the whole twelve weeks they had said not one word to him after the initial kidnapping, in any language. They'd refused to give him a television or a radio and the only time they showed him a newspaper was when they ran stories saying that the authorities were refusing to pay the ransom.

Over the three months he had six different guards, with

never less than two on duty at any one time. There were three of them in the house the day Howells came. One of them, a middle-aged swarthy thug with a wicked zig-zag of a scar under his left eye that had distorted the skin and given him a permanent leer, was the leader of the group. With him was a girl with long black hair who always had an automatic rifle in her right hand, and a young man barely out of his teens, a good-looking boy with a crew cut and fair white skin. They took it in turns to guard him, two sitting in the room while the other stayed upstairs. The basement had only one way in and out, a sturdy wooden door with a peep-hole, bolted on the outside and inside. All the room contained was a camp bed and a couple of army blankets for Edmunds, a plastic bucket for him to use as a toilet, and two easy chairs for his guards. Every second day they brought in another plastic bucket, this one half full of lukewarm water, and a rough cotton towel so that he could wash himself. Everything he ate or drank was brought in through the door on paper plates or in polystyrene cups. Twice they took photographs of him sitting on the camp bed holding a newspaper. Both times one of his guards stood by his side with a gun pointing at his temple.

He was nearing the end of his tether by the time Howells came on the scene. He was blindfolded so he wasn't sure who was in the room with him but he'd guessed that one of them was the girl by the way she'd padded across the floor. He heard her walk to the door and pause as she checked the peep-hole. He heard the rattle of the bolt and then he heard the crash of a foot against the wooden door and then a scream and two shots. Edmunds had panicked, rolling off the camp bed on to the floor clawing at the

331

blindfold, scared shitless that at any second he was going to get a bullet in the head. A third shot barked and he heard a simultaneous thud and grunt and he blinked in the light as the middle-aged man slumped to the ground. By the door was the young man, blood pumping from a gaping wound in his chest. The girl was lying at the foot of the bed, her long black hair spreading like a pool of oil behind her head. One of her eye sockets was filling with blood and as he watched he saw red flow among the black tendrils of hair. Her legs twitched as if she was sleeping but the bullet had cauterized most of her brain tissue.

Only then did Edmunds see the man at the door, the man who had done so much damage in a few scant seconds. Lean and wiry with a long face and deep-set eyes, two or three days' stubble on his chin, he held a large handgun in both hands, moving the barrel slowly from side to side, covering the three corpses in the room. Cancel that. Two corpses. The older man was still alive, breathing heavily and clasping his hand around his groin where he'd been shot. Howells looked at Edmunds and aimed the gun at him, face totally relaxed, no sign of the tension that he surely must have felt. Edmunds realized that he must have forced the young man to stand in front of the peep-hole and then pushed him into the room, probably shooting him in the back. One against three, crazy odds that no one in his right mind would go up against. The man didn't look crazy, he looked very, very cool. His voice when it came was cold and hard.

'Who are you?' The accent was English.

'American,' said Edmunds, looking into the barrel of the gun and wincing as he saw the man's finger tighten on the trigger.

'I didn't ask what you are.'

'Ralph Simmonds. I'm a businessman, I sell computers.' Edmunds knew instinctively that it would not be a good idea to tell this man that he was with an intelligence agency.

'Good answer. Stay down on the floor.'

He walked over to the man who was groaning on the floor and stood over him. He fired at the man's right leg and smiled as the bullet smashed through the kneecap and hit a chunk out of the floor. The man screamed and Howells shot him through the other leg. The man stopped screaming then, probably passed out, and Howells leant down and placed the barrel in the man's mouth before pulling the trigger for the sixth and final time. He stood up then, stretching like a cat in the sun, his eyes closed. He exhaled deeply and then turned to look at Edmunds. 'Tell nobody what you saw,' he said, lifting the barrel of the gun to his lips. 'Tell them you had your blindfold on all the time.' Edmunds nodded quickly, acting the part of the frightened businessman.

Afterwards, when he was being debriefed in Langley he was told that the man who'd been keeping him prisoner had been one of the most dangerous terrorists on the loose in the Lebanon; he'd killed three hostages and had been involved in at least half a dozen bombings. They told Edmunds how lucky he'd been. Two of the hostages had been killed after ransoms had been paid. They'd shown him countless pictures but he hadn't been able to identify the man who'd freed him, the man who'd taken such pleasure from torturing his captor. And, to be honest, Edmunds wasn't sure if he would have identified Howells even if he had been shown his photograph. He owed him. And as he looked down at the same deep-set eyes, and read the background information on the man called Geoff Howells, he knew that was as true now as it had been all those years ago.

Dugan waited until after lunch before calling Bellamy in the hope that he'd be in a better mood than the last time they'd spoken.

'Jeff. It's Dugan.'

'What the fuck do you want, Dugan?' Bellamy barked into the phone. Dugan held the receiver away from his ear. So much for his theory that a full stomach would soften his temper.

'Give me a break, Jeff. I just want some information.'

'Dugan, the way I feel at the moment I wouldn't piss on you if you were on fire.'

'I suppose this means you won't pass me the ball during the Rugby Sevens.'

Bellamy snorted and Dugan knew that he was smiling despite himself.

'Business is business, you bastard, but rugby is something else. I'll tell you what, Dugan, I'll give you one minute. For no other reason than the fact that you've got one of the best pairs of hands in Hong Kong. And the clock's ticking.'

'Petal?'

'She's gone. And be careful, Pat. She's trouble.'

'In what way?'

'Special Branch are on to the case. One of the dead

guys is some sort of Chinese intelligence agent, he was expelled from Taiwan a few years back and he'd been photographed a couple of times at Kai Tak. I think you're going to get a call from them today.'

'You think?'

'All right, I'm fucking certain you will.'

'You told them I knew her?'

'It wasn't a secret, old lad.'

'Yeah, I know. They think she was one of them?'

'What do you think?'

'It doesn't look good, does it?'

'For you? Or for her?'

Dugan ignored that. 'The gweilo,' he said. 'What's happening about the gweilo?'

'We've got his name and his passport number, and we're lifting his prints from the room. We've got a rough description from the hotel staff but no photograph. We've put a stop on him at the airport but if he's got a false passport we're buggered.'

'But he's hurt?'

'Yeah, there was plenty of blood so the chances are that he's gone to ground. We're checking all the hospitals and the surgeries, but that takes time. And anyway, there are plenty of underground doctors who'll treat him.'

'The question is, why did he run? If they were there to kill him, why run?'

'You tell me, Dugan. Maybe he thought they'd try again. Maybe he's got something to hide. Maybe he went out to buy a pack of cigarettes.'

'What's his name?'

'Howells. Geoff Howells.'

'Have you run a check on him?'

'We checked the name and it matches with the passport number and we're checking with the UK. There's no record of him in our files. He's never been to Hong Kong before, not on that passport, anyway. Your minute's up, Dugan. And we never had this conversation.'

'Understood. I appreciate it, Jeff. Next time I see you I'll give you a big, sloppy kiss.'

'My arse you will,' said Bellamy, laughing.

'Wherever you want it,' Dugan said and put the phone down. So the gweilo was still in Hong Kong, probably in need of medical treatment. His name was Geoff Howells, and for some reason he'd been hired to kill his brother-in-law. He sat staring out of the window, absent-mindedly drumming his fingers on the desk, as he tried to work out what to do next.

You could tell a lot about a country from the way the taxi system was organized, thought Edmunds, as he walked with Feinberg out of the arrivals area and through the electronically operated doors that led to the taxi rank. In a highly developed country only a fool would pay for a taxi – getting from Gatwick to London or from Narita to Tokyo cost an arm and a leg, and anyway it was quicker by train. If you arrived at some god-awful Third World country like Indonesia then the drivers attacked like jackals, grabbing at you and undercutting each other in an attempt to get you into their cab. The Thais were a bit more polite, but the taxis that waited outside Bangkok's airport were every bit as ramshackle and the meters, when they had them, never worked and you had to haggle over the fare before getting in. But they were still cheap. At Kai Tak the cabs queued patiently and the meters worked, but the fares were still affordable. The Jack Edmunds Theory of Economic Development in Relation to Taxis – the poorer a country, the cheaper and less efficient the taxi system. The richer it became, the better the quality of the taxi service until the standard of living of the drivers reached such a point that their cabs became priced out of the reach of most people. London was getting that way. The last time he'd been there he'd had trouble getting his expense sheet through; the accounts department had said he was only supposed to hire cabs, not buy one.

'What are you thinking about?' asked Feinberg as they joined the queue.

'Taxis.'

'Yeah, a bitch, aren't they? Them and death, the only two things in life that are certain. Who said that?'

'You did, Rick.'

'I meant originally.' Edmunds knew what Feinberg meant, but he couldn't be bothered to get into a long conversation about it so he just shrugged.

'Where did you book us into?' he asked the younger man.

There were a dozen or so people in front of them, businessmen in dark suits carrying briefcases and overnight bags, a German family sweating in the heat and a couple of turbaned Sikhs. Edmunds was dressed casually, cream linen slacks and a fake black Yves St Laurent shirt and a pair of brown leather moccasins that he'd picked up for next to nothing in Bangkok. Feinberg was wearing a pale blue safari suit and Nike training shoes and his Ray-Ban sunglasses. Edmunds knew that what the younger agent really wanted to do was to parachute in from 10,000 feet with an M-16 between his teeth, but the Ray-Bans would have to do. Christ, where did the CIA get him from? Obviously rode in on the gung-ho tide of Reaganism which gave the intelligence services back most of the kudos and glamour that they'd lost under Nixon, but which had allowed in a lot of men who would have been more at home in large institutions with bars on the windows and jackets with long sleeves.

'The Victoria Hotel, on the island.'

'We're doing this on the cheap?'

'We're not here officially,' said Feinberg quietly.

'What do you mean, we're not here officially?' said Edmunds, aware that a taxi queue outside an international airport wasn't the most secure environment for a conversation like this.

'Don't panic, for fuck's sake. When I say it's not official, I mean we've just got to keep away from the local office. They're not supposed to know we're here. Nobody is. In and out before anyone realizes we're even here.'

'But it's from the Company?'

'Of course it's from the Company. Do you think I'd take you on a freelance operation without telling you?'

Too right I do, thought Edmunds. Too fucking right. 'So?'

'Greg Hamilton is running this show. I was going to tell you when we got to the hotel.'

'It might have been nice if you'd told me before we got here.'

'Fuck it, Jack. Hamilton called me because he couldn't

get hold of you, that's all. I answered the phone and I got the briefing. I'm just passing on the information, that's all.'

They had got to the front of the queue and they walked across to the taxi. They had one bag each; Edmunds' was a folding job that doubled as a suit-hanger, while Feinberg carried a bright blue nylon holdall. They took them into the back with them rather than using the boot. They were both travelling light. Like Feinberg had said, in and out before anyone knew they were there. Anyone but Greg Hamilton. Feinberg told the driver where they wanted to go but he didn't seem to understand.

'Huh?' he grunted and screwed up his eyes.

'Victoria Hotel,' Feinberg repeated slowly. 'Hong Kong island.'

The driver shook his head. 'Me not know. Me not know.'

'Oh fuck,' said Feinberg. 'Now what are we going to do?'

'You could waste him,' suggested Edmunds dryly.

Feinberg slapped the headrest of the driver's seat. 'Victoria Hotel,' he said again. 'Victoria Hotel.'

Edmunds wound down his window and called over to a well-dressed Chinese businessman, forty years old or thereabouts with horn-rimmed glasses and a crocodile skin briefcase.

'I'm sorry to bother you but we're having a little trouble with the driver. Can you help?'

The man smiled and walked over, leaning down to get his head level with Edmunds. 'Sure,' he said, with a mid-Western drawl. 'Where do you folks want to go?'

'Victoria Hotel,' said Edmunds. The man spoke to the

driver in Cantonese and he nodded and grunted. 'Thanks,' said Edmunds.

'No sweat,' said the man. 'Enjoy your stay in Hong Kong.'

Edmunds wound the window back up and sat back as the air-conditioner did its best to cool the cab.

'Hamilton is in London,' he said.

'Right.'

'So why is he running an operation in Hong Kong?'

'He didn't say, and I didn't ask. You can call him if you want to, I suppose.'

'Sure. So what's the game plan?'

'According to Hamilton this guy Howells is injured, he's been shot, so it won't be too long before the police track him down.'

'You didn't tell me that.' Edmunds was starting to get annoyed. He didn't like going into an operation without a full briefing, but he hated even more the fact that the information had to come through a shithead like Feinberg. The least Hamilton could have done was to have spoken to him. He had seniority, when all was said and done.

'Like I said, I was going to sit down and discuss it when we got to the Victoria. Look, Jack, don't worry. This is going to be a piece of cake.'

'I still don't understand why the police shot him.'

'Not the police. He was attacked in a hotel room. Hamilton says he's killed an agent of ours and we have to even the score, but without offending our cousins. This is still British territory, even if there are more of us here than them.'

'So it's a revenge hit?'

'That's all there is to it. Howells hit one of ours, we hit him.'

'But Howells is a Brit. There's something not right here.'

'The Brits retired him, you read the file. Howells is a maverick, he's gone on the rampage. He's the disease and we're the cure.'

'You've been watching too many Sylvester Stallone movies.'

'Sly's my hero,' said Feinberg, grinning like a kid.

He would be, thought Edmunds.

'Look,' continued Feinberg. 'The local police are after Howells. Once they get him we hit him. There's no way he can leave Hong Kong and it's not an easy place for a white man to hide. Especially not with a bullet hole. But I think we can speed things up a bit.'

'What do you mean?'

'He's wounded and he's in an unfamiliar environment. He can't go to hospital so he'll need someone to hide him. He's working alone and as far as Hamilton knows he has no friends here.'

'Cherchez la femme?'

'It's the obvious, isn't it. Find a girl to shack up with.'

Edmunds nodded in agreement. 'So we check the bars and nightclubs. There must only be a few thousand of them.'

Feinberg raised his finger and waved it in front of Edmunds' nose. 'Hong Kong has changed since the days of the Vietnam War, you know. There are plenty of bars for the Chinese but he wouldn't go there, he's more likely to have gone to one of the tourist bars, Wan Chai or Tsim Sha Tsui. There's a few dozen of them at most. We can check them out in one night, just show his picture around and say we're looking for an old friend. We might get lucky. And even if we don't the police will get him eventually. Either way he's history.'

Feinberg seemed to relish the idea, and all but licked his lips Edmunds watched him, wondering who really was the psychopath, Geoff Howells or Rick Feinberg.

Amy was stiff all over when she woke up. There was only one bed in her tiny flat, and the gweilo was in that. She had no qualms about sharing her single bed but didn't want to risk hurting him. She came back just after four o'clock in the morning and Howells had been in a deep sleep, snoring soundly. She'd kissed him on the back of the head, and after placing a fresh glass of water by the bed she'd slept curled up on the small rattan couch in her lounge, covered with a woollen blanket.

Normally she slept until the late afternoon, but Dr Wu had said he would come round sometime after midday, so she set her small travel alarm for eleven o'clock. She made herself a pot of jasmine tea and sat on the couch drinking it as she thought about the night before. She had been lucky, a visiting businessman from Sydney had taken a fancy to her and had sat with her for almost three hours buying her drink after drink as he tried to slip his hand down the back of her dress. After he'd bought her a couple of drinks she'd taken him into one of the booths at the back of the bar where the lights were dimmer and the prices higher. There she'd let him kiss her and touch her breasts, outside her dress, and she'd stroked his thigh and speeded up her drink rate from one every twenty minutes to one every twelve. He'd smelt of stale sweat and tobacco and the whisky on his breath made her want to retch but she'd smiled and laughed at his stupid jokes and hung on his every word as his bill rose higher and higher.

As midnight approached he began asking her to go back to his hotel room with him but she'd coyly turned him down. He'd offered to pay her bar fine but she'd said no, and then he said he'd pay double the fine. It wasn't that she was averse to going out with customers, she did that at least once a month to boost her earnings, but the man disgusted her and she was choosy about who she'd go to bed with. Maybe as she got older she'd be less selective and grab each opportunity as it was offered, but she was still young enough and pretty enough to command a high price and while she was quite prepared to let the foul-smelling barbarian fondle and kiss her she'd rather die than spread her legs for him.

He called the mamasan over and told her that he wanted to take Amy out and the mamasan had asked her in Cantonese if she wanted to go and Amy said no, he was a pig. The mamasan gently explained that Amy was having her period, maybe next time, and that if he wanted a girl there were plenty more in the bar. The Australian decided to go instead. He paid with a credit card which meant that Amy wouldn't get her commission for at least two months. Her basic salary was about the same as a typist's, but she got to keep about one-third of the cost of every drink a customer bought her. The more drinks they bought, the more she earned, with the cashier giving her a handful of cardboard tickets at the end of each night signifying how many she'd had. If the customer paid in cash she got the money at the end of the week; if they paid with plastic then she got it when the credit card company settled the bill, and that usually took a minimum of two months.

She'd asked him to pay with cash, he had plenty of notes in his wallet, but he swore at her, called her a cock-teasing bitch. Amy walked away and told the cashier to add two more hostess drinks to his bill. The cashier grinned. 'Fuck the gweilos,' he cackled. 'Fuck the gweilos and fuck their mothers.'

Amy drank her tea, watching the leaves swirl around the bottom of the china beaker. There was more to it than money, she realized. Even if the Australian hadn't been such an ugly bore, even if she'd been attracted to him she wouldn't have gone with him. It was something to do with Geoff Howells, but she wasn't exactly sure what it was, something to do with being faithful – but that didn't make any sense. She hadn't even slept with the gweilo, she knew nothing about him other than the fact that he'd asked for her help and that something inside her had compelled her to agree.

All her life Amy had been used by people: by her father when she was barely into her teens; by a succession of boyfriends who had varied from cruel to callous; by the customers, and by the people who ran the bar. All had simply assumed that they had a right to use her and throughout her life she had gone along with them, taking the easy way out. And now this man was also using her, but in a different way. He needed her, it wasn't just that he wanted her help, he needed it, and that made a difference. It made her feel special.

She showered and dressed in a faded denim skirt and a white cotton blouse with short sleeves before making Howells a coffee. Without any effort she remembered how he liked to drink it, black with no sugar. He was awake when she went into the bedroom, but still lying face down. He twisted around and smiled up at her as she knelt down beside the bed.

'Good morning,' he said.

'Good afternoon,' she corrected.

'I can't tell with the curtains drawn.'

'To help you sleep. Dr Wu said best thing for you was to sleep as much as possible. And to drink water.'

Howells looked at the coffee and smiled. 'Thank you for the coffee,' he said. 'How do I say thank you in Cantonese?'

'*M goy*,' she said.

'*M goy*,' he repeated. '*M goy* for the coffee.'

'You better drink it soon, Dr Wu is coming and he will scold me if he sees I have given you coffee.'

Howells rolled slowly on to his left side and Amy helped raise him into a sitting position, pushing the pillow to support the small of his back.

'It'll be our secret,' he said.

For some reason that pleased Amy immensely, and she blushed. Howells raised the steaming cup to his mouth and drank.

'Lovely,' he said. 'How do I say delicious?'

'*Ho sik* for food,' she said. '*Ho yam* for drink.'

'*Ho yam*,' said Howells. '*M goy*.'

'*M sai m goy*,' said Amy. 'No need.'

Howells studied her over the top of the cup as he drank, wondering what he was going to do with the girl. For the moment he needed her to hide him, but what then? She knew who he was, and before long she'd know what he'd done. The shooting in the hotel would surely get into the newspapers and he'd used his real name. That was stupid, but he had trusted Grey completely. Still, no point in looking back, it was the future that counted.

'How you feel?' she asked.

'Much better,' he replied.

'Good,' she said. 'I am pleased.'

She looked it, too. Howells wasn't sure if it was because she was glad he was on the mend or because it meant he'd soon be getting the hell out of her flat. The doorbell rang, startling them both.

'Dr Wu,' she said, grabbing the cup and running into the kitchen before opening the door and admitting the elderly doctor. He greeted Amy and then walked into the bedroom.

'You seem much better than the last time I saw you,' he said.

'I heal quickly,' said Howells.

'I will decide that,' said the doctor, putting his leather medical bag next to Howells' feet. 'Lean forward, please.'

Howells leant forward while the doctor removed the dressing and peered at the wound over the top of his glasses.

'Hmm, it seems you are right,' he said. 'I see no problems. I will just change the dressing for you. Do you feel any pain?'

'A dull ache, unless I move the arm suddenly.'

'Do you want anything for that?'

'No injection,' said Howells. 'But if you have any tablets that I could take if it starts to hurt, I'd appreciate it.'

Dr Wu took a small plastic bottle from his bag containing half a dozen white tablets.

'I will leave these,' he said. 'Take one if the pain gets very bad, but on no account take more than two over a three-hour period. They are painkillers but they will also help you sleep. But if it hurts so much that you feel you need to take three tablets then you should call me anyway.' He put the bottle down by Howells' glass of water. 'And drink lots of water.'

'I am doing, Amy is looking after me very well.'

Amy came into the bedroom and stood behind the doctor, fidgeting nervously. Wu turned to her and spoke in Cantonese. She nodded and answered. Seeing the curious look on his face, Amy hurriedly said to Howells: 'Dr Wu is saying you can get up in two days, but he will come see you before.' There was no need to translate, Dr Wu's English was much better than hers, but she didn't want Howells to think she had been betraying him.

Howells looked at the doctor and nodded. '*M goy*,' he said.

Dr Wu smiled. '*M sai m goy*,' he said. 'Your Cantonese is very good.' Behind him, Amy smiled with pride.

One of the best things about being a chef was the fact that you always had afternoons free. André Beaumont knew there were plenty of drawbacks to the job: long hours, the pressure of always having to be on top form, the fact that he never got away before eleven o'clock at night, but he relished the free time between the lunchtime rush and the preparations for dinner.

Beaumont was the head chef at one of the top Kowloon hotels and whenever the weather was good and he didn't have a banquet to organize he'd drive his Golf GTI to Hebe Haven, the sunroof open and the stereo full on, and take out his yacht for a couple of hours.

He loved Hong Kong and the lifestyle it gave him: a salary almost double what he'd earn back in France, a 3,000 square-foot flat rent-free that was decorated every year to his specifications, the car, two first-class flights home every year, free hospitality in the hotel and a chance to be head chef at an age, twenty-eight, when his friends who had stayed behind were still *sous-chefs*.

Today was perfect for sailing; a cloudless sky, a fresh wind from the north, and in the seat next to him Caroline Chang, the hotel's public relations manager, who'd sneaked out of her office on the pretence of visiting their advertising agency. She had an easy-going boss and fancied André something rotten and she had no regrets about skipping off for a few hours. She reckoned that she gave the hotel more than enough in terms of hours, dealing with cantankerous customers, checking menus, sending out press releases and handling VIPs.

She raised her face to the sky and let the breeze play through her long black hair as André turned off the main road and drove towards the pier. There were plenty of parking spaces, as there always were on weekday afternoons. It was only at weekends that it got crowded, and then André stayed away.

'Which is yours?' Caroline asked as André closed the sunroof and locked the doors.

André pointed. 'The one with the white hull and the two masts,' he said.

'What's she called?'

'*Katrina*,' he said. 'It used to belong to a lawyer. He named it after his wife and she ran off and left him. He had to sell the boat to raise the money for his settlement. I haven't got round to changing the name yet.'

He walked behind her and slipped his arm around her waist. He rubbed his nose up against the side of her head, breathing in the warm fragrance of her hair. 'Perhaps I should call her *Caroline*.' She was the fifth girl he'd promised to name the boat after, and three of the previous girls had all ended up making love to him in the main cabin. For some reason the promise of having their name on a yacht seemed to act as an intense aphrodisiac. To be honest, André was quite happy with *Katrina*.

Caroline pressed herself against him. 'I'd like that,' she said, and turned to slip her arms around his neck and kiss him full on the lips. He was the first to pull away.

'Come on,' he said. 'We'll get one of the boatmen to row us out.'

They found a grizzled old woman with a dinghy and after a minute of bargaining she agreed to take them out to the *Katrina*.

'It's fabulous, so sleek, so feminine. I love her already,' said Caroline.

'Wait until you see inside,' said André, and held her gaze for a couple of seconds before smiling. She laughed and he knew she was his. For the afternoon, at least.

He climbed on board first and then helped her. 'Ask

her to come and collect us when we get back,' he said and Caroline spoke to her in rapid Cantonese. The woman cackled and rowed away.

Caroline leant over the side and watched the water below as André began to operate the winch to pull up the anchor. It seemed to need more effort than usual; maybe it was caught in something on the sea bottom. That was all he needed. Slowly, painfully slowly, it heaved the anchor up, at about half its normal speed. As he waited André admired Caroline's backside and her long legs. She had unusually long legs for a Chinese. When she screamed it was a blood-curdling yell that caused the old woman to drop one of her oars and wiped all thoughts of sex from André's mind.

Tomkins walked into Dugan's office as if he had an unpeeled banana up his backside. Dugan was eating Kentucky Fried Chicken and had grease all round his lips.

'Bloody Hell, Dugan, you're a pig,' said Tomkins.

'You should be glad I'm working through my lunch,' said Dugan.

'Yeah, yeah, I'm grateful, the Commissioner is grateful, the Governor is grateful, hell I bet the Queen herself will get to hear about this devotion to duty.'

Dugan reached for a sheet of typing paper and used it to clean his hands. The red and white cardboard box was full of chicken bones and a sprinkling of cold French fries. Dugan began to spoon coleslaw into his mouth with a white plastic spoon, the sort you used to feed babies. 'What do you want?' he said between mouthfuls.

'Me? I just want you to clear your caseload so I can dump another dozen or so on to your desk. But the boys in Arsenal Street seem to have other plans for you. I've just had them on the phone. They want you to go right over. What have you done to attract the attention of Special Branch, Pat?'

'Fucked if I know,' answered Dugan. 'They want me right now?'

'That's what they said. You're to ask for a Chief Inspector Leigh.'

'I didn't think there were any high-ranking Chinese left in Special Branch.'

'There aren't. He's a Brit.' He spelled out the name for Dugan.

Special Branch were also in Wan Chai, in a squat office block not far from the one where Dugan worked, so he walked over. The roads were crowded and noisy, trucks pouring out black exhaust smoke, chauffeur-driven limousines with high-powered businessmen on mobile phones in the back seats, taxis with impatient drivers banging their horns, bare-chested deliverymen on bicycles, one carrying dead, plucked chickens, another with large green gas cylinders, a mixture of old and new that typified Hong Kong.

The shops too were a rag-bag of ancient and modern: a herbalist with shelves full of glass bottles of mysterious green and brown plants and roots, sacks of dried mushrooms and deer antlers in display cases, a coffin maker with his wares stacked from floor to ceiling, an electrician's store with portable colour televisions and boxes of Japanese cameras, a noodle shop with five cluttered circular tables where Dugan sometimes bought beef noodles when he tired of gweilo fast food, a shop selling nothing but cosmetics. Some of the blocks were twenty years old or more, less than ten storeys high with flats above the shops and entrances blocked with ornate metal grilles, but gradually they were coming down and being replaced with glass and marble towers two or three times taller as the developers moved away from the Central office area in search of big profits.

The pavements were as busy as the roads, and there too could be seen a cosmopolitan mix: gnarled old housewives making their way home with pink plastic bags containing enough food for a day, businessmen with sharp suits and thin ties, the occasional poser walking along talking into a hand-held phone, shouting to make himself heard over the roar of the traffic and the blaring horns, schoolchildren with crisp white shirts and white socks, rucksacks full of books distorting their frail shoulders, mothers with babies on their backs.

Dugan walked slowly, partly because the crowds were so thick but also because he didn't want to arrive for an interview with Special Branch sweating like a pig. Occasionally he had to move off the pavement and into the road and he took care to avoid stepping in the piles of ash and rotting fruit left over from night-time ghost appeasing.

Chief Inspector Leigh looked to be a kindly man; greying hair, soft green eyes and folds of loose skin that gave him the appearance of a tired, but loyal, bloodhound. He seemed ill at ease in his light blue suit as if it had been the only thing hanging in his wardrobe when he got out of bed this morning. He smiled benignly when Dugan walked into his office and took him completely by surprise by offering to shake his hand.

'I've always been a fan of yours,' said Leigh. His voice had the lilt of a Welshman's and made Dugan think of congregations singing in frost-covered stone churches.

'I'm sorry?' said Dugan, flustered.

'You played a blinder during the last Sevens. That last try you scored, sheer magic. I remember telling my wife; Glynnis, I said, that boy could play for Wales.'

'I'm afraid not, sir,' said Dugan. 'I'm not Welsh.'

Leigh looked hurt but it was too late for Dugan to add the word 'unfortunately' without appearing to take the piss.

'Never mind, never mind. Please sit down.'

He waved Dugan to one of the two comfortable seats facing the desk. Leigh's office was much the same as Dugan's, albeit a bit larger. In one corner was a large metal safe, and on it was a brass bowl containing a bushy green plant with bulbous leaves. Leigh's desk was as cluttered as Dugan's though he merited a small table lamp. Dugan could see the back of a silver picture frame and guessed it contained a picture of Glynnis Leigh and probably a couple of children, too. Leigh was no doubt a devoted husband and family man, and a pillar of the church. God knows what he was doing in Special Branch. It must be a soul-destroying job, trying to stop Communist infiltration in a place which was gearing up to be handed over to Red China. Talk about a job with no prospects. Special Branch was due to be disbanded before the Communists took over and all their files gutted or destroyed. Most of the Chinese members had been promised British citizenship, unlike most of the other six million inhabitants, because even the British Government accepted that such men would not last long under the new regime.

Special Branch had other tasks, sure, they monitored CIA activity and any other intelligence agencies that tried to operate in Hong Kong, and they kept tabs on the local members of the Kuomintang, the hardline anti-Communist party that controlled Taiwan; but their main purpose was to identify Communists in Hong Kong and for that they had a network of contacts and informers throughout the colony, whose lives would also become dispensable after handover. That was one of the reasons there were so few Chinese in Special Branch, and none in top positions. The job was too sensitive to be trusted to locals.

'So,' said Leigh, steepling his fingers and leaning back in his chair. 'Tell me about this girl.' It felt for all the world like he was Dugan's father asking about his latest girlfriend.

'What is it you want to know, sir?'

Leigh smiled and his eyes wrinkled. He was obviously a man used to smiling. Dugan could imagine him on Christmas morning, helping grandchildren to unwrap their presents and basting the turkey while his wife looked after the vegetables. 'How long have you known her?'

'A few days, just a few days,' said Dugan.

'What was her name?'

'Was?'

He smiled again. 'A slip of the tongue, son. Of course, I mean *is*. What is her name?'

'Petal.'

'Her Chinese name?'

'I don't know. I only knew her as Petal.'

'You never asked for her surname?'

'It never came up.'

'She knew your name, though?'

'Sure.'

'Both names?'

'Both names,' agreed Dugan.

'Well, at least one of you knew what was going on,' said Leigh, and he laughed. 'Seriously Pat, how well did you know her?'

Dugan noticed the slick way the older man had dropped in his first name, trying to make it a chat between rugby fans rather than an interrogation.

'We were friends.'

'Do you know where she worked?'

'Bank of China. I called her there a couple of times.'

'And you got through to her?'

'Once or twice, yes.'

'You went to see her in hospital?'

'Yes.'

'What did she tell you?'

'She said she'd been attacked by a gweilo.'

'Did she tell you who her friends were?'

'Friends?'

'The two corpses in the room.'

Dugan shook his head. 'No sir, no, she didn't.'

'What else did you talk about?'

'That was about it, sir. She seemed pretty much out of it, she was badly hurt and she didn't make much sense.'

'She wasn't delirious?'

'No, but she seemed confused. I don't think she was sure what had happened.' Dugan could feel himself gradually enveloping the truth in layers of lies, building protective walls around the secret that Petal had given him, that she had trusted him with.

Leigh leant forward and put his arms on the desk. He adjusted his cuffs and studied Dugan.

'We have a problem here, Pat. This girl was in the company of two men, one of whom has already been identified as an agent of the Chinese intelligence service who we have tentatively linked to at least three assassinations in Taiwan. A syringe was found in the hotel room containing a drug that would have given an elephant a heart attack and her fingerprints were on it. She was taken out of the hospital, badly hurt as you pointed out, by a group of spooks from Xinhua, the so-called New China News Agency. Now while the rest of the world fondly imagines that the New China News Agency does nothing but put out press releases on the latest grain harvest, you and I know better, Pat. You and I know that they are Peking's official, and unofficial, representatives in Hong Kong. And we know that out of their offices in Happy Valley walk some of the meanest sons of bitches from China. And it is starting to look as if your friend is one of them.'

Leigh paused, looking Dugan straight in the eye as if his gaze could pierce the layers of lies. Dugan could feel his hands start to shake and he put them on his knees to try to steady them.

'So, what exactly did your friend tell you, Pat?'

'Like I said, sir, nothing.'

Leigh reached over and picked up a file from the left-hand side of his desk. He opened it and casually flicked through it.

'This is your file, Pat. It's not a bad record you've got. If it wasn't for your brother-in-law there's no doubt you'd have made chief inspector by now.' He put the file back on the desk. 'If there's one thing worse than having a triad leader as a brother-in-law, it's not being honest with your superiors, Pat. I would hate to see a career like yours come under any more pressure.'

'It's not as if I'm going anywhere now, is it?' asked Dugan, feeling the resentment grow inside, burning like a flame. He tried to stay calm, knowing that Leigh was just trying to rile him, trying to get him to open up.

'Believe me, it can get a lot worse. A lot worse. Now, what exactly did this Petal tell you?'

The senior officer was smiling still, but it seemed to Dugan that the green eyes hardened and that the kindly lines on the face were a mask. This man was not a friend, not to be trusted, and probably wasn't even a rugby fan. The rugby would be in Dugan's file. Dugan owed this man nothing. Fuck it, he owed the police nothing. They had killed his career, now they wanted his help. Dugan knew for sure then that his loyalty was with Petal. He would protect her and help her. He would lie to this man, he would lie all he could and he would enjoy doing it.

Dugan grinned sheepishly and rubbed his hand over his bald spot. 'It's a bit embarrassing, actually, sir.'

Leigh raised his eyebrows. 'What do you mean?'

'She wanted money.'

'Money?'

'For her hospital bills. She said she didn't think she had enough.'

'And why would she ask you for money, Pat?'

Dugan fell silent, and tried his best to look guilty and embarrassed.

'Why?' pressed Leigh.

'I'd given her money before, sir. She wasn't what you'd call a regular girlfriend.'

'She was a hooker?'

Dugan kept his eyes looking at the floor. 'Yes, sir. I met her at one of the bars the guys go to. I picked her up. At first I didn't realize she was on the game, it was only afterwards that she asked for money.'

'But you said she worked at the Bank of China?'

'That's what I told everyone, sir. I didn't want to admit that I'd had to pay for it. The guys would never have let me forget it.'

'And that's why you never knew her full name,' said Leigh.

'Yes sir,' said Dugan. 'That's why I can't understand why you think she's working with Chinese agents. She wasn't the brightest of girls, sir. A great body, but not a lot between her ears.'

Leigh nodded. 'I see,' he mused. 'I see.'

Dugan looked Leigh straight in the eyes, trying to keep his gaze even and his breathing steady. He kept his hands firmly on his knees, fingers rock-solid, trying to keep all the tension down below the level of the desk, out of sight.

Eventually Leigh seemed to reach a decision. 'OK, Pat, that's all for the moment. Let's call it a day. I'll give you a call if we need anything more from you.'

He didn't offer to shake hands when they parted, but stayed put in his seat and watched Dugan leave and close

the door behind him. Leigh drummed the fingers of his
right hand on Dugan's file.

'Senior Inspector Patrick Dugan, I don't believe a
fucking word you told me,' he said quietly.

Thomas Ng was standing outside the house, looking at the
harbour below when he heard the phone ring and then stop
as Master Cheng answered it. Cheng had arranged for a
large desk to be brought down from one of the bedrooms
upstairs and placed in the main lounge. On it he had put
the old-fashioned black Bakelite phone and a stack of
typing paper, a series of large scale maps of Hong Kong
and a couple of felt-tipped pens. Now he sat in a chair
taken from the set around the circular table answering the
phone which had been ringing non-stop since first light.
The maps had come from a property developer who owed
the triad a favour, several favours to be exact, and included
every single structure in the territory. As each tower block,
hotel or house was visited and the doormen questioned the
searchers rang back to inform Master Cheng. Cheng noted
down the building, the names of the men who had visited
it, and the time, which he took from a gold pocket watch
he kept by the side of the phone. Sitting by his side was
a young Red Pole who had formerly worked in a large
estate agents and was helping the old man identify the
properties.

The search had started early in the morning, and had
been going on for almost eight hours, and Cheng had
insisted on answering every call himself, pausing only

to drink cups of chrysanthemum tea, and once he ate a small bowl of plain white rice. Ng would insist that he rest soon. This was only the first wave; every building was to be visited three times to speak to all the doormen who usually worked eight-hour shifts. There was no point in just speaking to the men on the morning shift when the gweilo might have been seen late at night. A half-hearted search was worse than no search at all.

He heard footsteps behind him and then Cheng was at his shoulder, face grave.

'They have found him?' said Ng.

'They have found your brother. He is dead, Kin-ming.'

Ng had expected as much but the news still hit him hard. He tightened his hands into fists and slammed them against his thighs, cursing in English. Cheng put his hand on his shoulder.

'Where?' asked Ng.

'Hebe Haven,' said Cheng. 'He had been chained to the anchor of one of the yachts there.'

'He drowned?'

'Yes. And his wrist had been cut. It seems as if your brother tried to escape in the only way he could. He tried to cut off his own hand.'

'Oh no,' muttered Ng. 'No, no, no. Who found him?'

'The owner of the yacht, about half an hour ago. In a way it was fortunate, not many take their boats out during the week. At least we know that he is dead.'

Ng nodded. 'Fortunate is a strange term to use, but I know what you mean, Master Cheng. Can we keep this a secret?'

'I am afraid not, the police are there now. Our men at Sai Kung say they have stopped checking the boats, for a while at least. There are police everywhere and it would not be wise for our men to attract attention to themselves. I told them to withdraw, they can continue again tomorrow.'

'You are right, of course,' said Ng. 'Besides, the gweilo is unlikely to be keeping Sophie so close to where he killed my brother.'

The two men stood together, looking at the mist-shrouded hills of Kowloon. To their left a peacock shrieked as if in pain.

'You must tell your father, Kin-ming.'

'I know, Master Cheng, I know. I will also go and tell Jill. She will not take it well.'

'Neither of them will take it well. Your father is at your mother's grave,' said Cheng, and walked back into the house. The phone rang again.

Ng slowly climbed the eighty-eight steps up to where his father was, his hands dead at his side. The old man was sitting on one of the stools under the pagoda where they had sat together the previous day. This time, however, he had his back to the harbour and his eyes were on the stone dome. He turned to look at Ng as he reached the top and stood there, breathing heavily and not just because of the climb. Their eyes met and the old man knew at once.

'He is dead?' he said quietly.

'He is dead,' repeated Ng, tears stinging his eyes. 'Father, we must get the man who did it. We must, we must, we must.' The words degenerated into a series of sobs as the tears spilled down his cheeks.

'We will, Kin-ming. I promise you we will. Come and sit with me.' His voice was unsteady and he held out his hand towards Ng, palm upward like a beggar pleading for change.

'At least the budget runs to separate rooms,' said Edmunds. He was standing in Feinberg's room in the Victoria Hotel watching a hydrofoil set out for Macau.

'Too right – sleeping with you would cramp my style a bit,' said Feinberg as he flicked through the television channels. 'You hungry?'

'I guess so.'

'We might as well hit one of the hotel restaurants. It's what, four o'clock now? I say we shower, eat, and then hit the bars. We'd better change our money here, and for God's sake keep the receipts. Hamilton said he'd reimburse us but it's not to be done through official channels. And we're not to make contact with the local office.'

'No back up? No support? And our handler eight thousand miles away? It doesn't feel right, Rick.'

'Piece of cake,' said Feinberg. 'And Greg Hamilton is a good guy to keep in with. He's on the fast track and I could go a long way with him.'

Edmunds noticed how the young agent had slipped from the plural into the singular but he was past the stage of being annoyed by petty politics. If Feinberg wanted to jump a few rungs on his career ladder that was up to him. As for Edmunds, he'd long ago resigned himself to not going any higher within the CIA. He hadn't kissed the right arses and he'd been involved in too many dirty operations to ever be allowed a high-powered administrative position. In fact, during his more morose moods he sometimes worried about exactly what would happen to him, whether or not the CIA would actually allow him to retire and collect his pension. He knew where too many bodies were buried. He'd started taking precautions about five years earlier and compiled a diary of some of the murkier episodes of his career on a Macintosh computer and given three floppy disks to his younger brother in Chicago and sworn him to secrecy. Edmunds wasn't sure if it would do him any good, or if it was paranoia in the first place, but it made him feel a little more secure. He knew plenty of CIA operatives who'd taken early retirement and joined private detective agencies or joined law firms or even just opened a bar, but he was also aware of a few who had disappeared on missions that were, as Feinberg would have described them, pieces of cake. Edmunds had only three years to go before he could retire on full pension and spend more time with his wife and he was determined to make it. Like the short-timers in Vietnam he was starting to count the days before he would be back in The World, and that, he knew, made him vulnerable.

Feinberg sat on the bed and opened the telephone book. 'Police,' he said in reply to his partner's raised eyebrows.

Feinberg identified himself as a reporter with the *International Herald Tribune* and asked for the duty officer, eventually got through to someone who could speak English and again said he was a reporter.

'Anything new on the double murder at the Hilton?' he asked and was told there wasn't. 'What about the Brit who was shot? Has he turned up yet?' Again he was told no. Feinberg thanked the officer and hung up.

'Power of the Press,' he said. 'Howells is still on the loose. If he was in hospital they'd have him now. I feel lucky about this. Which side of the harbour do you want, Kowloon or Wan Chai?'

Edmunds shrugged. 'I'm easy.'

'OK, I'll take Kowloon. It's been a few years since I've been to Red Lips and Bottoms Up.' He passed the faxed picture of Howells over to Edmunds and said: 'Can you get a decent photocopy of that? It's pretty sharp so it should reproduce OK. I'm going to take a shower; I'll meet you downstairs in the lobby in half an hour.'

Edmunds agreed, though he was far from happy.

Dugan grabbed at the door handle of the taxi a second before the leather-jacketed Chinese youth who had raced across the road in an attempt to beat him to it. When Dugan pulled the door open the guy tried to slip into the back seat but Dugan side-stepped to block his way.

'Fuck your mother, gweilo pig,' the man cursed in Cantonese.

Dugan grinned at him as he got into the cab. 'Your mother was too ugly but your sister screwed like a rabbit,' Dugan shouted back in Chinese and slammed the door shut.

'Wah! Good Cantonese,' said the driver in admiration as he slammed the taxi into gear and drove off. 'Where to?'

When Dugan told him that they were going to the New Territories the driver began to whine. The tunnel traffic was too heavy at this time of night, it'd take almost an hour to get across the harbour and then he'd have to come back and he was supposed to be finishing his shift soon and had to hand the cab over to his replacement in Tin Hau. Please would the honourable gentleman mind switching over to a Kowloon taxi?

Dugan was too tired to argue, and it was such a long trip there was no point in going with an unenthusiastic driver. There were several unofficial ranks on the island where taxis from Kowloon waited to pick up passengers who wanted to cross the harbour. The driver took Dugan to a petrol station opposite the Excelsior Hotel where there were three taxis waiting, their roof lights on but with red cards covering the meter flags bearing the two Chinese characters Gow Lung, meaning Nine Dragons, the Cantonese name for the area which the British had transliterated to Kowloon.

The driver thanked Dugan profusely and drove off into the dusk. Dugan got into one of the Kowloon taxis and this time he met with no resistance when he said he wanted to go to the New Territories. They pulled out of the garage forecourt and forced their way into the queue of traffic edging its way to the tunnel entrance.

Dugan sat back and closed his eyes, massaging his temples with the palms of his hands. During the course of the afternoon he'd tried several times to get through to Jill, but without success, and he'd decided that the only way to find out for sure what was going on was to go round in person. It was a bitch of a taxi journey but the MTR didn't go anywhere near Ng's house and Dugan's salary barely covered his mortgage payments, never mind a car. They crawled along for the best part of half an hour before Dugan saw the tunnel mouth. They picked up speed once they were under the bright fluorescent lights and the tyres were singing on the road surface. The cars erupted from the end of the tunnel like water from a shower head, spraying out to pay their tolls at the line of booths where the money collectors were wearing white surgical masks to filter out the worst of the exhaust fumes, and then accelerating again, the harbour at their backs.

Dugan still wasn't sure what he'd say to Jill, or to Simon Ng if he was there. He would protect Petal, of that he was certain, but he would have to warn his brother-in-law that his life was in danger. He could tell them about the gweilo who had been attacked in the Hilton Hotel and tell Ng that the police had learnt that the man had been planning to attack him. He'd just have to be vague about the whys and wherefores and hope that the fact that the family would be on guard would keep them immune from harm. Assuming that is that they hadn't been harmed already. What was it Petal had said? She was to be the back-up, the second line of attack if the first failed, and that she thought that maybe the man Howells was the real assassin. He could tell them about Howells, but Petal's involvement would remain a secret.

He was so busy rehearsing in his mind what he was going to say that he missed the turn-off to the Ng compound and he leant forward and tapped the driver on the shoulder.

'We have to go back,' he said, and gestured the way they'd come.

'OK, OK,' said the driver, and he slowed the taxi and

did a reasonable approximation of a three-point turn. Dugan pointed at the side-road which angled off into the woods and the driver headed up it, switching his headlights on for the first time. He drove at full pelt up the track and had to slam on the brakes when he saw the barrier and its warning sign. The tyres squealed angrily and two men came out of the gatehouse before the car had even stopped. Dugan didn't recognize them but they were typical Red Pole thugs, wide shoulders, casual clothes and expensive jewellery; they were chewing gum and their hands swung at their sides as they walked. One of them approached Dugan's window and he wound it down, allowing the hot evening air to balloon into the cab. He could feel beads of sweat forming on his forehead almost immediately.

'Private road. You must go back,' the man said in English. He had a portable phone in his hand. His partner kept some distance away from the car and seemed to put a lot of effort into adjusting the buttons of his cotton jacket. There was probably a gun under it but Dugan wasn't on official business and under the circumstances he wasn't going to make an issue of it.

In Cantonese Dugan explained that he was Simon Ng's brother-in-law and that he wanted to go up to the house. The guard shook his head emphatically.

'Nobody home. You must go,' he said, still in English. He turned to the driver and switched to Cantonese, saying: 'Take the gweilo prick to wherever he came from or it will be the worse for you.' The driver grunted and put the taxi into reverse. Dugan flung the door open and got one foot on to the ground before the guard put his weight against it and tried to slam it shut on Dugan's leg. Dugan resisted and kicked it open with his other leg, knocking the guard off balance. Dugan grabbed him by the neck of his shirt and pushed him against a tree.

'Listen, you prick, don't you dare threaten me again or I'll stuff your balls down your throat. Understand?' He edged his forearm up under the man's chin and forced his head back so that it scraped against the bark. He tried to nod but the pressure on his throat stopped him so he groaned and blinked. The second guard began shouting at Dugan in English. 'Let him go! Let him go!' Dugan swung round, keeping his grip on the first guard so that he formed a barrier between them.

'Keep your fucking hands away from your jacket or I'll break this pig's neck,' Dugan warned and tightened his grip. The second guard looked confused, reached his hands up and then dropped them, then took a step forward.

'And don't move, just listen,' shouted Dugan. The taxi driver had stopped to watch, but he had a pretty good idea what was going on and didn't want to be around when this stupid gweilo got the shit kicked out of him so he began reversing down the track.

The second guard reached inside his jacket and pulled out a gun and held it unsteadily with his right hand, trying to aim at Dugan's head. Dugan kept moving from side to side, keeping his captive in front of him. He squeezed his neck tighter, wanting to keep him quiet but not so much that he'd pass out. He was fairly stocky and Dugan doubted if he could hold him up if the guard's legs collapsed.

'Listen to me,' said Dugan, speaking in Cantonese but speaking slowly, not because he wasn't fluent but because most Chinese couldn't get used to the fact that he could speak it; they just saw his white face and assumed that whatever language came out of his mouth would be English. 'I am Simon Ng's brother-in-law. Jill Ng is my sister. It is important that I speak to him.'

The guard with the gun kept it pointing at Dugan's head. 'We tell you already, he not here,' he said in halting English, refusing to acknowledge that Dugan spoke Cantonese.

'Can you reach him?' Dugan began backing away, step by step, trying to get a tree in between them. His prisoner's chest began to heave in spasms so he released the pressure, just a fraction.

The man shook his head.

'Look, I'm with the police. And I'm a good friend of Simon Ng's. That's two fucking good reasons why you can't shoot me. You put the gun away and I'll let go of your friend. Deal?'

'You let go first, then I put gun away,' said the guard. Dugan didn't trust him one bit, and he guessed that it was mutual.

He pressed his mouth close to his prisoner's ear. 'Throw him the phone,' he hissed. He did as he was told and it fell on the grass by the guard's feet. 'OK, listen to this. Call Simon Ng now and tell him I want to speak to him.'

Dugan could see by the confusion on the man's face that something was wrong and he realized suddenly what it was. Ng was already dead. Oh sweet Jesus, what about Jill?

'Where is my sister?' he yelled.

The guard pointed the gun up at the compound. 'She is in the house,' he admitted.

Dugan thought frantically. 'Who is the Dragon Head now?' he asked. The man remained stubbornly silent and aimed the gun at Dugan again.

Dugan was half-hidden by the tree now, and he leant against it for support. His prisoner wriggled but he swiftly yanked his arm tighter round his neck and the movement stopped. Dugan's arm was starting to throb and his elbow screamed in pain.

'Call Thomas Ng,' Dugan shouted. 'Tell him Pat Dugan is here and that I want to talk to him.'

The guard looked hesitant but eventually he knelt down and picked up the phone. He tried pressing the buttons while holding the gun but couldn't manage it so he tucked the gun under his arm while he dialled. Dugan couldn't hear what he was saying but after a few sentences the man held the phone out to Dugan. 'Throw it,' said Dugan. It landed at his feet and he pushed the guard he was holding forward towards the road and grabbed the phone before ducking back behind the tree.

The two guards stood together, his former prisoner massaging his throat. Dugan's right arm had practically gone to sleep so he held the phone to his ear with his left hand.

'It's Dugan here. Is that you, Thomas?'

'Patrick, my old friend. How are you?' There was not a trace of Chinese accent left in Thomas Ng's cultured American voice. They had met several times since the huge wedding almost a decade earlier, but calling him an old friend was pushing it a bit far. Dugan had never really liked him. Simon Ng had always been up front about what he did, take it or leave it, but his brother was always trying to pretend to be a legitimate businessman, acting as if the family fortune was based on hard work, initiative and enterprise rather than on extortion, prostitution and drugs. You knew where you were with the man Jill had married but Thomas was harder to read and Dugan had always kept away from him.

'Thomas, I heard you were back.'

'You should be a detective,' laughed Ng, but it was a harsh metallic sound as if knives were being sharpened.

'Yeah, very funny,' said Dugan, keeping a wary eye on the two thugs. They were whispering to each other but at least the gun was now directed at the ground rather than at his head. 'Look, have you called off your dogs?'

'They won't hurt you, Patrick, don't worry.'

'Hey, I'm not worried. I just didn't want to damage them,' replied Dugan, but he didn't feel anywhere near as cocky as he sounded. Whistling in the dark. 'They're trying to stop me talking to Jill.'

'They are protecting her.'

'From her own brother?'

'We are not sure what we are protecting her from.'

'Presumably from the man who killed Simon.' Ng didn't say anything. 'Simon is dead, then?' pressed Dugan.

'You haven't heard? I'd have thought the police would have told you already,' said Ng.

'Nobody is telling me anything at the moment, Thomas. What happened?'

'It's a long story, Patrick. Come round and we'll talk.'

'Where are you?'

'Golden Dragon Lodge. My father's house.'

'I know it. But I want to see Jill first.'

'I understand. Let me speak to my men again and I will

371

tell them to take you to her. But I must warn you that she is being sedated at the moment. Her husband has been killed . . .'

'Don't worry, I'll be gentle with her,' interrupted Dugan.

'Let me finish,' continued Ng coldly. 'There's something you don't know. Sophie has been kidnapped. At the moment we don't know if she is alive or dead.'

The news stunned Dugan. He didn't know what to say.

'Are you still there?' asked Ng.

'I'm here. I'm here. Christ almighty! Look, I'll be right over after I've seen Jill. Can you get your men to lend me a car? They've scared off my taxi already.'

'They'll drive you,' said Ng. 'Put them on.'

Dugan popped his head around the tree again. The gun had gone back inside the guard's jacket so he stepped out and handed over the phone.

'He wants to talk to you,' he said in Cantonese.

'Thank you,' said the armed guard, in English, and took the phone. After listening and muttering a few words he led Dugan up the track to the black iron gates where half a dozen more guards were standing, two of them with machine guns. Artillery like that was very unusual in Hong Kong, most triad soldiers stuck to knives and hatchets and when they did resort to firearms it was usually handguns. They opened the gate and two of the guards escorted Dugan to the house. Dugan rang the doorbell and it was opened by a Filipina maid whose name he couldn't remember.

'I'm Mrs Ng's brother, can you tell her I'm here please.'

'Mrs Ng is not to be disturbed, sir,' said the maid, her lower lip trembling.

'It's OK,' said Dugan. 'I've already spoken to Thomas Ng and he has said it's OK.'

The magic words 'Thomas Ng' seemed to do the trick and she stepped to one side to allow him in.

'I'll get her for you, sir,' said the maid, turning to go up the stairs.

'No, that's all right. I'll see myself up. Is she in the main bedroom?'

'No, sir, she's sleeping in Sophie's bedroom.'

Dugan left her at the bottom of the stairs and went up alone. He found Jill curled up on a single brass bed with pink sheets and pillowcases, cuddling the dog he'd bought for Sophie. On the bedside table was an empty brandy glass and a bottle containing green tablets. She moved in her sleep when he sat down on the bed and put his hand on her shoulder. She moaned and squeezed the dog, hugging it close and rubbing it with her nose. She looked terrible, her face drawn and pale, dark shadows round her eyes and puffy bags under them, lips cracked and dry. For a moment a picture of Petal lying in the hospital bed flashed through his mind; two girls that he loved, both of them normally so pretty and vibrant, both so full of life, both reduced to shells by the man called Howells, beating one almost to death, killing the husband of the other.

'Jill,' he said quietly. 'Are you awake?'

She murmured something and a hand appeared from under the sheet and brushed a lock of damp hair across her lined forehead. He called her name and her eyes opened slightly.

'Simon?'

'It's me, kid, it's Pat,' said Dugan, leaning forward and stroking her tear-stained cheek.

'Oh Pat, Pat,' she moaned and then she closed her eyes and slept again. Dugan tenderly put her arm back under the sheet and switched off the light before closing the door. On the way out he handed the bottle of tablets to the maid.

'Be careful with them,' he warned. 'Give them to her one at a time, and only if she asks for them. Whatever you do, do not leave them by her bed. Do you understand?'

She nodded and put the bottle in a small pocket in the front of her apron.

Outside two of Ng's men were waiting in a blue Mercedes, the engine running.

After visiting his third Wan Chai bar Edmunds had put together a workable model of the Jack Edmunds Theory of Economic Development as Related to Bars – the poorer a country the cheaper the booze and the younger the girls.

The cab had dropped him at a set of traffic lights on Lockhart Road and he'd gone first into the San Francisco Bar, followed by Popeye's and the Country Club. The layout varied but the music and the prices of the booze were the same, and the girls all had bored looks as if they'd rather be somewhere else, with someone else, doing something else. In each of the bars Edmunds had allowed himself to be shown to a stool and had sat there with a whisky on the rocks. Not one of the three stocked Jack Daniels and occasionally he grimaced as he drank.

Within seconds of his drink arriving he was joined by one of the hostesses with slackly-applied lipstick and bad breath, smiling like a simpleton and asking him his name, his job, how long he'd been in Hong Kong and if he would buy her a drink. In each case he lied to the first three questions and said yes to the last, which earned him an even bigger smile, usually one showing yellowed teeth encrusted with plaque, and twenty minutes of what passed for conversation.

Edmunds waited until they hit him for a second drink before he began to talk about his good friend Geoff, how he was supposed to meet him in one of the bars but couldn't remember which, and then he'd hand over the black-and-white picture and ask if she'd seen him. Three times he showed the picture and three times they'd said no. The women had all been keen to help and had passed the picture around for their friends to examine, but nobody remembered seeing Howells. It was a long shot, Edmunds knew that, but he also knew that Feinberg was right, a wounded man on the run in a hostile environment had few options, and they lost nothing by looking. They might even get lucky. Once he'd drawn a blank Edmunds would gather up his bill and the chits from the plastic beaker in front of him and ask for the check, paying in cash. Both he and Feinberg had changed a stack of traveller's cheques in the hotel before going their separate ways.

The Washington Club was the fourth bar Edmunds tried. As three others had done before him, the doorman jumped off his stool and held the velvet curtain open for Edmunds, waving him inside and promising 'many girls, full show.' A fattish woman in a too-tight black dress who barely came up to his shoulder gripped him by the arm and

STEPHEN LEATHER

virtually frog-marched him to an empty stool. Edmunds ordered a Jack Daniels, and received a confused look so he asked for a whisky instead.

'Whisky Coke,' said the woman, and walked away.

'No, whisky with ice,' he called after her but she didn't seem to have heard. What the hell, he was in no mood to drink it anyway. He looked around the bar but it had little to distinguish it from the ones he'd already visited, except for a large fish tank by the door. A boy barely out of his teens was admiring his crew cut in his reflection, smoothing it and patting it down. One of the fish was dying, swimming on its side and sinking to the bottom each time it stopped waving its fins. One of its bigger companions was nudging it, or biting it, Edmunds couldn't tell which.

A short girl, with an impish brown face and short black hair in a pageboy cut and wearing a lime-green cheongsam appeared next to him and smiled up at him, head on one side.

'Good evening,' said Edmunds, and motioned for her to take the stool next to his.

'You American?' she asked.

'Yeah, do you want a drink?'

'Thanks,' she said and gave her order to one of the women behind the bar.

'You're not Chinese, are you?' he said.

She pulled a face as if she had a sour taste in her mouth. 'Filipina,' she said. Edmunds chatted with her for the best part of an hour, during the course of which she racked up four blue chits in the tumbler in front of him. She seemed to enjoy herself, laughing at his jokes and asking question after question about his life, ninety per cent of which he answered with lies; but every time the curtain was pulled back to admit another punter her eyes flicked to the door. She was always alert, and Edmunds knew that as soon as he paid his bill and left she'd be by someone else's side.

He started telling her about his friend Geoff and took the black-and-white picture out of his jacket pocket and showed it to her.

'Have you seen him?' he asked.

She studied it carefully and said no, she hadn't. Edmunds wondered how many customers she fleeced in a night and how many she remembered ten minutes after they'd stepped out of the bar. He asked her if she'd show the picture to her friends and she went from girl to girl, mostly getting quick uninterested shakes of the head, occasionally pointing to him.

Edmunds pretended not to look but as he toyed with his tumbler of adulterated whisky his attention was focused on the girl and the reaction she was getting. He struck gold when she had gone to the far side of the bar, directly opposite where he was sitting. She handed the picture to a young Chinese girl with sleek black hair that curled above her shoulders, a small silver brooch at the neck of a peach-coloured blouse. She was talking to an overweight balding man in a cheap grey suit, laughing with her hand over her mouth, but when she saw the picture her lips closed like steel gates slamming shut. She glared at the Filipina and although he couldn't hear them over the pulsing beat of the dance music he guessed that she was demanding to know where the picture had come from. He looked down as the Filipina pointed and then checked them out in a long mirror above one of the booths. The Chinese girl's eyes narrowed as she studied him across the bar and then she began to question the Filipina.

Edmunds looked at her as she glared down at the shorter girl, hands on her hips. The Filipina kept shaking her head and then the Chinese girl put a hand on her shoulder and spoke to her. Edmunds could see the urgency on her face, and he wasn't in the least bit surprised when she came back and said that none of the girls could remember seeing the man in the bar. Edmunds put the picture back in his jacket pocket and thanked her anyway.

'Why don't you give me your card and write down where you're staying and I'll give it to him if he comes in,' said the Filipina, and Edmunds was one hundred per cent certain then.

'No,' he said. 'No point. I'm leaving Hong Kong tomorrow. I'll catch Geoff next time.' He yawned and stretched. 'I'd better be going,' he said.

'What hotel are you staying at?'

'Hilton,' he lied. 'Can you get me the check, please?'

She didn't seem as friendly now; there was an edge to her voice and a wall behind her eyes, but the smile was still there and she swung her hips as she went over to the cashier. Edmunds suddenly realized just how much he missed his wife. He wanted to be back home with her, sharing a bed with her, no matter how cold it was.

He paid the bill and walked through the curtain out into the hot night air. A couple of hundred yards down the road he flagged down a taxi and got into the back.

'How's your English?' he asked the driver.

'English or American?' he replied with a grin.

'You'll do,' said Edmunds. He opened his wallet and

handed the man two $500 notes. 'I want to hire you for the rest of the night.'

The driver took the notes and examined them under the dashboard lights. 'Where do you want to go?' he said suspiciously.

'At the moment, nowhere,' he said. 'Drive a little way down the road and park. I'm waiting for someone.'

The red doors swung open as the Mercedes approached, and the twin headlights cut through the night, swerving from side to side as they drove up the path to the double garage and parked. The two men escorted Dugan up the steps and over the wooden bridge to the house. The stone dragon scowled at him, illuminated by hidden spotlights under the water, and he scowled back.

Thomas Ng was waiting for him in front of the house and they went inside together. Two men, one old and one young, were sitting at a large desk in the centre of the main reception room, drawing lines on large maps.

'Do you want a drink?' asked Ng, and Dugan shook his head. Ng took him through into the room where only twenty-four hours earlier the triad leaders had pledged their loyalty to Ng Wai-sun. All trace of the ceremony had been removed, now it was a family room once more. Even the lamps had been taken away and the room was now illuminated by the electric lights set into antique brass fittings around the room. Ng sat down at the circular table and told rather than asked Dugan to sit down. Dugan took a seat three away from where Ng sat. He didn't like the way Ng was trying to dominate him so he decided to go on the offensive.

'What the fuck's going on?' he asked.

'My brother is dead,' said Ng. 'And whoever did it still has Sophie, though at the moment we don't know if Sophie is alive or dead.'

'What happened?'

Ng told him how Sophie had been abducted from her school, how the gweilo had demanded a ransom, and how instead of taking the money he had taken Simon Ng instead, and left him to die handcuffed to the anchor of a yacht at Hebe Haven.

'And what happens now?' asked Dugan.

'Now we find the gweilo. And then we find Sophie. We know what he looks like. We have a photograph. We have men at all the ports and at Kai Tak, and we are now searching every block in Hong Kong.'

'Every block in Hong Kong?' said Dugan, surprised. 'You don't have enough men.'

'We do now,' said Ng, but he didn't elaborate.

'It'll be like finding a needle in a haystack,' said Dugan.

'Not at all,' said Ng. 'There are fewer than six million people here, and ninety-eight per cent are Chinese. There is a finite size to this haystack, Patrick, and the needle is different enough to make it clearly visible. It is just a matter of time.'

'Do you know who he is? Or why he killed Simon?'

'No,' said Ng. He did not trust the gweilo cop enough to tell him about his brother's contact with the mainland or the fact that he had begun spying for them. What he wanted from Patrick Dugan was information about how the police were getting on with their investigation. Nothing more.

'If you catch him, what are you planning to do with him?'

'First we will get him to tell us where Sophie is. Then we will ask him why he attacked our family.'

'And then?'

Ng smiled coldly. 'We are not planning to hand him over to the police, if that is what you mean.'

'I suppose not,' said Dugan. He sat with his elbows on the table and ran his hands through his hair. God, it was hot. His hair was damp with sweat and he could feel it running down the back of his neck and soaking into his shirt. Why didn't Ng switch the air-conditioner on?

As if reading his mind Ng said: 'I am sorry about the heat. My father doesn't believe in air-conditioning.'

'Is he here?'

'Upstairs. Polishing his jade, he said, but really he just wants to be alone. He is not a man to share his grief.'

'He has caused enough in his time,' said Dugan bitterly.

'Now is not the time for that,' answered Ng.

'I suppose not,' said Dugan. He looked at Ng, his jaw set tight. He had to help Jill and that meant helping Ng catch the gweilo so that they could get Sophie back, but he was worried about how far he would have to go. He had little loyalty to the police force that had treated him so badly because of his brother-in-law, that wasn't what was troubling him. What was playing on his mind was Petal and what would happen to her if Ng found out that she would have killed Simon Ng if the gweilo had failed. He breathed out, long and deeply, and looked at Ng.

'His name is Howells. Geoff Howells.'

Ng looked shocked. 'The police know who did it? Already?'

'There's more,' said Dugan. 'He's been shot. Somebody tried to kill him in his hotel room at the Hilton. They shot him but he got away.'

Ng stood up and walked up and down the room, past the lines of photographs.

'Do you know why?'

'Why they shot him? No. Nor do the police. Two Chinese guys were behind it. Robbery maybe.' He knew that it didn't sound too convincing, and he knew too that Ng would have his own informers within the police. Hopefully, if he told him as much as he could he'd be too busy going after Howells to bother checking up on what actually happened in the hotel room and that there had been a girl there, a pretty girl with jet-black hair and soft lips.

'When?'

'Last night. He killed the two men and got away before the police arrived. They've put a stop on him at the airport but as they don't know what he looks like they think he might get out using a false passport. They don't know that you have his picture. But they are checking all the hospitals and doctors. They don't think he's going anywhere without medical treatment.'

Ng laughed. 'The police are stupid,' he said. 'Do they imagine he will just walk into a Government hospital with a bullet wound? This man, this Geoff Howells, is a professional killer, an assassin.'

'So what do you think he will do?'

'If he does need medical attention he will get it from

an underground doctor, one without the necessary qualifications to practise legally, from the mainland perhaps. They are not too difficult to find.'

'If they are not difficult to find, then the police will find them too.'

'There is a big difference between finding them and getting them to talk. Such men have no reason to tell the police anything. But they will tell us.'

'I bet,' said Dugan. 'I just bet they will.'

Ng sat down again. 'There is one thing I do not understand. How do they know this man Howells killed my brother?'

That was the question Dugan had been hoping Ng wouldn't ask, because for the life of him he didn't know what to say because as things stood at the moment the police had no way of connecting Howells with the death of Simon Ng; that connection had come from Petal.

'I don't know,' Dugan lied. 'They won't let me anywhere near a murder investigation, you know that. I'm stuck in Commercial Crime. I only got the information second-hand, but it's kosher.'

'I'm sure it is,' said Ng. 'Look Patrick, what you've told me is going to be a big help, a really big help. But can you do me a favour? Will you keep tabs on the police end for me, and if anything comes up, let me know?'

'Sure,' said Dugan, and he practically sighed with relief. If he wanted him to act as a source of information on the investigation into Howells then the chances were that he wouldn't start asking anyone else. So long as they depended on him to keep them informed then he could make sure Petal stayed out of it.

'I want something in return,' Dugan added. 'I want to

be in on this. I want to be there when you catch him. And I want to help get Sophie back.'

'You will be more use to us staying at work and keeping tabs on the investigation,' said Ng.

'I can do that on the phone. I want to help,' insisted Dugan.

Ng looked at Dugan thoughtfully, weighing him up, and then nodded.

'OK, Patrick, I don't see why not. So long as I have your word that nothing you see or hear will ever be used against us, as you cops are so fond of saying.'

'To be honest, I think my days with the police are almost over anyway,' said Dugan. 'But I'm not switching sides. I'm doing it for Jill, and for Sophie.' And for Petal, he thought. Especially for Petal.

'I'll have a room made up for you upstairs,' said Ng. 'We're controlling the search from here. I'll get on to the men and tell them that we are now looking for a man who has been shot. There is also an outside chance that he will call again about Sophie. If he does he'll call Simon's house and the call will be transferred here. Either way all we can do now is wait.'

'I'll wait,' said Dugan. 'I'll wait for ever,' he added as Ng left the room.

Edmunds had thought he'd have to wait until closing time before Amy went home, and he almost missed her when she came out of the Washington Club at about two o'clock in the morning. She looked different in her jeans and leather bomber-jacket. Younger. He knew that his visit to the bar and Howells' picture had upset her and she was in a hurry to warn him but even so he'd assumed that the mamasan would have made her stay until the end of the shift, and he knew from asking the girls that they didn't shut their doors until after four o'clock.

She waved goodnight to the doorman and stood at the side of the road and hailed a taxi. Edmunds kept his head down until her cab drove off and then he pointed after it.

'Follow that taxi,' he said.

'Like in the movies?' said the driver.

'Yeah, just like the movies. Hurry up before you lose them.'

The driver laughed and jerked the car away from the kerb. There was something hanging from the driver's mirror, a sort of upturned horseshoe, a gold-coloured ingot hanging beneath it, and below that brass rings tied to a red cord that swung back and forth with the motion of the cab. Every thirty seconds or so it emitted a couple of bars of disjointed metallic music. Edmunds had no idea what purpose it served, whether it was religious or just to bring good luck, but it was as annoying as hell. The roads were fairly clear and they had no trouble keeping the taxi in sight as it headed towards the harbour and through the tunnel. More than half the vehicles on the road were red and grey taxis so Edmunds knew that there was no chance of their being spotted and he relaxed a little.

The traffic was thicker in Kowloon and Edmunds' cab moved closer, leaving just two or three cars between it and the one they were following. They passed by the airport, its runway lights switched off, and then they burrowed through a maze of housing and commercial blocks, until they were the only two cars on the road and Edmunds told his driver to drop back. Eventually their quarry stopped and they waited at a distance while Amy paid her fare and got out of the cab. She walked to the entrance of a grimy, soot-stained building, shops with their shutters down on the ground floor, a dozen floors of flats above with tiny metal-framed windows, some with clay plant-pots standing ill at ease on fragile-looking wrought-iron balconies that appeared to have been tacked on to the outsides of the flats as an afterthought.

'Wait here,' said Edmunds, and he opened the door quietly and ran down the road to the building where she had entered. The metal gate at the entrance was not locked and though it was rusting and the purple paint was peeling off it opened easily. An old man in a white vest that had seen better days was slumped over a wooden table, snoring and spluttering in his dreams.

Edmunds slipped past him. A quick look round confirmed that there was no lift so he headed up the stone stairs on the balls of his feet, pausing at each turn to check that the next flight was clear. He moved quickly up to the second floor but then he heard her footsteps and he began to move more slowly. She passed the third floor and by then he was one flight behind her and breathing with his mouth wide open and taking extra care whenever he put his feet down. When she got to the fourth floor he heard her open her handbag and heard metal jingling as she took out her keys. As he heard the key being slotted into the lock he risked a quick look around the stairwell and saw her push open the door. He ducked back, his heart pounding in his ears, but she hadn't seen him; he waited until he heard her step across the threshold and then ran up to the door and followed her inside, grabbing her shoulder and pressing his hand across her mouth.

Before she could scream or struggle he hissed: 'It's all right. I'm not going to hurt you, or him. Do you understand?'

She nodded, her eyes wide with fear, but she didn't look as if she was going to struggle so Edmunds slowly took his hand away.

'Where is he?' he asked.

She looked at the bedroom door, her reflexes taking over, so Edmunds didn't wait for an answer. Amy followed him in. Howells was asleep, lying on his front.

'How badly is he hurt?' asked Edmunds, keeping his voice low. Howells came awake immediately and began rolling off the bed, hands moving to fighting position, ignoring the pain. Edmunds stepped back, holding his arms out to the side, showing he was unarmed. 'I'm here to talk, Howells, that's all. Back off.'

Howells carried on moving, oblivious to the fact that he was stark naked. He looked behind Edmunds to the room beyond, and then when he saw that the man was alone side-stepped across to the doorway so that he was between him and the exit. His face was calm and relaxed, the same as it was when Edmunds had last seen him, when he had killed three people and saved his life. Howells had no weapon but if the file was right then he didn't need one – even with a bullet wound he'd still be fast and strong enough. He knew his own limitations and hand-to-hand combat with someone almost half his age was one of them, unless Howells was a lot weaker than he looked.

'Who are you?' Howells asked, his voice rock-steady, his feet evenly spaced on the wooden floor, toes digging in for balance, heels up ready to move fast, hands poised to strike. The bandage was on his right shoulder so Edmunds knew that if the attack came it would be from Howells' left side so he drew back his right leg, ready to block with his own left hand, shifting position slowly so it wouldn't alarm the Brit. One of the first things they taught you about interrogation was that when you take away a man's clothes you take away his confidence and his identity, but Howells was no less of a killer naked, and it was the American, clothes and all, who was the more nervous.

'Edmunds. Jack Edmunds. CIA.'

'What does the CIA want with me?' His eyes narrowed. 'Do I know you?'

'You saved my life a few years back in the Lebanon,' explained Edmunds, keeping his hands low and avoiding any gesture that could be interpreted as threatening. 'I was being held hostage and the Company was dragging its feet on the ransom.'

'I remember,' said Howells. 'You said you were a businessman.'

Edmunds smiled. 'Yeah, you were a bit slow in identifying yourself. And Americans didn't have friends in too many parts of the world just then. I saw what you did to the three bastards who were guarding me, remember?'

Howells nodded. 'Yeah, you never know who to trust in this business, do you?' He seemed to relax a little. But only a little.

'So you've come all this way to thank me?' Howells asked.

'You wish,' said Edmunds, dropping his hands completely. 'Look, can we sit down and talk about this, you're making me nervous.'

Howells weighed up the American and then shrugged. 'Sure,' he said, turning away and walking into the lounge. He realized for the first time by the way Amy looked at him that he was naked. He opened his mouth to ask her for his trousers but she nodded before he could speak and half ran to a cheap wooden wardrobe and took out his pants and his new shirt. The pants had been washed and pressed. He sat on the sofa and she helped him on with the trousers and then draped the shirt around his shoulders.

'*M goy*,' he said, and she beamed at him.

'*M sai*,' she said. 'Is everything OK?'

'Everything is fine,' he said. 'This man is a friend. Amy, I have to talk with him alone, do you mind?'

She shook her head, eager to please. 'I'll go in the kitchen.' She kissed him on the forehead. 'Do you like coffee or a cup of tea?' she asked Edmunds, who said no, neither. Howells also declined and she left the two men, Howells sitting on the sofa, Edmunds standing by the bedroom door, arms crossed across his stomach.

'Is the bullet out?' asked Edmunds.

'How did you know I'd been shot?' asked Howells quickly. There was no way of telling from the bandage whether he'd been shot, stabbed, burnt or attacked by a swarm of killer bees.

Edmunds began pacing up and down, walking slowly between the bedroom door and the window that over-looked the street below, three paces there, three paces back, his head hung in thought as if he'd forgotten that the Brit was there. Edmunds wasn't one hundred per cent sure just what the hell he was doing alone with the man he'd been sent to kill, but he knew it was something to do with honour, about a debt that deserved to be repaid.

But it was more than that. It was about a lifetime spent doing things he regretted, that made him feel sad and unclean, and that when all of it was behind him and he was retired or dying, he wanted to be able to look back at some things and to think that maybe, just maybe, he'd really done the Right Thing, whatever that was. This man had saved his life; now he was hurt, and it was obvious that he had been betrayed by his own organization. He was a Brit and the CIA operation was being run from London. Maybe that was part of it too, the fact that one day Edmunds might also be betrayed by his own masters and that he'd open his door to a couple of grey-faced men with cold eyes, young men who didn't have bad dreams. Men like Feinberg.

Edmunds continued to pace up and down. Howells sat and watched him, knowing that whatever it was the CIA man wanted, he was no threat. Not just then, anyway. He'd had ample opportunity to take Howells out, so the best thing to do was to let him walk, and talk, in his own time.

Eventually Edmunds seemed to come to a decision; he stopped pacing and stood in front of Howells, linking his fingers and pressing them outwards until the knuckles cracked like breaking bones.

'The man who sent us wants you dead,' Edmunds said quietly.

There were two things Howells wanted to know immediately – who was the man and what did Edmunds mean by us? But he kept quiet, and waited.

'They told us you had killed one of our agents. Is that right?'

'I was doing what I was told to do,' said Howells.

'By who?'

Howells sneered. 'You show me yours and I'll show you mine.'

'I don't freelance,' said Edmunds. 'I'm working for the Company.'

'I haven't done anything that would cut across the CIA,' said Howells.

'What about London?'

'What do you mean?'

'Feinberg said that our operation was being run from London rather than from the States.'

'Feinberg?'

'My partner. And you're lucky it was me that found you first, believe me.'

'How did you find me? The girl?'

'How else? You'd been shot, you couldn't stay in a hotel and you obviously wouldn't want to go near a hospital. You'd have to go to ground, and you needed someone to take care of you.'

'That easy,' mused Howells, looking at the ground. 'Fuck it.'

'Partly luck, partly carelessness,' said Edmunds. 'You should have kept her home.'

'You knew what hotel I was staying at? And you knew I'd been shot?' asked Howells.

Edmunds nodded and Howells knew for sure then that Grey had set him up. But he still couldn't make sense of the sequence of events. First he was attacked by three Chinese, shortly after telephoning London. And then when he'd escaped two CIA agents came after him. What next? The fucking KGB?

'Do you know why?' he asked Edmunds.

'Because of the man you killed, our agent,' said Edmunds.

'Nobody told me he was one of yours,' said Howells. 'I was told he was about to betray one of ours.'

'Life's a bitch,' said Edmunds. 'You never know who to trust.'

'Only yourself,' said Howells.

'Only yourself,' agreed Edmunds.

'So where do we go from here?'

'I go back to the Victoria Hotel and tell Feinberg that I couldn't find you. I owe you one for what happened in the Lebanon. But then we're quits. The rest is up to you. You've got to get out of here, out of this flat and out of Hong Kong. If I can find you so can Feinberg. So can the police.'

'Easier said than done. They're sure to be watching the airport, my passport is fucking useless.'

'You don't need a passport to get on a boat out of here, not if you've got enough money.'

'Yeah, well there's the rub. I've got a few thousand dollars and that's not going to buy me a ticket out of here, is it?'

'That's your problem,' said Edmunds, but as he said it he reached into his back pocket and pulled out his wallet. He gave Howells a handful of notes. 'That's still probably not enough, but it's the best I can do. It's all I can do.'

Howells took the money. 'Thanks, Jack.' He tucked the notes into his own back pocket, using his left hand.

'I'd better go,' said Edmunds. Howells got to his feet unsteadily and called Amy out.

'Jack is going,' he said to Amy. She opened the door for the American and said good night as he left.

'He seems nice,' said Amy as she closed the door and carefully locked it. 'He came to the club and showed your photograph to the girls. I didn't tell him I knew you. I thought perhaps he might want to hurt you. How did he know where I lived? Did y u tell him?'

'No, Amy. I think he must have followed you. But it doesn't matter. He only wants to help me.'

'I thought perhaps he was the man you call Grey.'

Howells looked at her, stunned. He'd never mentioned Grey to her. 'You talked in your sleep,' she explained. 'You were shouting, saying he had betrayed you.'

Howells nodded. 'No, that wasn't Grey. Grey is a man I used to work for. And yes, he is the man who betrayed me. He's the one who had me shot.' He wasn't sure why he was telling her, but part of it was because he was so bitter about the betrayal that he wanted to share it.

'Is Grey a bad man?' she asked.

'Yes. I was very loyal to him, but he wanted to have me killed. He works for the Government in a place called Century House in London.'

Amy slowly repeated the words, Grey and Century House, as she'd memorized the word 'fridge' in the bar.

She sat down on the sofa next to him and rested her head against his shoulder, his good shoulder. 'Can you tell me what is wrong? Can I help?' No and yes, thought Howells. The problem was, how could he get her to help him? And how far would she go?

'I have to go out soon,' he said. 'Jack promised to give me some money so that I can get out of Hong Kong.'

'You can't go out,' she said. 'You are still weak. Let me go.'

He stroked her hair with his left hand, curling it around

his fingers. 'No, I have to go. I won't be long. You can help by making me some sort of sling to support my arm. Do you have some spare material?'

'I'll use one of my old pillowcases,' she said. She went into her bedroom and he heard the sound of a wooden drawer being opened and closed and then she walked through to the kitchen and came back with a plastic-handled butcher's knife that she used to carefully slit it down the seams.

'Help me put the shirt on first,' he said. Together they eased his bad arm through the sleeve and pulled the shirt down, the pain making his eyes water. She folded the cotton material into a triangle and knotted it behind his neck.

'How's that?' she said.

'It's fine. It's really fine,' he said and she smiled.

'Do you want one of the tablets that Dr Wu left you?'

'No, no thanks. They'll only make me sleepy. Maybe later.' She rested her head back on his shoulder and stroked his left thigh. 'Amy?'

'Hmm?'

'Do you have any friends who can get me out of Hong Kong? Secretly?'

She sat upright and looked at him seriously. 'I know somebody who might help you. But he is not a good man. He is a smuggler. I used to work for him.'

He frowned. 'Worked for him? How?'

'I was a, what is the word, a courier?'

'Courier, yes. Carrying what?'

'Drugs sometimes. Sometimes taking gold into Thailand. I didn't do it many times, I wasn't very good at it. I looked too nervous, I always used to feel very sick. I needed the money, Geoff. I didn't do it many times.' It was suddenly important for her to convince Howells that she wasn't a criminal, she didn't want him to think badly of her.

'But the man you worked for, you know how to get in touch with him?'

'Sometimes he goes to Washington Club. But Geoff, he is not a good man. He will want a lot of money.'

He smiled easily and kissed her on her forehead. 'Amy, there's no need to worry. Jack will give me more money later tonight. Can you do me a favour and make me a cup of coffee?'

She smiled again, pleased that she could do something for him. As she went into the kitchen Howells slipped the knife into the sling.

Sophie drank a little water from the tap, scared to take too much because her mother had always warned her against drinking tapwater. She'd done it sometimes and never got sick but her mother always made her drink bottled water. She was ravenous, the thoughts of food crowding out everything else except the fear of what was going to happen to her. Occasionally she'd start to panic when her imagination ran riot – what would happen if the boat caught fire? If it sank? If the man never came back and she starved to death? Once she'd almost gone into a fit, screaming and kicking at the door until she'd collapsed exhausted on the floor. It was hot, so hot that she felt as if she was going to melt. Despite being born in Hong Kong she lived most of her life in an air-conditioned world; her house, school and the family's cars provided a stable environment that protected her from the colony's often stifling heat and humidity. Now, locked in the junk's washroom, she was hot and sweaty and uncomfortable. She couldn't sleep for more than an hour at a time before she'd wake up, gasping for breath, her throat dry and aching. She kept soaking a towel in cold water and rubbing it over her face, sometimes sitting with it draped over her head, enjoying the coolness of it. She tried chewing it slowly to see if that would make the hunger pains go away, but it seemed to make it worse, she could feel her stomach rumbling and groaning. She wished her dog was with her, the one Uncle Patrick had given her, at least then she'd have someone to talk to. But most of all she wanted her mother. And her father. She wanted to go home.

Edmunds was in the shower when the doorbell rang. 'Is that you, Rick?' he yelled above the sound of the water. He grabbed a bathrobe hanging on the back of the door and padded across the carpet. He opened the door and his eyes widened as he saw Howells standing alone in the corridor, his arm in a sling.

'I need your help,' said Howells. 'Can I come in?'

Edmunds stood to one side and let him in. Howells walked over to the window, slowly as if in pain, while Edmunds shut the door.

'You shouldn't have come,' he warned. 'If Feinberg sees you . . .'

'Is he here?'

'Not at the moment.'

'Where is his room?'

Edmunds nodded at an adjoining door next to the bathroom. 'Through there. If I know Feinberg he's having a whale of a time in the bars of Tsim Sha Tsui. But he could be back at any time. You said you wanted help?'

'I need money. I have to get out of Hong Kong. I know someone who can get me out but he'll need money. More money than I have. And it's not as if I can go out and stick up a bank in my present condition, is it?'

Edmunds shivered. He'd tried adjusting the aircon earlier but it had made no difference, and now the combination of cold air and water on his skin chilled him. He took a thick white towel from a metal rack above the bath and began to rub it through his hair. 'How much do you need?'

'Five thousand dollars, US.'

'To go where?'

'That'll get me to the Philippines. I can hide out there for a few months until I'm fit.'

'I don't know how much I've got on me,' said Edmunds. He went to the dressing table and opened the top drawer to get his wallet. Howells came up behind him as he rifled through the traveller's cheques. Edmunds felt rather than saw the arm go across his throat because he was looking down but he lifted his head in time to see the knife being drawn across the throat of his reflection in the mirror, and saw the blood pour down his neck and chest. So much blood, and yet no pain, just a spreading coldness around his throat. He opened his mouth but it felt numb and the wallet dropped from his hands and a red film passed over his eyes. The last thing he saw before the red turned to black was the smiling face of an old Vietnamese man, grinning with chipped and stained teeth, laughing silently as he went to his death.

It wasn't quite light when Rick Feinberg returned to the Victoria Hotel, humming to himself as he paid off his taxi and rode the lift up to his floor. He'd had no luck showing the picture of the Brit in the dozen Kowloon bars he'd visited, but he'd enjoyed himself, chatting up the hostesses and touching them up whenever they'd let him. It didn't come close to Bangkok or Manila, they all kept their clothes on for one thing, and they were a darn sight more hard-faced, but it was still better than drinking in the States. He wondered how Edmunds had got on and thought of banging on his door and waking him up but then in an uncharacteristic gesture of friendship decided that he'd let him sleep instead. The old guy needed all the rest he could get. Feinberg couldn't imagine why a guy as old as Edmunds, he must be fifty-five at least for fuck's sake, was still working as a field agent. He must have got somebody back at Langley mighty pissed at him, or there must be some deep dark secret in his personal file that kept him from going any higher.

He unlocked his door and switched on the light. He'd left his curtains open and he switched the light off again and stood for a while watching the harbour. Even at such a late hour the harbour was busy, with motorized sampans chugging to and fro, a couple of large freighters, stacked

HUNGRY GHOST

high with containers, sounding their horns, a floating crane being nursed along by an ancient tug, and two American frigates bobbing silently at anchor, light bulbs outlining their superstructures.

Watching the black water made Feinberg realize how much he wanted to go to the toilet. The last time he'd taken a piss he'd felt a slight burning sensation, nothing too painful, a slight smarting, but it had been uncomfortable and he wanted to put off going through it again. He hoped it was just something he'd eaten. Please God don't let him have the clap. Or AIDS. If those fucking whores had given him the clap he'd go back to Bangkok and give them hell. They'd asked him to wear a condom but he'd insisted on going without, told them that he didn't wear boots when he went paddling. They hadn't understood and they had tried several times to open a packet and slip one on him but he held one of them face down on the bed and forced himself inside her as she yelled at him in Thai. Once he'd had her the other one gave in without a struggle and when he took them both again a few hours later they didn't even bother asking him. Now he regretted it. Not the fact that he'd taken them to bed, but the fact that he hadn't bothered to wear protection.

Edmunds was so lucky. When he'd been screwing his way around South East Asia the worst you could get would be a dose of VD and a couple of jabs of penicillin would put paid to that. This AIDS business had taken a good deal of the fun out of fucking.

A police launch carving through the water below sounded a blaring siren and drew alongside a fishing boat in the middle of the harbour. As he watched two policemen climb from the launch into the junk

399

he became aware of somebody standing behind him. Reflected in the window was a thin clean-shaven face, short hair and deep-set serious eyes. It was the face in the photograph. Feinberg didn't move. There was no point.

'You're Howells?' he said.

'And you're dead,' said the reflection, and it smiled.

The Red Pole assisting Cheng was asleep, his head on the maps, when the phone rang. The phone had been silent for three hours and Cheng had gone upstairs to rest, to gather his strength for the coming day. Ng was also upstairs, but unlike Cheng he was wide awake, lying fully dressed on his bed. Dugan had taken an upholstered chair out of the house and was sitting in it, deep in thought. The phone made him jump as it shattered the silence.

The boy answered sleepily in Cantonese and then switched to English. He listened and then went running up the stairs, calling for Ng. Dugan walked into the house as Ng came down the stairs, rubbing his forehead. 'The gweilo,' he said to Dugan. The two men stood together as Ng put the receiver to his ear.

'Who are you?' said an English voice.

'Thomas Ng. I am Simon Ng's brother.'

'I tried to speak to Mrs Ng but I was told to ring this number. Is she there?'

'Mrs Ng is not taking any calls. You can talk to me.'

'OK. Then listen to this. I still have the girl, and I am prepared to release her if you do exactly what I tell you. I want thirty-two ounces of gold and I want a quarter of a million US in diamonds – stones, not jewellery. I will call you tomorrow afternoon to tell you when and where you are to hand them over. Do you understand? Thirty-two ounces of gold and $250,000 in diamonds. I will phone this afternoon.'

'I understand,' said Ng, but before he could say anything else the line went dead.

Dugan caught some of the conversation but not all, so Ng repeated it for him.

'What do you think?' asked Ng.

'Did he ask specifically for you to carry the ransom?'

'No. But that might come next time he phones. You think he might be after me?'

'It's possible. We still don't know why he killed Simon. If he asks for you to deliver it then I think we can assume he's after you. Look, I think you should suggest that I hand over the money. There's no way he could want to hurt me.'

Ng nodded thoughtfully. 'I agree,' he said. 'It's good of you, Patrick. It's good of you to help.'

'Sophie's my niece, too,' said Dugan.

Ng put his hand on Dugan's shoulder. 'You'd better get some sleep,' he said.

'I'm OK,' said Dugan. 'I'll stay outside for a while longer.'

Ng Wai-sun appeared at the top of the stairs wearing a dark blue silk kimono and Ng went up to tell him what had happened.

Howells knocked on the door and within seconds Amy was there, a worried frown on her face.

'Is everything all right?' she asked as she let him in.

'Everything's fine,' he said. 'He gave me some money, but I still don't think it'll be enough.'

'Does your arm hurt?'

'It's fine,' he said, sitting on the sofa. 'Can I have a cup of coffee, please?'

'Of course,' she said, and went to the kitchen. While she was out of the room he slipped the knife out of his sling and placed it on the floor, next to the sofa, where she was sure to find it at some point. She'd probably think it had fallen there after she'd cut the pillowcase apart. The knife was spotless now, he'd cleaned it carefully after phoning Simon Ng from Feinberg's hotel room.

He leant back and rested his head. God, he was tired. He closed his eyes and breathed deeply, listening to Amy opening and closing cupboards and the sound of the gas hissing under the kettle. There was no doubt that he was going to need her help later on when he went to collect the ransom. But he was having second thoughts about using her contacts to get out of Hong Kong. Better to drop her as soon as possible, he decided. With US$250,000 in diamonds he'd have no trouble buying a passage on a ship, any ship. Howells knew that when he left the colony it would be vital that he left no one behind who knew where he was going – or at least that he left no one alive behind. He had no choice.

She came back into the room and handed him a yellow mug of coffee.

'*M goy*,' he said.

'*M sai*,' she replied and sat down next to him, one leg curled underneath herself so that she could face him. She rested her arms on the back of the sofa and placed her chin on them, looking up at him with wide eyes.

'What is happening, Geoff?' she said.

He reached across with his good arm and brushed her cheek. He had already worked out how he was going to get her to help him. He'd told her about Grey but from here on he'd have to be careful, because there was no way she'd help him if she found out that he'd kidnapped a child. He'd have to lie.

'That man who gave me the money tonight, Jack Edmunds, is a thief. And he's a friend of mine. He's what they call a safe-breaker, do you understand?'

She shook her head.

'He opens safes, sometimes in banks, sometimes in offices. He is one of the best in the world. And I'm a friend of his.'

'You help him steal?'

'Not steal. But I help him get rid of what he has stolen. I help him sell the things he steals. That's why I was attacked. The man Grey thought I had some diamonds and they were going to kill me and steal them. But I didn't have them. Jack had given them to another friend of his. This afternoon Jack wants me to collect the diamonds and to get them out of Hong Kong. It's very dangerous, Amy, because if they find out I have the diamonds then they are likely to attack me again.'

She nodded, her brow furrowed. 'My friend can help you leave Hong Kong.'

'Good. I'll be able to pay him in gold. Will that be all right?'

'Of course. In Hong Kong gold is better than money. But how will you get gold?'

'It was with the diamonds. Jack said I was to use it to pay for my fare. Thirty-two ounces.'

'Wah!' she said in surprise. 'So much.'

'Amy, I am going to need your help. I cannot do this on my own. I will need your help. Will you help me?' He looked at her earnestly and gave her a half-smile, trying to look as if it was the most important thing in the world to him.

'Of course I will help you, Geoff,' she said. 'What do you want me to do?'

'Thank you,' he said, and leant forward to kiss her softly on the lips. Her mouth opened immediately and she pressed herself against him, careful not to put pressure on his right arm. She moved her head from side to side as she kissed him on the mouth, and then she moved to kiss him above each eyebrow, the way she'd soothe a child. She looked deep into his eyes then and solemnly promised that she'd do anything he wanted, and then she kissed him again, opening her mouth wide to allow his tongue to move between her teeth and she moaned and said his name.

Howells tentatively reached for her breasts with his left hand, gently smoothing them with his palm before beginning to unbutton her blouse, slowly because he didn't want to frighten her; he wanted this to be perfect, he wanted her to enjoy it like she'd never enjoyed it before.

Because then she really would do anything for him. And because it would be her last time.

Getting the diamonds and the gold was no problem for Ng Wai-sun. The old man had some fifty taels of gold in the safe set into the floor under the wood panelling at the foot of his bed, and he could call in plenty of favours among the colony's diamond dealers to lay his hands on $250,000 of good quality stones, especially when he was paying for them in cash. The first dealer he woke up was around at Golden Dragon Lodge half an hour later with a selection. Ng Wai-sun held them in his palm and looked at them in the early morning light.

'What do you think?' he asked his son.

'I think we should use fakes rather than risk real diamonds,' said Thomas.

'They are a small price to pay if they get back my grandchild,' said Ng Wai-sun.

'It will not come to that, Father. This time we will catch the gweilo.'

'Beware the over-confidence that comes from under-estimating the enemy,' said Ng Wai-sun, carefully pouring the diamonds from his hand into a small green velvet pouch with a draw-string at the top. He handed the bag to his son.

The two were standing at the round table, on which were lined up thirty-two small oblongs of gold bearing the imprint of the Hang Seng Bank. Thomas Ng put the gold and the diamonds into a small brown leather attaché case. He zipped up the top and passed it to Dugan, who was sitting at the opposite side of the table.

'Be careful with it,' he said. 'That's a lot of money.'

'I'll try not to lose it,' said Dugan. He looked dead tired, bags under his bloodshot eyes, his clothes rumpled. He'd fallen asleep in the chair outside and had been woken up by screaming peacocks just before dawn.

Lin Wing-wah appeared at the double door wearing brown cord trousers and a green and brown camouflage jacket over a white polo neck. He'd carefully arranged his small ponytail so that it lay over the collar of his jacket.

He nodded at Ng Wai-sun. 'Good morning, Lung Tau.'

'Good morning, Lin Wing-wah,' the old man answered. Thomas noticed how easily his father had slipped back into the role of Dragon Head. It was as if he had never stepped down. 'Come in and sit down.'

When all four of them were seated, equally spaced around the table, Ng Wai-sun said: 'There must be no mistakes today. None at all. I have lost one son to this gweilo, there must be no more deaths.' He spoke in Cantonese, knowing that Dugan was fluent. 'We must continue the search this morning; if we wait until this afternoon then he will have the advantage of surprise. Cheng Yuk-lin, can you relay this to the other triads and ask for their co-operation?'

'I shall, Lung Tau.'

'Mister Dugan has brought us valuable information. We know that the gweilo has been shot and must be receiving medical attention from somebody.'

'We have already checked the hospitals, Father. Today we begin to question the legal and the illegal doctors,' said Thomas Ng.

Ng Wai-sun nodded. 'Good. Again, we must move quickly. I think we must assume that once the gweilo has the ransom he will leave Hong Kong. That brings us to the next problem. If we do not track him down before we are due to hand over the ransom, then we must decide how we handle it. At what point do we try to take him? Do we do as your brother planned to do and try to seize him when the ransom is handed over? Or do we follow him after we have given him the diamonds and we have Sophie back? Or do we simply give him the ransom and assume that he will keep his word?'

'The gweilo did not keep his word last time,' Cheng said slowly. 'We must not trust him on this occasion.'

'I agree,' said Thomas Ng. Dugan did not know whether or not he was supposed to contribute to the discussion, but he nodded in agreement with Cheng and Ng.

'That is also my feeling,' said Ng Wai-sun. 'Do we agree therefore that we try to capture the gweilo and then force him to tell us where he has Sophie?'

They all nodded.

'So be it,' said Ng Wai-sun. 'Lin Wing-wah, you must have our Red Poles prepared. I think it best that we do not involve the other triads in the actual ransom, I think we must keep that firmly under our control. It would be best if we have our men spread around Hong Kong so that we are sure to have some men close to where the handover is due to take place. As soon as we know when and where you must be able to contact our men and get them in position. This time there must be no mistake.'

There was no malice in his face but Lin flinched at the subtle reprimand and he was overwhelmed with shame at having failed Simon Ng. This time there would be no mistake, he swore to himself. He would have the gweilo, or die in the attempt.

'I have a suggestion,' said Dugan, speaking for the first time. Ng Wai-sun raised his eyebrows in surprise, but then smiled and asked him to speak.

'I think you should have a fallback position,' he said. Though they had invited him to sit in on their war council, he was still reluctant to say 'we' while in their company.

'What do you have in mind?' said the Dragon Head.

'Bearing in mind what happened last time, I think you should bug the ransom. Place a transmitter, a homing device of some sort, in the case with the gold and the diamonds. Then if he does get away you still have a chance of following him.'

'But what if he finds it?' asked Thomas Ng.

'We can stitch it into the bottom of the case. The CCB technical department has some ultra-thin models that they've been testing. They use small batteries that are only good for twelve hours or so but they can be detected up to a distance of two miles. You pick up the signal with a radio directional finder, a small hand-held job. It would mean that you could have men in cars close to the handover point and they could follow him at a distance.'

'Could you get us the equipment?' asked the Dragon Head.

'I am sure of it,' said Dugan.

Howells woke up slowly, drifting up through layers of sleep, until he became aware of his arm being kissed, just above the elbow, slowly and sensually, a tongue licking the flesh in small circles, warm and wet. He became aware then of Amy's hair lying across his upper arm, shielding her face as she caressed him with her mouth like a vampire preparing to feed. He became fully awake then and felt the warmth of her lithe body, her legs entwined with his, her shoulder against his hip, her lips on his skin.

'Good morning,' he said sleepily. 'What time is it?'

She looked up and smiled at him, and this time she didn't put her hand up to cover her teeth.

'It's eleven o'clock,' she said.

'That was the sexiest alarm call I've ever had,' he said.

'I don't understand.'

'Kissing me like that. It was a lovely way to wake up.' He was lying on his left side, his left arm up on the pillow, his right lying across his chest. The sling lay on the floor, along with the rest of his clothes that Amy had so carefully taken off him hours before. Her clothes were on top of his, because she'd stripped him naked and kissed him all over his body before undressing and slipping on top of him, careful to keep her weight away from the upper half of his body, so that she wouldn't hurt him. She was a gentle and considerate lover, matching her pace with his, taking him first slowly, then moving faster and harder, timing it so that she came a second or two before him and then slipping off him and lying next to him, exhausted but happy. Happier than she'd been in a long time. Now she was his, body and soul.

'Do you want coffee?' she asked.

'Please,' he said.

She slid out of bed and put on his shirt before going to

the kitchen. Howells sat up and gently rotated his arm, the injured one. It hurt, it hurt like hell, but it was healing, and so long as he didn't put too much strain on it he reckoned he could do without the sling. The painkillers were still in the plastic bottle, untouched.

Amy came back into the bedroom and handed him a mug of coffee. She rubbed her hand through his thick hair as he drank, enjoying the feel of it as it ran through her fingers.

'Do you think I'd look Chinese if I had black hair?' he said.

She laughed. 'Maybe,' she said. 'You want to be Chinese?'

'No. I want to look Chinese. And you can help. I need something to dye my hair black. Can you get some?'

She nodded eagerly. 'I go now. I will buy some food for breakfast as well.' She changed into a clean dress, carrying it from the wardrobe to her lounge and making sure that he couldn't see her, suddenly shy and not knowing why. Then she rushed back to kiss him before going out to shop. Howells watched her go, with a smile.

Dugan got out of the lift at the 26th floor, C Division's territory. He walked along the corridor and passed a stuffed camel, its haughty head almost scraping the ceiling. The camel was one of C Division's little mysteries; nobody knew what it was doing in the corridor, nor how it had got there in the first place. To Dugan's knowledge it had been there for at least four years, possibly longer. He'd asked one of the C inspectors once but he'd just shaken his head mysteriously and tapped the side of his nose. Dugan was damned if he'd give them the satisfaction of asking again.

He found Dave Rogers bent over the innards of some electrical equipment that looked as if it had dropped from a great height and bounced badly.

'Whotchya, Dugan,' he said. They were good friends, drinking partners and both were on the police rugby team.

'Hiya, Dave. Can you do me a favour?'

'Sure.' Rogers was like that, helpful and trusting to a fault. You wanted something, he'd give it you; you needed help, you got it – no questions, no comebacks. He was a lousy copper, but he had a degree in electronics from some Scottish university and after a few years working out of a poxy station in Sha Tin they'd realized that he'd be of more use on the technical side than he was chasing villains.

'You remember those bugs you were telling me about, the slimline model? Can I borrow one for a while?'

'Yeah, little beauties. Expensive little beauties. You won't lose it, will you?' he said.

'Listen to yourself, you daft bastard. How the fuck am I going to lose a homing device?'

Rogers laughed and opened a drawer under his workbench. 'I suppose you're right,' he said. He took out a small stainless steel cylinder about the size of a lipstick, but slightly thinner. Rogers held it in his palm, turning it from side to side.

'See the black button? Press that and you activate it. Push the one next to it to turn it off.'

'You said the battery lasts for twelve hours?'

'About that.'

'And how do I keep track of it?'

Rogers took out another piece of equipment, this one about the size of a small voltmeter, black plastic with a clear plastic dial at one end. He switched it on, and then pressed the black button on the transmitter. He showed Dugan how the needle on the dial followed the transmitter as he moved it.

'Simple,' said Dugan.

'A child could use it,' agreed Rogers. 'I don't want to pry, Pat, but when are you going to give it me back?'

'Tomorrow. Either that or your money back.'

'You any idea how much that baby costs?' Dugan shook his head. 'About as much as you earn in three months.'

'Fuck me, Dave.'

'If you lose it, I might well do,' warned Rogers, only half joking.

Dugan had taken pains to make sure that no one saw him enter CCB headquarters, and he was equally careful when he left. A Mercedes was waiting for him around the corner.

Howells waited until he was sure Amy had left the building before making the call. The phone was answered by an old Chinese man and he asked to speak to Thomas Ng. When he came to the phone Howells asked him if he had the diamonds and the gold ready.

'It is here,' said Ng.

'You are to take the ransom to the same place as last

time, to the pier at Hebe Haven. At four o'clock this afternoon. I want there to be just one man there, do you understand?'

'Yes,' said Ng. 'But you'll forgive me if I don't appear in person. After what you did to my brother, I'm sure you'll understand my reluctance.'

Howells snorted. 'I don't care who you have there. My only concern is the money. And I would have thought that you would have been more concerned about your niece than your own skin.'

'Think whatever you like, someone else will be there with the diamonds.'

'And the gold.'

'And the gold,' repeated Ng.

'Whoever is there must be alone and unarmed,' said Howells. 'I want him to be wearing nothing but a pair of shorts. And the tighter the shorts, the happier I'll be. I don't want there to be any place where he can conceal a gun, do you understand?'

'Yes,' said Ng, feeling the anger grow inside. He wasn't used to being spoken to as a child. He was a giver of orders, not a taker.

'I will send someone to collect the ransom, a girl. She knows nothing about your niece or where she is. If you make any attempt to prevent her leaving with the diamonds your niece will die. If you attempt to follow her your niece will die. Only after you allow her to leave Hebe Haven safely will I call you and tell you where Sophie is. Do you understand?'

'I understand,' said Ng.

'If anything goes wrong, anything at all, I will kill your niece and you will never hear from me again.'

The arrogance of the gweilo finally got to Ng, and he snapped. 'And where do you think you can hide, Howells? Where do you think you can fucking well go where we can't get to you? And when we get you the pain we'll inflict on you will be nothing to what you're feeling just now.'

If Howells was surprised that Ng knew his name he gave no sign of it, other than a slight pause before he spoke.

'Just have the diamonds there,' he said coldly and hung up.

Ng could feel his cheeks reddening as he put the phone down, a sick feeling in his stomach. He saw Cheng looking at him and he averted his eyes from the old man's withering stare. Losing his temper had been a mistake. Telling the gweilo how much they knew had been a mistake. Damn the gweilo, damn him for ever.

Dugan arrived back at Golden Dragon Lodge in the Mercedes and walked up the path to the house. Thomas Ng was there to meet him.

'You have it?' he asked. Dugan showed him the homing device and the directional finder. 'It is so small, are you sure it will work?' Ng asked. Dugan gave him a quick demonstration.

'Has he called?' asked Dugan.

Ng nodded. 'He wants the money at Hebe Haven. The pier again.'

'That doesn't sound good, does it? One thing that

diamonds and gold have in common – they're both unharmed by salt water. Makes you think, doesn't it?'

'It gets worse,' said Ng. 'He wants you to wear nothing but shorts. He said that was because he wanted to make sure you weren't armed, but . . .' He left the rest unsaid. Dugan knew what he meant – everything pointed to Howells coming out of the sea. And all the indications were that the ransom, if not Dugan himself, would be taken back into the water.

'So what are you doing about it?' Dugan asked Ng.

'We'll be better prepared this time. I've already arranged for our men to sail a dozen or so boats into Hebe Haven, and we'll have the whole bay sealed off. We've also drafted in four of our members who have scuba-diving experience. They're already on their way; we'll put them on a boat and drop them off a half mile or so from the pier with spare tanks. They're going to sit on the sea bottom until we know where the gweilo is.'

Ng Wai-sun came out of the house behind his son. He greeted Dugan but made no move to shake hands.

'Do not let the obvious blind you to the unexpected, my son,' he said quietly. 'If all the signs are that the gweilo will come from the water, it could be that he plans to come from the road.'

'Yes, Father, we will have our men staking out the pier too. And Patrick has brought his transmitter. I'll have it stitched into the bag.' He took it inside, leaving his father alone with Dugan.

'Thank you for helping us,' said the old man in halting English. 'It cannot be easy for you.'

'I love my sister, and Sophie,' said Dugan, also using English, but speaking very slowly so that Ng Wai-sun could follow him. 'I also liked your son. He was a good husband and father.'

The old man smiled and looked at him with watery eyes. 'Be careful today,' he said.

Chief Inspector Leigh put down the file he had been holding and looked at the photograph of his wife.

'Well now, Glynnis, what are we to make of this?' he said softly. It had long been the Special Branch officer's habit to talk to his wife's picture; it helped him get his thoughts in order, but he was careful to do it only when he was alone in his office. His wife smiled at him as she had done for the past twenty years, when the photograph had been taken, her head tilted to the left, her eyes looking right through him.

The blue file on his desk contained the details of a messy double killing in the Victoria Hotel. Not that murders fell automatically within his brief, but the two barely cold corpses discovered in adjoining rooms were both CIA agents, Jack Edmunds and Rick Feinberg, and dead CIA agents most definitely were of interest. Both had been killed with a knife, both had been attacked from the back by a left-handed man. For more than that he'd have to wait for the coroner's report, and with the way the brain drain was affecting the coroner's office that could take two days.

Robbery appeared not to have been the motive; both men still had their wallets and their passports, and it had none of the hallmarks of a triad execution, just one slash across the throat and not the wicked multiple hackings that the local thugs preferred. There was one item in the report, however, that made the chief inspector sit up and take notice. At about the time of the killings, give or take half an hour, two phone calls had been made from one of the rooms, one to the home of the recently deceased Simon Ng, and one, a few minutes later, to the home of that pillar of the community Ng Wai-sun.

It was almost too much for one day, thought the chief inspector. First two dead Chinese agents in the Hilton, with a third spirited away to China, and two CIA agents dead in the Victoria. And a fifth death, a triad leader found handcuffed to the anchor of a yacht at Hebe Haven. It was like a puzzle, and Leigh took great satisfaction in the knowledge that if the file had dropped on to anyone else's desk except for his, the puzzle would probably never have been solved. But Leigh knew what the link was between the five deaths, knew that the single connecting factor was Patrick Dugan the rugby player, the CCB officer who claimed to be infatuated with a hooker called Petal. Patrick Dugan, whose hooker girlfriend seemed to be an agent working out of Beijing. Patrick Dugan, whose brother-in-law was brutally murdered. Patrick Dugan, whose in-laws were telephoned from the room of a dead CIA agent. Patrick fucking Dugan. Leigh reached for the phone and rang Tomkins.

'Is Dugan about?' he asked.

'No, he rang in earlier. Family problems. His wife's husband has been killed and he said he needs time off to arrange things. Something up?'

'I'm not sure. Have you got his home number?'

Tomkins gave it him, but when Leigh dialled the

number there was no answer. He wasn't surprised; he had a pretty good idea where he'd be. The second call had been to Golden Dragon Lodge, and Leigh would bet a season ticket to Cardiff Arms Park that Dugan would be there.

He called for his car and summoned a sergeant and two armed constables to meet him outside. He checked his own gun carefully before adjusting his holster. 'Times like this when I'm glad I'm not a British bobby, Glynnis,' he said to the picture. There had already been five deaths linked to Mr Dugan and Leigh was going to make damn sure there wasn't a sixth.

There were no problems at all in persuading old Dr Wu to give them the address where he'd treated the injured gweilo, no problems at all. Kenny Suen knocked on the door of the doctor's 14th floor flat in a Mong Kok residential block with two other Red Poles and his wife, a frail sixty-year old, bow-legged and slightly hunched, let them in. Suen did the talking; at twenty-five, he was a couple of years older than his companions, and half a head taller. He was the one carrying a gun, tucked away in a holster under his left armpit, hidden by his American football jacket, but there was no need to show it to the doctor as he sat at his dining-table in stockinged feet, his shirt sleeves rolled up, a glass of hot tea and a racing paper in front of him. He polished his glasses nervously on a white handkerchief as Suen introduced himself and told him what they were after. Wu was just a name on a list, and a long list at that, before Suen knocked on the door, but immediately he saw Wu's reaction he knew that the search was over.

The doctor began trembling slightly, and when Suen described what had happened to the Dragon Head his breathing began to deteriorate into short, rasping gasps. He invited the three visitors to sit at the table and asked them if they would take tea with him. Suen and the two Red Poles accepted his hospitality and waited until the old woman had poured three glasses of tea and retired to the kitchen.

'I had no idea, no idea at all,' muttered Wu, shaking his head and replacing his glasses.

'We understand,' said Suen. He knew there was no need to threaten the doctor. He was not a stupid man, he knew what would happen if he lied or if he did not offer them every assistance. Triad justice was swift and sure. They helped and rewarded those who were loyal, they killed those who betrayed the organization. Wu knew that, there was no need to insult him by stating the obvious. So they took tea and offered him the respect that was due to an elderly doctor. He told them everything, apologizing profusely all the time.

Leigh sat in the back of the black Rover with Sergeant Lam. One of his constables, Chan, was driving while the other, Lau, was in the front passenger seat. The traffic was heavy and they moved at a crawl through Wan Chai, hemmed in by double-decker buses and open-sided trucks laden with goods. A man on a bike, his carrier full of green vegetables, cycled by, making better progress than the Rover. Even with the windows up and the aircon on the car was still filled with the bustling noise of Hong Kong, the rattle of trams, the judder of jackhammers biting into concrete, the shouts of hawkers, the roar of engines, the shrill whistle of a traffic policeman on point duty where a traffic light had stopped working. Wherever you went in Hong Kong there were people, and wherever there were people there was noise.

Leigh sat patiently, knowing there was nothing the driver could do to speed things up. It was one of the first things he'd learnt when he arrived in the colony almost a quarter of a century earlier, that the quickest way to a coronary or a stroke was to waste one's energy fighting Hong Kong. That went for the people, the traffic, and the climate. There was no way any of it could be defeated by confrontation, you had to go with the flow. And you had to learn to relax.

He looked across at his sergeant and pulled a face. 'Wrong time of the day to be driving through Wan Chai,' he said.

'Soon be out of it, sir,' said the man in accented English.

Leigh wondered what would happen to Lam come 1997. If he had any sense he'd be out of it then, out of Special Branch and out of Hong Kong. The Chinese had long memories, bloody long memories, and there would be no favours granted to Special Branch after handover. As early as 1989 they'd stopped Chinese officers having access to delicate or sensitive police files, more for their own protection than anything else.

Part of the reason was that the Government didn't want sensitive information getting into the hands of Beijing, but it also meant that there was less reason to put pressure on any former officers who were still around after 1997. They wouldn't know anything, so hopefully the Chinese would leave them alone. Sure, believe that and you'll believe anything.

The top-ranking Chinese officers had already been promised UK passports or resettlement in other countries where they would be safe, and all had been told that under no circumstances were they to come back after Hong Kong became part of China. They had been promised hefty compensation packages and had been issued with secret identification numbers, memorized and on no account to be written down, which would give them priority in the event of an emergency evacuation, much as the Americans had done with trusted South Vietnamese personnel prior to the pull-out of Saigon. Leigh hoped it wouldn't get as ugly as it had in Vietnam, but he had been working against the Communists for long enough to know that it could still all go very wrong, despite all the promises from Peking. What then would happen to the likes of Sergeant Lam and the two constables? No foreign passports for them, no sanctuary in the UK, or Canada, or Australia. God help them.

They eventually escaped from the traffic jamming up Wan Chai and headed up the Peak, Leigh shielding his eyes from the bright sunlight as they ascended, the car whining up in third gear, the driver's foot flat on the floor. They were about a quarter of a mile from Ng Wai-sun's house when Leigh saw the motorcade heading towards them, eight cars driving together.

'Slow down,' he said to the driver, and he craned his neck as the cars shot past. The third car from the front was a large Mercedes and in the back sat Patrick Dugan, his face set as if in stone, unsmiling and clearly worried. The rest of the vehicles contained enough triad fighters to start a small gang war.

Leigh told his driver to turn around and follow them, but at a distance, and he told the constable in the front passenger seat to radio for reinforcements, three more unmarked cars and officers in plain clothes. Four Speical Branch cops in a black Rover wouldn't be able to tail a triad army for long without being spotted. Leigh didn't feel so calm anymore and his stomach began to churn. He reached down to his side and checked that his gun was there. It was, but its weight provided little comfort.

Grey fumbled for the ringing phone while still asleep, trying to stop the noise before it woke up his wife. He checked the time on the clock radio by the bedside, squinting to make out the red figures because his glasses were out of reach. Half past seven – almost time to get up, anyway. He pressed the receiver to his ear. 'Grey,' he said.

'Grey?' The voice was American.

'Yes,' he said, sitting up in bed. His wife stirred next to him, a shapeless lump hidden under the quilt, snoring loudly.

'It's Hamilton.'

'What's wrong?' asked Grey. If the CIA man was

ringing at this time of the morning it wasn't a social call, and good news would have waited until a more civilized hour.

'Everything,' said Hamilton, and it sounded to Grey as if he was talking between clenched teeth. 'Two of my best men are dead.'

'Howells?'

'Of course it was Howells. I've just heard from Langley that my agents, Feinberg and Edmunds, have been found dead in Hong Kong. In their hotel rooms. Their throats had been cut.'

'Good God!'

'I don't think God had anything to do with it,' said Hamilton.

'I don't know what to say,' said Grey.

'There's something else. The girl who tried to kill Howells before, the Chinese girl?'

'What about her?'

'Her name is Hua-fan, yes?'

Grey frowned. He hadn't told Hamilton her name, or even the fact that the assassin was a girl. 'Yes. She's one of their best.'

'So I gather. She also killed one of my agents in Beijing two years ago during a Presidential visit. We thought it was natural causes, but our technical boys reckon that the same stuff was used to kill him that the girl tried to use on Howells in Hong Kong.' Grey said nothing, but he closed his eyes and cursed silently. 'We don't know why he was killed, but it's quite possible that he was on the track of your agent. And that it was your agent, your so-called goldmine, who got Hua-fan to kill him. Does that sound possible to you?'

'I don't know, I really don't know. But yes, it is possible. But I didn't know, I swear to God I didn't know.'

'Whether you knew or not makes no difference. Look, Grey, all bets are off. Feinberg and Edmunds were acting unofficially – I don't think it'll be traced back to me, though it could get a bit too close for comfort. But you are in deep shit. Howells is still alive and I'd think he's going to be pissed at you. And if he gets caught he's bound to tell everything. But that's not my problem, Grey. You and I never spoke, do you get my drift?'

'I understand.'

'I'm going to do everything I can to protect my own back, Grey, and I suggest you do the same. But if you so much as whisper my name . . .' He left the threat unfinished. The line went dead.

'Who was it?' murmured Grey's wife from the depths of the quilt.

'Nobody,' said Grey. 'Nothing for you to worry about.'

The traffic heading towards the tunnel seemed surprisingly heavy, especially as rush hour was still an hour or so away. Dugan sat in the back of the big Merc feeling a bit exposed wearing his too-tight shorts. Ng had scoured the house for a pair that would fit, but the only pair that came close to accommodating Dugan's expanding waistline were still an inch or so too tight and he couldn't get the zip closed up to the top. He sat looking down at his legs, scarred and mottled from too many bad tackles. At his feet was the leather attaché case containing gold and diamonds worth something like US$275,000. Dugan was very conscious of the fact that it would take him more than ten years to earn that much. The triad had raised it with one phone call. It didn't seem fair, but Dugan had long ago learned that the meek inherited nothing, certainly not the earth. He was wearing a red and black cotton T-shirt, but that would have to come off when they got to Hebe Haven. High fashion it wasn't.

Thomas Ng was sitting next to him, immaculate in a sharp grey suit and white shirt and a red tie, the sort that would allow him to dominate breakfast meetings. In the front seat, next to a driver in a chauffeur's cap, was the old Dragon Head, who had insisted on coming along. Thomas Ng had protested, but Ng Wai-sun had been adamant and that was the end of it.

Dugan had made it clear that when the car dropped him at Hebe Haven it should drive well away from the area; it was far too conspicuous to hang around. Lin Wing-wah would be responsible for tailing the girl until she handed the ransom over to the gweilo, and he would be in a battered old off-white delivery van with Franc Tse and Ricky Lam. They had taken the directional finder and had gone ahead of the motorcade so that they could be in position before Dugan arrived. The car moved slowly along and Dugan rubbed his hands together anxiously. Despite the cold air blasting from the aircon he was sweating heavily.

Ng noticed Dugan's discomfort. 'Don't worry, our men will be all around,' he said. 'There will be four under the water around the pier and we'll have half a dozen small boats close by. There'll be three men in the van up close and they're all armed, and they'll be in radio contact with the rest of us. Nothing can go wrong.'

Dugan nodded, but he didn't feel any more secure.

'You know what your biggest problem will be?' asked Ng.

'What?'

'Not getting arrested for indecent exposure in those shorts,' Ng laughed.

Dugan forced a smile. The entrance to the tunnel came into view and they could see what was holding up the traffic. A lorry had run into a taxi on the approach road and both drivers had got out to wait until the police arrived. They each stood by their own vehicles refusing to look at each other. It was a matter of face, neither wanting to admit they were in the wrong, neither wanting to be the first to pull over to the side and allow the cars behind to pass. They just stood and waited, and to hell with the rest of the world. Eventually the Merc passed the taxi and Dugan looked across. There was no damage to be seen, other than a slight denting of the taxi's rear bumper.

'Face,' laughed Ng. 'The strength and the weakness of the Chinese.'

That sounded great coming from a Chinese, thought Dugan, albeit one with an American passport.

Once the accident was behind them the Merc picked up speed and a few minutes later they were Kowloon-side, heading for Hebe Haven. One by one cars left the motorcade, parking on the approach roads leading to the bay, effectively sealing off the area. By the time they were travelling along the Clearwater Bay Road there were just two cars left accompanying the Merc.

Dugan looked at his watch. Half an hour to go before

the deadline. His mouth felt dry and uncomfortable and swallowing was difficult. He wanted something to drink but didn't want to ask Ng. Face, thought Dugan ruefully, didn't only apply to the Chinese.

Leigh's car kept close to the motorcade until he heard over the radio that an unmarked Special Branch car had Ng in sight. They dropped back then and let the undercover boys do the work. Two elderly Toyotas and a Nissan took it in turns to take the lead, rotating regularly so that the triads wouldn't spot them. Eventually the call came over the radio that the Merc had pulled into Hebe Haven, by the sea. Leigh told them all to drive past and asked his own driver to pull into a side road.

He thought for a while, and then radioed the men in the Nissan, telling them to get into the Toyotas. The driver of the Nissan could then go back to the pier and check it out. One of the Toyotas was to wait about a mile away from Hebe Haven along Hiram's Highway, while the men in the other were to take the high ground and find a vantage point where they could look down on to Ng and the triads.

'Have you got any binoculars?' he asked.

'Negative,' was the reply. Leigh just shrugged; there was no point in getting upset, it was his own fault for not reminding them before setting out. If they could think for themselves they wouldn't be constables.

He waited patiently until one of the men radioed back to say he was in position, overlooking the pier at Hebe Haven. At the same time the Nissan turned into the road and drove down to the line of parking spaces. Both reported that Ng's Mercedes had gone, leaving behind a slightly overweight gweilo wearing nothing but a pair of shorts and carrying a leather case.

'Dugan,' said Leigh under his breath. He told his men to stay where they were. He looked at his watch. Ten to four. None of this made any sense. What the hell was Dugan up to?

Lin Wing-wah was standing on the same spot he had occupied only days earlier when Simon Ng had been waiting at the water's edge. He studied Dugan through his binoculars and sneered at the way the gweilo's stomach bulged over the top of his shorts. He could see that he was sweating profusely under the afternoon sun and already his skin was beginning to redden. Dugan paced up and down slowly, his eyes scanning the horizon.

Lin watched a dirty red Nissan drive towards the pier and park. He checked out the driver. A young Chinese, scruffily dressed, reading a newspaper and eating a chocolate bar. Lin turned the binoculars back on Dugan. As he watched he took a toothpick from his shirt pocket and began to work at the gaps between his teeth. Down below, Tse and Lam were parked at the roadside with the detector. He called Ng on his walkie-talkie: 'Nothing so far,' he said. He called up the teams out in the bay one by one. All had nothing to report. He stopped picking his teeth and looked at his watch. Two minutes to four.

Dugan wiped his forehead with the back of his hand and it came away soaking wet. There was no shade and he could feel the hot sun burning his shoulders. He wasn't used to the sun; he disliked sunbathing and rarely went to the beach, and while his legs and arms were tanned from playing rugby, his upper body rarely saw daylight and was white and pasty, and his skin would burn easily.

He swung the bag by his side, hoping that the homing device was working. He'd switched it on before getting out of Ng's Mercedes, but there was no way of telling if the detector was picking it up. He walked to the top of the steps leading down to the water at the side of the pier and looked down. He wondered what he would do if Howells appeared and demanded that he go underwater with him. Would he go? Dugan didn't know how he would react; he had to get Sophie back, but the thought of how his brother-in-law had died under the waves made his blood run cold.

He heard a car and turned around to see a taxi driving down the road. He shielded his eyes from the sun to see better. There was a girl sitting in the back.

Lin watched the taxi turn off Hiram's Highway and head down towards the bollards where Dugan stood. He spat out the toothpick and called Ng. 'There's a taxi stopping near the pier. Only one girl in it. She's getting out and going over to Dugan.'

'Any sign of the gweilo?' asked Ng.

'No, no. She's on her own – they are talking – she's trying to take the bag from him but he's keeping it away from her. They're arguing. What is the prick playing at? Now they're both walking back to the taxi. This is it.'

Over the radio came Ng's voice, calmly telling him to go back to the van. Lin jogged down the hill, the binoculars banging against his chest. Tse was in the driver's seat and he switched the engine on when he saw Lin. Ricky Lam stayed crouched in the back. 'Here you are, Elder Brother,' he said, and handed over the receiver. Lin thanked him and told Tse to stay on the alert; they had no way of knowing which way the taxi would go when it left with the ransom.

The girl who got out of the taxi and walked towards Dugan was casually dressed in faded denims and she wore wrap-around sunglasses. She had a small canvas satchel, the strap across her shoulder. She kept her hand on the top as if frightened someone would steal her purse. The girl looked nervous, moving her head left and right as she walked, but there was no doubt it was Dugan she was heading for. She stopped a few feet away from him.

'I've come for the diamonds,' she said, and held out her hand.

'Where is Sophie?' Dugan asked.

The girl frowned. 'I don't know anybody called

430

Sophie.' She stepped forward and tried to take the case from him.

'No,' said Dugan sharply, holding it out of her reach. 'No you don't. Not till I know Sophie is all right.'

The girl seemed totally confused; she moved back, and then stepped forward again, but Dugan refused to let her take the attaché case. The girl looked over her shoulder at the taxi, and then at Dugan.

'You must give me the case,' she insisted. 'You must.'

'Where is Howells?'

'Please,' she said, and he could sense the urgency in her voice. 'Give me the case.'

'Take me to Howells first,' insisted Dugan. 'No Howells, no diamonds.'

The girl began biting her lip and her hands were shaking. She put both hands on top of her canvas bag and gripped it tightly. Dugan wondered if she had a gun. There was enough room.

'Come with me,' she said eventually, and walked back to the taxi. Dugan followed her, sweat trickling down his back.

The plainclothes constable in the Nissan watched over the top of his newspaper as Dugan got into the cab, but made no move to use his radio. He knew that one of his colleagues would already be relaying the information to Chief Inspector Leigh. He waited until the taxi had pulled away before starting his car, and slowly followed them up the road. The taxi indicated left and headed for Tsim Sha Tsui. So did the Nissan.

'They're coming this way,' said Ng. He told Hui Ying-chuen to start driving back towards Tsim Sha Tsui, so that they could keep ahead of the taxi. Hui had practically begged to be allowed to drive, even though Ng Wai-sun had told him it meant handling the Mercedes and its automatic transmission. Hui said he would put up with it. Lin had said the trace was working perfectly so all the triad cars were able to keep their distance until the girl handed over the diamonds to the gweilo.

'Something wrong?' asked his father, twisting his body round in the front seat.

'Dugan was arguing with the girl and refused to hand over the case. He got into the taxi with the girl.'

'Perhaps he wanted to check that Sophie was unharmed before handing it over.'

'That's probably it,' agreed Ng. 'I hope he doesn't get in the way. He is, when all is said and done, still a policeman.'

The taxi driver hadn't waited for the girl to speak; as soon as Dugan closed the door he drove off, turning left on to the main road. He was wearing grubby white woollen gloves with the fingers and thumbs cut off, a black jacket with the collar turned up and a flat cap, the sort that gamekeepers wear when out shooting rabbits. He didn't bother asking for directions so he obviously knew where he was going. The girl leant forward to speak to him, but as she did the driver cleared his throat noisily and accelerated, throwing her back into the seat. She looked as if she was about to burst into tears.

'He wouldn't give me the bag,' she whimpered.

Dugan thought she was talking to him. 'I won't give it to you until you tell me where Sophie is,' he said in Cantonese.

'Speak English,' snapped the taxi driver. 'Who the fuck are you?'

Dugan sat stunned, looking from the back of the driver's head to the girl and to the driver again, trying to work out what was happening. The driver turned round to look at Dugan, the eyes hidden by black sunglasses. With the glasses and hat it was hard to tell what nationality he was, but the accent was one hundred per cent English. 'I won't ask again,' the man said and turned back to concentrate on the road, accelerating out of a curve.

'Dugan. Pat Dugan.'

'The brother-in-law,' said Howells. 'I should have guessed.'

'I'm Sophie's uncle,' said Dugan. He lifted the bag up. 'And you're not getting this until I know she's safe.'

'If you do as you're told she'll be fine.'

'I know what you did to her father.' Dugan was conscious that Howells was speaking very quickly, obviously so that the girl wouldn't be able to follow the conversation. Few Cantonese could keep up with English at speed, especially when native speakers dropped into slang.

'You don't know why I did it. You don't know what you're talking about.' He fumbled in the pocket of his jacket and pulled out a small plastic bottle containing six white tablets which he tossed at Dugan. 'I want you to take three of those.'

'Do you think I'm stupid?'

'I'm starting to wonder, Dugan. Look, if I wanted to put you out of your misery I'd just stick something sharp between your ribs.' He pulled the handle of a knife from the inside of his jacket, just enough to show Dugan that he was serious. 'Look at the label on the side; they came from a doctor, they're not poison.'

'So what are they?'

'They're sedatives, they'll slow you down. I'm not going to hurt you, and I'm not going to hurt the girl. I just want to get away from Hong Kong, and for that I need the stones. What I don't want is to have to fight you. Take the tablets and I'll feel a whole lot easier. And as soon as I know I'm in the clear I'll tell you where the girl is.'

Dugan unscrewed the top of the bottle and picked out three of the tablets. He put one in his mouth and swallowed but his throat was so dry it stuck there until he tried again. He felt like throwing up.

'All of them, Dugan.'

He swallowed the other two with difficulty. He waited anxiously for something to happen, but there was no dizziness, no numbness.

Amy watched as he took the tablets, a frown on her face as she tried to work out what Geoff Howells was up to and why he was giving Dr Wu's medicine to the big, sweating gweilo.

'Can you see them?' asked Leigh.

His car was stuck behind a labouring double-decker bus that ground its gears as it assaulted the hill. Behind them a green Mitsubishi played chicken with their rear bumper.

'No, sir. And at this speed he's going to be leaving us far behind.'

I know that, thought Leigh. He didn't say so, the man was only trying to help. He'd ordered the Nissan to hang back in case they recognized it, so the two Toyotas were taking it in turns to tail the taxi. He radioed his men and was told that they could see it, and that they were some two miles away from the crawling bus. 'Damn this bus,' he cursed under his breath. 'Damn this bus and damn Patrick Dugan.'

Thomas Ng's Mercedes was about as far in front of the taxi as Leigh was behind it. He was talking on his walkie-talkie to Lin, checking that the Hung Kwan official hadn't lost Dugan or the diamonds. He hadn't. One of the Red Poles broke in on the radio to say that there was a carload of uniformed police on the road to Tsim Sha Tsui, heading their way.

'Where are they?' asked Ng.

'Stuck behind a China Motor Bus. We're right behind the police.'

'Keep an eye on them. It's probably a coincidence.'

'Something wrong?' asked his father.

'There are police on the road, but they're some way behind us. I don't think it's a problem.'

'And still no sign of the gweilo?'

'No. Just the girl and Dugan. But the gweilo can't be far away.'

Dugan rested his head against the window. He was starting to feel drowsy and the vibrations made him want to retch – or maybe it was the effect of the tablets on his empty stomach. He opened his eyes wide and shook his head from side to side. He felt like he normally did after drinking six or seven pints of San Miguel. He heard Amy talking to Howells, but it seemed as if he was listening down a long tube that distorted her voice.

'What's happening, Geoff?' she asked. She was leaning over the back of the seat, her arms folded under her chin.

'Don't worry, Amy, it will be all right.'

'Who is he? And why won't he give us the diamonds? You said they would give them to us so we can sell them?'

'We can, Amy. And we will. And then we can both leave Hong Kong.'

She smiled, pleased that he'd said 'we', pleased that he intended to take her with him. She wanted to kiss him, but at the speed he was driving she couldn't risk distracting him. They were racing down Argyle Street, past the grey squarish building that housed the Kowloon Regional

Police HQ. Amy felt a twinge of anxiety, knowing that the building was packed with police and that she was breaking the law, though in exactly what way she wasn't sure.

'Who is Sophie?' she asked.

'A friend of ours,' lied Howells without a second thought. 'He's worried about her, that's all.'

'A girlfriend?'

'No, just a friend.' Over his shoulder he called to Dugan. 'Let her check the stuff, Dugan.'

Dugan did as he was told, not sure if he could resist if he wanted to. He picked up the bag and handed it to Amy. She unzipped it and gasped when she saw the small gold ingots.

'Wah!' she exclaimed. 'So much gold!'

'The diamonds, check the diamonds, Amy.'

She took the small pouch out of the attaché case which she placed on her knees while she poured the stones out carefully, almost reverently, into the palm of her delicate hand. They glittered and shone in the sunlight, and she pushed her sunglasses up on the top of her head while she admired them, open-mouthed.

'They are beautiful,' she said softly. Howells took a quick look over his shoulder as he drove.

'Pick two of the biggest and give them to me.'

She selected two and handed them to him. Howells studied them as best he could with one hand on the wheel.

'They're real all right,' said Dugan. 'I wouldn't let them take any risks with Sophie's life.' Howells believed him. They looked genuine enough.

'I haven't hurt her, Dugan, but I'm quite prepared to. You are going to have to be one hundred per cent honest with me because if I don't get away then she stays locked up where she is. She'll starve to death, Dugan, and take it from me that's not a pleasant way to die. Now tell me, is there a trace on this stuff?'

Dugan closed his eyes and rubbed his forehead. He wanted to sleep, he wanted to lie down in a big, comfortable feather bed. With Petal.

'What?' asked Howells sharply.

Dugan realized he must have spoken her name out loud. He opened his eyes again and looked at the back of Howells' head. He couldn't take the chance of lying; if Howells scrutinized the attaché case he'd soon find the homing device. 'Yes,' he said.

'I'd have been surprised if there wasn't. Amy, put the diamonds back in the pouch and give it to me.' They were driving through a high-rise residential area, blocks and blocks of flats, balconies covered with potted plants and washing, many shielded with ornate metal grilles that bulged outwards as if to proclaim dominance over as much space as possible, even if it was just empty air.

She did as she was told, taking great pains not to drop any. The taxi stopped at a set of traffic lights and she kept her hands low so that the people in the next car couldn't see what she was doing. She gave the pouch to Howells and he put it on the seat next to his leg, then he handed her the two diamonds over his shoulder.

'Keep them,' he said. 'I'll get them made into earrings for you.' She didn't understand so he squeezed his left ear with his fingers. 'Earrings,' he repeated slowly. 'For you.'

Amy protested, but not too vociferously, and then she wrapped them in a paper tissue and slipped the small parcel into her jacket pocket.

The traffic was heavier now as Howells drove through a built-up area; more high-rise housing and a growing number of shops, so he had to concentrate on driving, switching from lane to lane, looking for the gaps and the hold-ups, knowing that the triads wouldn't be too far behind him. They went up a flyover and Howells saw the airport to his left. With a screaming and a roaring a 747 swooped low on its final approach, its landing gear down, so close that Howells ducked involuntarily.

'Do you know where we are, Amy?' he asked.

She nodded. 'Coming up to Yau Ma Tei. This is Waterloo Road. Then it's Jordan and then Tsim Sha Tsui and the harbour.'

'Is there an MTR station close by?'

'Yes, after the YMCA. Not far.'

'OK, listen, Amy. I'm going to drop you there and I want you to go down and catch the first train you see. The men I told you about are after us and I want you to be safe. I'll get away from them and when I've sold the diamonds I'll go back to your flat.'

'I want to stay with you, Geoff,' she said, beginning to tremble.

'I want you to be safe,' he repeated. 'I don't want to have to worry about you. I want you to take the gold and keep it safe for me. It's very important. Will you do it for me?'

Amy nodded, but even Dugan could see that she wasn't convinced.

'I need you,' said Howells quietly, and that seemed to make her mind up for her. She clasped the attaché case to her chest and pointed at the junction ahead.

'There, MTR station.'

'OK,' said Howells. 'Now, when I stop I want you to run, and don't stop running until you're on the train.'

'I will,' she promised. 'Be careful.' She leant forward and kissed him on the cheek, and spoke to him hurriedly in Chinese. Howells slammed on the brakes and the car behind him sounded its horn as he screeched to a halt. Amy flung the door open and ran for the entrance without looking back. Howells reached over the back of the seat with his left arm and closed the door behind her before driving off. Dugan had his head slumped back and he was breathing heavily, almost snoring. As Howells accelerated again Dugan's head rolled forward on to his chest.

'What did she say?' asked Howells.

'She said she loved you. You're a bastard. You know they'll catch her.' He slurred his words as he spoke.

Howells grinned. 'Maybe,' he said. 'But it's rush hour so she's got a fighting chance. And she'll keep them occupied. While they're following her, I'll dump the taxi and disappear into the next MTR station. Then you can go and collect your niece.'

Howells thought it best not to mention the fact that just feet behind Dugan, lying in the boot, was the body of the owner of the taxi, his neck broken. He hadn't told Amy, either. He'd gone out on his own and returned with the taxi, telling her that he'd paid a few thousand dollars to borrow it. He'd considered just knocking the man out but he couldn't take the chance of him coming round and calling the police, so he'd told the driver to take him up a deserted sidestreet behind a foul-smelling dyeing plant and he'd grabbed his head and twisted, feeling the neck crack and enjoying it.

'She's out of the taxi,' Lin screamed into his walkie-talkie.

'What about Dugan?' said Ng, his voice crackling in Lin's ear.

'He's still there. Heading your way.'

'Where are you?'

'Yau Ma Tei MTR. At the junction of Waterloo Road and Nathan Road. She's in the station.'

'With the case?'

'Yes, she's . . .'

Ng didn't let him finish. 'Go after her. Don't lose her. We'll pick up Dugan.'

Lin threw the door open and jumped on to the pavement, the detector in his hand. Lam scrambled over the seat and ran after him. 'Come on,' Lin screamed at Tse. 'Leave the fucking van where it is.' Tse did as he was told and as the three stormed into the entrance of the MTR station the drivers blocked in behind the van began to sound their horns impatiently.

The three triads stood outside the door to Amy's flat. Suen had his gun in his hand, cocked and ready, while the two Red Poles had large knives by their sides. Suen knocked on the door and listened carefully for footsteps. Nothing. He knocked again. Still nothing.

'Break it down,' he said to Ah-wong, the bigger of the two heavies. Ah-wong stepped back and kicked the door hard, just below the lock. It gave a little and there was the sound of tearing wood, then he kicked it again and it sagged on its hinges. It caved in on the third go and the three men spilled into the small flat. It took only a few seconds to see that there was no one there, but they spent some time searching it thoroughly for a clue as to where the girl and the gweilo had gone.

Ah-wong found a blood-stained pillow case at the bottom of a black plastic bag of rubbish in the kitchen and he brought it triumphantly into the lounge. Suen went through the bathroom cabinets. He found a half-empty bottle of hair dye there and he noticed that the sink was stained black in places, though someone had tried to clean it with a cloth. There was a pair of scissors in the cabinet, too, and the drain in the sink was clogged with bits of hair.

'Look at this,' called Ah-wong. 'Look what I've found.' Suen went back into the lounge and Ah-wong waved the blood-stained material under his nose. 'We're in the right place,' he said to Suen.

'But at the wrong time,' replied Suen.

'Let's get back to the car,' said Ah-wong, heading for the door.

'Fuck your mother,' said Suen. 'We phone Ng first.'

One by one Ng called up the cars that had been following behind Lin, told them the girl had taken the diamonds down the MTR station and gave them instructions to get there as soon as possible and follow her down. While he was talking to the Red Poles the car phone rang. Ng Wai-sun leant over and picked it up. It was Kenny Suen.

'We found where the gweilo was hanging out,' said Suen, obviously pleased with himself. 'He was with a girl from one of the Wan Chai bars. She'd let him stay in her flat while Dr Wu treated him. They're not there now.'

'The girl, what does she look like?' the old man said.

'Medium height, high cheekbones, she looks a bit Shanghainese. Dr Wu says she's about twenty-four years old.'

'We have seen her,' said Ng Wai-sun. 'We are pursuing her now.'

'Oh,' said Suen, sounding disappointed.

'She collected the ransom for the gweilo,' Ng Wai-sun explained. 'But we have not seen the gweilo yet. We think she is on the way to see him.'

'Did she look twenty-four?' asked Suen. 'I mean, could she be older?'

'No, she was a young girl, dressed more like a teenager than anything else. Why?'

'There was hair dye all over the sink, it was a real mess. I thought maybe she had dyed her hair. But if it wasn't her . . .'

'Then it must be the gweilo,' said the old man, finishing the sentence for him. 'You have done well. Very well indeed.'

He replaced the phone and waved his finger to attract his son's attention. Ng took the walkie-talkie away from his ear to listen. 'The gweilo has dyed his hair,' said Ng Wai-sun softly. 'Black.'

'The driver!' hissed Ng. 'And he's behind us.'

'How far?' asked his father.

'Less than half a mile.' He told Hui to stop the Merc, no matter how much it annoyed the drivers behind. 'Put the hazard warning lights on, let them think we've broken down. He'll be here within two minutes.' He asked his father to open the glove compartment and the old man reached in and handed over the handgun that he found there. Ng took out the clip and then banged it home again, checking that the safety catch was off. He caught his father looking at the gun with a worried frown. 'It will be all right,' he said. 'As far as we know he is not armed. But we can take no chances. The man is a killer.'

'Be careful,' said Ng Wai-sun. 'I have already lost one son.'

Ng began calling up his triad soldiers, ordering Lin and his team, and one other group of Red Poles who had already arrived at the MTR station, to keep after the girl. The rest were to catch up with the taxi as soon as possible. But from the sound of it the gweilo would reach the Mercedes at least a minute or so before any of the Red Poles would be close enough to make a difference.

Amy was fumbling for her MTR card as she ran into the station, and it was in her hand by the time she got to the barrier. She slotted the plastic card home and then collected it from the return slot at the top of the ticket machine before pushing the barrier and running for the down escalator. As always the Hong Kong commuters seemed reluctant to walk down the moving metal staircase and Amy had to push and shove her way down, all the time repeating '*m goy, m goy*', but even so she was cursed and glared at.

It seemed to take a lifetime before she reached the platforms. The one to the left was for trains heading for Tsim Sha Tsui and on to Central, that on the right was for those going out to the New Territories. She felt a warm wind on her right cheek and knew that that signified a train coming. She ran to the edge of the platform and stood there, her legs shaking and her chest heaving, panting for breath. She looked behind her at the escalator, but all she saw were lines of impassive faces, nobody seemed to be chasing her. She heard the roar of the train and it sped out of the blackness of the tunnel and into the light. It growled to a stop and the doors gushed open, disgorging its passengers. Amy forced her way through before the last of them had got off and leant against the steel pole in the middle of the carriage. From where she stood she could see right along the line of connected carriages, two hundred metres or more. People flooded in, diving to get a place on the long, polished metal seats or a space to the side of the door so they could be first off at their station. The people of Hong Kong treated their mass transit system the same way that they lived their lives – the strong got the best places and got where they were going, the weak were left behind, standing on the platform when the doors closed. That's what it would be like come 1997, Amy thought. Those that pushed and fought would get out, those apathetic or incapable would be swamped by the one billion Chinese on the mainland. Amy knew that alone she would never be able to escape, but with Geoff Howells, maybe, just maybe, she would find a way out. He was strong, he was confident, and he had money. And she was helping him. In return, she knew, he would help her. But first she had to get away from the men who were chasing her.

She saw them then, at the top of the escalator. She heard the driver warning passengers to stand clear of the doors, first in Chinese and then in mumbling English, as three hefty men began shouting and pushing people out of their way as they scrambled down. One of them, a big man with bulging forearms and a small pigtail, almost made it, using his sheer bulk to force his way down. He leapt on to the platform but at the same moment the doors hissed shut. He ran forward and tried to claw his way into the carriage next to where Amy was standing but he was too late; the train pulled away, slowly at first and then picking up speed until the advertisements on the walls blurred. The man with the pigtail screamed and kicked out at the moving train and then Amy was in the black tunnel, heading for the New Territories with the attaché case clasped to her chest.

Behind her on the platform, Lin watched helplessly as the needle on his receiver slammed over to one side. 'Fuck your mother, bitch,' he cursed, and put the walkie-talkie to his mouth.

'They've lost her,' Ng said to his father. 'She got on to the MTR. I've told Lin to catch the next train and go after her, but she could be anywhere by now.' He looked out of the back window at the queue of cars waiting to pass.

'Any sign of the gweilo?' said Ng Wai-sun.

'Not yet,' said Ng. 'But he is not far behind. Hui Ying-chuen?' The elderly driver stopped waving at the cars behind to overtake and turned round. 'When I give you the word I want you to put the car in reverse and ram the taxi.'

Hui's face fell and he looked as if he was going to protest. In all the years he had been driving for the Ng family he had never, ever, been involved in an accident. It was a record he was proud of, but he did not argue. He just nodded and thanked the gods that he was in the Mercedes and not his beloved Daimler.

Ng told his father to make sure he was well strapped in and that his head was against the headrest. 'The Mercedes is much bigger and heavier than the taxi, we'll barely feel it,' he said. 'But better to be on the safe side. Once we've stopped them I'll hold the gweilo until our Red Poles get here.'

He held the gun down near the floor of the car, his finger clear of the trigger so that it wouldn't go off accidentally when the cars collided. The rest of the traffic was now streaming past the parked Mercedes and its flashing hazard warning lights.

Chief Inspector Leigh was becoming more confused by the minute. His men in the Toyota closest to Dugan's taxi had told him how it had stopped near Yau Mat Tei MTR station and how the girl had run into it carrying his case. The Special Branch man had continued after the taxi, but the officer in the Nissan following behind had called in to say that a group of cars had converged on the station and that more than a dozen triads had gone haring down after her.

Dugan was now heading towards Tsim Sha Tsui, alone. Leigh tapped Chan on the shoulder and told his constable to get a move on, to get closer to the taxi so they wouldn't lose him in the rush-hour traffic.

'Get up behind the Toyota,' he ordered. 'Keep that between us and Dugan's taxi and he won't see us.'

Chan put his foot down and began overtaking, thumping the horn as a makeshift siren. He had little trouble making headway and they soon left the green Mitsubishi behind. The Red Poles knew they couldn't follow the Rover without attracting attention to themselves, especially when the police sped past the airport and drove through two sets of red lights before reaching the neon signs of Yau Ma Tei. They drove past the MTR station and the cluster of badly parked cars outside it. The lights at Nathan Road were against them, but Chan edged the car through, carefully because it was one of the busiest roads in Hong Kong. Every second car seemed to be a taxi now and Leigh knew they'd have no chance of spotting the one Dugan was in, but they soon caught up with the Toyota and edged up behind it. The traffic had slowed down to a virtual crawl.

'Where is he?' radioed Leigh.

'Three cars ahead of us,' came the reply from the Toyota.

'What's the hold up?'

'I don't know. Some sort of accident up the road.'

At least it meant they wouldn't lose Dugan, thought Leigh. At last something was going his way.

'I see them,' said Ng. 'Third car behind us. Be ready, Hui Ying-chuen. Put it into reverse now, and as soon as the two cars have passed us, hit him. Hard. Are you all right, Father?'

His father grunted and settled back into the seat, his head pressed against the headrest. Ng lay down, his face against the leather upholstery.

Howells was beginning to get impatient. The traffic hardly seemed to be moving in his lane. Eventually he saw the source of the trouble; a large Mercedes had broken down and in typical Hong Kong fashion the driver had made no move to get it off the road, the passengers just sitting there waiting for someone to come and sort it out for them. During his short time in Hong Kong Howells had seen several accidents but had yet to see a Hong Kong Chinese with his head under the bonnet or pushing his vehicle off the road.

He could see the entrance to Jordan MTR station up ahead and considered leaving the taxi where it was. Then the car ahead indicated it wanted to pass and Howells did the same, but the vehicles in the right-hand lane were reluctant to let them in, deliberately keeping close, bumper to bumper, the drivers keeping their eyes fixed straight ahead. The car in front managed to squeeze in between a delivery van and a minibus and Howells tried to do the same. The reversing lights of the Mercedes came on, shining whitely next to the flashing yellow lights.

'What the fuck's he playing at?' asked Howells.

Dugan leant forward to see what was happening, and as he did the big car leapt backwards, rushing towards them. Dugan yelled and groggily threw himself down on the seat. Howells grabbed at the door handle but realized he wouldn't have time to open it so he dropped across the front seats, the handbrake handle biting into his stomach as he pulled his legs up out of the footwell, his knees up against his chest.

The Merc slammed into the front of the taxi, smashing the lights and crunching the bumper, forcing the air from Howells' chest. The thin metal of the Toyota cab screamed and buckled, the mass of the bigger German car seeming to meet no resistance. Water hissed and spurted from the radiator and still the Mercedes reversed, pushing the taxi back as Ng's driver kept his foot to the floor. There was a second bang then as the rear of the taxi crashed into the car behind it, and only then did the Merc stop. Water flooded around the front of the taxi and bits of metal and glass tinkled to the ground. The distorted car groaned and shuddered like a dying animal. Dugan pushed himself up and looked groggily around, his reactions dulled by the combination of the sedatives and the crash.

He could see startled faces watching from the pavement: an old woman with grey, crinkly hair and her front teeth missing; a young couple in matching T-shirts and stone-washed denims; a man in a grey pinstripe suit with a portable telephone in his hand, a bare-chested teenager carrying a refill for a distilled water dispenser on his shoulder. All were staring at the accident with wide eyes. Dugan smelt petrol and suddenly had a vision of himself and Howells engulfed in flames. With a mounting sense of panic he clawed at the left-hand door, but it had warped in the crash and wouldn't move. He shuffled along to the opposite side of the cab, his legs wobbling as he moved, his arms numb. Howells groaned in the front seat and then pulled himself up, using the steering wheel for leverage. He kicked open his door and fell into the road. He got to his feet to see Ng get out of the Mercedes, gun in hand.

'Stay where you are,' Ng shouted, pointing the gun at Howells' chest, holding it steady with both hands. He was eight feet at most away from Howells, and he knew he wouldn't miss.

'There's been an accident, sir,' said Constable Chan. 'The taxi's hit the car in front.'

Leigh stuck his head out of the window in time to see a well-dressed Chinese man threatening to shoot the taxi driver while Dugan staggered out of the cab into the road wearing nothing but a pair of shorts. The plainclothes officers in the Toyota pulled out their guns, one stepping on to the pavement and steadying his gun arm on the roof of the car, another crouched down behind the driver's door. Leigh's sergeant got out of the Rover and also drew his gun, telling his constables to do the same. Leigh left his in his holster. They had more than enough firepower. The pedestrians began screaming then and running for cover –

the Hong Kong police had a reputation for firing first and asking questions later.

'Drop the gun,' Leigh yelled. 'Drop the gun or we'll fire.'

The surprise showed on Ng's face and his aim wavered. Howells turned to see who was shouting and he too looked stunned to see so many police only yards away. Dugan was the last to turn and he almost lost his balance when he saw Leigh, his stomach wobbling over the top of his shorts. He looked like a drunken bull seal, thought Leigh. Dugan opened his mouth to speak and then shut it again. He was dribbling and he wiped his chin with the back of his hand.

'Drop the gun. This is your last warning,' shouted Leigh.

Howells stepped to the right, getting Dugan in between himself and the police and then stepped up behind him, drawing the kitchen knife from inside his jacket. He grabbed Dugan with his weak right arm and held the blade close to Dugan's neck with his left. 'Don't move, Dugan, or I swear to God I'll kill you,' he whispered.

Howells dragged him over to the taxi. The boot had sprung open in the crash and through half-focused eyes Dugan could see the body of a man inside, his head at an unnatural angle and a wet patch on the front of his jeans. There was no room to get through and Howells didn't want to go any nearer to the cops so he pulled Dugan back, trying to head towards the MTR station. That brought him nearer to Ng, which made him feel equally uncomfortable. Dugan started to complain that the blade was cutting him and Howells told him to shut the fuck up.

Leigh's men looked at him for guidance. In the chief inspector's mind there was no confusion. The Chinese with the gun could kill a lot of people, and the only person the taxi driver was going to hurt was Patrick Dugan. In Leigh's present frame of mind that was no great disaster.

'Keep your guns on Ng,' he ordered.

To Ng he shouted a final warning. Realizing he stood no chance against so many police, Ng threw his pistol to the ground and raised his hands.

Howells saw the gun clatter to the tarmac. He knew he had only seconds to act. Police reinforcements were sure to arrive soon, and he was already outgunned. The roads were too busy so there was no point in trying to hijack a car, and besides, he wasn't sure how effective a hostage Dugan would be. He looked as if he was about to pass out and he wouldn't be much of a shield if he slumped to the ground. His best chance, his only chance, was to get to the MTR and try to do as Amy had done and disappear in the crowds. The Special Branch officer standing by the Rover shouted that he was to drop the knife. He pushed Dugan into the road and dived for the gun, dropping the knife as he moved. Dugan fell to his knees as Howells got the gun in his right hand and then rolled over, howling as he jolted his injured shoulder. He felt the wound open and bleed but he kept on moving, coming up into a crouch, aiming the gun at the police and firing off two quick shots, the recoil burning into his shoulder. The bullets hit Chan in the neck and he fell back, blood streaming down his chest.

'Shoot him,' shouted Leigh, though his men needed no encouragement.

Howells leapt on to the roof of the taxi and rolled over it, dropping on to the pavement in a smooth movement. The crowds of pedestrians scattered like startled sparrows finding a cat in their midst. Sergeant Lam stepped away from the car and aimed at Howells' chest. As Howells raised his gun Dugan staggered to his feet, bellowed and threw himself across the bonnet of the car. He managed to tackle Howells around the waist with his flailing arms and brought him down to the ground. Howells slammed the butt of the gun against Dugan's head but he barely felt it. His grip slackened a little and Howells wriggled away, but Dugan grabbed his left leg and hung on for all he was worth, his eyes closed and his mouth wide open.

'Let go, you stupid bastard!' yelled Howells, but Dugan seemed not to hear him. All Dugan could hear ringing in his ears were the cheers of the crowds at the Rugby Sevens and he hung on for all he was worth, waiting for the ref to blow his whistle.

Howells pointed the gun at Dugan's head and started to pull the trigger, but as he did Sergeant Lam fired. The bullet ripped into Howells' chest and knocked him backwards, the gun falling from his hand. Dugan's eyes opened at the sound of the gun-shot. He drifted in and out of consciousness but kept hold of the leg and crawled slowly up the body as it lay on the pavement. There was a hole the size of a fist in Howells' chest, filling with blood, bubbling in time to his breathing. His eyes were open but seemed not to see Dugan's face.

Ng came running over and shoved Dugan away. He began going through Howells' pockets until he found the bag of diamonds. He waved them triumphantly over Howells' head until Dugan pushed him away angrily. He knelt down beside Howells, conscious that the police were running up and that he didn't have much time. Neither did Howells, that was clear enough.

'The girl,' mumbled Dugan, his voice thick and the words slurring. 'Where is Sophie?' Howells seemed to become aware of Dugan for the first time and he almost smiled. 'Where is the girl?' Dugan asked again, not wanting to beg but knowing that he would if necessary. There was no need. Howells told him and then died.

Dugan sat back heavily on to the road, shaking his head to try to clear it. He felt elated at knowing that Sophie was safe, but he felt cheated too. He had no idea who the killer was, or why he'd wreaked such havoc. Maybe when his head was clearer he'd be able to think and put it all in perspective, but all he wanted to do was to sleep, to curl up in the road and close his eyes and dream of Petal.

Leigh came up behind him and put his hand on Dugan's shoulder. 'Great tackle, Dugan.' Dugan shook his hand away. He got unsteadily to his feet and slowly and carefully went over to see Ng Wai-sun.

The two labradors jumped up and down with excitement as Grey opened the back door to let them out into the night for their last run before turning in. His wife had banned them from the bedroom but had grudgingly allowed them to sleep in the kitchen. While the two dogs did whatever they had to do Grey poked the embers of the fire and looked at the flames. When he was a child he'd spent hours gazing into the fire, making stories out of the twisting shapes; knights fighting dragons, angels against demons. Now when he looked into the fire he saw nothing, just burning coals.

He heard the dogs barking, probably fighting over a long-forgotten bone. Stupid animals – their sole aim in life appeared to be to have a full stomach. Whenever he forgot to put the lid on the dustbin they'd be in, rooting for scraps as if they were strays rather than well-fed pampered pedigrees. Dogs never seemed to appreciate when they were well-off. Neither did people.

Grey's career was finished, he knew that. Less than a week after the abortive attempt to kill Howells, his agent in Beijing had disappeared. There was no trial, no charges, no announcement in the *People's Daily*. With Hong Kong jittery enough in the run up to 1997, the Chinese had no wish to bruise what fragile confidence remained. Already 60,000 of Hong Kong's brightest and most able were flooding out of the colony each year, emigrating to Australia, Canada and the United States. They had no wish to make it worse. A show trial of a British agent, even one who was Chinese, would do more harm than good. He had just vanished, and so had his family. The assassin who had survived would have told them where the order to kill Howells had come from, a trail that led straight to Grey's man. He would have been tortured, Grey was certain of that, and he was equally sure that his man would have told them everything. So what next? There were, in Grey's mind, two possibilities. They would send a man to eliminate him, as an act of revenge. Or they would release the information to the British authorities. Either way Grey was finished. He had decided not to wait and had handed in his resignation, blaming ill-health. It had not yet been accepted, and there would be a long period of debriefing and arranging to hand over to his successor, but his mind was made up. Maybe that would satisfy them. He poked the fire savagely.

One of the dogs had stopped barking, probably the victor chewing on the bone. He straightened his back and put the poker back on its stand. He'd have to get them in. His wife would give him a hard time when he eventually slipped into their bed if he allowed them to bark too long.

He walked through the kitchen, opened the door and whistled quietly. He heard Lady barking but she remained in the darkness, by the sound of it somewhere near the orchard.

'Lady,' he called, but she continued to bark.

He switched on the outside light, set into the wall to the left of the door, but its hundred-watt bulb only illuminated a dozen steps and most of the lawn was still pitch-black. If anything, the light only made the night seem darker. He pulled on his Wellington boots, grunting with the exertion, and then wrapped a red wool scarf around his neck.

He called for the dogs again but they ignored him. One of his collection of walking sticks, a Victorian example with a brass knob on the end in the shape of a swan's head, was leaning against the door jamb. He picked it up and stepped outside.

He stood on the edge of the pool of light and whistled, swinging the stick in his right hand as if it was a golf club. Lady had stopped barking. 'Damn dogs,' he muttered under his breath and headed down towards the orchard. He thought he could hear Lady whining but when he stopped and listened carefully there was only silence.

There was a lump in the lawn to the right of one of the trees, like a pile of wet soil. He headed towards it, the stick held in front of him. He knelt down and reached to touch it. It was warm and wet and when he took his hand away and held it close to his face he could see it was blood. It was Tramp, his brown Labrador. Dead.

He heard a noise, a rustling or an intake of breath, he didn't know which, but he turned round in a crouch to see a man bent down holding Lady's collar with one hand, the other clamped around her muzzle.

'What are you doing with my dog?' Grey asked. The man took his hand from around Lady's mouth and immediately she started barking, her eyes wide and panicking. The man was Chinese, Grey realized with a start. He pulled a wicked-looking curved knife from behind his back. He smiled, and before Grey realized what was happening he drew it across Lady's throat with a jerk and the dog's legs collapsed from under her. She lay on the grass, chest heaving as blood gushed from her neck, her eyes fixed on Grey.

'No!' cried Grey, stepping forward and raising his stick. 'No, no, no.'

Something hit him on the back of the right leg and then on the left; sharp lines of pain burned behind each knee and he felt blood pour down his calves. The strength went out of his legs and he fell on his knees, the pain making him scream. The sound had barely escaped from his mouth when a hand grabbed his chin from behind and stifled his shrieks. He reached up to hit the man with the stick but a man stepped from the side, another Chinese, a cleaver in his raised hand. He brought it down hard, slashing at Grey's forearm. Grey saw in horror the way it sank a good two inches into the arm and then the wave of pain hit him and he almost passed out. The stick dropped from his nerveless fingers. His legs had gone numb below the knees, but he could feel strips of pain and knew that he'd been hacked with knives, probably cutting his tendons. He was going to die. Oh God, he was going to die. He tried to use his left arm to pull the hand away from his mouth and then he felt rather than saw another blow and that arm too fell uselessly by his side. He started to shake as if he had a fever; convulsions racked his body.

The man who had killed Lady stepped over the dead dog and stood before him, the knife pointing at his nose. I'm going to die, was the one thought in Grey's mind. The man stepped forward and the hand round Grey's mouth twisted his head up sharply so that he was looking towards the sky. The man fumbled in his pocket and pulled out a piece of tattered paper. He looked at it for a few seconds before speaking. They were being well paid for this job, and although it had been ordered by somebody more than eight thousand miles away the instructions had been quite specific and the man was determined to carry them out to the letter. The woman who was paying the money, paying in taels of gold, would never know whether or not the instructions had been obeyed. But the man would, and he had professional pride. It had taken more than a week to track down the man called Grey, the man who worked in a building called Century House. Soon the job would be over and he could return to Hong Kong.

Slowly, carefully enunciating every word, he repeated the message on the piece of paper, written there in capital letters. 'This is for Geoff Howells,' he said, pushing his face up close to Grey's. 'For Geoff Howells. Do you understand?'

Grey could feel his life's blood pouring down his arms and pooling around his legs. He felt elated, light-headed, almost happy, as the blood drained from his brain. He smiled. The hand moved away from his mouth and his chin flopped down, saliva dripping from his lips.

The man standing in front of him repeated the words. 'Do you understand?'

Grey tried to speak, tried to say that yes, he understood, that he was sorry he couldn't speak, but his mouth wouldn't work. He felt like giggling. He nodded and groaned, trying to form the words.

The man in front of him looked at his two companions, standing behind Grey, blood-wet hatchets in their hands, to check that they had seen the reaction. They nodded silently and the man smiled. As one they raised their hatchets in the air and brought them down one at a time into Grey's neck.

The flushing water was off again, the handle swinging uselessly in Dugan's hand. 'Piss, fuck and shit,' he cursed.

'Fuck this flat, fuck this place, fuck this whole fucking town.' He didn't feel any better getting it out of his system. He slammed down the lid. There was no problem with the water supply to the shower, thank God, so he pissed gratefully down the plughole and watched the yellow liquid swirl in circles and disappear.

He was in no hurry to get to the office; he'd lost all enthusiasm for the job since Petal had gone. Worse, he'd lost enthusiasm for everything. He'd been out drinking a few times but took no pleasure in it, and he'd spent the best part of the three weeks since she'd gone sitting in his flat watching videos. Not the television, there was precious little point in that, what with the sweeping cuts that took out all but the most innocuous sex and violence and interspersed what was left with adverts every ten minutes or so. He took out three videos a night from one of the Circle K convenience stores and watched them.

He towelled himself dry and put on his grey suit. He couldn't be bothered cooking breakfast, or even making himself coffee. There seemed to be no point – no point at all.

He locked the door behind him and paced up and down the corridor as he waited for one of the three lifts to haul itself up to his floor. On the way down he leant his forehead against the gap between the two doors and sighed deeply. What the hell was he going to do? He'd sent off at least a dozen applications for jobs in the past fortnight, everything from a credit agency in Singapore to an estate agents in Tsim Sha Tsui, but nothing had come of it. An unemployment rate of less than two per cent and he still couldn't get a job. What was wrong with him? 'Oh Petal,' he moaned quietly. 'Where are you?'

He'd never before felt so alone. He didn't even have

Jill to lean on, because she and Sophie had returned to England. Maybe that was the only decent thing to have emerged from the whole sorry episode, the fact that their parents had flown over and re-established contact. They'd whisked Jill and Sophie out of the triad compound into the Mandarin Hotel and flown with them back to the UK, all thoughts of the past forgotten. Jill had been too exhausted to argue, and although Thomas Ng had told her that she was welcome to stay, Dugan reckoned she'd done the right thing. Sophie's prospects would be better in England, too. Hong Kong over the next few years would be no place for children. The tension was building by the week and police riot squads were being trained with tear gas and rubber bullets in the New Territories.

The doors hissed open and he stepped out into the ground floor lobby, turning his face to the large wall-mounted fan and letting the cold breeze play over his damp skin.

Just before the reception desk where a blue-uniformed security guard slept with his head down on his folded arms were the racks of letter boxes, one per flat. He unlocked his. Inside was his electricity bill and a circular from a credit card company. And a postcard, a view of the Oriental Hotel in Bangkok, the best hotel in the world, on the banks of the Chao Phraya River. He'd never stayed there, but he'd had a drink in the Author's Wing once. His name and address were written on the back in a handwriting he didn't recognize. But to the left of the address was something that made his heart leap. No words. Just a flower, carelessly drawn.

STEPHEN LEATHER

THE SOLITARY MAN

'Masterly plotting . . . rapid-fire prose'
Sunday Express on *THE DOUBLE TAP*

'Action and scalpel sharp suspense'
The Daily Telegraph on *THE BIRTHDAY GIRL*

'Will leave you breathless'
Daily Mail on *THE CHINAMAN*

Chris Hutchison is a man on the run. Imprisoned for a crime he didn't commit, Hutch escapes from a British maximum security prison and starts a new life in Hong Kong. Then a ghost from his past catches up with him, forcing him to help a former terrorist break out of a Bangkok prison. Or face life behind bars once more.

Meanwhile the Drug Enforcement Administration wants to nail the vicious drug warlord responsible for flooding the States with cheap heroin. And decided to use Hutch as a pawn in a deadly game.

Hutch's bid for freedom takes him into the lawless killing fields of the Gold Triangle, where the scene is set for one final act of betrayal . . .

HODDER AND STOUGHTON PAPERBACKS

STEPHEN LEATHER

THE VETS

Hong Kong. The British administration is preparing to hand the capitalist colony back to Communist China with the minimum of fuss.

But Colonel Joel Tyler has other plans for the British colony, plans which involve four Vietnam War veterans and a spectacular mission making use of their unique skills.

Vietnam was the one thing the four men had in common before Tyler moulded them into a team capable of pulling off a sensational robbery.

But while the vets are preparing to take Hong Kong by storm, their paymaster, Anthony Chung, puts the final touches to an audacious betrayal. At stake is the future of Hong Kong . . .

HODDER AND STOUGHTON PAPERBACKS

STEPHEN LEATHER

THE TUNNEL RATS

Praise for THE TUNNEL RATS

'Stephen Leather should be nestling in your bookshelves alongside Frederick Forsyth and Jack Higgins' *Daily Mail*

'A well-constructed and fast-moving plot . . . stunning . . . another top-notch thriller'
Yorkshire Evening Post

Two murders, thousands of miles apart: one in London, one in Bangkok. The bodies brutally mutilated: an ace of spades impaled upon their chests.

In Washington, a US senator receives photographs of the corpses. And realises that his past has come back to haunt him.

Nick Wright is the detective trying to solve the mystery of the double killing. His hunt for a motive takes him to the tunnels in Vietnam, where the American tunnel rats fought the dirtiest battle of the war against the Viet Cong.

But his search places him in grave danger with a killer determined to protect the secrets of the tunnels. At whatever cost . . .

HODDER AND STOUGHTON PAPERBACKS

STEPHEN LEATHER

HUNGRY GHOST

'Very complicated. Fun'
Daily Telegraph

'The sort of book that could easily take up a complete weekend – and be time really well spent'
Bolton Evening News

Geoff Howells, a government-trained killing machine, is brought out of retirement and sent to Hong Kong. His brief: to assassinate Chinese Mafia leader, Simon Ng. Howells devises a dangerous and complicated plan to reach his intended victim – only to find himself the next target . . .

Patrick Dugan, a Hong Kong policeman, has been held back in his career because of his connections – his sister is married to Simon Ng. But when Ng's daughter is kidnapped and Ng himself disappears, Dugan gets caught up in a series of violent events and an international spying intrigue that has run out of control . . .

Tough writing, relentless storytelling and a searingly evocative background of Hong Kong in the aftermath of Tiananmen Square make *Hungry Ghost* a compulsive read.

HODDER AND STOUGHTON PAPERBACKS